Candy waited, flinching at every little sound. An internal voice told her to keep quiet and absolutely still, but somehow the silence was unignorable. If she didn't challenge it, it would engulf her.

'Robert,' she cried sharply, 'where the hell are you?'

The silence pressed in. She whimpered. She no longer cared about finding proper shelter. All she wanted was to be in a human presence.

'Please whistle,' she whispered. 'Whistle and I'll come to you.' The words kept repeating themselves and finally petered out.

After that she didn't call again.

Something bad had happened to Marriot.

Something had got him.

Windsor Chorlton was born in the north of England and worked for an international publisher before taking up full-time writing. A wilderness expedition to study a Tibetan Buddhist community in a remote Himalayan valley inspired his first acclaimed novel *Rites of Sacrifice*. Since then he has written two further thrillers. Windsor Chorlton lives in Dorset.

BY THE SAME AUTHOR

Rites of Sacrifice
Canceleer
Blind Junction

LATITUDE ZERO

Windsor Chorlton

ORION

An Orion Paperback
First published in Great Britain by Orion in 1997
This paperback edition published in 1998 by Orion Books Ltd,
Orion House, 5 Upper St Martin's Lane, London WC2H 9EA

A CIP catalogue record for this book is available
from the British Library.

ISBN: 0 75280 921 0

Typeset by Deltatype Ltd, Birkenhead, Merseyside
Printed and bound in Great Britain by
Clays Ltd, St Ives plc

Not in Utopia – subterranean fields – Or some secreted island, Heaven knows where.

William Wordsworth, *The Prelude*

We will now discuss in a little more detail the struggle for existence.

Charles Darwin, *The Origin of Species*

For Alan Lothian and Mike Newth

At 16.47 on 14 December, the duty radio officer of the liner *Gloriana* picked up an SOS traced to latitude 5.50 S. and longitude 113.39 E., about 80 miles north of Java and two days' cruise from Singapore, the next port of call. The radio officer informed the officer of the watch, who passed on the information to the intelligence officer, who decided that the distress signal justified interrupting the captain's game of tennis.

Geoffrey Ainsley, master of the world's most luxurious cruise ship, was one set down and serving to save the second when Ancram appeared on the sidelines. In the presence of passengers, Ainsley's officers were expected to demonstrate the non-verbal communication skills of a casino pit boss, and from the finely calibrated tilt of Ancram's eyebrows, the captain gauged that his business wasn't so critical that it couldn't wait until after the point.

'Match conceded,' he called to his opponent. 'Duty calls, I'm afraid.' Wearing what he thought of as his hotelier's smile, he strolled off court. 'What is it, Stephen?'

'A Mayday. We've got the vessel on radar. Small, probably a fishing boat, about thirty miles south by south-west.'

'What kind of trouble are they in?' Ainsley asked, towelling his face.

'Don't know. They're not responding to our transmissions.'

Ainsley zipped up his racket. 'Any other shipping in the area?'

'Nothing closer than us. The signal's very weak. I suspect nobody else has picked it up.'

Ainsley looked out to port. Java lay over there, its coast signalled by a squadron of stationary clouds. The decision to go to the rescue should have been simple, but when you were responsible for the safety and comfort of eight hundred souls, nearly all of them wealthy, some with the home numbers of congressmen and ministers, nothing was straightforward. This was Ainsley's last voyage before retirement and he didn't want any blemishes. He gave his racket a backhand swing. 'Very well. We'll take a look. I'll join you on the bridge in a few minutes.'

By the time he had showered and changed, the range was down to twelve miles and the vessel was visible through high-resolution binoculars. It looked like an insect. At eight miles, Ainsley identified it as a schooner of primitive cut and distinctive rig – like a dhow, with sharply raked bow and a high stern. The sails were black.

'Not from these parts,' he said. 'Have you heard of the Bugis?'

'Bugis?'

'Sulawesi pirates. At least, they were pirates when I first sailed these waters.' Ainsley lowered the glasses. 'You'd better ask our security friend to step up. And find an interpreter.'

The sea was calm, gentian blue, the angles of the schooner sharply printed. The vessel was running under motor – a powerful one. Ainsley could make out three figures on deck and a cargo lashed down under tarpaulins.

'Paddy's here.'

2

'Ah, Paddy.'

Only a certain watchfulness of expression betrayed the man's calling. Ainsley handed him his binoculars. 'We've got an SOS from that boat, but we don't know the nature of their problem. Any reason why we should steer clear?'

'No intelligence alerts,' Paddy said. 'But the way the world is going ...' There was no need to expand the warning. With the millennium approaching, all kinds of groups were trying to fulfil their doomsday philosophies. He adjusted focus and peered long. 'Trim even, everything fine topside, running nicely. She's a long way from sinking.'

'Quite. I'm sure it's unnecessary, but perhaps you could arrange to have your team standing by. Maximum discretion, of course.' Ainsley turned to his First Officer. 'Keep the bow area clear except for Paddy's men. We'll close astern to within hailing distance.'

A young Asian of collegiate appearance entered tentatively. 'This is Syed, sir, the interpreter. I've explained the situation.'

'Come in, Syed. What I'd like you to do is ask those chappies what's wrong.'

'Just speak into here,' the radio officer told him, indicating a mike on the console. 'No need to shout.'

Syed looked anxious. 'How do I hear what they say?'

'No need to worry about that.'

Paddy had retired to a corner and was muttering into his lapel. Ainsley concentrated on the schooner. Dolphins arced in its bow wave. As the distance narrowed, the vast difference in the scale of the vessels became apparent. Foreshortened by height, the Bugi sailors stared up as if God had parted the heavens above them. They wore baggy black trousers and headbands.

'Go ahead,' Ainsley told Syed.

Passengers looked up, startled by the hugely amplified

voice booming over them. The Bugis jabbed towards a shadowed bundle under the stern awning.

'Looks like one of the crew is ill,' Ancram said. 'Maybe dead.'

The bridge filled with the tinny sound of Bahasa Indonesia.

'Did you get that?' Ainsley asked the interpreter.

'He says it's not dead person. One live woman. White woman.' He looked at the captain.

'Ask them where they found her.'

'Some place on Sumatra. They don't know the name. Captain, they're asking you to take her. They say she's very sick. Think she soon die.'

Ainsley exchanged a long look with his First Officer. 'Full astern all engines, please. Syed, order them to keep five hundred metres ahead and wait for our launch. Stephen, alert the hospital.' Ainsley turned to his security officer. 'Paddy, I'm assuming that this is genuine but, just so we're on the far side of safe, I want three of your people among the boarding party.'

'I'll go myself.'

'But for God's sake, don't show weapons unless absolutely necessary.' Ainsley gestured to the deck below. The rails were lined with passengers, camcorders trained on the schooner.

'Shall I order them to move away?' enquired one of the midshipmen.

'*Order*, Mr Clarke? If you had paid twenty thousand pounds for a grandstand seat, would you give it up?'

'Yes sir. I mean, no sir.'

Even with engines at full astern, it took the *Gloriana* the best part of three sea miles to lose way. In that time the rescue launch was readied and its squad briefed. When the launch reached the schooner, the day was ending as serenely as it had begun, the sea turning navy, the

4

western horizon streaked with parrot colours. Paddy kept up a radio commentary as the party boarded.

'She's carrying timber. They say they loaded in Padang and are headed for Sulawesi.' Ainsley watched Paddy make his way aft. 'Approaching the body.' Ainsley saw him crouch, then there was a long pause. 'Female. Estimate late twenties. Northern European. Very bad shape. Unconscious. Over.'

'Any identity?'

'Nothing. She's naked.'

'Ask the crew if they have her possessions.'

'Nix. They say this is how they found her.'

'Where?'

'Some village. I don't think they have a name for it.'

'Try to find out what happened.'

Three of the Bugis clustered around Paddy, gesticulating.

'Captain, they're pretty spooked. I'd say their cargo's not completely legit. Do you want me to search the vessel?'

Captain Ainsley's responsibility was to his ship, not the world's rain forests. In a few minutes it would be dark. 'Let them go. Get the woman on board.'

Passengers pointed when they saw the woman being lowered into the launch. As the last sailor jumped down, water boiled at the schooner's stern and it heeled sharply, heading north-east. By the time the launch was alongside and the woman had been hoisted aboard, the Bugis were beyond recall, their black sails swallowed by the blacker equatorial night.

Ainsley turned to Ancram. 'Check for reports of vessels missing in this area. I think we could be looking for a yacht.'

He remained on the bridge for another hour before asking his First Officer to take over. 'I'll be in the hospital.'

The *Gloriana*'s sick bay was equipped to handle any operation short of major neurosurgery. At present it was occupied by a child with a grumbling appendix, a seventy-year-old man with a broken femur (disco casualty), a deckhand with a dislocated shoulder and a woman with a threatened miscarriage. Ainsley paused with words for each before making for the emergency room.

Through the window he could see the rescued woman lying wired and plugged to a battery of life-support equipment. Dr Penny Laing, a slim Scottish woman in her late forties, was bending over her. Ainsley tapped to attract her attention. She beckoned him in.

'How's our castaway?'

'Poorly. We got her just in time.'

Ainsley was shocked by the patient's condition. Her face was puffed and cratered, her lips split and scabby. The arm crooked across her chest was mottled and as thin as a peeled stick. Her hair might once have been dark blonde but was now bleached and lifeless.

'Will she live?'

'She's taken everything nature can throw at her – heatstroke, dehydration, a lot of insect bites and a nasty leg wound. But her pulse is surprisingly strong. Yes, I think she'll come through.'

'Has she spoken?'

'Incoherently. Something about tigers. And about killing someone. Or someone trying to kill her. She's obviously been through a terrible ordeal. Do you know who she is?'

'No idea. What language did she speak?'

'English. It sounded like English English.'

Ainsley checked his watch. In half an hour he was due at dinner. The ritual of the captain's table was eagerly anticipated by the passengers and it wouldn't do to let tonight's guests down. 'Okay if I stay a while?'

'So long as you don't disturb her.' Dr Laing turned away. 'I'll be next door.'

It was dead quiet in the emergency room. Ainsley had begun to drowse when he became aware of some faint shift in the atmosphere. The woman's eyes had opened. They were dark blue and drugged, but in their depths Ainsley sensed fear and confusion.

'You're safe now. You're in hospital.'

Slowly her eyes slid half-shut.

'Can you tell me your name?'

There was no response. Ainsley glanced at the door and leaned closer. 'Who are you?'

The dry lips parted, closed and parted.

'Andy? Did you say Andy? Where did you come from, Andy? Where did those men find you?'

'Greenland.'

'Andy, were you with anyone else? Should we be looking for anyone else?'

'Killed them.'

'Killed who?'

The door banged open and Dr Laing stormed in. 'Captain, what are you doing? Please leave my patient alone.'

Ainsley straightened up. 'If she was shipwrecked, there may be others.'

'I'm sorry, but you'll just have to wait.'

A discreet cough made Ainsley turn. Ancram was at the door, a sheet of paper in his hand. Ainsley stepped outside. 'Come up with anything?'

'Nothing recent. Only this.'

It was a list of names faxed from Singapore.

> Leo Jaeger, 37, American
> Aquila Corrigan, 32, American
> Jay Boucher, 29, American
> Dexter Smith, 30, American

7

Nadine Wells, 24, American
Kent Bartok, 23, American
Candida Woodville, 26, British
Ronnie Trigg, 39, British
Robert Marriot, 33, Australian
Sixt Haimendorf, 44, Austrian
Josef Fieser, 35, German

Ainsley frowned. 'A yacht crew?'

Ancram shook his head. 'Passengers on an airship that disappeared over the Java Sea six weeks ago. They were members of some environmentalist group called Wildguard.' Ancram tapped the list. 'This chap Dexter was a big rock star – their main supporter. He was on board with his girlfriend, a fashion model. It made world headlines.'

Six weeks ago Ainsley had been in Arctic waters, but the news of the missing airship hadn't passed him by. 'I thought they were all dead.'

'Except one. He turned up in Singapore about two weeks ago.'

Ainsley studied the list again. Candida Woodville was the only female British passport holder. Ainsley eyed the unconscious figure behind the glass.

'The doctor thinks she's English. She said something that sounded like "Andy". I think she was trying to tell me her name.' He stared at the list. 'Candida ... Candy.' He looked up. 'My God, I think it must be her.'

'Captain, the survivor said no one else made it.'

'Well, who else could it be?'

Ancram shrugged.

'Did they find the bodies?'

'I'll check.'

'Wait.' Ainsley pondered a moment. 'Come with me.'

'You *are* expected at dinner,' Ancram reminded him.

The ship's library had been modelled on the one at Chatsworth. When Ainsley entered, it had two occupants – one writing, the other asleep. With nearly six hundred men and women under his command, including cabaret artists, beauticians, children's entertainers and an astrologer, Ainsley could be forgiven for not recalling the name of the librarian, a middle-aged gentleman of Indian origin. His security tag said he was called Jimmy Kuparam.

'Jimmy, what British newspapers do we keep?'

'*The Times* and *Sunday Times*, the *Telegraph* and *Mail*.' Jimmy spoke with a Tyneside accent.

'I'm a *Telegraph* man myself,' Ainsley told Ancram. 'You take *The Times*. Jimmy, would you dig out all the issues going back to, say, the last week of October?'

Jimmy ferried eight large bundles to their table. For the next ten minutes the silence was broken only by the shuffling of broadsheets and the rhythmic snoring of the slumbering passenger.

'Here it is,' Ancram said. 'Fifth November, dateline Hong Kong. "Fears Mount for Missing Airship."'

'Read it out,' Ainsley said, continuing his own search.

'American rock musician and environmental campaigner Mr Dexter Smith is among eleven people aboard an airship reported missing off the coast of Borneo. Radio contact was lost during violent storms that struck the southern part of the island on Wednesday night. The airship had been chartered by the radical conservation organization Wildguard, whose American founder, Mr Leo Jaeger, was among the passengers. Other passengers include Mr Smith's girlfriend, the American model Nadine Wells. Unconfirmed reports say that at least two British nationals were on board. An air and sea search has been launched, but ...'

Ainsley stiffened. 'Look at this.'

Ancram came and stood behind him, studying the large portrait photograph of a young woman. It was a well-bred face, the sort you might expect to see in *Country Life*, but there was nothing vacuous about the expression. Her eyes showed intelligence and an undimmed zest for life. The name under the picture was Candida Woodville.

'Lovely girl,' Ancram said. 'Do you think it's her?'

Ainsley read out the copy.

'Miss Woodville, 26, recently graduated in zoology. Friends say she had a particular interest in the big cats and was thrilled at the chance of working with the Wildguard team in South-East Asia. At her family home in Hampshire, General Adrian Woodville expressed concern over his daughter's safety but refused to give up hope.'

Ainsley sat back, unsure how to proceed. Ancram consulted his watch. 'Do you want me to carry on while you go up to dinner?'

Irritation nipped. 'Stephen, I'm the captain of a liner, not a bloody professional entertainer. My passengers can do without me for one evening.'

'Yes, sir. You haven't forgotten that you're hosting the Millennium Ball.'

'Damn. Oh, all right. I'll be there. In the meantime ...'

'Sir?'

Ainsley stood up. 'Comb the rest of the papers.' He headed for the librarian's office. 'I have to make a call.'

As he dialled, he realized his hands were trembling. Bloody silly, he thought. Completely irresponsible.

'Doctor, does our patient have any distinguishing marks? Scars, that kind of thing?' He began to jot down Dr Laing's response. 'Large surgical scar on left elbow. Curved scar on the ball of right thumb. No, that should be enough. Thank you.'

When he returned to the library, his expression was

opaque. 'Carry on, Stephen. I'll be in my cabin if you turn up anything interesting.' He held up the newspaper. 'Okay to borrow this, Jimmy?'

Almost surreptitiously, he made his way to his suite. His private secretary was waiting with papers requiring attention. He waved them away. 'Can you find a private number in Hampshire? General Adrian Woodville.'

He shut his office door behind him. In England it would be four on a dark winter morning, but if it had been *his* daughter, he wouldn't care what time of night he was woken. On the other hand, if he was wrong – God, it didn't bear thinking about. What he was doing was extremely foolish. He should pass the information on to the embassy and let the FO sort it out.

His intercom bleeped. 'I have that number. Do you want me to connect you?'

Ainsley eyed the phone and felt sick. 'If you would.'

Electronic speed outstripped his misgivings. Within seconds the connection was made.

'Woodville,' a curt English voice said.

'I'm sorry to call at such an ungodly hour. My name is Geoffrey Ainsley, captain of ...'

'What do you want?'

'I'm captain of the liner *Gloriana*, en route from Bali to Singapore. Late this afternoon, we received a ...'

'Is it about Candy?'

Ainsley registered the diminutive and plunged in. 'Did your daughter have a scar on her left elbow?'

There was a huge silence. 'Why do you ask?'

'Please.'

Another silence yawned. 'She had a bad riding accident when she was fifteen. She needed a pin. Look ...'

'And on her right hand?'

'What is this about?'

11

'Did your daughter have a scar on the ball of her right thumb?'

'She was bitten by a dog – a foxhound, of all things. She was always getting into scrapes.' Woodville hesitated, and Ainsley plainly read the thought taking shape in his mind. 'Have you recovered her body?'

Ainsley drew a breath. 'Today, at 1800 hours, we picked up a young woman from an Indonesian schooner one hundred miles north of Java. She was suffering from extreme exposure, but she's alive and receiving treatment in the ship's hospital. She has scars that match those you've described. She gave her name as Candy.' Ainsley shut his eyes. 'I believe it's your daughter.'

'I'm sorry. That's not possible.'

'I assure you it's the truth.'

'Let me speak to her.'

'Unfortunately, she's sedated.'

'How do I know this isn't a hoax? You wouldn't be the first sick individual to call since the papers started printing that garbage.'

'I can only repeat that we have rescued a young woman whose description matches that of your daughter. I was at her bedside less than an hour ago.'

'What colour are her eyes?'

Ainsley was startled. 'Blue – a kind of smoky blue.' He stopped, checked by an observation that hadn't made an impression at the time. 'One eye was a slightly different colour. I'm not sure.'

There was no response, or none that Ainsley could hear.

'General?'

When Woodville spoke again, his voice was choked up. 'He said he saw her drown. He told me himself.'

It took Ainsley a moment to realize that he must be referring to the other survivor.

'He was wrong. Your daughter is in hospital on board my ship.'

'Is she badly hurt?'

'Her main problem is dehydration and malnutrition. The doctor's confident of a full recovery.'

The general gave a little sob of laughter. 'I always said that girl was indestructible.'

Hearing the pride and pain in the man's voice, Ainsley decided it was time to withdraw. 'You'll want to make arrangements. In two days, at 1100 hours local time, we'll be arriving in Singapore. I shall inform the British embassy and my company headquarters. They'll give you all the information you'll need.'

'Do you know what happened to her?'

'I'm afraid not. Not yet. But I'm sure she put up a bloody good show.' A knock at the door obliged him to break off. 'Excuse me,' he said, and muffled the phone.

Ancram entered, grimacing. 'I thought you'd better see this.'

It was a copy of the *Daily Mail*, only a week old. Under an EXCLUSIVE! banner and a photograph of a gaunt young man superimposed on a jungle montage, complete with snarling tiger, the headline screamed: 'Greens Turn Predator: Airship Survivor Describes Rock Star's Last Horrifying Moments.'

Ainsley took in the first paragraph. 'The only survivor of the Wildguard airship disaster spoke tonight of the nightmare desert island ordeal that killed all eleven of his companions. For four weeks, while search parties ...'

Ainsley shoved the paper away. 'Not now.' He uncovered the phone. 'I'm sorry, sir.'

'I can't begin to tell you how ...'

'Please, there's no need. I have a daughter of my own.'

When Ainsley finally put down the phone, he felt faint.

'So it *was* her?'

13

'Yes.' Ainsley let his breath go. 'I think I need a drink, Stephen. You'll join me, I hope. Whisky, isn't it?' He poured himself a gin and raised his glass. 'To Candy.'

'Candy. Wait until the reptiles get hold of her.' Ancram slapped the paper. 'Talk about a holiday in hell. Man-eating tigers, crocodiles, pirates, sex, murder. Time Warner has signed this man up. They're talking about making a movie. He's on to a fortune.'

Ainsley had no time for tabloid fantasies. 'Well, it's not exclusive any more, is it?' He glanced at the staring-eyed man in the newspaper. 'And I know whose story I'd prefer to hear.'

ONE

1

As the millennium spluttered to a close, Jay Boucher found rich pickings to be had in the fault lines that opened up in the American consciousness. For many citizens, the year 2000 marked the expiry date of old certainties; to these people, the past seemed like so much useless baggage to be carried on a journey to an unknown destination they would never reach. But for others, the big 2K promised exciting new possibilities, with no shortage of guides to show the way. Cults sprang up like dragons' teeth, and it wasn't just over-the-rainbow types who signed up. Top business leaders spent five minutes a day chanting under tepees for lower interest rates; a mainstream women's magazine ran a piece on how a more intense orgasm could project you through the space-time continuum.

Interesting times, and no one was more finely tuned to them than Boucher. An unsuccessful musician turned rock critic turned guru of the lifestyle pages, he was now much in demand as a sifter of cultural detritus and decoder of blips. His first book, a collection of magazine pieces called *Dissecting Aliens*, had just been published to enthusiastic reviews. 'Mercilessly exposes the uncertainties of the age,' *New York Times Book Review*. 'The leading chronicler of the rockalypse,' *Rolling Stone*.

To celebrate publication, which coincided with his twenty-ninth birthday, Boucher invited five friends to dinner at the apartment he shared with Lydia, a cellist with the Chicago Symphony. After the meal they played poker – dollar-ante, pot limit, dealer's choice.

All the guests were male. Lydia was in Cleveland on the first leg of a six-week tour, and though Boucher liked the company of women, he hadn't yet met one who could play poker worth a damn. Dealing clockwise, the first three players were all achievers of about his own age. Marvin Finn was a prize-winning architect, Ben Lief a dramatist whose second play was in rehearsal, Conrad Jacobsen an assistant professor of modern history at the University of Chicago, and also a mountaineer of prowess.

Next round the table was Tom Brack, whose glory days were over. In the Sixties, he'd been a *Life* correspondent, but after the magazine folded, he had started juicing in a big way and his career had nose-dived. Rescue had arrived in the shape of a woman sixteen years younger than him, and now he worked as a sub on a trade magazine and had a four-year-old son.

Last in the deal was Henry Ritter, Boucher's oldest friend and therefore still his greatest rival, despite the fact that Ritter's three novels remained resolutely unpublished. He was a morose soul dressed in thrift-shop clothes who worked shifts as a shelf-filler in an auto parts warehouse because he thought a proper job would get in the way of his writing.

This particular night, the cards were tepid and the players filled the slack with gossip and the salty-edged banter that playing for stakes provokes in otherwise well-mannered men.

'Are you saying Lydia can't cook,' Lief asked, 'or won't?'

'Can't,' Boucher said proudly. 'She can't cook, can't drive, and has no small talk whatsoever.'

'If it's a style accessory you want,' Ritter said gloomily, 'why didn't you get a saluki?'

As Boucher was preparing a response, the phone rang. 'Leave it,' he said. 'The machine's on.'

'Hey, Jay. Rich Caldwell. I'm in LA and I've landed you an assignment. Call me.'

Rich Caldwell was the high-adrenalin editor of the magazine that had got Boucher's career rolling.

'He sounds excited,' Lief said.

'Rich has the metabolism of a small carnivore. He lives at double time.'

'Aren't you going to call him?' Finn asked.

Boucher looked at his hand – a ten high. 'Well,' he said, 'it's a slow game.'

He dialled Caldwell's number.

'Jay? Great. Listen. I just lunched at *Chez Panis* with a potentate called Delta Glenn. She's real connected, wired into everybody. Among her list of clients is Dexter Smith, and it turns out that he's a big fan of your work.'

'Dexter Smith,' Boucher said. He turned towards his guests and widened his eyes slightly. 'I'm flattered.'

'He's offering us an exclusive.'

'Rich, you know I don't do celebrity interviews.'

'Gosh-darn,' Jacobsen whispered. 'Jay Boucher's gotten so big he won't let the world's biggest rock star interview him.'

'Not an interview. Listen, Dexter's a passionate supporter of the environment. You heard of the Wildguard movement?'

'Nope.'

'Eco freaks, but not your average tree-huggers. They're run by some guy called Jaeger who used to be a warrior with the Fresno Angels. Wildguard are putting together a campaign to save a piece of Borneo rain forest threatened by a dam. Dexter Smith's gonna be there with them, shoulder to shoulder. What do you think?'

'My heart isn't exactly going pit-a-pat. I mean, apart from Dexter Smith being an international name, I don't see the storyline.'

'Intrinsically, it's got to be about Dexter, but these motorheads for nature are kind of intriguing.'

'It's still not a big plot.'

'Saving the environment? What's bigger than that? If the dam goes ahead, an area the size of New Jersey is going to be drowned. Millions of furry creatures will perish, including some unknown to science. Do you want that on your conscience?'

Boucher sighed. 'What's the tie-in?'

Caldwell paused only fractionally. 'Dexter's been fighting a contractual battle for the last fifteen months. That's a long time to be out of the spotlight. Right? So it's important his latest cut gets maximum publicity. It's called *Dirty Old Man* and Delta says it's a scorching indictment of man's rape of Planet Earth. But what the fuck? I'm not asking you to review it.'

'You're asking me to fly halfway round the world to plug a rock musician's next album.'

'Jay, you can have four thousand words. How you fill them is up to you. Plus, you get top rate, a round-the-world ticket and two weeks' expenses. Even Tintin never got a better deal.'

'It's not that. I've got a novel to finish.'

'Who reads novels?'

'It's a penance for all the stuff I've written for you.'

'Jay, I anticipated enthusiasm. I practically promised Delta you'd come across. Don't let me down.'

It was out of the question, but Boucher didn't want to get into a trans-continental row. 'Rich, I'm in the middle of a poker game. Let me sleep on it.'

'Well don't lie in, because they've got short attention spans in Tinseltown.'

Boucher made a face as he returned to the table. 'Dexter Smith and some conservationists he's bankrolling are going to save the Borneo rain forest.'

'You gonna cover it?'

'Nope. It doesn't engage my interest.'

'Borneo could be neat.'

'It's a jungle. Jungles aren't neat.'

'What about Dexter Smith? He's huge.'

'So he doesn't need me to polish his image.'

'You could always make him look like an asshole.'

Boucher threw his hand in. 'I'm not interested in making Dexter Smith look like anything. He's a dude who can carry a tune. Who cares what's underneath?'

'Millions of fans.'

'Let's play cards,' Boucher said. The call had unsettled him. 'Who's dealing?'

'You are,' Jacobsen said, sliding the deck across. 'Your choice.'

'Seven-card stud. No frills.'

Boucher dealt two cards down, the third face up. The act of committing himself to chance steadied him. His up card was a king. He looked in the hole – another king and a jack. It was a solid start, but Lief also had a king, and Ritter, showing an ace, bet six – the pot. Boucher called and so did everyone else. On the next deal, he collected an unhelpful nine to Ritter's queen. Ritter bet twenty, but only Finn folded. It looked like a game was shaping up.

Brack tossed in some chips. 'What outfit is Dexter Smith funding?'

'Wildguard. Caldwell says they're run by a Hell's Angel.'

Jacobsen looked up. 'Leo Jaeger. Yeah, the Sierra Club had a run-in with Wildguard over their scheme to set

21

aside most of the Rockies for grizzlies and cougars. They're active in the campaign to re-establish wolves. The rumour is they imported some from Canada and released them in Idaho. They go in for monkey-wrenching, too – spiking trees with nails, blowing up power lines. In Big Sky country, the ranchers have a bounty on anyone showing a Wildguard sticker.'

'What sort of recruitment do they have?'

'Not big, but their hands-on tactics make good copy.'

'They must have something going for them to attract a star like Dexter Smith.'

'Enviro-fundamentalism sweetened with hippy-dip spirituality. The world is an indivisible whole, each creature living in harmony, blah-de-blah. Their slogan is "Look after the wild and the wild will look after you."'

'That's not much of a manifesto.'

'It's enough. The less people believe in, the more fiercely they believe in it. Those kooks who say the world will disappear into a black hole at the stroke of New Year's midnight have fewer doubts than the average quantum physicist. And people without doubts attract disciples.'

'You make Wildguard sound like a fascist cult.'

'Hitler was a vegetarian animal-lover; Himmler adored his chickens. A lot of Greens share the Nazis' notions of a degenerate culture being saved by a hierarchy based on survival of the fittest. Look at Earth First; they say that if AIDS didn't exist, environmentalists would have to invent it.'

'C'mon, Conrad, someone's got to stop the shit. The world's getting mighty dirty and mighty crowded.'

'Sure, and Wildguard loves it. Without the filthy, ignorant masses, you can't have a pure and enlightened élite. Basically, Wildguard's solution is a lifeboat for ten on a ship carrying a thousand passengers.'

'What I hate,' Finn said, 'is when rock 'n' roll singers turn preachy. Their lyrics go to shit.'

'I'll go along with that,' Boucher said, but only in response to Ritter, who had paired his ace and bet fifty on the strength of it. Having failed to improve his hand, Boucher called the bet against his better judgement. Everyone else folded except Jacobsen, who looked like he was chasing a straight or flush.

Boucher dealt the sixth card and forgot Dexter Smith and the trashing of the planet. 'Three of spades for Conrad – possible flush. Another damn queen for Henry. Dealer gets a jack – no apparent help.'

'Put not your faith in kings and princes,' Ritter told him, 'because I've got three of a kind.'

From the way he'd been betting, he probably had. Boucher was an intuitive player, sometimes a rash one, but even he couldn't ignore the odds when they were so manifestly stacked against him. Two pairs hidden was a sucker's hand at any time, but when those pairs were beaten on the table by aces and queens, he was on a hiding to nothing.

'It'll cost you a hundred,' Ritter told him.

'Okay.'

Jacobsen called too, which certainly meant he'd got his flush or straight. Suddenly, Boucher's palms were damp.

'Down and dirty,' Ritter said.

Boucher dealt the last cards and didn't look at his own.

'Pass,' Ritter said, his face impassive.

'Pass,' Boucher echoed feebly, still not looking at his last card, knowing that Ritter was only postponing the moment of retribution.

'Sandbaggers,' Jacobsen said, and shoved a hundred in. 'To keep you honest.'

'Your hundred,' Ritter said inevitably, 'and up two hundred.'

All eyes turned to Boucher. He lifted one corner of his last card and the king of hearts looked back at him. The thrill was immediately succeeded by panic. Against the odds and in defiance of sensible play, he had made his full house, but for all he knew, Ritter had aces over queens or even four of a kind. He considered folding, but he'd never thrown in a full house before. The right and proper thing to do was match Ritter's raise and minimize his losses. He reached for his chips.

'I'll call your three hundred and raise the pot.'

Jacobsen folded with much head-shaking. 'This is a pissing competition.'

Ritter laughed. 'Your ass is sucking wind, Jay.' He began to count the pot. There was nearly fourteen hundred dollars and Ritter didn't have that much cash.

'Take my marker?'

'Sure,' Boucher said, feeling physically sick.

'Show time,' Finn said.

Boucher fanned his cards out. 'Full house. Kings over jacks.'

Deadpan, Ritter turned his last card over – a two. He turned his first hole card – queen of spades. He turned his second hole card – a useless three.

'Looks like mine,' Boucher said, when his victory had sunk in.

'You fluky bastard,' Jacobsen told him. 'You filled your house with the last card.'

Ritter gave a fractured laugh, his face draining from red to white. 'You had no right to be in the game.'

Boucher needed both hands to scoop in his winnings. 'I took my chances.'

The blood had flooded back into Ritter's face. 'Christ, Jay, that's cheque-book poker.'

Boucher smiled at him. 'I'm a winner. You're a loser. Accept it the way it is, the way it's always been.'

He regretted the words before they were out of his mouth, but there was no recalling them. Ritter went belly up. Mouth trembling, he looked at the space where his chips had been. 'That's me wiped out,' he said. With what dignity he could muster, he stumbled to his feet and in a general silence headed for the door. When he reached it, he stopped, shoulders hunched. 'Your book,' he said. 'I forgot it.' Glassy-eyed, he picked up his copy of *Dissecting Aliens*, opened it to the title page and pulled out a ballpoint.

'Let's leave it for some other time,' Boucher said, acutely apprehensive. 'I can't think what to write.'

'How about what you just told me?'

Boucher squirmed. 'Hell, Henry, that was just the adrenalin talking.'

'Okay,' Ritter said. 'Put the date.'

Boucher wrote it out.

'And then,' Ritter said, '"In memory of old times."'

Boucher wrote and handed the book to him without looking up. After a few seconds, it was tossed on to Boucher's pile of chips. He heard Ritter walk out and the door close behind him. Embarrassment charged the atmosphere.

Lief yawned. 'I guess that's as much pity and terror as I can take for one night.'

Suddenly they were all rising, bidding Boucher thanks and goodnight, not quite engaging his eyes. In a couple of minutes only Brack was left, shuffling the cards, dealing to invisible players.

'Henry's right,' he said. 'That pot was his.'

Knowing it was the truth, Boucher blustered. 'You only collect what you win.'

Brack looked at him thoughtfully. 'What you said about him being a loser – that was shitty.'

'Unforgivable,' Boucher agreed miserably. 'I'll call him tomorrow.'

Shaking his head, Brack prodded the book. 'That was goodbye, *amigo.*'

'I'll make up. We always do. You want some coffee?'

Brack rose. 'In four hours, Junior will be climbing over me.' He tapped the book again. 'Smart prose.'

'But?'

Brack considered his criticism. 'You always write after the event. That way you can shape the piece any way you like. I'd like to see you do a story where you don't know the ending.'

'Working backwards helps you get closer to the truth.'

'Hindsight's for historians. Journalists are hunter-gatherers, snuffling out the raw material. This book, these stories – they're autopsies.'

Boucher's ego was as fragile as any writer's. 'I know it's not your style of journalism.'

Brack laughed. 'You're thinking, who's this old burn-out telling me how to write?' He reached under the table. 'I got you something.'

The bulky package he'd brought along turned out to hold a vintage typewriter.

'I picked it up in France. Who knows? Maybe it belonged to the *Paris Review* crowd.'

Boucher was embarrassed. He used tape and honed his copy on a laptop. There was no place in his method for intermediate technology. 'Tom, I can't take it.'

'It's a magic typewriter. Stories write themselves on it. It's been everywhere – the Congo, Cambodia, Carnaby Street.'

In that case, Boucher wondered, why are you dumping it on me? 'You think it'll magic up a story out of Dexter Smith?'

'If anything can, that little old Smith-Corona will.'

Before leaving, Brack took a mouthful of water and swallowed a pill. At the door, he paused with a sad smile. 'Don't fritter it away, Jay. Today it's all pat hands. Tomorrow, you're chasing inside straights.'

After he'd gone, Boucher sat looking at the typewriter sitting amid the chips and the glasses and the beer cans. In some indefinable way it gave him the creeps. It seemed to him that Brack's parting words had been in the nature of a malign prophecy.

When he'd cleaned up the poker wreckage, he opened the window to ventilate the room and stood listening to the rise and fall of city sounds. The aircraft warning lights blinked on the Sears Tower. He felt too restless for sleep and it was too late to call Lydia. He looked at his book with dissatisfaction. Not all the reviews had been good. 'Trite and exploitative,' is how the *Washington Post* had dismissed it. He thought of his novel, less than half written – all those words to be hacked out before it even got to the weigh-in, before the first critical punch was thrown. By literary temperament, he was a sprinter, not a marathon man.

His eye was drawn back to the typewriter. He fed a sheet into the rollers. The action was oiled and smooth. He stood with his fingers poised over the keys, then found himself typing, 'Look after the Wild'. On reflection, there were angles to the Wildguard venture that might be worth exploring. Checking his watch, he saw that it was a little after midnight, only ten California time. He dialled Caldwell, expecting to find him absent on the drugs and party circuit, but he must have been having an early night or a late start.

'I changed my mind. I'll do the Dexter Smith story.'

'You took a beating at poker, right?'

'Wrong. I cleaned up. When does the expedition leave?'

2

On the morning of her Wildguard interview, Candy got up early and took her father's gundogs for a walk up to his pheasant release pens. When she got back to the house, she found him in the kitchen, dressed in an old army sweater and a silk cravat, eating toast by the Aga. He had been retired for a year, but he was still fit and handsome, and Candy sometimes wondered if he might marry again and how she'd feel if he did.

He kissed her. 'How are my pheasants?'

'They're beginning to feather up at last,' Candy said, pouring herself a cup of tea. 'I flushed a sparrowhawk on the way down. It had caught a pigeon twice its size and was eating it alive. I had to kill it myself.' She could still see the little hawk's demented saffron eye and the pigeon, half-plucked, slowly opening and shutting its beak.

'Nature's cruel,' her father said. 'I hope these Wildguard people know that.'

Candy half-turned her head. 'Of course they do.' The truth was, she had only a vague idea of what Wildguard stood for. She had picked its name out of a directory – just one of the dozens of wildlife conservation and research organizations she'd applied to on graduating from Edinburgh University three months ago. She had almost forgotten Wildguard's existence when the letter arrived from its Co-Director, a woman called Aquila Corrigan. Aquila was going to be in London to look into the possibility of establishing a European branch, and she would be pleased to see Candy on 29 September to discuss a project in Borneo.

Panic. That gave Candy only three days to prepare. Frantic phone calls and a trawl through her local library revealed that Wildguard was an environmental pressure group that advocated direct action against despoilers of nature. It was enough to make Candy think twice about taking up the invitation, but it was the first positive response she'd received in forty-one applications, and Borneo had an allure she couldn't resist. At the very least, she told herself, the interview would be good practice.

After breakfast, she went upstairs to bathe and then stood naked in front of her dressing-table – a woman in a child's room that was still cluttered with soft toys, teenage fiction, Pony Club rosettes and pop pin-ups a decade out of fashion. Look at you, she told her reflection – twenty-six years old, still living at home, and going for your first proper interview.

Her gaze dropped to the photograph of her mother and grew wistful. They had been very close, so alike in looks that strangers occasionally took them for sisters, but her mother had died of cancer more than four years ago, three weeks before Candy's wedding day.

'Such a bloody nuisance,' she'd told Candy two days before she died, 'but of course I'll be watching you walk up the aisle from the best seat in church.'

With a sigh, Candy turned back to the mirror, assessing herself for signs of deterioration. Skin good, hair okay – thick, oat blonde and wavy. Breasts modest, firm and mathematically round, hips fuller, legs *just* long enough to keep everything in proportion, but not as long as she would have liked.

She opened her wardrobe and grimaced. The right approach might be to dress up as an ecological guerrilla, but she didn't have the clothes for that, let alone the nerve, so in the end she settled for a cotton shirt, silk waistcoat, a wool skirt below the knee and minimal make-up

'A bit casual, isn't it?' her father said when she came down.

It was an Indian summer's day, and in a fit of friskiness, she decided to drive to London in her convertible – a powder-blue 1957 Lancia Aurelia Spyder that had been left to her by her mother, who had inherited it from her uncle, a privateer racing driver and wastrel. Driving up the motorway with the top down, she attracted a lot of attention. Truck drivers flashed their lights, and fast-lane reps in fleet saloons slowed as they passed, their stares ranging from fond or wistful to downright lecherous. Candy kept a polite smile on her face and her eyes on the road.

She parked the car in Belgravia, where she'd arranged to spend the night with her great-aunt Peggy. Then she tubed and bussed up to Hornsey – a hideous trek that took half as long as her drive from Hampshire. Her interview was for 3.15 and the address turned out to be a maisonette in an Edwardian terrace. As she reached for the entryphone her eye fell on a poster in the window advertising a Druid gathering.

'Here we go,' Candy murmured, activating the entry phone.

'Hi, Candy,' a disembodied American voice said, 'come on in.'

'I was completely useless. Absolutely the last person they wanted.'

Over supper in a West-Eleven brasserie, Candy was explaining how the interview had gone to Gemma – living proof that if you make a close friend in youth, you're stuck with them for life. They had been opposites at school, and they were polar opposites still. For every virtue Candy possessed, Gemma had the corresponding vice; she was chaotic, tarty and an indiscriminate substance abuser. Work for her was an extension of her social life; at present she was some kind of assistant on a glossy woman's monthly, and disastrously entangled with an Uzbeki warlord's son whom she suspected of being a bullion smuggler or worse. Candy supposed that whatever vicarious pleasure she got from Gemma's lurid lifestyle was matched by the satisfaction her friend got from Candy's provincial stodginess.

Gemma eyed her closely. 'What were you wearing?'

Candy glanced down. 'As a matter of fact, what I've got on.'

Gemma was aghast. '*Darling*, you look like one of those Jaeger ladies employed by estate agents to show house buyers around damp old rectories. Why didn't you call me? I know this place in Fulham that does these wonderful *faux* hunt-sab outfits. I could have got you discount.'

'I really don't think my clothes were the problem.'

At the next table, a beautiful young couple were poring over a marine chart. From snippets of conversation, Candy gathered that they were planning a winter cruise in the Maldives.

'How grisly,' Gemma said when Candy told her where she'd been interviewed.

'The house was perfectly decent, but Aquila was rather out of the ordinary.'

'Cropped hair and plastic sandals? Smelling of mildew?'

Candy laughed. 'Tall, statuesque, long black hair. Black everything. Black clothes, black eyes. And she had tattoos on her shoulder. Oh, and she's a pagan.'

When Gemma's eyes rounded, Candy couldn't help

observing that they were puffier than when she had last seen her.

'Aquila's her spirit guide,' she explained, 'a Sioux holywoman who was killed in Canada. Before that she was an Irish witch. She's led a very persecuted existence.'

'She sounds crackers.'

'I rather liked her. She was so sincere, and ... I don't know ... pure.'

'So why didn't she go for you? Wrong birth sign?'

Candy smiled. 'It all started sensibly enough. She asked me why I'd gone to university so late.'

'Did you tell her about Roger?'

Candy's smile went out. Roger – Captain Roger Yuill – had been the man she had come within three weeks of marrying. The perfect match, her friends had sighed – handsome, independently wealthy, heir to a large farm twenty miles from Candy's own well-padded home.

'Of course not,' she said. 'It wasn't relevant. We talked about my course.'

'You scraped through, I assume.'

'Yes.' Candy hesitated. 'Actually, I got a First.'

Gemma's eyes widened. 'Golly, I had no idea you were *that* clever.' Her tone was one of alarm.

'Oh, I just slogged – in the library from morning to night. Absolutely no social life.'

'No men?'

'The other students had just left school. The age difference seemed phenomenal.'

'Yum-yum. I shagged a seventeen-year-old last year. God, he was delicious – so big for his age.' Gemma's tone became wheedling. 'Candy, you must have met *someone* – some hairy Highlander.'

'Nobody you could call a proposition. Anyway,' she said, 'things went wrong when Aquila asked me why I'd applied to Wildguard. You see, I knew next to nothing about them.'

'How did you get around that?'

'I didn't. I came clean.'

Gemma stopped chewing. 'Candy, that was silly. To get a job these days, you need attitude.'

'It wouldn't have mattered, because then Aquila gave me a personality test.'

'Golly. What sort of things did she ask?'

'Oh, who's the most important influence in my life? Am I frightened of germs? Did I agree with keeping pets? Pretty weird stuff.'

'How did you do?'

'Apparently, I'm a very centred individual, but my centre's in the wrong place.'

'I expect you told her you had dogs and rode to hounds.'

'Funnily enough,' Candy said, beginning to enjoy herself, 'I did.'

'That's it; you're unemployable. You'll just have to get married.'

'What finished me off was telling her that I wasn't a vegetarian. Meat is murder as far as Aquila's concerned. She gave me a gruesome account of slaughterhouse procedure, describing how the animals go to their deaths terrified, adrenalin pouring into their systems, poisoning the meat with the essence of fear. Basically, if you eat meat, you're consuming negativity.'

Gemma eyed her pork and seaweed dish. 'Candy, I hope it was a super job.'

'It wasn't a proper job – only a three-weeks' expenses-paid trip to Borneo. Wildguard's going to survey a part of the rain forest that's threatened by a hydro-electric scheme. They weren't interested in my zoological skills. All they want is a cook and bottle-washer.'

'You had a jolly lucky escape. Imagine being stuck in the jungle with that woman spouting on at you.'

Candy's attention strayed to the couple studying their charts. 'Yes, but Borneo would have been such a thrill.'

Gemma lit a cheroot. 'What next?'

'Carry on job-hunting.'

'Remember Nathalie? Her father's bought a block of flats in Chelsea and she wants someone to help do them up.'

'I don't want to be an interior decorator. I want to work with animals.'

'Horses no good? You used to be passionate about them.'

'Wild animals, Gemma.'

Gemma took a drag. 'Mm. Any chance you and Roger...?'

'None whatsoever,' Candy said, trying to bury the subject.

'He's still absolutely loopy about you, you know. I met him at a drinks party a couple of weeks ago and he talked about nothing else.'

'He's wasting his time.'

Gemma blew smoke ostentatiously. 'Sex no good?'

'Distinctive.'

'Well, that's something.'

'Distinctive, not distinguished.'

Gemma examined the tip of her cheroot. 'Remember the night you broke off the engagement? We were all at some dreary ball and you took Roger off to tell him the bad news.'

A sort of blank screen fell across Candy's mind. She nodded.

'Well,' Gemma said with a guilty laugh, 'for reasons far too sordid to explain, a friend and I also needed privacy

34

34

and we followed you upstairs. Unfortunately, the first bedroom we tried was already occupied.'

For a moment, Candy's mind remained blank, then the entire, awful scene flooded back – Yuill thrusting and grunting above her, the door opening, a gasp followed by a giggle, and then muffled laughter growing less restrained as the intruders made off down the corridor.

'Don't look so furious, Candy. I thought it was awfully sweet of you to soften the blow like that.'

Quaking, Candy leaned forward, the force of her emotions sucking the smile off Gemma's face. 'I didn't have any choice, you idiot. He was raping me.'

Gemma stared stupidly back. 'Roger? You? Christ, Candy.' Automatically, her hand reached for her drink.

'Now you know why I want nothing more to do with him.'

Slowly, Gemma resumed an upright posture. Distractedly, she turned and raised her hand to summon a waiter. 'My God,' she murmured. 'That's my last illusion shattered. I thought that sort of thing only happened to slappers like me.' Suddenly she was in a hurry, digging into her bag, calling for the bill, thrusting her credit card at the waiter. 'Anyway,' she said gaily, 'you can't stay buried in the country. You must move to London. Break a few hearts.'

'My father ...' Candy said, but broke off at Gemma's squeak of alarm. Candy glanced behind her and stiffened. She glared at Gemma.

'Cross my heart,' Gemma hissed. 'I had no idea.'

'You'd better go,' Candy told her, then turned with a perfectly judged smile. 'Roger, what a surprise.'

'Candy, how wonderful to see you. Hello, Gemma.'

Yuill was with a party of six, including a tall blonde woman, who looked down on Candy with undisguised hostility. Yuill didn't introduce her and the party moved away to their table.

'Oh gosh,' Gemma said, scrambling up. 'I promised I'd phone Gavin to see if we could use his place for a fashion shoot.'

As she bolted, Yuill lowered himself into her chair. 'More beautiful than ever,' he said.

'You look very well yourself, Roger.'

It was better than the truth. Though still handsome, Yuill's features had thickened into a suggestion of jowliness, accentuated by late-night shadow. He seemed a little drunk.

'I thought you never came up to town,' he said.

'I had an interview.'

'Successful?'

'No. Completely fluffed it.'

'How's the general?'

'Oh, flourishing. He's started a shoot and he's fussing about his pheasants.'

'Please give him my regards. And love to your brother, of course. You know I resigned my commission.'

'Yes, I was surprised.'

'Soldiering's dull work these days. When all's said and done, you join the army to shoot and be shot at. The only place left to make a killing is the City, so that's where I'm going. I've decided I may as well be rich.'

'Roger, you *are* rich.'

'Land-rich. It's not the same thing.'

Candy caught the blonde's baleful eye. 'Roger, your friends are waiting.'

'Candy, will you forgive me?'

She looked away, her mouth set in a line. 'Yes.'

'I was such a bloody fool. I don't know what came over me.'

'I'd rather not talk about it.'

'There's something I must ask you. Would you have gone through with the marriage if your mother hadn't died?'

Candy's answer came out shaky. 'I suppose I would.'

'And do you think we would have been happy?'

Candy looked him in the eye. 'I would have tried. I'm not sure it would have been enough.'

Yuill smiled around as if he was mildly amused by the other diners. 'Found anyone else?'

Candy could hear the tall blonde woman's voice raised in indignation. 'No, but ...'

'Nor me. If anything, my feelings have grown stronger.'

The only way out was straight forward. 'But *I've* changed, Roger. Four years ago, marriage and children were the height of my ambitions. I still hope to have a family eventually, but I also want a job – a career. I want to do something with my life.'

'I wouldn't stop you. I could help you.'

'I've only just graduated. I may work abroad. The interview I failed was for a job in Borneo.'

There was a commotion behind her and the blonde woman stalked out, trailing clouds of anger. Yuill didn't seem to notice her departure.

'Candy, can we go somewhere to talk? I promise there'll be no more lapses of behaviour on my part.'

'I'm sorry Roger. I'm staying with my aunt and I haven't spent enough time with her.'

Yuill's smile twisted. 'That woman's a witch. I think it was her who poisoned you against me.'

'She did no such thing,' Candy said. 'You did that all by yourself.' As she rose to leave, Yuill trapped her hand. She didn't try to pull it away; she stared down at it and didn't speak until he looked up.

'You don't understand, do you? That night ... what you did ... if I'd had the means, I would have killed you.'

Candy walked fast, trying to outpace memory, her breath smoking in the autumn air. Roger had sunk into the grave of her consciousness, and seeing him again had been like meeting a stranger. Imagining that she might now be his wife, she shuddered and glanced over her shoulder.

Raped by the man she had intended to entrust with the rest of her life, the man she had dreamed would help create a replica of her parents' blissfully happy marriage. How little she understood people, she thought, anger washing over her. Gemma was right: nobody would employ a silly little fool like her.

It was past eleven when she let herself into her aunt's flat. The sitting-room light was still on. Tired after the long day and the emotional wear and tear, Candy tried to creep past.

'Is that you, darling?'

Candy took a breath and formed a smile.

Peggy sat in an armchair, almost walled in by London Library books. She was old, dotty and as shrewd as a stoat.

'Pleasant evening, Candy?'

'Very pleasant.'

'You look a bit pale.'

She hesitated. 'I bumped into Roger.'

'Oh yes? How is he?'

'He's put on weight and decided to become rich.'

'Never go back to old lovers. At least not until you've discovered that all the new ones are worse. Fortunately, by then it's too late.'

'I've no intention of going back.'

'Very glad to hear it. Never marry a man in uniform.'

'He's left the army.'

'They never grow up, you know. They live such pampered lives – people waiting on them hand and foot,

38

every minute of their day organized. Overgrown school-boys, your father included. Now, dear, Adrian's a lovely man, but utterly hopeless. Your poor mother ...'

Candy clenched her fists. Peggy, though she loved her dearly, could be a right bitch.

Candy smiled brightly. 'It's been a bit of a day. I think I'll go to bed.' She leaned over, lips pursed in a kiss.

Peggy raised her cheek. 'Oh, that American girl phoned – Aquila. She wants you to call her.'

'What, now?

'In the morning. She's meditating now.' Aunt Peggy smiled at Candy's astonishment. 'Interesting girl. We had a very pleasant chat.'

Candy took a wary step backwards, feeling for a chair. 'What about?'

'All sorts of things, witches – she calls them wiccans – paganism. She explained that pagans aren't Satanists; the word comes from the French *pays*, like peasant. Isn't that interesting? We talked about holistic medicine and she recommended I try myrtle oil for my arthritis.' Peggy frowned. 'Do you think Harrods will have it?'

Candy's head had begun to spin. 'I expect so.' She placed her hands flat on her knees. 'Peggy, did Aquila tell you why she wanted me to call?'

'About the position you applied for.'

'And?'

'She asked me if I thought you'd be suitable. I told her that you'd be very suitable indeed.'

Candy clutched her knees. 'What did she say?'

'She's worried that you might not get a visa in time. I told her my godson works in the Foreign Office and could probably oil the wheels.' Peggy smiled fondly. 'Well, then, where is it that you're off to?'

'Borneo,' Candy said faintly.

'That'll be nice, dear. Gerald was there in the war,

training headhunters to kill the Japanese. Charming people, he said. Absolutely darling little men. Provided they liked you, of course.'

3

Wildguard's plan was to rendezvous in Pontianaka, on Borneo's western seaboard, but after two stop-overs, Candy reached Jakarta late in the evening to find that the onward flight had been cancelled and the next plane didn't leave until dawn. Woolly with travel fatigue, she was gathering up her luggage when she noticed a young man smiling in her direction. She looked behind her, but there was no one else in his sights. He came forward, his wide-set smiling gaze inviting reciprocal warmth. American.

'Wildguard?'

'Yes,' she said, offering a carefully weighted hand. 'Candida Woodville. Everyone calls me Candy. How do you do?'

'Jay Boucher,' he said, 'and I'm doing just fine.' He regarded her with the hint of a question mark. 'I'm the journalist covering the story.'

'Oh,' she said, not sure what story he was talking about.

'You speak Indonesian.'

'That was Malay. I spent some time in Sarawak and Brunei.'

'This is my first time in the tropics,' Boucher confessed. His gaze roamed about for a second. 'Looks like we're stuck for the night. What say we head downtown, find a hotel, then go for a meal?'

Candy wasn't used to falling in with the plans of strangers at the drop of a hat, but Boucher's suggestion was perfectly sensible, and he didn't look threatening. On the way to the taxi rank, she completed her appraisal. Fashionably-cut linen suit, blue cotton shirt and snazzy tie. Soft brown hair rather foppishly cut. Clever eyes, a clear tundra grey and placed at an intriguing upward slant. Slim build, above medium height, but not tall compared to the men in her life. Not her type. Far too pleased with himself.

Jakarta was a reeking steam bath, choked by people and traffic. To Candy the cops at the intersections seemed to be on the point of nervous collapse or mass shoot-out.

'My kind of town,' Boucher said, sniffing appreciatively. 'Feel the energy. Hell, imagine being mayor.'

'Are you an environmental writer?'

He grinned disarmingly. 'Contemporary cultural side-bars. My words are written on water. And you?'

'I'm a zoologist,' she said, and immediately regretted the claim.

'How long have you been involved with Wildguard?'

'Hardly any time at all. I wrote to them on the off-chance about three months ago.'

'So this is your first campaign?'

'Yes. Aquila Corrigan's the only one I've met.'

Boucher nodded with disconcerting slowness.

'You're looking at me in a strange way'

'Sorry, it's just that you're not quite what I expected.'

'And what was that?'

'Oh, I don't know – a homespun hippy with happy-clappy eyes.'

Alarm bells began to ring in Candy's head. 'Is that the typical Wildguard member?'

Again Boucher flashed his smile. 'Damned if I know.

42

You're my only example so far, and you're so normal it's almost disappointing.'

Candy gave him a look that could have opened a clam at fifty paces. 'Thank you.'

He was impervious. 'Let's hope Leo lives up to his billing.'

'What do you mean?'

'Didn't Aquila tell you?'

'Tell me what?' Candy demanded, beginning to feel thoroughly cheesed off.

'About Jaeger's Hell's Angels' days. The guy's got a sheet a mile long – assault with a deadly weapon, indecent exposure, innumerable traffic violations.'

Candy stared blindly out at the street. 'How interesting,' she said in a far-off manner.

'I guess he's reformed. He's the guy who got Dexter Smith to open his wallet. His gang used to handle security for his concerts, and when he turned Green, he went backstage and put the squeeze on him.' Boucher hesitated, then cleared his throat. 'You *do* know about Dexter Smith?'

Candy eyed him coldly. 'I'm not that out of touch.'

'I meant about him coming on the expedition.' Boucher's insufferable smile changed to a concerned frown. 'That's why I'm here. Dexter's the hook. Didn't they ...? Ah, I see they didn't. I ... ah ... guess they didn't want word to get out in case it attracted undesirables.'

Candy stared at an overloaded bus, wishing she could throw herself under its wheels. 'Who else is coming?' she asked dully.

'The usual bunch of psychotic ideologues,' he said, then registered her expression. 'Just kidding,' he said hastily.

Candy took a cold shower then, with great reluctance, anticipating fresh humiliations, she joined Boucher in the lobby and they set off into the night.

43

They ate at a *warung*, a food stall parked at the edge of a main thoroughfare. The night was turbid, the sky tinged the colour of rotten shellfish and charged with fumes and electricity. Traffic brayed on one side and pop music blared from the other. In the centre of this bedlam, the *warung* was an oasis of medieval calm. Moths beat at kerosene lamps under which sat dignified men with smooth leathery faces smoking clove-scented cigarettes.

'What's your particular area of zoological expertise?' Boucher asked.

'Ethology – animal behaviour. Cats are a special subject of mine. I helped on a tiger population survey in Nepal last year.'

Boucher sampled a dish of spicy dumplings. 'You hoping to pursue your interest on this trip?'

Candy tried to keep her voice steady. 'I'm afraid I must have given you the wrong impression. Wildguard hasn't employed me as a zoologist. Aquila took me on as a general assistant.'

'You said you'd been to Borneo before.'

'During my school holidays. My father was stationed there – in the army.'

'So what were you doing before Wildguard signed you up?'

'I only finished my degree four months ago,' Candy admitted. She wondered if she could pass for twenty-two, then rebuked herself for her cowardice. 'I went to university late.'

'And before that?'

'You mean work?'

Boucher nodded.

Candy looked away, her gaze coming to rest on an altercation between a pedestrian and a pedicab driver. 'I've never had what you'd call a proper job. I was a chalet girl in Switzerland; I schooled horses in New

Zealand; and I've worked in an art gallery. That's about it.'

Boucher had stopped eating. He appeared bemused.

Candy's face tingled. 'You think I'm incredibly naive, don't you?'

Boucher grinned. 'It's okay. I'll look out for you.'

They had adjacent hotel rooms, and before parting, Candy asked Boucher if he happened to have a copy of his book with him. He had and was flattered by her interest.

The pieces didn't resemble journalism as Candy knew it. The title story was about a Michigan teacher and his wife who claimed to have recovered an extra-terrestrial being and performed a post-mortem on it in their garage. Candy gave up on this nonsense halfway through and skipped randomly through some of the other stories.

Laying the book down, she looked at the ceiling. Next door, Boucher was clacking on a typewriter. The longer she lay there, the more she became convinced that he was writing about her. She even began to provide the text.

Slipping a cotton robe on, she went into the corridor, lifted her hand, lost her nerve and regained it, then knocked. Boucher came to the door, still dressed.

'Was I disturbing you?'

She saw the typewriter on the bed. 'That's rather antique.'

Boucher grimaced. 'A veteran foreign correspondent gave it to me. I brought it along out of sentiment.' He directed a rueful glance at his book. 'Not your kind of thing.'

'The stories. Did you make them up?'

Boucher was startled. 'No, they're true. Everything happened.'

'Did the characters know you intended writing about them?'

'Most of them. Maybe not all.'

'Are you writing about me?'

'What gives you that idea?'

Candy felt her ears redden. 'The questions you ask, the way you look at me.'

'There are other reasons a man might want to look at you.'

Candy's blush spread and there was nothing she could do to stop it. 'I'm serious.'

'So am I,' Boucher said. He scratched his head. 'Look, we're both here to do a job. Mine is writing about this expedition. You're part of it, which makes you a legitimate subject.'

'So anything I say might appear in your story.'

Boucher smiled condescendingly. 'Like what?'

'How about foolish Candy Woodville running off to Borneo without knowing anything about her companions?'

'Never crossed my mind.'

'Don't patronize me, Mr Boucher.'

Boucher sighed. 'At the risk of denting your self-esteem, I'd better point out that you're not central to the story. Dexter Smith and the Wildguard leaders are the main players.'

Desperately, she hung on. 'But you won't give me your word.'

'That I won't mention you? No. You never know, you could turn out to be the star of the show.'

'In that case, it would be best if we didn't speak.'

Boucher squeezed the back of his neck and gave a short laugh. 'Candy, you're taking ...'

'Goodnight,' she said. Thrusting the book into his hands, she dashed for her room.

Lying in bed, feeling more than a little bit foolish, she heard the screech of Boucher's typewriter and then, a couple of seconds later, the faint *ping* of balled-up paper hitting the waste bin. Smiling guiltily, she turned over and fell fast asleep.

A gecko unsplayed itself from the wall and darted behind a mirror as Candy erupted from bed. She banged on the wall. 'Hurry up! They forgot our alarm call.'

She ran into the shower, turned on the taps, took off her robe, swore, hurried back into the bedroom and pounded on the wall again.

'Wake up! We're going to miss the plane.'

There was no response.

Dragging on her robe, she burst out of the door, straight into Boucher's arms. For a moment they were in full body contact, she wearing a flimsy gown, he fully dressed and groomed, fragrant with aftershave and wearing his most sinuous smile.

'Mm,' he said.

Candy pulled free. 'What do you think you're doing? Why didn't you wake me?'

'I knocked half an hour ago, but you were out of it. I thought you could use the rest, so I told the bellboy I'd call you myself.'

'I'll bloody well decide who wakes me.'

He raised his hands and backed off. 'Hey, I'm sorry.'

She gave a little growl. 'Call a taxi.'

'All done. I also ordered coffee and juice.' He looked past her into her room. 'Go take your shower.'

As Candy soaped herself, she berated herself furiously. She was never late, never overslept, but now Boucher had marked her down as a slothful incompetent along with everything else. What sharpened her anger was the recognition that there had been a sexual component in their skirmishing.

'Coffee,' he called. 'Okay if I bring it in?'

'Leave it, thank you.'

But when she came out of the bathroom, towelling her hair, he was standing with the pot poised to pour, wearing that cocky smile. 'Java,' he said. 'How do you take it?'

'Alone.'

'It's okay. I'll look the other way.'

'No you won't. I'll meet you downstairs in ten minutes.'

Eyes veiled slightly, he backed out.

Rubbing her hair dry, she recognized how uptight and crabby she must seem, but she didn't care. She wasn't going to have some bloody American journalist taking notes while she dressed. She threw on her clothes – underwear, cotton shirt and slacks, rope sandals. She gathered her hair in a comb, gulped down a malaria pill with her coffee and left the room at a run.

Boucher was subdued in the taxi. Serves him right, Candy thought. It was still dark when they reached the airport, the city already throbbing; but the sun rose as they took off, and Candy's spirits lifted with it, soared as they lifted clear of emerald green hills and silver paddy fields. Bewitched by the tropical abundance, Candy forgot about her companion.

'You really going to stick to your vow of silence?'

Part of Candy was aware that she was taking her resentment too far. 'With you I am, yes.'

'Boy, you are *prickly*,' Boucher said. He lay back, eyes closed. 'Listen, I know we haven't got off to a flying start, but I don't see why we can't be friends.'

'As the spider said to the fly.'

Boucher regarded her with what appeared to be amusement. 'You've had bad experiences with journalists, have you?'

'My father has. I've seen how they distort and invent.'

Boucher's forehead creased. 'What rank is he?'

'General.'

48

Boucher studied her closely. 'It figures,' he said at last, and looked away, his eyes flinty. 'Have it your way. Obviously, it's what you're used to.'

Candy's toes had just started to uncurl from that snub when the sight of the Kalimantan coast swimming through mist induced fresh collywobbles. Boucher was right; it wasn't his fault that she hadn't done her homework.

Pontianaka sprawled into view – a grey blight lapped by monsoon green.

'I expected an airstrip hacked out of jungle,' Boucher said.

Stealing a look at him, Candy wondered if now was the time to call a truce. But the moment passed and then they were landing, buffeting down through layers of turbulence. As she left the plane, the heat closed round her like a scorching poultice.

'I wonder what the plan is,' she said after they'd cleared Customs.

'Grab a shower, a sleep and a change of clothes. Let's find a cab.'

'No need,' Candy said, spotting a Chinese man holding aloft a Wildguard placard. 'We're expected.'

At her wave, he hurried over, tapping his watch. 'Quick,' he ordered, 'follow me. Leave your luggage. It will be taken to your hotel.'

'Hold on,' Boucher protested. 'Where are we going?'

'Hurry, please. Your friends are about to take off.'

Trotting after him, Candy looked back to see that Boucher hadn't moved. 'What are you waiting for? We can catch them if only you stop dawdling.'

Boucher groaned. 'We only just touched down. I've been in the air for two days. I don't want to get on another airplane.'

Good, Candy thought, glad to be rid of him. 'I'll tell

them you're not feeling well.' She slung her bag over her shoulder. 'See you this evening.'

She nearly made it.

'Wait.'

Damn, she thought.

'What do I need?'

'Oh, just come as you are.'

4

Muttering curses, Boucher jogged in Candy's wake as their escort led them out on to the runway. He was seriously disenchanted – weary of all this shuttling about, pissed off at Candy treating him like a contagious disease. He piled into a Suzuki pick-up, crammed hip to hip and knee to knee with her, and wiped sweat from his brow. 'They must have chartered a private plane.'

Candy pointed through the smeared windscreen. 'Look!'

At the far end of the runway, a huge silver balloon shimmered in the vortices like an alien gastropod. On its canopy, Boucher made out the Wildguard logo above Rousseau's painting of a tiger slinking through lush jungle.

Candy pulled a face. 'That's not very appropriate. There aren't any tigers in Borneo.'

'Environmentally right-on, though.'

They caught up with the main party in the shadowed entrance of a rusting hangar. A couple of crisply uniformed pilots were addressing them, and Boucher, usually so snappily turned-out himself, wished that this meeting could have been more propitiously timed. He felt wrung out, limp, uncool.

A large man detached himself from the group. '*Selamat datang,*' he called, stretching wide his arms like an Old Testament prophet. He was massive, a force of nature himself, with a full red beard that grew almost up to light blue eyes set deep behind wireframed spectacles. His hair, what remained of it, was pulled back in a pony-tail. 'Leo Jaeger,' he declared, and Boucher felt the underlying strength of his grip. 'Hey, Candy, terrific to meet you, terrific to have you along. Jay, this is Aquila Corrigan, my life partner and the rock on which Wildguard stands.'

Boucher looked back into jet-black, rather protuberant eyes aimed intently at him along a nose that was indeed aquiline. Great face, he thought – like a Medici portrait. From the neck down, though, the effect was more martial arts student or Vietnamese peasant, and when Boucher shook Aquila's hand, he noticed that her shoulder was tattooed with what looked like runic symbols.

'No need to introduce Dexter Smith.'

In Boucher's experience, many performers of Dexter's stature were mythomaniacs, incarnations of their own hype, but Dexter sang for the common people, and in this setting he almost passed for one. Boucher knew how to read the clues though – the octagonal shades guarding the poetically vulnerable face, the baggy designer pants and overshirt, the discreet but indubitably 22-carat Rolex. He checked Dexter's aura for the faint lustre that the true star, no matter how intellectually dim, emanated. There it was.

'Glad you could make it,' Dexter Smith said, the voice husky and deep, raising tuneful echoes of emotional woundings, doomed loners and youthful angst.

'Glad you asked me,' Boucher said with honest deference.

'And I bet you've seen Nadine Wells before,' Jaeger said.

'Only in my dreams,' Boucher smirked, then thought: Damn, why did I say that?

Because Nadine was indeed the American dreamgirl made flesh – tall and leggy, full-lipped and big-eyed, glossy-skinned, with a thick plait of honey-coloured hair hanging to the waist of her artfully draped sarong. She was so flawless that, beside her, Candy looked dumpy and Aquila plain grim.

'Hi, Jay,' she sighed, apparently rather hot and bored.

'Hi, Candy.'

When Jaeger moved to the next man in the line-up, Boucher began to wonder if Wildguard's supporters were recruited entirely on celebrity status or pin-up looks. This guy was six-two of tanned muscle topped off by a determined jaw, dazzling toothwork and sun-streaked blond hair.

'G'day, mate,' he said affably. 'So you're the journo. Looking forward to talking to you over a beer.'

'Robert Marriot's our consultant,' Jaeger explained. 'He's a wildlife biologist and one of the world's leading experts on rain forest ecology.'

Boucher could see now that Marriot's physique hadn't been honed in the gym or health salon. His arms were corded by hard toil, not pumped up by isometrics, and the skin around his ferrous eyes was crinkled by sun. An outdoorsman, without doubt.

'Kent Bartok,' Jaeger said, turning to the next man. 'Kent's one of our volunteers.'

Bartok's face lit up in the sunniest smile Boucher had seen this side of Salt Lake City. He had yellow curls and a gymnast's physique, and he wore Bermuda shorts and a T-shirt illustrated with a map of the universe and an arrow saying YOU ARE HERE.

'Disco,' Jaeger announced, moving down the line. 'Disco's our latest convert. We only met last night, at a beach restaurant. He's doing a solo tour of the East, and when it turned out he shared our ideals, it seemed only right to invite him along for the ride.'

The lone traveller was as slim as a duellist, dark and good-looking, with raisin-coloured eyes. 'I'm thinking of writing a book, too,' he said. 'Hey, maybe you can give me some tips.'

'Sure,' Boucher said, offhand, already moving on to the last of the Wildguard team – a wiry, long-haired cultural throwback with the sort of parched, nocturnal face Boucher associated with the music biz.

'Our sound and vision man Ronnie Trigg – plain Trigg to his friends. Trigg will be putting together some film of our expedition. Ronnie's another Brit, Candy, but he's lived in LA for a long time.'

'Wotcha,' Trigg said.

Finally, Jaeger turned to the aircrew. 'Captain Sixt Haimendorf and Josef Fieser. They were just briefing us on today's trip.'

'We're going up in that balloon?'

Jaeger laughed. 'Balloon? Hellfire, you're looking at the world's most advanced airship.'

'Yeah?' Boucher said, eyeing the ponderous craft. 'What happens if you stick a pin in it?'

Fieser, the co-pilot, stepped forward. He was a studious-looking beanpole, in contrast to Haimendorf, who was stout and bearded and looked like an operatic tenor.

'The envelope is constructed of six layers of Tedlar and neoprene inflated by four buoyancy bags containing inert, non-inflammable helium gas. There are also two air ballonets. The pressure of these can be altered to adjust the trim.'

Boucher nodded as if he understood the technical ramifications. 'How do you steer?'

'Computer-aided fibre-optics control the rudders and elevators. The engines can be rotated through two hundred degrees to assist take-off, landing and other aerial manœuvres.'

'State of the art,' Bartok added happily. 'Twin Porsche engines producing four hundred horses. Cruising speed seventy miles per hour. Maximum altitude around ten thousand feet. Boy!'

'What we're planning on doing,' Jaeger said, 'is to fly up the Landak river, have an in-flight picnic, get to know each other. We'll leave the serious talking until tonight.'

He had to raise his voice to compete with the buzz of a two-stroke motor bike that came smoking across the tarmac and slithered to a stop beside them. An airport official dismounted importantly, took the pilots aside and pointed into the heatwaves boiling off the tarmac. The crew nodded soberly at what he had to say, and then Fieser beckoned Jaeger, who frowned and stroked at his beard before addressing his party.

'Minor adjustment,' he said. 'We've got a report of bad weather brewing out east. Nothing to stop us flying, but we've decided to change our flight plan. You'll be seeing plenty of jungle in the next few days, so instead of heading inland, we'll cruise down the coast, take a look at some offshore islands. Hey, maybe we'll get a sight of some whales.'

'Are you sure it's safe?' Nadine demanded. She had an emphatic New York delivery – sandpaper issuing from velvet.

'The storm won't reach here before nightfall, and by then we'll be back at the hotel.'

'As a matter of curiosity,' Boucher said, 'what kind of weather can the airship handle?'

Fieser hesitated. 'In a wind greater than sixty kilometres, we will not fly.'

'You're grounded by a gale.'

Jaeger showed a trace of impatience. 'Right now, there ain't enough wind to stir a feather and it's forecast to stay that way until after sunset. But if any of you wants to miss out, say so. How about you, Nadine?'

Nadine stuck out her bottom lip. 'I don't want to sit round that crummy hotel on my own.'

Jaeger turned: 'In that case, let's get lift-off.'

From a distance the passenger gondola looked tiny – a succubus clamped to a huge mammary. Close up, though, it was the size of a city hopper. A blessed draught of chilled air doused Boucher as he entered and, looking through the partition into the flight cabin, he was heartened to see instrumentation that wouldn't have disgraced a NASA Space Shuttle.

He chose the rearmost seat, level with the engines, stowed his hat and camera, but kept his tape recorder and notebook to hand. Candy boarded last and looked for a seat away from him. They were all filled.

'No escape,' Boucher said, standing up. 'Here, you take the window.'

'Thank you. I'm fine here.'

'I didn't come for the sights.'

At idle the air-cooled engines sounded like nails jumping inside a can. They hardened in pitch, vectored to increase downward thrust, then the airship rolled only a few yards before making a fuss-free launch. Slowly the city sank away, and Boucher got his first sight of the rain forest – a rumpled canopy spreading with hypnotic monotony to the horizon. Gradually, the undulating green gave way to flat blue as the airship pivoted south over the sea. When they had settled on their stately course, Boucher decided it was time to go to work. Dexter Smith was his intended first call, but as he rose, Jaeger caught his eye and beckoned him up front.

Aquila was sitting next to Jaeger, and she didn't offer to move, forcing Boucher to squat in the aisle.

'You get a chance to read the background material we sent you?' Jaeger asked.

'Sure, but before we talk about your organization's aims, I wonder if I can ask ...'

'... how I made the move from Hell's Angel to nature conservationist.' Jaeger chuckled. 'Hell, it ain't as big a jump as all that – leastways, not according to the last judge I saw. He told me that in his opinion the Angels are a pack of wild animals.'

Boucher glanced at Aquila. Her attention seemed to be on far-off things.

Jaeger shifted his bulk. 'A couple of years ago I got into some strife in San José. My legal adviser told me to take an out-of-state holiday, so I tied a sleeping roll on the Harley and headed on up into Idaho.

'One day I got myself lost on a backroad along the Snake River. It's ranching country there and all along the fence were signs saying trespassers will be shot first and prosecuted after. I came to a crossroads and there was a post with a dog hanging on it, like a big German shepherd. Except it wasn't no dog. It was a wolf, and round its neck was a sign saying: "Keep your vermin in the city."'

Jaeger's expression became reflective. 'I never seen a wolf before, Jay, but when I saw that beast hanging there I got a real strange feeling, like I'd been hurt deep in a part of me I didn't know was there. I cut the wolf down and covered it with rocks and that's all I could do for it. Then I rode into the nearest town.

'Nowheresville – a couple of houses, a store, a gas station and a bar. Outside the bar were a few pick-ups with rifles racked in the back, and the guys inside were cowboys, wearing fancy boots and stetsons. I told them about the wolf and they eyed me up in that mean country way, and one of them said: "You got any trouble with that, mister?"

'Well, boys,' I told them, 'I got more feeling for a timber

wolf than I got for a bunch of shit-kickers getting paid a whack of tax-payers' dollars to grow food no one wants anyway.'

'That was provocative,' Boucher said.

Jaeger gave a rumbly laugh. 'It provoked about six of them to come down on top of me with pool cues and bottles and any shit came to hand. To cut a long fight short, I woke up in a ditch with half my ribs popped and my arm broke and shit knows what else. No point going to the sheriff, even if I was the complaining type, so I dragged myself on the Harley which those dudes had kindly left me and made it to hospital back in Twin Falls.'

Jaeger ruminated for a moment. 'Lying in bed there, I figured on coming back with my outlaws and putting cowboy city to the torch. But I knew if we did that, there wasn't no hope of making it back across the state line. First day out of hospital, walking through town, considering my vengeance, I passed a pagan restaurant and bookstore, and in the window was a poster showing a poisoned wolf.'

'I'm sorry,' Boucher said, 'did you say "pagan" or "vegan"?'

'Dietetically speaking, they're pretty similar. Anyway, I went in and got talking to the lady who runs the place. I told her about the wolf and she said the ranchers shoot them from planes and drop strychnine bait for them. And worst of the bunch, this lady said, is the rancher who owns the spread where I found my wolf. I asked the lady what folks are doing about that. Ain't nothing they can do, she said. The ranchers got the law in their pocket and all the conservationists do is sit round wringing their hands.'

Jaeger's blue eyes shone bright. '"I ain't no hand-wringer," I told her.

'She took me in. I was slow to heal, and she explained

that's because I ate all wrong, filling my tissues with toxins and bad radicals. She put a healing spell on me and within a week I was back on the road, but it was a different road to the one I been travelling.'

Boucher glanced at Aquila again.

'After six weeks, I was ready to pay a call on the rancher. He lives on his own and this particular night he was attending some Cattleman's Association jamboree in Boise. I went out there and let myself in.'

Jaeger laughed. 'What a place! The house is full of hunting trophies – stuffed bears, bighorn sheep, moose, wild boar, buffalo, polar bear, elephant, wild yak, sambur. It's like this guy is on a crusade, like he's set himself to exterminate every creature on the planet except cows.'

Jaeger's eyes altered focus, replaying the moment. 'About midnight, he walks in. I hold him close.'

Boucher found himself pinioned by Jaeger's great hands.

'"Mister," I say, "it's old Wolfie come to pay you back."'

Jaeger stared into Boucher's eyes and gave a mournful howl.

Memory softened his gaze. 'It'll be a long time before that rancher does any more safari-ing.' Jaeger released Boucher from his grip. 'And that, Jay, is how I came to be a conservationist.'

Boucher cleared his throat.

Jaeger stood up, eyes twinkling. 'Now if you'll excuse me, I have to speak to Dexter. Anything more you want, ask Aquila. She's the real inspiration behind Wildguard.'

'I guess you must be the lady who owns the pagan restaurant?'

Aquila acknowledged the fact with minimal head movement.

Boucher decided to explore this intriguing byway later.

'I've been reading the Wildguard literature and I have to confess I find some of your ideology pretty uncivic. For example, you compare humans to maggots feeding on a corpse. You call for a massive reduction in population, the destruction of cities, a return to pre-industrial agriculture.'

'That's not rhetoric,' Aquila said. 'In the last fifty years, the global population has grown faster than in all previous history. Do nothing, and it could double again within the next thirty years. By then there'll be no forests, no wilderness except desert, no fresh water, no large animals except genetically engineered hybrids.'

She spoke in short rhythms, her voice uninflected by passion.

'And Wildguard's solution?'

'Give the world back to nature and redefine our niche in it. People must be educated to understand that they're not special, not God's chosen ones, that they're no more sacred than any other species.'

'You'll have a job convincing the voters that armadillos have the same rights as people.'

'There you have the root of the problem. Individualism's the curse of Western society. "I am" equals "I *mean*", equals six billion personality cults. That's the disease of ego that allows whale species to be exterminated so a few Japanese and Norwegians can make a profit. That's the corrupted Christian ethic that encourages scientists to torture healthy chimpanzees so they can manufacture new drugs that might make the terminally sick and senile live a few months longer.'

'You advocate euthanasia, killing the crippled and defective – a mass cull?'

'I don't believe a human life should be bought at the expense of another individual, human or animal. I wouldn't allow *my* life to be saved if it meant sacrificing another warm-blooded creature.'

'Even a rat?'

'That's a cheap journalistic equation. But yes – even a rat.'

Boucher wondered how far down the evolutionary tree Aquila was prepared to take her altruism. 'You talk about equal rights for humans and animals, but if the stories are true, Wildguard is prepared to use violence against people to achieve its ends. I'm talking about the logging workers who have been injured by your alleged monkey-wrenching tactics.'

'Since animals are an oppressed minority that can't protect themselves, it's legitimate for people to come to their defence. Those timber companies were warned of the consequences of their actions and chose to put profits first.'

From Aquila's patient, patronising tone, Boucher knew he wouldn't find any chinks in her armour. 'What level of population do you believe we should be aiming for?'

'No more than five hundred million.'

'Tough on the other five and a half billion. How do you persuade us to lay down our lives, or are you relying on war, disease and famine to do the job?'

'I believe a universal mind shift will occur, just as it did two thousand years ago. It's already happening. For me, the Year 2000 is Year Zero – a chance to start over again.'

'History's against you, Aquila. Humans aren't going to vote themselves out of existence.'

'History's just a habit, reinforcing our previous perception of reality and blinding us to new possibilities. History closes doors.'

'You're a fan of William Blake.'

'I seek wisdom in many places.'

'But not in science.'

'I believe in mystery not mastery, an organic universe

61

not a mechanical one.' Aquila's voice grew more animated. 'Ask yourself something, Jay. Do you want to live in a world with standing room only, a world where no birds sing and the environment's entirely a by-product of industry? Think about it.'

'I don't have to,' Boucher said. 'It sounds like Humboldt Park, the neighbourhood where I grew up.'

As Boucher flexed his cramped legs, Kent Bartok, the curly-headed volunteer, engaged him with his eager smile.

'You work full time for Wildguard?'

'No, I'm a core teacher in a positive peer culture program for adjudicated youths. This is a real exciting break for me.'

'I bet.'

On Bartok's lap was a Bible, on Disco's a mag opened at a photo spread of a glowering platinum blonde in a studded leather jacket falling open around her tits. He looked up with a lazy grin. 'I'm tempting Kent from the ways of righteousness.'

Despite Disco's friendly manner, Boucher found himself downgrading his own smile. Observing his cheap, flashy clothes and nylon sports bag, Boucher wondered about his claim to be an ecologically friendly globe-trotter. Still, he wasn't going to be around after today, and it cost nothing to be pleasant.

'Where are you from, Disco? How did you fetch up in a burg like Pontianaka?'

'That's a true-life adventure story. One day I'll tell you.'

'I guess today is your last chance.'

'Didn't Leo tell you? He's invited me along for the whole trip. Him and me kind of hit it off.'

Boucher glanced at the soft porn mag. 'Another champion of the biotic community.'

'Sure, I love animals.'

'What kind of work are you escaping from?'

'Escaping?'

'You know – job, nine-to-five.'

Disco frowned up from under long lashes. 'You ask an awful lot of questions, Jay.'

'It's what *I* do for a living,' Boucher told him. He paused. 'Now your turn.'

'A hundred bucks says you'll never guess.'

Boucher wondered why he was wasting time on the man. 'No bet, Disco. You're not *that* interesting.'

Disco's features froze, then expanded in an intense smile. 'Say, a writer's got to have a point of view – an angle. Right?'

Boucher shrugged. 'It helps.'

'So what's your angle on Wildguard?'

'I don't have one. Not yet.'

Disco looked dubious. 'Seems to me Leo's taking a big risk. How can he be sure you're gonna be on their side?'

'If he's worried about bad publicity, he shouldn't have asked me along.'

Disco leaned across the aisle. 'Hey, Leo, you'd better run Jay's copy past you when he's finished.'

Boucher felt his temper rising. He placed a hand on Disco's shoulder. 'You won't tell me what your business is, so I sure as hell don't intend to have you interfering in mine.'

Disco raised his hands. 'Shit, now I've pissed you off. Sorry, man.'

Boucher nodded.

As he turned, Disco took hold of his sleeve and cast a speculative glance past him.

'That English girl,' he whispered. 'You got a romance going?'

'Candy? What's it got to do with you?'

63

'Hell, now don't get mad again. I just want to know the state of play.'

Boucher kept his anger under restraint. 'I only met her yesterday.'

'Hell, I laid eyes on her for the first time an hour ago, and already I'm wondering if she tastes as sweet as she sounds.'

Boucher drew a deep breath and unhooked Disco's hand. 'I don't think you're her type.'

'Opposites attract,' Disco said, and flicked to another photo.

After this, it was with a certain grimness that Boucher made his way back to Dexter Smith. They shook hands again.

'Delta sent me the album. It's good. The instrumentation on some of the tracks. What did you use?'

'Gamelan orchestra. We recorded some of the backing on Bali.'

'Bali was delicious,' Nadine said.

Her sweet lustre took away the taste left by Boucher's exchange with Disco. 'You here to lend your name to Wildguard's campaign?'

'Frankly,' she said, 'I had a week's break in my schedule and Borneo sounded like a neat vacation destination. I'm only here five days and then I'm flying to Milan. For the Galliano collection.' Nadine appeared restive. She turned to Dexter Smith. 'You think it's okay to smoke?'

Dexter grimaced. 'I guess this isn't the place.'

'Dexter, honey, who's paying for this trip?' She raised her head. 'Anyone object if I smoke?'

'Yes,' Aquila said as if she'd been poised to jump on the request from the moment she'd boarded.

'It's not as if this thing will explode if I light up.'

Jaeger stood. 'Sorry, Nadine, but it's no.'

Nadine crammed her cigarettes back in her purse.

'She's so im*pacted*,' she hissed. 'No smoking, no salt, no milk, no booze, no coffee.'

'She looks pretty good on it,' Boucher said.

'You know why? Because she's on a diet of pure bullshit.'

Deciding he had enough to be getting on with, Boucher returned to his seat. Candy was talking to Marriot, the hunky Australian, and was showing considerably more animation than she'd demonstrated in Boucher's company. The sea on his side was so empty that the sight of it made him yawn. He lay back and closed his eyes. With luck, he could wrap up the assignment in a week. Maybe he could fly out with Nadine and spend a few days in Europe. Now that was a thought.

5

Boucher woke in a state of mild arousal, some discomfort and a fair degree of confusion. His right arm had pins and needles from using it as a pillow. He massaged it back to life and lifted his wrist. Past three. He'd been asleep for nearly two hours. He yawned. 'Have we reached the island yet?'

'We didn't get that far,' Candy told him. 'One of the engines was overheating. The pilot shut it down. We've turned back.'

Boucher straightened in his seat. Blinking at the starboard engine, he saw the blades static in their duct. 'What do you mean, shut it down?'

'It's just a precaution. The airship can fly perfectly well on one engine.'

He inspected the cabin. Everyone was in their place, everything was orderly. He scrutinized Candy – unruffled forehead, calm eyes, relaxed mouth. Panic on his part, it appeared, was uncalled for. 'How far are we from Pontianaka?'

'Less than two hours.' Candy reached under her seat. 'I saved you some lunch.

Boucher accepted a bottle of mineral water and a cardboard carton containing herb-flecked rice balls heaped on a leaf. 'I guess Aquila's in charge of the catering,' he said, sampling the rice. It made zero impact on his taste buds. 'A witch's picnic. Warm over a blaze of self-righteousness and serve with a generous scoop of high moral fibre.'

Candy's astringent look told Boucher he'd just earned another black mark. He sighed. 'Don't tell me you share Aquila's vision of a new world order in which bats and lizards get the same constitutional rights as humans.'

She put her nose in the air.

Boucher laughed to hide his annoyance. 'Still not speaking, huh? No need to worry, Candy, with the cast of characters I've got here, you'll be lucky to get a footnote.'

She looked at him then. 'I'm here at Wildguard's expense. I'm not in the habit of criticizing people I've taken money from.'

'I'll remind you of that when they send you up against a crowd of Third World construction workers waving billy clubs.'

'Oh yes,' Candy said, colouring slightly, 'you'd love that, wouldn't you?'

'There's always an element of cruelty in writing,' Boucher agreed, and drank thirstily. He laced his hands behind his head and leaned back. 'But it'll never happen. This whole project is nothing more than a big-budget photo-opportunity for Dexter's benefit, and I'm just the caption writer.'

Candy's flush deepened. 'Excuse me,' she said, and stood and stretched for the luggage locker.

Idly, Boucher registered the taut curve of her hips, then raised his eyes and blinked as he saw her breasts firmly outlined through the flimsy stuff of her shirt. She flopped down and began to read. The top button of her shirt had come undone. Boucher averted his eye, but the image of that creamy declivity and swell continued to tantalize. Disco's gamey comments had stirred a frisson of lust, and though it was no more than animal reflex, it seemed to communicate itself to Candy. On the pretext of studying something interesting on the horizon, she buttoned herself up.

No opportunities there, Boucher thought. Not that he had any sexual designs on her. Fast and loose wasn't his style, and Lydia, in bed or out, was quite enough for any man. Nevertheless he found himself recalling the pliant sensation of Candy's body when she'd collided with him that morning. He wondered what she would be like stripped of her English reserve – stripped, not to put too fine a point on it, of ...

'Please, your attention. Thank you.'

Candy laid down her book.

Fieser seemed reluctant to start and then spoke in a rush. 'We have received a radio alert. The storm is coming quicker than expected. For this reason we have decided to make an alternative landing on Belitung.'

Tension broke in a hubbub of questions from which Boucher heard his own voice emerge. 'Where the hell is Belitung?'

'It is a large island 180 kilometres south-west. There is an airport.'

'Christ, man, that's halfway to Sumatra. Borneo can't be more than an hour away. Why can't we run for the coast?'

'There are no facilities for landing except at Pontiana-ka.'

'Okay,' Jaeger shouted, waving down another outburst. 'Okay.' He breathed deeply. 'How long will it take to reach this island?'

'At our present speed, four hours.'

'That means we'll be landing after dark.'

'We have radar and night navigation aids.'

Disco rose, his stance aggressive. 'Hold it.' After a glance to confirm he spoke for the passengers, he took aim on Fieser. 'You said this airship was failsafe and one of the engines craps out. You said the storm was on the other side of Borneo, and now you tell us it's just over the horizon. You said we'd be back by nightfall, and now we find we're floating in the opposite direction to some island we've never heard of. What the fuck else is gonna go wrong?'

'We're gonna crash,' Nadine said, a thread of hysteria in her voice.

Jaeger raised his hands to forestall a general collapse, but before he could speak, Trigg called out: 'Course it's going to crash. That's why it's got such a bleeding big airbag.'

Even Fieser raised a smile. 'Okay,' he said, 'there have been accidents, but now I think we will have no more.'

'He looks scared,' Boucher said softly, watching him retreat into the flight cabin.

'Poor Josef.'

'Candy, if it's got to the stage where we're feeling sorry for the crew, then it really *is* time to panic.'

She eased out from under his gaze and turned her attention back to her book.

The sky remained clear and their progress smooth. Boucher was fretful, unable to settle between fear and boredom. He had nothing to help kill time. 'What are you reading?'

Candy displayed the title: *Why Big Fierce Animals are Rare*.

'Good?'

'I don't think it's your kind of thing.'

'Maybe not, but if we're still drifting by the time you've finished, could I borrow it?'

'I've got a handbook on the birds of South-East Asia if you want.'

'Anything.'

Boucher skimmed colour plates of darters and lorikeets

and sunbirds. He had no change of clothes, no luggage, not even a razor or toothbrush. All the time he fretted about these trivialities, dread sat like a stone in his stomach.

Fieser addressed them on the intercom, anouncing that their ETA at Tanjungpandan airport was 19.50.

It was now five-ten, the sun in steep decline. Boucher kept glancing out of the window. Trails of cirrus had appeared high up.

'Are those storm clouds?' he asked Candy.

'Yes.'

'Please fasten your seatbelts,' Josef announced. 'There may be some turbulence.'

The milky streamers had spread above them and there were still two hours before they reached the island. It's going to catch us, Boucher thought, a hollow opening inside him. He felt chilled and sweaty, tight-throated and dry-mouthed. Candy was scared, too, though the only way he could tell was because though her eyes were fixed on her book, she wasn't turning the pages.

Half an hour passed in anxious limbo. The sun began to melt back into the empty sea. In front of them, the sky was teal blue and very peaceful. Boucher pressed his face to the glass and looked back.

'Sweet Jesus,' he whispered.

Behind them, an engorged mass of purple towered up from a solid black base. Lightning arced between thunderheads and waves of light quaked fitfully in complex chain reaction. Boucher heard a subdued rumbling above the drone of the engine. He watched in horrified fascination as a mushroom of cloud sprouted before his eyes. The storm was still building, feeding on the super-saturated air, increasing in energy with every second.

Boucher locked eyes with Candy and saw his own

terror reflected there. He yanked his tie loose. 'I guess that slams the door on us.'

'God be merciful unto us, and bless us: and show us the light of his countenance, and be merciful unto us ...'

It was Bartok who was praying, his voice composed. The last pastel afterglow had faded in the west and the tempest had merged into the darker cloud of night, its progress heralded by brilliant lightning chains and thunderclaps. Boucher's temples throbbed. His neck muscles burned from the effort of craning round.

He faced forward, pulled his belt tight and pushed back in his seat. Beside him, Candy sat like an astronaut strapped in for blast-off, her lips faltering in silent entreaty.

Steadily the barrage overtook them. The thunder and lightning were continuous now. A flash seared Boucher's eyes and the interior of the gondola expanded with violet light.

'Holy shit!'

Boucher clutched the seat ahead as the airship lurched. There was a rustling that sounded like something scrabbling to get in and he saw rain crawling across the window – crawling from bottom to top.

'Hey!'

He gasped, his own gasp drowned by someone else's shriek. Then he couldn't speak because he was dropping – down and down until the airship hit the bottom of the pocket with a force that drove breath from the pit of his stomach. The next thunderclap seemed to explode in his skull. They were in the middle of the reactor, separated from a maelstrom with more energy than a hundred nuclear warheads by nothing more than a synthetic membrane. He envisaged the gondola tearing loose and spinning end over end like a seed capsule.

Lightning illuminated the cabin brighter than day, strobes freezing the passengers in attitudes of terror – necks corded, eyes sealed or fixed wide and bolting.

'Please,' a voice moaned. 'Oh please.'

Another bolt burst and raw electricity sheathed the engine in blue flames and danced on the window frame. Boucher was weightless again, and then heavy, his weight doubled by gravitational force. He was slammed like a doll against Candy and heard her grunt under the impact. A moment later the two of them were flung the other way. He groaned and was sick.

Rolling and tumbling, pitching and yawing. He was on a roller coaster to hell, his senses haywire and then mush, scrambled in the chaos. The last image he had before he blacked out was of a small boy on a carnival ride, laughing and screaming to be let off.

6

Eerie silence, the ride so stable that Candy couldn't tell if they were moving. It was pitch black inside and out, sky and sea merged invisibly. She rubbed her arms and her hands rasped on gooseflesh.

Someone groaned. Someone else laughed. It sounded more like a laugh than anything else.

'Who's hurt?' Jaeger demanded. 'Dexter?'

'I think so. I mean no. I'm not hurt.'

'Nadine?' There was a silence. 'Nadine?'

'She's been pretty sick.'

Dim emergency lights came on. In the feeble glow, Candy couldn't tell whether Boucher was conscious.

'Jay?' she whispered.

'I'll live,' he mumbled. 'Why's it so cold?'

'The power's failed,' Candy said. 'Both engines have packed up.'

Nadine looked round at her, huge-eyed in the gloom. 'What does that mean?'

Dexter laughed weakly. 'It means my next car isn't going to be a Porsche.'

'It means we can't steer,' Marriot said. 'We're part of the wind now. Where it blows, we blow.'

'Where? Where are we?'

Jaeger pulled himself up. 'I'll find out.'

'Look on the bright side,' Boucher said. 'If this had been an airplane we'd already be dead.'

'If we'd been on a plane, we wouldn't have gotten into this mess.'

'We're alive,' Bartok said, 'and for that we owe someone a prayer.'

'God,' Disco said in a strained voice, 'don't you pull a fucking stunt like that again.'

Fieser's gangling figure stooped through the cabin door. In the eerie dimness, Candy could make out patches of sweat ringing his shirt and a livid bruise on his cheek. He held on to a seat for support. 'Both engines are no longer operating. You have probably noticed that it is no longer so warm. That is because Captain Haimendorf has climbed to maximum altitude, nearly three thousand metres. Our situation is stable.'

'What happened to the island?' Disco demanded.

Fieser lifted one hand in a defeated gesture. 'It is behind us. We are drifting south-west at eighteen kilometres. Our position is less than two hundred kilometres east of Sumatra.'

'Is help on its way?' Boucher demanded.

Fieser hesitated. 'The storm has damaged the radio. At this moment we have not been able to repair it. That was a bad storm, you know.'

'You're saying no one has any idea where we are?'

'Please,' Fieser said, again raising his hand. He let it flop. 'The Indonesian air force has our last position. They will track the storm and find us.'

'They'll assume we crashed.'

Fieser tried to smile. 'But we are not crashed. If we maintain present course and speed, we will be over land by dawn.'

'The question is,' Jaeger said, 'can we last that long?'

'Of course. The buoyancy bags are fully inflated. You can take off your lifejackets. Why do you not try to sleep? You have had an exhausting day and much excitement.'

74

Fieser gave an odd little bleat. 'Too much excitement, I think.'

Heavy silence filled the gondola. Jaeger stood up. 'Let's clean up in here.'

For the next half hour, Candy helped stow luggage and mop up the mess. Everybody had been violently sick. Nadine sprayed air-freshener. There were blankets in the lockers. Candy wrapped herself in one, took out her book again and tried to decipher the print. Her co-passengers had begun to talk quietly among themselves.

Boucher rolled his head. 'Why *are* large, fierce animals rare?'

'It's to do with the second law of thermodynamics.'

'Is that the one that says whatever goes up must come down?'

Candy didn't answer. A dozen times during the storm she thought her last moment had come, and now she had to face it again.

Soon after midnight, Fieser appeared again. His manner was more collected, more guarded.

'Is the radio fixed?'

'There is something else.'

'Let me guess,' Marriot said. 'A slow puncture.'

Fieser didn't smile. 'A puncture, no. But a dirigible is not an ordinary balloon. It makes use of two kinds of lift: static and dynamic. The dynamic lift is produced by our speed relative to the air. Since our air speed is zero, we have no dynamic lift.'

'We're sinking.'

'Slowly, not much – only five hundred metres since my last report. There is nothing to be alarmed about, but we have jettisoned our fuel and now I must ask you please to remove all unnecessary possessions.'

'What possessions?' Trigg demanded. He stood up.

'Look, mate, this was supposed to be a trip around the bay. All we've got are the clothes we stand up in.'

'Do what he asks,' Jaeger ordered. 'Start with the recording equipment.'

'I'm not chucking away thirty grand's worth of video camera.'

'Do it, Trigg. Keep the palmcorder.'

The alloy cases were slid towards the gondola door, where Fieser had buckled on a safety harness. 'Please, stay in your seats,' he ordered. He slid open the door.

Candy expected a rush of air, an icy draught but, apart from a slight deepening of the chill, there was no change in atmosphere. It was hard to believe, sitting there in the dark and stillness, that beyond the black hatch was a drop into the void.

She went through her sack: change of clothes, passport, money, make-up, basic medicines, maps. The only items to sacrifice were her two books and her camera. She passed them forward.

Boucher hadn't stirred. Candy gave him a quizzical look.

'Nothing to declare.'

'What about your camera?'

'Essential equipment. Until the shark's jaws snap shut, I'm on assignment.'

'A writing assignment,' she reminded him. 'Trigg's our cameraman.'

'Offloading my camera isn't going to make a millimetre of difference.'

She made sure she had his eye and held out her hand.

Sighing, he handed it over. 'To hell. None of my pictures turns out the way I hope.'

Candy woke to find her head resting on Boucher's

shoulder. He smiled at her – a tender smile that caught her off-guard.

'You were sleeping like a baby. You're a cool lady.'

'Freezing,' she said, struggling upright. She checked her reflection in the window and tidied up her hair. When she turned, she saw that Boucher had filled a page of his notebook.

'Letter to my girlfriend,' he explained. 'She's called Lydia, and plays cello with the Chicago Symphony. It was her cello I fell in love with first.' Boucher's mouth set in a line. 'If I don't make it and you do, will you tell her sorry and ask her to think of me next time she plays Elgar's Cello Concerto?'

Candy opened her mouth to say something heartening, but the idea of Lydia playing a requiem stopped her throat. 'Yes, of course.'

'How about you? Anyone special in your life?'

'Only my family.'

Pain cut to her heart as she realized what her loss would mean to her father. Her mother's death had taken a huge chunk out of his soul, but what was left he had re-invested in her, and without that she knew the core of him would be extinguished.

She gave a little mew of laughter. 'My father always said I was accident-prone.'

Jaeger emerged grave-faced from the flight cabin. 'We're down to less than six thousand and we're still a couple of hours from land. There's a possibility we'll have to ditch. We've got a raft plenty big enough to take all of us and there's food and water for a week. Now don't get excited, Nadine. We've still got every chance.' He dropped heavily into his seat.

Adrenalin began to beat in Candy's blood. 'It's true, isn't it?' she said to Boucher. 'It's the waiting that's so awful.'

'Death in slow motion,' he said, then tensed. 'I've got an idea.' He raised his voice. 'Let's play the balloon game.'

Candy turned in incomprehension. So did everyone else.

'You know – everyone explains what qualities they think justify their claim to a place on a sinking balloon.'

'That's sick,' Nadine snapped, and looked furiously at Jaeger.

'Maybe not,' he said slowly. 'I've been checking out the map. It looks like we'll hit the Sumatran coast right in the middle. There's a lot of wild terrain in there, and it could be a while before the cavalry show up. We've been teamed up for less than a day. It makes sense to hear what each person has to say.'

'How about you kicking off?' Boucher suggested.

'I guess you've done my justifying for me right there.' Jaeger looked around, searching out each passenger's eye. 'I'm the leader of this expedition and that responsibility doesn't weigh heavy on me. Those of you who've ridden with me before will tell you I look after my team.'

There was a murmur of assent from Bartok.

Boucher scribbled something in his notebook. 'How about you, Aquila?'

'Sacrifice one individual, you sacrifice all. No form of life needs to justify its existence. That's why we're here. That's the Wildguard philosophy.'

Boucher murmured: 'A skylark wounded in the wing, a cherubim does cease to sing.'

Marriot shifted in his seat. 'What we're looking for, Aquila, are practical survival skills.'

'I'm a woman. Women are born survivors.'

'Aquila's the strongest individual I know,' Jaeger stated. 'She's got strength for us all.'

'Dexter?'

'Hey,' Jaeger said in alarm. 'Whoo! Think what the

public would say if they heard we kicked Dexter Smith out of the balloon.'

'Okay, Dexter, no need to jump.'

'I don't want to hide behind an image,' Dexter said. 'We're in this together.' He took a breath. 'I can't claim much disaster experience. None of us can. But I'm fit and strong and I ... I'll do whatever's necessary.'

'Same go for you, Nadine?'

'I'm not playing this awful game.'

'It isn't a game,' Aquila said. 'We need to know we can rely on each other. We need to know how we can help each other.'

Nadine eyed her with malice. 'I guess even with my disgusting eating habits, I weigh twenty pounds less than you, Aquila. If you're worried about shedding weight, I'd look a little closer to home.'

'Knock it off,' Jaeger ordered. He nodded at Bartok. 'I'll vouch for Kent. He's a solid man in a crisis.'

'Trigg?' Boucher said.

The cameraman appeared to be asleep. 'Wherever we end up, you'll want a good rate of exchange for your dollars. Wake me when we get there.'

They all laughed, then fell quiet, waiting for Marriot.

'A few years ago I was doing a small-mammal survey in the Simpson Desert. That was the year of the big wet. When the floods came, me and my mate were stuck on a dune for three weeks with rations for three days. We ate lizards and grubs and came out better fed than we went in. I tell you, Sumatra's got better tucker than the bush, but you'll need someone to find it – someone who knows the difference between what's good to eat and what will kill you.'

There was a humble silence and Candy realized it was her turn. Her voice trembled only slightly. 'I'm a qualified first-aider. I can use a compass. I can cook. I don't mind taking orders. I don't give up easily.'

'Candy's from a soldiering family,' Boucher added gratuitously.

Marriot turned to him. 'Jay, I didn't hear you earning your ticket yet.'

'I've got no backwoods skills,' Boucher admitted. 'I never was a Boy Scout or went to wilderness camp. I'd get lost and starve in City Park. Unlike Candy, I'm not too good at taking orders.'

'So tell us why we shouldn't dump you.'

'Because someone has to get back with the story.'

'Is that how you see it?' Marriot demanded. 'A story laid on for your benefit?'

'What's on the front page right now? "Fears Mount for Missing Airship. Rock Superstar Feared Dead in Airship Crash." You're already news. You're going to be bigger news when they find you. I intend to be around for that. This exclusive has my name on it.'

'You make it sound like you're on some other airship.'

'Sure. Forget I exist.' Boucher leaned back complacently. A few seconds went by. 'That leaves our lone traveller,' he said. 'Time you took off the mask, Disco.'

'I can take care of myself.'

'We want to know what you can do for *us*.'

Disco looked hunted and Candy felt sorry for him. 'Oh, leave him alone,' she said.

'No,' Boucher said, 'everyone else has spoken up. Come on, Disco, don't be shy. We don't care what you do for a living.'

'All sorts of things,' Disco muttered.

'Like what?' Boucher said, edging a grin at Candy.

'Like movie work.'

'Really?'

Disco turned all the way round. 'You don't believe me?'

'Maybe if you were a little more specific.'

Disco seemed about to speak, then he threw himself back into his seat. 'Fuck you.'

'Well,' Boucher said, after a strained pause, 'I guess we just found our excess baggage.'

The moment he said it, Candy knew there was going to be trouble. She shot Boucher a furious glance. 'Idiot.'

Disco rose and, watched by all, walked down the aisle. He stopped by Boucher and leaned over him. 'You think you're more important than me, Jay? You think you're smarter? Is that what you think?'

'All I asked is what you do.'

Disco knocked Boucher's notebook from his hand. 'So you can put me down in that.'

Keeping his eyes on Disco's, Boucher leaned down and picked up his book. 'Stay cool, man.'

Disco dropped to a crouch, his face level with Boucher's. 'You don't want me along? Fine, try pushing me off. Then we'll see who's tough.'

'All right, Disco,' Candy said, touching his arm, 'that's enough.'

Disco straightened up and pointed a trembling finger. 'Nobody puts me down, Jay. Nobody.' In silence, he went back to his seat.

Boucher gave a shaky laugh. 'Looks like I touched a sensitive nerve.'

'Well that's something *you* lack completely,' Candy snapped. Part of her anger stemmed from the fact that she had just about made up her mind that Boucher was nicer than he had seemed at first. She consolidated her original judgement: he was a smug, arrogant, odious ... *American*.

A few minutes later, Dexter half stood. 'It's getting light.'

Everyone peered at the rising orange glow.

'At least the weather's calm.'

81

'Don't be fooled. Fifteen knots – that's what Josef said.'

With the onset of day, tension broke at a new level.

'I'm gonna sue the pilot,' Nadine blurted. I'm gonna sue the airship company. I'm gonna sue ...'

'Look! The sea!'

Candy stared down. The ocean was petrol-coloured and combed into lines of surf.

'God, it's awful close.'

'Running rough, too.'

'Hold it,' Jaeger said. 'Isn't that land out there?'

Candy made out a grey-green smudge on the curvature of the earth.

'Allelujah!'

Second by second the world grew lighter. The airship's envelope blushed pink in the sun and seemed to breathe in and out.

'Come on, babe,' Disco said. 'You can make it. Push!'

Now that salvation was in their sights, Candy was able to set the clock running on her fears. Sumatra, she estimated, was at least thirty miles off, and she guessed their height couldn't be more than three thousand feet. If they were losing height at the rate of only ten feet every hundred yards, that meant they would sink 170 feet every mile, which meant ...

Fieser appeared in the door. 'We are approaching the coast of Sumatra.'

'Which part?'

'Are there any airports?'

'No, there are no airports.'

'So what's the plan? Put down in a field?'

'Ja. Exactly. In a field.'

For several minutes, Candy was sustained by an image of the airship descending gently to alight in a rice paddy, watched by astonished batik-clad peasants. She found herself imagining how she would describe her adventure to friends and family when she returned home, and her mood flipped from fear to disappointment. Her expedition was over before it had begun.

The coast had become more distinct – a tilt of lush green fringed with surf. Straining for details, Candy spotted an offshore island surrounded by waters in six gorgeous shades of blue and green. It looked everything a tropical island should be.

'There aren't any fields down there,' Marriot said. 'That's prime jungle.'

Fieser came back. Something about his manner had changed again. 'Has everyone got on their lifejacket?'

'Sure,' Jaeger said. 'But what do we need lifevests for?'

'Please. You can see for yourself. There is no place to land on the coast. It is a forest, a swamp.'

'How big a space do you need, for chrissakes? You said a field.'

'It is not so simple, you know. We need a big space to make our approach, We cannot say how far we will have to go before we find such a space. It is too risky. The sea will be much safer.'

Nadine jumped up. 'I'm not going down there. You can't make me.'

'Please. Please. The captain will make a landing in the water by the beach. We will not be going so fast. Now, excuse me. I must help him.'

Boucher wrenched at his tie, though it was already undone.

Jaeger took up a position in the aisle, facing them. 'Time's short, so answer up quick. Can everyone swim?'

Nadine shook her head very rapidly.

'Not at all?'

'Hardly.'

Boucher gave a short laugh. 'And I thought from all those swimsuit ads that she was a regular water babe.'

Candy kicked him. He gave her a 'What did I do?' look.

'Robert, you look after Nadine. Anyone else a poor swimmer? How about you, Candy?'

Candy could swim, but that wasn't the point. Fearless of heights, aggressive dogs or shifty horses, she had no phobias except one – a profound terror of death by drowning. At the age of three she had fallen into a neglected swimming pool in Malaysia – a soupy green pond. It had been several minutes before her *amah* had found her, and by then she was unconscious.

'I'll manage, thank you.'

'Okay, we evacuate in pairs. Nadine and Robert, you're first. Dexter, you're with me. Aquila and Trigg are next, then Kent and Disco. Jay and Candy are last out. Try and stay together.' He clapped his hands. 'Look out for each other.'

'What happened to women and journalists?'

Candy had had enough of Boucher's drolleries. 'Would you mind awfully?'

'Awfully what?'

'Keeping your comments to yourself. They're not helpful and they're not funny.'

Marriot stood. 'Take what belongings you can – medicines, skin protection, that kind of thing. No shops or hospitals down there. Hang on to your passports, too.'

'Oh my God,' Nadine quavered. 'Look at the sea. The waves are *huge!*'

Candy nursed her sack. The airship had sunk low enough for her to gauge speed and perspective. The sea was advancing in lazy sweeping rollers. Close to the littoral the surf became confused and angry. There seemed to be two lines of reef separating the island from the sea. She stared at the whites of her knuckles.

'We're headed straight for the island.'

'Are there sharks?' Disco wanted to know. 'I fucking hate sharks.'

'No sharks,' Jaeger told him.

'Yeah, there'll be sharks,' Marriot said, 'but they won't be expecting us.'

Candy felt light-headed and sick in her stomach. She opened her mouth for air and a little squeak escaped. Boucher touched her arm. 'Yes?' she demanded.

'We're going to land short,' Marriot said, a flat statement of fact.

'The pilot knows what he's doing.'

'This blimp goes where it wants. The wind and pressure will be different close to land. He's got no way of compensating.'

'If we hit the reef, we're purée.'

'Climb, you moron!' Nadine shouted. 'Climb!'

'He's doing the best he can.'

'Please go up. Oh puhleeze!'

Candy glimpsed a sucking trough between the waves. She bowed her head.

'Grab your knees,' Jaeger shouted. 'Brace!'

Head down, Candy heard through the hull the greedy roar of bursting surf. Spray brushed the underside and she felt the airship drag.

'Goodbye and amen,' Boucher said.

'Oh G-arrrrrd!' Nadine screamed.

The next wave caught them but the bag's buoyancy pulled them clear. Candy raised her face and saw the rear swell of a blue breaker rising smoothly in front, its crest above eye level. She held her breath, waiting for impact. The gondola skimmed the spray and for a moment Candy thought they would bounce clear over the reef. Then the next wave reached up and the horizon spun and that was the end of thought. Her head whacked into something and she was vaguely aware of windows bursting.

Another collision shocked her forward. Water surged around her. There had been no gap between impact and sinking, no time to collect her wits. She scrabbled for the seat-belt release, frustrated by the slow motion that had overtaken her. Boucher was already scrambling up. He turned and pulled her arm.

'We're on the reef!'

'We're going over. Get out!'

Candy saw Jaeger hauling himself towards the door like a man climbing an escalator the wrong way. It was only then that she worked out they were jammed on the reef crest. Something cracked and the gondola tilted and she toppled sideways.

'Go!' Jaeger shouted, pushing Nadine out. 'Go!'

The gondola lurched again, throwing her into someone's empty seat. Dexter Smith and Aquila leapt clear. Candy had dropped her sack.

'Leave it!'

Boucher was already at the door, pressing behind Bartok, his arm outstretched to Candy. She lurched after him. Trigg jumped, then Disco and Bartok. Boucher turned and Candy saw him torn between helping her and saving himself. 'Another one coming!' he shouted. 'Jump!'

He disappeared. Candy reached the door and glimpsed the wave poised to break. Boucher was kicking away through foam, looking back at her, shouting soundlessly. She grabbed for a hold and the wave toppled and the gondola lifted and shot forward. Water closed over her head and she felt herself going backwards, away from the door. Sound was extinguished and she knew that the gondola was submerged and she was going to die. Her breath was used up before she had even begun to fight.

Her mouth opened and she sucked air. She was still in the gondola. Through a window she had an underwater view of the stump of an engine mounting and the reef behind it. She was at the rear, by her own seat, in an airpocket. She had to get out but didn't know how. Something firm but yielding bumped her side. A man broke surface beside her.

It was the pilot, unconscious or dead.

A spout of air erupted. The gondola was still settling. It wasn't on the bottom. Ducking underwater, she saw the door. She couldn't get to it with her lifejacket on. As she struggled to remove it, the pilot's body seemed to deliberately impede her. Even if he was still alive, she couldn't do anything for him. Other wreckage hampered her – drinks cartons and clothes and cushions. As she pulled the jacket off, the gondola swung again. She tried to dive but got only a foot or two. She floundered back up. Any second and the pocket would fill. She pounded the window with her fist but it held. Her shirt had half come off. She tore it away, then forced herself to breathe deep, conscious that there wouldn't be another attempt. When she was a kid, she and her brothers had competed to see who could hold their breath for longest. She'd managed over a minute.

Taking another lungful, she braced her feet against the rear bulkhead and pushed down. She began counting. One ... and ... two. Her hands found a seat back and she pulled, propelling herself towards the next hold. Five seconds. Her eyes strained towards the door. Seat by seat she dragged herself towards it. She was nearly there and she'd only used up twelve seconds. She groped for the opening and it seemed to float away. Fifteen seconds. She tried again and missed and she stopped counting as panic took hold. She kicked and pulled once more, knowing it was her last chance, and this time her fingers clawed round the frame and gave her the leverage she needed.

She was out, floating up through a skein of suspension

cables. The surface light got no brighter. A stream of bubbles escaped from her mouth.

She half broke surface and was pushed back under immediately, swallowing more water than air. She had come up under the ripped envelope. It was pressing her down. She thrashed blindly. Something caught around her leg – one of the broken cables. She jerked free and something else grabbed her. She kicked out and contacted a body. A hand grabbed her wrist. She saw a distorted face and she had enough wits left not to fight.

She burst into blinding light. In the moment before everything went black she glimpsed the deflated envelope and clutched hold. She clung on to her strange rubbery island, her breath sawing in and out and a dark red veil over her eyes. At last her vision cleared and she saw a glittering strand and a green frieze against a sky so huge she couldn't see the end of it. Her rescuer clung beside her, his hair plastered over his brow so that for a moment she didn't recognize him. It was Boucher. She couldn't see anyone else.

'Let's go,' Boucher said.

'A moment,' she gasped.

'Candy, you're bleeding.'

She put her hand to her face and it came away red. 'It's only my nose.'

'I was thinking of sharks.'

She nodded but still didn't move. Her ears felt funny and sound was muffled.

'It's only a hundred yards. Just float. I'll be beside you.'

She let go, Boucher side-stroking alongside. The water was warm and gin-clear. She could make out more than one person on the beach now. Dexter was standing in the shallows, arm outstretched. It seemed to take forever to reach him. Ignoring his arm, she staggered past and fell full stretch on to the sand. Weakly she retched.

She lay there while the humming in her ears resolved itself into voices.

'I've lost my glasses. Shit! Anyone see my glasses? Damn!'

'Josef's hurt. I think his leg's broke.'

'Anyone see the pilot?'

'Look, there's the liferaft, stuck on the reef.'

Candy absorbed the voices and the warmth of the sand and the radiance of the sun on her back. The realization that she was alive seeped through her. Alive! She opened her eyes and was conscious of each grain of sand. She opened her mouth to laugh and then found she was crying. Boucher was standing over her.

'Thank you, Jay.'

'Any time. You okay?'

She nodded. She felt woozy, everything out of register.

He gave his sinuous smile. 'Just as well. Because my mouth-to-mouth technique is rusty.' He shaded his eyes and laughed. 'Nadine, you've been here before.'

Nadine looked at him with zombie eyes.

Boucher spread his arms. 'The sand so white, the sea so blue, the trees so green, so green-o. It's a gem of a location for a perfume ad. I bet we find the film crew having a beer down the beach club.'

By a conscious effort, Candy managed to sit up. Blood dripped on to her breast and only then did she discover that her bra had slipped off and was hanging around her waist. With wooden fingers she covered herself up. Her stomach hurt. Her face hurt. Everything hurt. Aquila was beside her, hugging her knees, staring out to sea. Her gaze seemed to be fixed on something significant, but Candy could see only bits of flotsam from the airship and the obscene swell of the ruined envelope.

'The pilot's still inside,' she said. 'He's dead.' The

memory of being trapped in the gondola stuck in her throat.

Aquila gathered her in her arms. 'We are so lucky,' she sobbed. 'We are *so* lucky.'

TWO

7

Boucher sat on the sand and marvelled. In a few scrambled minutes they had crashed out of the late twentieth century and landed in a place primeval, a place utterly wild, spiced by exotic scents and filled with outlandish sounds. And yet it all seemed familiar. Wherever he looked, his eye was filled with the saturated colours he associated with the cinema screen. The fluting birdcalls and insect static had the clarity of a high-fidelity soundtrack. And to heighten the impression that they had washed up on to a movie set, Trigg was filming the cast of castaways with his camcorder.

Boucher became aware that his senses were functioning selectively. There seemed to be a plate-glass sheet between him and the other survivors. In a kind of trance he watched Aquila, Candy and Jaeger kneeling around Fieser, both Aquila and Candy partially naked from the waist up, Aquila's tunic undone, Candy wearing a bra – a much lacier confection than he would have anticipated. Jaeger was shirtless too, his torso front and back covered by an alarmingly dense pelt of orange hair. Standing bedraggled beside them were Disco and Bartok. Disco was supporting his left arm and seemed to be in pain. Nadine and Dexter clung together on the beach like babes in the wood.

Boucher took stock of his own condition. He was still clothed in jacket, shirt and tie. Even his loafers had stayed on. He was the best-dressed survivor on the island. Laughter bubbled in his throat. Shock. Understandable. He tried to put his wits in order.

From the airship he had framed a picture of the island. So far as he could recollect, it was small, maybe a mile long and less than half as wide, thickly forested and shaped like an elongated comma, the broad head furthest seaward and the tail separated from the mainland by a narrow channel. South, the mangrove coast curved in a dark green sweep to a headland at least ten miles away. The beach on which he sat was white coral grain, the lagoon turquoise blue, planted with iridescent clumps of emerald green where patches of coral touched the surface, darkening to sapphire near the reef. A more beautiful place to wash up on would be hard to imagine.

Fieser cried out in pain and Jaeger said something, his voice filtered by distance though he was only a few yards away. Boucher shook his head and tried to stand up. Stars spangled his vision.

'Oops.'

Groggily, he joined the group around Fieser.

What he saw made him flinch. The co-pilot was splayed on the sand, his face crumpled by pain, his right thigh bent at a shocking angle. While Jaeger cupped his head and Marriot supported his lower back, Candy was struggling to bare his thighs. Boucher glimpsed flesh pushed into unnatural contours and his groin cringed.

'It's bad,' he heard Candy murmur. 'The femur's broken in more than one place and the lower end has nearly pierced the surface. We can't possibly set it. He needs surgery.'

'Let's get him into the shade.'

'Not without a stretcher.'

'No time.'

'Splints.'

'Later,' Marriot said. He noticed Boucher. 'Don't just stand there. Take an arm.'

As they lifted him, Fieser screamed at a lacerating pitch and kept screaming, each cry piercing Boucher to the quick. He helped lay Fieser down and stepped back, biting his lip. The co-pilot had lapsed into semi-consciousness. 'You'll be all right,' Boucher said helplessly.

'A ship! There's a ship out there!'

Down at the water's edge, Dexter was semaphoring his excitement. Miles up the coast, Boucher picked out a tiny shape stitched into the horizon. Forgetting Fieser, he ran down the beach.

'Looks like a naval vessel.'

'Do you think it's searching for us?'

'Could be. How do we let them know we're here?'

'A fire,' Nadine cried. 'Light a fire.' She began to run towards the forest, holding up the sodden drapes of her sarong. Nobody followed.

'Nadine,' Boucher called, 'it's heading the wrong way. We don't have time.'

'There are flares on the raft,' Bartok said.

Boucher looked at the rectangle of yellow canted up on the reef crest.

'Too late.'

They watched the ship dwindle. When it was just a pinpoint, Jaeger turned to Disco. 'How's your shoulder?'

Disco squinted sideways. 'Dunno. Dislocated, I guess.'

Gently, Jaeger manipulated the joint, drawing a hiss of pain. 'Yeah, sprung all right.' He glanced round. Without his glasses, his face stood out pink and naked amid his general hairiness. 'Robert, hold him tight round the chest and his good arm. Hold him good.' With Disco immobilized, Jaeger gripped the patient's damaged arm by wrist and elbow and splayed his feet for balance, as if he was about to engage in a throwing contest. 'Disco,' he said, 'I've done this before and ...'

'It's gonna hurt like fuck.' Teeth gritted, Disco stared at the sky. 'Do it.'

Jaeger pulled down and Boucher heard a fibrous grating. Only a gasp escaped Disco. When Boucher opened his eyes again, Disco was gingerly flexing the shoulder. He blew out his cheeks, stamped the ground and whistled. He saw Boucher boggling and gave a pallid leer.

'Anyone else need treating?' Jaeger asked.

'We ought to recover the raft before the tide takes it,' Marriot said. 'I'll need help to lift it off. Jay, you swim pretty well.'

After braving the deep once, Boucher considered he had done enough in that element. And he was about to say so when he saw that Marriot's expression held a deeper message.

'Convince me there aren't sharks.'

'Only small ones in the lagoon, and they won't bite unless you do something stupid, like picking them up. The big ones – tiger sharks and hammerheads – hang about the other side, in the drop-off zone. There may be sting rays sitting on the lagoon bottom, so keep your shoes on if you're feeling tender.'

'It's gone,' Nadine wailed. 'The ship's gone.' And she burst into tears. Aquila put her arms around her.

Boucher could still hear her sobs as he waded into the lagoon.

'Hey,' Disco called, 'if you see a blue sports bag, it's mine.'

'And don't mess with anything on the boat,' Jaeger added, as Marriot launched into an easy crawl.

Boucher breast-stroked behind. Near the crash zone a reek of fuel washing from the airship's ruptured tank clung to the water. The raft was at least fifteen feet long and about eight wide. One buoyancy compartment had collapsed and the bottom was ripped across where it had hung up.

'Stay in the water,' Marriot told him. 'I'll try to lift it from above. Watch yourself. This coral will cut to the bone and reef wounds don't heal easily.'

Boucher trod water while Marriot picked his way on to the crest. As he hoisted the raft, Boucher took hold and kicked, but the boat hardly budged. He kicked again and his ankle snagged a coral branch. A moment later pain cut him, sharp as a knife and then dulling to an ache. A wisp of red drifted from his foot.

'I said pull,' Marriot cried.

'I've cut myself.'

'It's not sharks you need to worry about. This time – after three.'

Boucher took another grip. He glanced over his shoulder, half expecting to see a dozen crescent fins cleaving the surface.

'One, two, and ... pull!'

Neck sinews straining, Boucher launched backwards, trying to support the raft's weight. It slid clear in a rush, pushing him under. Spluttering, he grabbed the thwart and wriggled and heaved aboard. A moment later the craft tipped under Marriot's weight. It listed steeply, one side almost submerged, the torn bottom awash.

Boucher lay gathering his breath. 'What do you mean – it's not sharks I should be worrying about?'

'Forget it, Jay. Let's see what we've got in the lockers.'

'Jaeger said to leave alone.'

Marriot ignored him. 'Fresh water – a hundred litres. Survival rations. A big sack of rice. Space blankets, stove, knife, *parang* ...' he brandished a machete '... fishing tackle – good – matches, flashlight, flare gun and cartridges, mosquito nets, compass, whistle ... Hell, there are even charts. The Germans certainly pack a nice hamper.' Marriot looked up, a rueful smile on his face. 'But they forgot the radio.'

'Is that serious?' Boucher asked. He registered Marriot's patient smile. 'Okay – stupid question.'

Marriot stropped the knife against the ball of his thumb, then slid it into his pocket.

Boucher hesitated. 'Don't you trust Jaeger?'

'Trust isn't the right word. Confidence is closer. He's tough enough, but he's out of his element.'

'Why don't you put yourself up as leader? I reckon the majority would be happier if you were in charge.'

'You heard him on the airship. He's not going to put it to a vote.'

'Yeah, but ...'

'Listen, Jay, leadership's not about competence or practical skills. If it was, we wouldn't have ratbag politicians. It's about group dominance – the will and ability to wield power. Jaeger's high dominance. I'm not. If that makes you unhappy, stand against him yourself.'

'I'm just an observer.'

'And I'm a hired hand.'

Boucher was disgruntled. 'You're a proper scientist. Why did you sign up with this lot?'

'I love the rain forest, Jay. Each trip, I get eaten alive, pick up malaria, end up feeling like shit. And each time, I can't wait to get back. But expeditions are expensive. When Wildguard offered me full bed and board, I jumped at it.'

Boucher eyed the alien shore. 'Jaeger's signalling us to get back.'

'Relax. This could be your last few minutes of peace.'

'What happens if he screws up?'

'It won't come to that. We've been here only a couple of

hours and already we've seen one boat. If we're close to a shipping lane, it's odds on we'll be rescued within a couple of days.' Marriot released an oar. 'Now, let's collect some of this wreckage.'

Rowing the waterlogged raft was hard toil, but Boucher's mood settled into serenity. He had acquitted himself better than he could have expected. It wasn't an exaggeration to say he had probably saved Candy's life. Everybody had behaved well. Even Nadine hadn't lost it completely. A glow of solidarity filled him.

Flotsam dotted the surface in the crash zone. They retrieved a vacuum flask, a rope sandal, a plastic bottle.

'Let's salvage some of the envelope before it sinks,' Marriot said. 'It'll make ideal shelter material.'

Laboriously, he sawed and hacked while Boucher tried to keep the boat steady. The stiff breeze that had blown them here had died and the heat was intense. Salt crusted on Boucher's skin and he felt his face beginning to burn. He was parched and famished. Aquila's low-impact rice balls were the only nourishment he'd had in the last twenty-four hours.

'Wait,' Marriot said.

When the surface had settled back into placidity, Boucher saw the gondola apparently close enough to touch.

'About twelve feet deep,' Marriot said.

It had come to rest slightly nose down, tilted to port, its tail propped against the reef wall. Boucher could see where the flight cabin had smashed on impact. Fish that seemed to emanate their own light shoaled around the wreck as if it had always been a fixture. One specimen with a deep red body and a head like a fat cardinal floated through a smashed window and hovered by a white disc.

'I can see the pilot,' Boucher said.

'Too risky,' Marriot said in answer to the unspoken

question. 'The eels and crabs will take care of him. Once night falls, the reef will be crawling.' The image of the gondola crazed over as he began to haul in the material. 'We've got as much as we can manage for one trip.'

On the way back, Marriot gave his easy-going smile. 'Well, Jay, you've got your story, but if I were you, I'd keep a low profile. People under stress don't like to be under scrutiny, especially if they know they'll see themselves in print later. That goes for me, by the way.'

'Don't worry. I've pencilled you in as hero.'

Marriot laughed. 'So what does that make the rest?'

Boucher gave the question serious consideration. 'I think you're wrong about Jaeger; without Aquila, he's just a brainless bear. She's the – what do you biologists call it? – the alpha female. The only other person I've got a take on is Candy. She's level-headed, cool under pressure, old-world colonial. She'd have made a great imperial memsahib – you know, rallying the servants when the natives come over the wall with knives between their teeth.'

'The way you two were cuddled up, you seemed pretty close.'

'Opposites thrown together by the whirlwind. She's been trying to lose me ever since we met.'

'You like her, though?'

'Yeah,' Boucher said, surprising himself. 'Yeah, I do.' He laughed. 'But I guess we're not on the same emotional frequency. Actually, I got the impression that you're more her type.'

'No holiday romances for me. I've got a wife and kid back in Melbourne. Married young.' Marriot seemed to be on the point of saying something else, then gave himself a sort of mental shake. 'How far have we got in the pecking order? You think our showbiz pair will hold together?'

'Dexter will try. Nadine displays a refreshing lack of

grace under pressure, but I suspect she's tougher than she looks. I don't know about Trigg. Bartok's an eager puppy. And Disco ... well ...' Boucher stopped, aware that the lone traveller was the fly in the ointment, but not sure why. 'I think we'd be better off without him.'

'So we noticed. Why were you riling him?'

'Trying to find out who he is. I don't buy that eco-friendly globe-trotter shit any more than his claim to be an actor. Did he give you any biography?'

'Said he came out East to find adventure.' Marriot chuckled. 'Looks like he's got more than he bargained for.'

'I don't know about that. He acts like he's really warming to the situation, and I find that strange, because he strikes me as more of an urban rat than I am.' Boucher hesitated. 'Also, I don't like his attitude to Candy.'

Marriot looked at him thoughtfully. 'I smell a whiff of testosterone.'

'What?'

'Admit it, Jay, the reason Disco gets your hackles up is that you've both got your eyes on Candy.'

Boucher found himself flushing. 'Hell, I'm not squaring up for a fight over a woman.'

Marriot didn't smile. 'Good, because if we're stuck here more than a few days, things could turn primitive.'

Jaeger peered in short-sighted suspicion as they landed. His face was already boiled tomato red by the heat. 'What were you guys doing out there?' he demanded, hauling the inflatable ashore.

'Cutting balloon fabric for shelter. We'll need more, though. We can use it for hammocks, clothing, even shoes. We've got all the other essentials. The raft's loaded.'

'You'd think they were expecting to crash,' Boucher added, as Jaeger inspected the contents of the lockers.

'You take anything?'

Marriot produced the knife. 'I always carry one in the bush. I'm naked without it.'

Jaeger's eyes hardened. 'Next time, ask.' He reached into the locker and hefted the long-bladed parang, then turned to Boucher. 'How about you? You help yourself while we weren't looking?'

Boucher kept his tone easy. 'No. There's a notebook in there. If you don't mind, I'll take it. I lost everything in the crash.'

'Except your story,' Disco said, smiling. Still smiling, he uncoiled from the sand. 'Dexter Smith and Nadine Wells marooned on a tropical island. That is fucking *monster*.'

Sensing the barbs beneath the surface, Boucher knew that Disco hadn't forgotten the confrontation on the airship. He parodied a smile of his own. 'You want to write your own account? Go ahead.'

Jaeger tore the notebook down the spine and tossed one half to Boucher. 'Don't anyone else come shopping for personal favours.'

'Is there any antiseptic?' Nadine asked. 'I've cut my toe.'

'Who cares about your toe?' Candy blurted. 'Josef's leg is smashed.'

'What does he need?' Jaeger said. 'There's a full kit.'

'Antibiotics and painkillers – the more powerful the better. Morphine if there is any.'

'No morphine.'

'Later, I'll do a healing spell,' Aquila said.

Candy sorted out the medicines and hurried over to Fieser.

'Don't use them all up,' Disco called. 'Other people may need doctoring before we're through.'

Boucher had the disquieting impression that it was him Disco had in mind. Keep your head down, he told himself, and pretty soon his resentment would die.

Dexter wiped his mouth with the back of his hand. 'We're awful thirsty, Leo.'

Struck by Dexter's wheedling tone, Boucher realized how drastically the social dynamics had been upset. Here was one of the biggest names in the rock pantheon virtually begging for a drink from a guy who, back in civilization, would be lucky to hold down a job in a car wash.

Jaeger doled out about half a pint of water and a biscuit for each survivor, then closed the lockers. 'Nobody touches the contents without my say-so. Okay, now I want everyone to lay out their personal possessions.'

Boucher uttered a caustic laugh.

Candy and Disco had also landed with nothing, but most of the others had managed to save some kit. Nadine had come off richest. Not only did she have a change of clothes and enough malaria tablets, insect repellent and water purifiers to equip an expeditionary force, but she also had a carton of Marlboro Lites that had survived immersion, and a bag of cosmetics and toiletries. Bartok had hung on to his Bible. Aquila had a collected edition of William Blake.

'All medicines go into the pool,' Jaeger said.

Nadine looked mutinous. 'I don't think that's right.'

Jaeger levelled his gaze at her. 'You want to keep them? Then set up house on your own.'

With an angry flounce, she spilled her pharmacy on to the sand.

'We ought to make a camp,' Marriot told them.

Jaeger squinted at the sun. 'First, let's explore this island. I'll take Disco and Aquila. We'll head straight across, then see if we can work round the shoreline. Candy, you stay with Josef. Jay and Kent, collect wood. Dexter and Trigg, cut as much balloon fabric as you can. Nadine, look for somewhere we can sleep.'

Nadine eyed the forest boundary. 'There are wild animals and snakes in there. And viruses. AIDS came from the tropics, and that disease that eats your internal organs.'

'Maybe I'd better ...' Dexter began, his request wilting under Jaeger's myopic stare.

'You do what I say. Now let's go.'

'I'd like Candy along,' Marriot said. 'Apart from me, she's the only one with bush experience.'

Jaeger sighed under the weight of all these demands. 'Jay,' he said, 'keep an eye on Josef.'

Not relishing the role of nurse, Boucher wandered over to Candy. 'What do I do?'

'There's not much you can do. Talk to him. Reassure him.'

A sheen of sweat covered the swell of her breasts. Boucher noticed the subtle hollows in her shoulders, the damp curls on her neck. The feeling that overcame him was sexually located, but spread into a more tender emotion.

'For a while there, I thought we'd lost you. I'm real glad you made it, Candy.'

A stillness entered her eyes.

'Are we pals now? Are we on speaking terms?'

Candy wiped a curl from her brow and smiled. 'After what you did, it would be very churlish of me to say no.'

'Hey,' Disco called. 'Hurry it up.'

Boucher glanced at him and his expression clouded. 'Candy?'

'Yes?'

'Watch yourself.'

She frowned and moved off to join the others. When they'd gone, Boucher settled beside Fieser. His eyes were pits of pain in a face dulled to the colour of tin.

'Can I do anything?'

Fieser moaned. 'I couldn't get Sixt out.'

Boucher had an image of the face at the window. 'You did everything you could.'

Fieser's eyes filled with tears. 'My wife is expecting a baby at Christmas.'

'Hey,' Boucher said, holding his hand, 'we'll be home long before then. Did you see the ship that came past? I bet it was looking for us.'

'No.'

'Sure it was,' Boucher said, rubbing Fieser's hands. 'Sure it was.'

Fieser shook his head, breathing rapidly. 'I did not tell the truth. My last radio message. Near Belitung. We were close to the sea. Not more than five hundred metres. I said we were attempting a crash-landing. They will not be looking for us here, I think.'

Boucher straightened and his gaze drifted offshore. As he envisaged the thousands of square miles of ocean, a charge collected on his skin. He worked up a smile. 'They'll look everywhere, Josef. We've got the flares now. Tomorrow at the latest, I guarantee.'

Fieser shut his eyes. 'Your friends are angry with me, *ja*? They think it is my fault.'

'Nobody blames you,' Boucher lied. Even he harboured some resentment about the crew's spectacular misjudgements. He came to a decision. 'Josef, there's no need to tell them about the radio message. Nadine's about ready to flip as it is.'

'She is very beautiful. All the women are beautiful.' Fieser sighed and looked up as if an unattainable vision filled the sky.

Boucher squeezed his hand. 'Try to sleep now. I'll be here if you need anything.'

Sitting down, he looked at his note-pad. The blank page blinded him and his hand trembled slightly. He stole a guilty glance at Fieser, but the pilot was too racked by pain to notice his excitement. Boucher swallowed a breath. Disco was right. This was a monster of a story. He was sitting on the scoop of a lifetime.

But to write it he had to survive, he told himself, his thoughts hardening. To survive he would have to keep his wits about him and make sure he wasn't caught up in any animosities. Marriot's advice was sound. He would talk softly and merge into the background. He would become an invisible spectator. And if that meant giving up his interest in Candy, it would be a worthwhile sacrifice.

8

Day 1

Inside the rain forest the air grew musty and the light level dropped to a watery green. On all fronts huge trees pressed in, some massively buttressed, their boles rising straight and branchless for at least seventy feet before merging into the canopy. Every limb and crook was clothed in parasitic plants – mats of creeper and gardens of sickly-pale flowers. Giant ferns and palms sprouted through the leathery leaves carpeting the forest floor. Light slanted through the canopy in thin beams and insects patrolled these spotlights. Their harmonics filled the air – layer upon layer of buzzings, hummings and dronings.

Candy saw Aquila standing mouth parted, staring up with the awestruck expression of a pilgrim inspecting the vaulted interior of a cathedral. Moisture filmed her face. Everyone wore the same reverential expression. Candy was aware of each breath she took.

Far away a hornbill called on a note of rising intensity that climaxed in a cackle of hysterical laughter.

Disco's eyes swivelled slowly. 'Maybe you should tell us what to look out for.'

Marriot's manner was relaxed. 'Anxious about running into something nasty?'

Disco laughed nervously. 'Well, yeah.'

'Don't be. I spent three months in Sarawak and the worst thing that happened to me was I got bitten by a centipede. Hurt like hell, but it wasn't life-threatening.'

'What about snakes?'

'Nine out of ten species are harmless. The ones to watch out for are cobras, vipers and kraits.'

'Great. What's a krait look like?'

'Small, with yellow and black bands. They'll shoot off if you give them a chance. But there are some things that won't get out of your way. In fact, a pair of them are headed towards you right now.'

Candy looked down to see two leeches looping across the leaf mould with horrid briskness. Disco executed a rapid two-step. 'Shit.'

'It's the little things that can kill,' Marriot said, 'leeches, mosquitoes, thorns, ants. Small bites and scratches fester quick in the jungle.'

'Any big predators?' Jaeger asked

'Not on land, no.'

Candy frowned. 'There are tigers on Sumatra.'

Disco's mouth curved in a smile. His gaze slid down to her breasts. 'Thanks, honeybun, but I was asking the expert.'

Candy flushed in annoyance, certain that he wouldn't have spoken to her like that if she'd been properly dressed. Then she saw the pale gape between Aquila's tunic and realized that, despite her semi-nudity, Disco's attitude to her was unfailingly, almost comically, respectful. If anything, her nakedness only served to enhance her authority. That must be because she wore it unselfconsciously, Candy decided, half tempted to tear off the flimsy bra that seemed only to draw attention to what it was supposed to conceal.

'Candy's right,' Marriot said. 'But we won't meet any tigers here. Not enough for them to eat.'

'The mainland's only a few hundred yards away,' Candy pointed out, 'and tigers can swim.'

'Only if they have good reason to,' Marriot said. 'You can forget about tigers.'

Candy dropped her eyes to hide her irritation. From her conversations with Marriot, she knew that his fieldwork had been confined to Australia, New Guinea and Borneo. Much as she respected his experience, she suspected that she knew more about the big cats than he did.

'So what's the most dangerous thing on this island?' Disco persisted.

'We are,' Candy said rattily. 'And don't call me "honeybun".'

Marriot smiled. 'And the most vulnerable.'

This time, Disco looked at her without derision, nodding, turning the paradox over in his mind.

'What about fresh water?' Jaeger asked.

'There won't be a permanent source on the island. We've got enough in the boat for a litre each per day for a week. That's not enough, so one of our first tasks is to rig up a collection tank with some of the balloon fabric. Until it rains ...' Marriot went over to a tree colonized by tubular plants the colour of veal. 'Bromeliads,' he said, breaking one off. He turned it upside down and a murky liquor spilled out. 'Insect soup, but we've got sterilizing tablets.'

'Food?'

'Shouldn't be a problem. The reef's teeming with fish. There'll be crabs and probably turtles. There are mouse-deer and monkeys in the forest and maybe wild pigs.'

'We don't eat meat,' Aquila said.

'That's a lifestyle choice. You can't be picky now.'

'We don't eat meat,' Jaeger said.

'None of you?'

'None of us.'

Startled by this false claim, Candy was about to challenge it, then bit her tongue. Group discipline was vital, and with rescue probably only a matter of hours away, diet was hardly an issue.

Marriot wouldn't let it go. 'You a vegetarian, Disco?'

'Me? I eat whatever's going.'

'We don't eat meat,' Jaeger repeated, 'and we don't kill animals.'

Marriot responded with restraint. 'Okay, but things will look different when you're hungry.'

Aquila peered around at the riotous greenery. 'There must be plenty of edible plants.'

'Up in the canopy there are fruits and nuts and honey, but you'd need wings to reach them. Don't be fooled by all that luxuriance. Most of it's inedible at best, poisonous at worst. If you're lucky, we'll find wild figs and maybe durians. Ever taste a durian? It's like slurping nectar through a sweaty sock. Even if that's to your taste, it won't keep you going.'

'We'll see.'

'Let's hope we don't,' Marriot said with finality.

Storms had torn gaps in the forest and these were places of creative chaos, crammed with trees competing to reach the light before their neighbours. Toppled hardwoods, moss-covered and sprouting orchids, blocked the explorers' path like the carcasses of dinosaurs. Lianas as thick as a man's wrist hung in fantastic loops.

The forest subdued them, soaking up their voices so that Candy caught only the tag ends of words. Jaeger blundered along in front of her, swiping at the creepers, and she realized that without his glasses he was virtually blind. Aquila followed Marriot, occasionally diverting to examine a particular plant or insect and exclaiming excitedly. She gave the impression of the world's most enthusiastic consumer given free run of a gigantic supermarket. Disco moved with graceful caution, watching on all sides.

Butterflies in extraordinary profusion and colours attended them. Some wafted like scraps of silk caught in an eddy; others tacked and weaved as if they were battling a current; and a few rowed along with bird-like directness. Aquila held out her hand and within seconds it was enamelled by swallowtails.

Somewhere about halfway across, Marriot froze in concentration. Very, very slowly he turned and pointed up, then sank to his haunches. Everyone followed suit, staring into the forest roof, trying to separate the real from the illusions created by the leaf tangles.

If the gibbon hadn't moved, Candy wouldn't have seen it. Sixty feet over her head, it ran upright along a branch, paused, looked down at them, dropped, casually took hold of a branch with one muffed paw, swung up and cartwheeled away with wonderful speed and fluid grace. Candy was left with an image of a dark little manikin with pale eyebrows.

Aquila squealed with delight and clutched Jaeger. 'Did you see that? It looked right at us. It wasn't scared.'

Really, Candy thought, you couldn't resent such open-heartedness.

Candy made the next discovery. Climbing over a toppled tree, she almost put her hand in it.

'Robert.'

Marriot crouched and whistled softly. 'In five years, I've never run into one of these, and then half an hour in this tiny patch – bingo!' He looked up. 'Strewth, this could be a rich habitat. I'd love to do a proper survey.'

'What you find?' Disco asked.

'Clouded leopard dropping.'

111

'Leopard shit?' Disco said, stiffening. 'You didn't say anything about leopards.'

'It's a small arboreal species,' Candy told him, proud to display her knowledge. 'They live on birds and monkeys. They're beautiful and rare.'

'Perhaps Trigg could film it,' Aquila said.

'They're very shy,' Candy told her. 'This one won't stay long with us around.'

Aquila looked up into the lattices. 'Don't go,' she called softly. 'We won't hurt you.'

Marriot caught Candy's eye and smiled, boosting her morale. 'Better keep moving,' he said. 'We've still got to make a camp.'

It took nearly an hour to cross the island. The last part was the toughest, and to reach the landward shoreline, Jaeger had to slash a path with his parang. They clustered in the gap, sobered by the sight that greeted them.

On this side the lagoon was stained an unhealthy brown, its surface flat and as still as glycerine. Across it, the mangroves stretched in unbroken monotony for as far as Candy could see. At this point they were about three hundred yards away, but even at that distance she could smell their foetid breath. The heat was crushing.

'Do you think anyone lives in there?' Aquila asked, her voice hushed.

'Nobody lives in the mangroves. I don't know how far back they go, but if we're where I think we are, the region is one big swamp.' Marriot tapped the nearest trunk. 'Ebony,' he said. 'If people could get to the island, they would have clean-felled it. But they can't get in by sea and the mangroves cut it off by land. I'd say we're the first people to set foot on it for years, maybe centuries.'

'Maybe since the beginning of time,' Aquila said, and a sigh escaped her. 'It's so beautiful, so peaceful. This is what Eden must have been like.'

Candy was touched by her emotion, then she caught a movement near her arm and turned to see a leech blindly feeling for her. She swatted it away.

Marriot was scouring the far shoreline through the glare. 'What are you looking for?' she asked.

'Crocodiles.'

Disco was plainly startled. 'I thought crocodiles lived in ...'

'Africa? There are more than twenty species and the big daddy of them all, *Crocodylus porosus*, the salt-water croc, lives in these seas.'

'Big, you say?'

'Up to nine metres. In the Philippines, they killed one so large it took forty men to drag it ashore, and when they cut it open they found a horse inside – in seven pieces. That was a while ago. One brute shot in the fifties was better than eight metres long. Biggest I've trapped was just on five metres.'

'You trapped them!'

'To attach radio transmitters for tracking.' Marriot laughed. 'That was some chore. Turned out the only way to sedate them was to pump alcohol down their throats. When they were knocked out, we screwed solar-powered tags on to their cranial domes.'

Aquila registered disapproval. 'How cruel.'

'Takes more than a one-inch bolt to hurt a croc. We did it that way so the sun kept the tags charged when the crocs basked on the surface. We picked up some of those brutes twenty kilometres out to sea and fifty kilometres upriver. I found three crocs in a billabong where you wouldn't expect to find anything bigger than a goldfish.' He surveyed the muddy lagoon. 'Yeah, they turn up in funny places.'

'And they're man-eaters, you say.'

'It's not personal. There's not an animal alive they

won't eat if they get the chance. In the Territory, they kill more people than sharks – mainly Abo fishermen, but also a few tourists who decide to take a dip from a boat or wade across a creek. Worst croc attack happened about twenty-five years ago. A river ferry capsized and the crocs took forty of the passengers.'

'This happened in Australia?'

'Sulawesi – next island east of Borneo.'

Even Candy felt a prickle of unease. She concealed it under a laugh. 'Are you trying to frighten us?'

'They breed in coastal mangroves – sheltered places where predators can't get their eggs and young and there's plenty of food.' Marriot nodded at the brooding wall across the water. 'Nurseries don't come cosier than that.'

'When *is* the breeding season?'

'Coincides with the wet,' Marriot said, and looked at the sky. 'Starting about now. If you want to go swimming, do it the other side of the island, in the clear water.'

'What happens if one of them grabs you?'

'I believe the theory is to poke them in the eye.'

'You're not serious.'

'Got any better ideas?'

'If we respect their territory,' Aquila said, 'they won't bother us.'

'They're not interested in your respect,' Marriot told her.

9

Day 1

Soon after the scouting party returned to camp, the sky went dark and all the creatures in the forest fell silent. For a few moments there was a breathless hush, then the trees all sighed at once and fat water bombs splattered down. In seconds the rain had merged into a sheet so thick that Boucher couldn't make out the lagoon fifty yards away. He sat out the downpour under a fold of airship fabric, staring blankly out to sea. He had made a brief foray into the forest and found it disorientating and claustrophobic. His jacket was already a mould culture. Marriot had impressed on them the need to keep their soft body parts clean and dry, but Boucher had no spare clothes or any other grooming aids. *Tristes tropiques*, he thought despondently.

An hour later the sky cleared as if a curtain had been pulled aside and the survivors emerged sodden from their makeshift shelters. For a few minutes the air had a delicious coolness and clarity. Water tip-tapped through the canopy. Every leaf was tipped by liquid crystal. A bird sang. A series of booming cries resonated in Boucher's diaphragm. A shriek followed and then a series of barks. Just when Boucher thought it was all over, a final scream curdled his blood.

'Siamangs,' Marriot said. 'Black gibbons. They're marking their territory. We'd better establish ours before the sun goes down.'

Watching Marriot construct sleeping platforms Boucher realized how fortunate they were to have his expertise to call on. First he felled a dozen saplings which he trimmed to different lengths. He cut four uprights about two feet long and lashed side and end beams to them with strips of rattan, then tied cross-pieces to the main frame and padded it with palm fronds collected by the women. He stuck more branches in the ground on each side and pulled together their tops to make a support for a fabric roof. Two hours' labour produced only three of these tented beds. Fieser was laid on one, Nadine got another, and Jaeger insisted that Candy take the third.

'Tonight, the rest of us will have to sleep on the sand.'

Candy placed her bed close to Fieser. The others paired up according to preference. Boucher found himself on the outside, furthest from the fire that Jaeger and Disco had made.

'Hey, guys,' Bartok called from the beach, 'take a look at this.'

Against the cooling sky, Boucher picked out a twist of black smoke. As it coiled towards them, strands peeled off and disappeared into the forest. The streamer passed overhead with a dry rustling and squealing.

'Fruit bats,' Marriot said. 'They live in the mangroves. And before you ask, Nadine, there are no vampires.'

'I don't care,' she said sullenly. 'I hate bats, whatever they eat.'

Night fell fast, the material of the sky changing from blue satin to black velvet within minutes. Frogs burped and cheeped and pinged like a warehouse of electronic cash registers going off simultaneously. Looking south,

Boucher saw the entire mangrove coast pulsing with light. Fireflies.

By the time he turned, the world had shrunk to the tiny circumference of the campfire. Aquila crouched beside the guttering flame, shadowy as a sorceress, stirring a mess tin of rice. Nadine moped on the other side, massaging skin cream into her neck. Jaeger and the other men had withdrawn a few yards and were examining the charts by flashlight. Candy was tending Fieser. Boucher was happy to sit with his thoughts, reviewing the day's events.

Nadine's cigarette lighter flashed, illuminating the planes of her face.

'You shouldn't,' Aquila told her.

Nadine took another drag. 'I didn't see any no-smoking signs.'

'This island is such a spiritual place. It's completely uncontaminated. It's sacrilege to spoil it.'

Nadine exhaled theatrically. 'Are you declaring it a no-smoking zone?'

'I think we ought to respect the spirit of the island.'

'The spirit of the ...!' Nadine poked the fire savagely. 'What do you call that? Why don't you object to that? Or is the only smoke you hate the one that gives me pleasure?'

Aquila adopted a placatory attitude. 'I'm sure you'd like to give up, but never found a good reason. Well now you have a clear starting point, a chance to break the habit.'

'Oh yeh,' Nadine said, nodding violently. 'Oh yeh. I get it. You're like those creeps who ask you to dinner and when you ask for salt they smile at each other like you're a child. They don't use it, they say; it's bad for you. But it isn't enough that they've discovered the secret of eternal life. They've got to inflict it on you, because if not eating salt makes them good, stopping other people eating it makes them even better.'

Aquila dropped her mollifying tone. 'I just don't like people smoking around me.'

Nadine leaned forward, her eyes glittering maliciously. 'We're stuck on a desert island without any plumbing or work surfaces, and one man is dead and one seriously injured, and the only thing spoiling your outlook is me puffing on a cigarette.' Her manner suddenly grew gay. 'Jay, you hear about the couple on the subway who had sex in the rush hour? And I mean, *sex*. They're at it all ways – backwards, forwards, hanging from the straps ... And you know what?' Nadine drew on her cigarette until the tip fizzled. 'No one said a word of complaint until they lit up afterwards.'

'Jay,' Aquila said sharply, looking for support.

'It really doesn't bother me.'

Before Aquila could rally, Jaeger and the others joined them and the dispute went on hold.

'We think we've worked out our position,' Jaeger said. 'We're on the south-east coast of Sumatra, not far from the equator. It's a wild corner – no towns closer than a hundred miles and mostly swamp between us and them.'

'Someone must live in the forest.'

'Maybe a few hunter-gatherers,' Marriot said, 'but to find them we'd have to get through the mangroves, and I'm not prepared to chance that. Leo and I agree the wise move is to stay put. We can hang on for weeks if necessary.'

Nadine ground out her cigarette. 'I don't want to stay for weeks. It's dirty and spooky.'

'You won't have to,' Jaeger promised. 'You and Dexter are VIPs and the Indonesians will be shifting heaven and earth to find you. They'll have tracked the storm and they'll know which way we headed and where we're likely to have come down.'

'I've been looking out for planes,' Dexter said. 'I didn't

see any. I mean, if they had an idea where we are, I'd have expected some activity by now.'

The same worry had been plaguing Boucher. He opened his mouth to speak.

'Something bothering you, Jay?'

Boucher guessed how Nadine would react if he told them about Fieser's admission and firmly shut his mouth. 'It's a big area,' he said. 'It could be a day or two before they get round to this spot.'

'But how long will they keep looking?' Dexter said. 'Every day that goes by, the more they'll think we're dead. Then what?'

'Then we wait for a passing ship.'

Aquila looked up dreamily. 'I'd like to stay forever,' she murmured. 'Our own miniature rain forest, a little microcosm of the richest habitat on earth. There are so many things to discover, so many things we can learn.' She frowned. 'I think we were meant to come here. I think this island has something to teach us, some message we can carry back.'

'It's been a pretty tough lesson for the pilot and Josef,' Marriot pointed out.

'I know it,' Jaeger said. He pondered a moment. 'Aquila's right, though. We can turn this into a positive experience. Tomorrow, or the day after that, we're gonna be picked up, but until then here's our chance to live the Wildguard philosophy for real – to show that we can live at one with nature.'

Across the fire, Marriot stirred uneasily. 'Don't get carried away, Leo. That might sound okay on a back-packing weekend in California, but this is real wilderness!'

Even in the dark, Boucher could see Aquila's face shining with excitement.

'I know I'm idealizing our situation. I mean, I realize that in a sense we're voyeurs, that we can't fully participate in the wild, but this is the closest any of us will come to it. Trigg, is your camcorder still working? Do you have batteries?'

Boucher silently guffawed. There wasn't an ironical nerve in Aquila's body. She was perfect unto herself, the embodiment of a flawless principle. He wondered how he could do justice to her in his write-up.

'Yep. At least an hour's worth.'

Aquila clapped her hands. 'Let's make a video diary.'

'Brilliant,' Jaeger said. 'Great promotional material, Dexter. For you, too, Nadine.'

'I'm not gonna be filmed in this state. Look at my hair, for heaven's sake. It's *caked*. It'll be weeks before I dare show myself in front of a camera.'

'You'll be incredible,' Jaeger promised. 'You'll launch a new look.'

'Scene one, take one,' Disco said. 'What's the schedule for tomorrow?'

'First priority, we run up a signal flag,' Jaeger said. 'The north tip is the best place. There's a big tree out on its own. Get a flag up there and any ship passing within miles will see it.'

'If it's the tree I'm thinking of,' Marriot said, 'it's more than a hundred feet high. Nobody could climb it without ropes and irons.'

'Hear that?' Jaeger said, addressing Bartok.

'Technically, it's easy.'

'Easy?'

Jaeger laughed. 'You said the only way to reach the canopy was with wings. Well, tomorrow you'll believe a man can almost fly.' He winked. 'Wait and see.'

'What about a flag?'

'Show them, Dexter.'

Dexter proudly unfurled a large section of airship fabric

and there, snarling in the firelight, was Rousseau's tiger. Everyone laughed and clapped.

'Dexter's idea,' Jaeger said. 'You've all done great.' He squeezed Dexter and Bartok in his bear's grip. Emotion dampened his eyes. 'I'm proud to be alongside you guys.'

'I think this rice is just about cooked,' Aquila said.

It wasn't, but everybody was too ravenous to care. Even the survival biscuits, which had the texture of fibreboard, were greedily eaten except by Aquila, who ruled that they contained animal products and industrial poisons injurious to physical and spiritual well-being.

'Tell us what else we should do tomorrow,' Boucher asked Marriot.

'Hold it,' Disco said. 'Leo's the guy who decides what to do.'

Boucher gritted his teeth. Every intervention Disco made acted on his nerves like fingernails scratching on board.

'I ain't too proud to take advice,' Jaeger said, chewing hard. 'Go ahead, Robert.'

'Finish the sleeping frames. Collect more fabric and anything else floating about. Gather wood. And when all that's taken care of, I propose to go fishing.'

Jaeger's mood clouded. 'I told you. No fishing. No hunting.'

'We don't need to hunt,' Aquila added. 'We've got rations for at least a week.'

Marriot stirred the fire. 'You don't realize how lucky we are to be sitting here with food in our bellies. If that raft had hit a bit harder, we would have nothing to eat, nothing to cook with, no medicines. Nothing! And I guarantee you wouldn't be talking the way you are.'

'But we *are* alive,' Aquila said. 'And we do have food.'

'We have to plan for the future. Think forward a week. By then the rations will be used up.'

'In a week, we'll be home.'

'We probably will, but I'm not going to bet my life on it.'

'Robert,' Aquila said with quiet earnestness, 'I'd starve before I take a life.'

'That's your privilege,' Marriot said, his voice trembling slightly. 'But I came here as a consultant biologist, not the member of a vegetarian cult.'

Aquila shook her head. 'When you join a Wildguard expedition, you abide by its rules.'

'You think you set the rules out here?' Marriot cried, jumping up. His hand stabbed into the clamorous night. 'Hear that? Billions of creatures going about their business without any reference to us. All that concerns them twenty-fours a day is how to eat and how to avoid being eaten.' Slowly, Marriot sat down. 'Ignore my advice if you want, but don't try telling me what I can or can't eat.'

'Anyone else feel that way?' Jaeger asked, dangerously quiet.

'Yeah,' Trigg said, 'I do.'

Boucher decided to pass.

'Hey,' Disco said, grinning at him. 'For a guy with so much to say, you've gone awful quiet.'

Flushed out of his bystander's role, Boucher shrugged and held up his biscuit. It had been manufactured in Scandinavia and had an eat-by date well into the next century. 'Now I know why Norway isn't rated as one of the great national cuisines.' He laughed, downplaying any implied dissent. 'Hell, I think we'd be pretty foolish to employ a jungle expert and not listen to what he has to say.'

For a moment he thought that he and Trigg were

Marriot's only supporters, then Candy spoke out. 'Surely,' she said, 'living with nature means feeding off nature.'

Somehow, her intervention broke the deadlock. 'Look,' Marriot pleaded. 'In the lagoon there are fish by the thousands. There are crabs and mudskippers in the mangroves. However many we catch, we won't tip the balance one scrap.'

'It's the principle,' Aquila said.

'Bugger principle,' Marriot snapped. 'On this island it's *us* who are the endangered species.'

Jaeger bowed his head, coming to judgement. When he spoke, his tone was deceptively mild. 'Okay, you can catch enough fish for your own needs. No more.'

'Leo,' Aquila protested, 'give way on this and God knows where it will end.'

'That's the truth,' Disco said. 'You're the boss, man, and you got to make that clear.'

Boucher gulped on his annoyance. Two days ago, Disco had never even heard of Wildguard, and now he was acting like he was Jaeger's most loyal lieutenant.

'This isn't a power struggle,' Marriot declared. 'We're trying to agree a strategy for survival.'

Jaeger raised a hand, silencing him, silencing everyone. A lengthy pause added weight to his pronouncement. 'That's my last concession. You can catch fish. Everything else – birds, monkeys and God knows what else ... is left alone. *Everything*. When we leave here, nothing's gonna be changed, nothing damaged. We're a radical conservation group dedicated to preserving the wild. Wildguard. Think what that name means, and then imagine what would happen to our image if the world found out we trashed one of the last virgin pieces of rain forest.'

Boucher wished he was getting this down on tape. He didn't dare use his notebook. There was a lot he would have to commit to memory.

'One more thing,' Jaeger said, spacing the words so that no one would be foolish enough to think he was about to deliver a casual afterthought. 'Disco's right. There's only room for one leader, and if any of you has a problem with that, you'd better speak up.'

Nobody did.

'Okay,' Jaeger said, 'then this is how it works. We live by Hell's Angels' rules. Don't look so startled, Candy. They're a damn sight straighter than the laws that come out of Washington or London. Living the Hell's Angel way means everybody has their say, everybody gets equal shares, everybody gets equal protection. But it works the other way, too. Anyone taking advantage of anyone, anyone caught stealing, anyone harming wildlife, is punished.'

Boucher glanced at Disco, and as if the same current had passed between them, he found the drifter's eyes already looking back at him. Disco winked, as if they were in collusion on some enterprise not yet declared, and Boucher's mouth went dry as he finally accepted that the drifter wasn't going to forget his grudge and had payback in mind. Shit, Boucher thought.

'In any dispute,' Jaeger said, 'the final decision is mine. And so I know we're all reading from the same piece of paper, I want to hear you say "aye".'

One by one, with varying degrees of enthusiasm or reluctance, they acknowledged Jaeger as supreme arbiter. Marriot and Candy were the last to pledge their allegiance.

Afterwards, though it was only a little after nine, there was nothing left except sleep, and Boucher realized that long days and longer nights would be the rhythm of his existence for the foreseeable future.

'Kent, how about reading to us from the Book?' Jaeger suggested.

Bartok opened his Bible and started at the right and proper place.

"'In the beginning when God created the heavens and the earth, the earth was a formless void and darkness covered the face of the deep ...'"

Listening to the story of the Creation, Boucher understood how vital a divine plan must have been to the pioneers of civilization.

"'... So God created the great sea monsters and every living creature that moves, of every kind with which the waters swarm, and every winged bird of every kind. And God saw that it was ...'"

'Jesus!'

From deep within the forest came an agonized creaking and groaning. Reports rang out, sharp as pistol shots, and then there was a terrible rending, slow at first, accelerating and deepening into a deafening roar. The ground shivered under a resounding crash.

Boucher found himself on his feet, dry-mouthed and trembling.

Disco uttered a short laugh. 'I guess whoever runs this place doesn't like competition.'

'Don't,' Aquila whispered, her eyes burning.

Several seconds of silence elapsed. 'Us men had better keep a watch,' Jaeger said. 'Three hours each, alternate nights. I'll take the first watch, until midnight. Disco, you're after me, and Jay, you're on the grave shift. Three through to dawn.'

Before turning in, Boucher wandered down the beach to relieve himself. The clamour of the frogs had settled into a rhythmic throbbing. The lagoon lay lacquered in silence. Looking across it, Boucher filled the air with a sigh that expanded into nothingness.

Just as he was about to head back, he did a double take.

He blinked to make certain that what he was seeing wasn't the residual glow of the fire.

'Hey,' he called softly, 'there's some kind of light out here.'

In the dark the others gathered around him. 'What do you think?' Dexter Smith asked. 'A town?'

'Can't be. It's way out to sea.'

'It's the gas flare from a rig,' Marriot said. 'There's oil all along this coast.'

'How far off would you say they were?'

'Over the horizon – thirty kilometres at least. Too far for them to see a fire.'

'They might spot a flare,' Dexter said. 'They'll have a helicopter.'

In the dark, everyone looked at Jaeger. 'Not tonight. We're not prepared. Tomorrow, we'll hoist the flag and build a bonfire.'

The distant glow cancelled out Boucher's fear that the Indonesians might have called off the search. It set the seal on their hopes of an early deliverance. Even Nadine perked up.

'I am so *relieved*,' she declared. 'Maybe I can still get back in time for Milan.'

After a few moments, they drifted back to the fire. Boucher remained for a while, contemplating the artificial dawn. Now that he knew rescue lay just across the horizon, he worried about it coming too soon, before his story was complete. A week would be perfect, he thought. Long enough for characters to flesh out and plot to gel, but not too long for hardship to set in. And of course, he thought belatedly, it was essential that Josef get hospital treatment. Yes, a week would be ideal, he decided, stepping back into the narrow radius of the campfire.

10

Day 2

Drifting between sleep and waking, Candy listened to the tropical orchestra tuning up. First came the jarring overture of the cicadas, then the plaintive woodwind of the gibbons, and finally the brassy notes of the hornbills.

Stiff from the battering she'd taken yesterday, she crawled out of her shelter. In the light that preceded dawn, she contemplated the sleeping shapes of her companions. Jaeger and Aquila lay sprawled together, his hairy arm thrown across her waist. Really, Candy thought, he wasn't such a brute. Actually, she felt a bit sorry for him; he'd found paradise, but without his specs it was just a blur.

Looking at Aquila, Candy didn't know what to think. What could you make of someone who, hours after a fatal air crash, seemed to have been transported to a state of religious ecstasy – a woman who worshipped nature but was such a poor naturalist that she couldn't tell a hornbill from a spoonbill? And, Candy thought, a little sourly, Aquila's compassion for dumb animals didn't leave much over for humans. True to her word, she had performed a healing spell over poor Fieser, but once that was finished, she seemed to think her duty was done. Not once had she offered to nurse him.

Candy eyed Marriot's form. Having grown up in the company of virile, quietly commanding men, she naturally looked to Marriot for leadership, but apart from his rather badly managed confrontation last night, he seemed reluctant to assert authority.

Oddly enough, he seemed to have struck up a friendship with Trigg, who Candy found a bit shifty.

She looked towards Nadine's shelter with amused exasperation. Nadine was perfectly awful – selfish, demanding, bitchy. And yet Candy liked her – liked her wry metropolitan asides and almost admired her implacable refusal to see the slightest thing good about their situation. Anyway, she was beautiful, and beauty absolved its owner of responsibility. The same went for fame, she supposed, thinking of Dexter Smith, who was a bit of zero in the flesh. Night and day he wore his dark glasses, as if trying to preserve his anonymity against an anticipated invasion of screaming fans.

She looked at Bartok's curly head. He was quite appealing in his wholesome muscularity, but his equally muscular religious convictions were a bit of a turn-off. Candy subscribed to the Anglican tradition of moderation in all things, including devotion to God.

She couldn't see Disco, but she knew he was awake. He had got up before dawn and mysteriously disappeared into the dark, returning only a few minutes ago. Disco unsettled her, and she knew that the root of her unease was sex. He was always looking at her, favouring her with his insidious smile. At first she'd smiled back, wanting to be friendly, but after a while she'd found his attention wearing and had adopted a look of haughty indifference. It didn't have any effect; he just went on smiling, as if he had a secret she'd catch on to in the fullness of time.

Treetops hung ghost-like in the mist smoking up from the island. The eastern sky caught alight.

Boucher came down the beach. In his stained jacket and tie he looked like a late-night reveller who had been mugged and was putting on a brave face. Candy smiled, glad to see him, then felt a bit guilty. He had saved her life, but since the crash she had hardly spoken to him – had, in fact, gone out of her way to avoid him. Why was that? she wondered. Their trivial antagonism back in Jakarta seemed a lifetime ago. She watched him sit down by the remains of last night's fire and hold out his hands to the cinders. In repose, his world-wise sharpness ironed out and he looked altogether more vulnerable. Recalling some of the barbed remarks she'd made, it occurred to her that there was a discrepancy between how she spoke to him and how she actually felt. He had a girlfriend, of course, a rather glamorous one by the sound of it, but there was no reason why they couldn't be friends.

'See anything, Jay?'

'Negative.'

Disco propped himself on one elbow and grinned at Candy. 'How could he see anything if he was asleep?'

Boucher slowly sat up. 'Who says I was asleep?'

Disco laughed. 'I sneaked right up behind you and you didn't know a thing about it.' He sank back. 'Lucky there ain't any dangerous animals on this island.'

Candy's gaze jumped from one to the other, registering Disco's smirk, the hapless look of loathing on Boucher's face.

'Course,' Disco told her, 'it's possible our writer doesn't want to get off too soon.'

Boucher half rose. 'You think I want to stay on this atoll longer than I have to?'

'Only for as long as it takes.'

Disturbed by the undertow of hostility in this exchange, Candy was about to tell them to cut it out when Fieser whimpered, erasing all other considerations from her mind. She went to him. Half a dozen times she had tended him in the night, but now, in the light of day, she hesitated – not so much squeamish as frightened because there was so little she could do to ease his suffering.

At least he was still conscious. He even managed a weak smile.

'Let's take a look at you,' she said, automatically falling into bedside manner.

It was worse than she'd feared. His right thigh from knee to hip was the colour of raw meat and grotesquely swollen. There was no doubt he had suffered internal haemorrhaging, but she had no way of knowing if important blood vessels were involved. Infection was the greatest danger. She felt his forehead. Hot and damp. She took his temperature. More than two degrees above normal – a little higher than yesterday, still not dangerously high, but worrying. She gave him water and another dose of antibiotics. What he really needed was a massive shot of penicillin.

He looked at her, his eyes lucid. 'I think I will lose my leg.'

The same sickening possibility had already occurred to her. 'Of course you won't.'

His eyes turned to the sea and dulled. 'Today you must find help.'

Jaeger sat up and scratched like a bear emerging from hibernation. 'Hey, looks like it's gonna be a great day.'

After breakfast, Candy went bathing with Aquila and Nadine. A small bay beyond a spit of sand about two hundred yards up the beach was designated the women's area. Already the sun was at full strength.

Aquila stripped naked – 'skyclad', as she put it. Her breasts were large, her body as white as an altar candle. She ran into the water with top-heavy exuberance.

Candy, unable to shed her Anglo-Saxon inhibitions, removed her bra but kept her pants on. Nadine, as befitted a woman whose catwalk appearances were worth $20,000 a strut, opted for even more discretion. Hips tilting regally beneath her sarong, she sashayed in and didn't disrobe until she was waist deep.

Sticky from the night's heat, Candy submerged herself. She swam under cool dappled water, past coral antlers and over miniature dunes. Fish coloured like hussars fussed around her. She surfaced into the glare and floated on her back, surrendering herself to elemental sensations – the sun beating down on her eyelids, the water cradling her body. She knew that ten minutes after leaving the lagoon she would be tormented by itchy heat. For now, though, she was swathed in satin.

Hearing splashing, she opened her eyes to see Aquila wading towards her, breasts swaying. Candy found her feet and Aquila came intimately close, almost nipple to nipple. She put out her hand as if she was reaching for something delicate.

'Candy, where did you get that *skin*? It's perfect.'

Under Aquila's touch, Candy tingled. She was confused and excruciatingly embarrassed. 'I inherited it.'

'Anyone who eats like you shouldn't have such a lovely complexion. It's unfair. Look, Nadine.'

Nadine eyed Candy's body with professional detachment. 'Hmm, it won't be so dewy after a week in this goddam climate.'

To Candy's disappointment, not that she'd ever admit it, Nadine didn't offer to share her cache of body lotions and creams.

'Oh-oh,' Nadine said, 'the cavemen are on their way.'

Up the beach trooped the men, rag-bag and motley, led by Jaeger at his most paleolithic.

'Coming to the flag-raising ceremony?' he called.

'Trigg, put that camera away *now!*' Nadine shouted, crossing her arms over her breasts.

Candy defended her modesty likewise, but Aquila walked naked and unabashed from the lagoon, every tremor and jiggle filmed by Trigg. Most of the men reacted with studied coolness, but poor Bartok blushed and turned to hide the bulge in his Bermuda shorts.

'Stupid bitch,' Nadine said.

'She can't help it.'

'Like hell she can't. It's not her fat butt she's flaunting; it's her power. She's saying, look at me, boys. How would you like some of this? But she knows none of them would dare come on to her while that Neanderthal is around. Or maybe she's hoping one of them gets so carried away he'll fight over her. I'm telling you, she's *primitive*.'

'I'm sure ...'

Nadine laid her elegant hand on Candy's arm. 'Honey, body language is something I do know about. It's my job.'

Rather unsettled, Candy surveyed the men on the beach. At this distance they weren't individuals. They were just a group of half-naked males and she was the only woman on the island who wasn't spoken for. In the same moment it struck her that by now news of their disappearance would have reached England. Her family would be frantic. The sense of well-being created by her swim evaporated.

When the men had gone a decent distance, she dressed and prepared to return to camp. She was rather annoyed that the men had simply abandoned Fieser.

'Don't you want to see the flag show?' Nadine asked.

'I'd better get back.'

'I'll take over.'

'Are you sure?'

'Sugar, I'm gonna find a nice piece of shade with no creepy-crawlies and sit there until a ship takes me away.'

Secretly pleased to be let off, Candy hurried after the flag-raising party, catching them up at the north tip. On this headland storms had thinned the forest. From the scrub layer rose a solitary giant that soared to a crown well over a hundred feet high. Although vines had got the trunk in a stranglehold, to Candy's eye it looked unassailable.

'I hope you know what you're tackling,' Marriot told Bartok.

Bartok nodded and massaged his palms, like a wrestler preparing to grapple with an outsize opponent. Today, his T-shirt portrayed an alpinist bathed in a biblical light, and read: NEARER MY GOD.

'Kent's a free climber,' Disco told them. 'His idea of recreation's crawling up a thousand-foot rock face without ropes.'

'Rock-climbing's one thing,' Marriot said. 'That tree's half-dead and those vines could harbour a lot of unpleasant wildlife.'

'I'll take care.'

As Bartok began to ascend, Candy's apprehension turned to awe. Arms and legs articulating in smooth diagonals, he swarmed up the trunk as if it had sprouted steps. Soon he was foreshortened by height and Candy's neck ached from keeping track of his progress. She moved back. He looked tiny. The tree was even taller than she'd thought.

Where the trunk divided, Bartok halted and inspected his surroundings. Having chosen a suitable branch, he shinned along it and unrolled the flag. Using cord from the raft, he secured it by its top corners. In the breeze the tiger came alive. Candy joined in the cheer.

'Wildguard lives,' Aquila shouted. 'The flag flies.'

'We ought to give our island a name,' Jaeger said.

'Ecotopia?' Boucher suggested, with what struck Candy as excessive irony.

'Too uptight.'

'Then how about Greenland?'

Aquila clapped her hands. 'Right. Perfect.'

'Hey, Kent, can you see the rig?'

Bartok's voice floated down. 'No.'

'See anything at all?'

Bartok scanned through the compass. 'Solitude all directions. The forest goes on for ever. It's real awesome.'

'Okay, you come on down.'

Up or down were all the same to Bartok. He made a fluent descent, jumping the last eight or nine feet, his body absorbing the shock of impact like a spring. He looked around shy and pleased, barely out of breath.

Marriot shook him by the hand. 'Could you build some kind of observation platform up there? From that height we'd be able to see three or four times as far.'

'No problem.'

11

Day 2

Tired after her disturbed night and a morning of chores and nursing duties, Candy stole an afternoon nap. She woke from a doze to find Boucher smiling in at her. Feeling slightly crowded, she scrambled out and glanced around. Nadine, true to her word, had established herself in deep shade and was plaiting a sunhat from palm leaves. Down the beach, Marriot was loading something into the inflatable.

'Where's everyone else?' Candy asked.

'Spying on the shy denizens of the forest. We're going fishing. Nice if you came along.'

She wiped her forehead with the back of her hand. 'I can't leave Josef.'

Boucher turned. 'Nadine, would you mind sitting with Josef?'

Nadine raised a torpid hand. 'Sure. Go catch fish.'

It was the first time Candy had been alone with Boucher, and walking at his side, she felt awkward, unsure if they were silent because they were shy or because they had nothing to say to each other. But once they pushed off from shore, her reticence vanished. She found herself invigorated and ready for adventures. Disturbed by the shadow of the boat, a small ray wafted across the bottom, raising lazy whorls of sand.

'I'm glad you took a stand last night,' Boucher told Marriot.

'Had to be done.'

Candy came to Aquila's defence. 'Even if you don't agree with her views, you must try and respect them.'

'Life's too complex for certainties,' Boucher said. 'And I've never understood why you have to pay homage to cranky doctrines just because someone else swallows them whole. Besides, with people like Aquila, respect's a one-way street.'

'So what do *you* believe in?'

'I'm a libertarian humanist. I'd go to the stake for my beliefs.'

'Ha-ha.'

'I respect your right to laugh at me and I'd die to defend it.'

'Be serious,' Candy said. 'At least Aquila acts according to her convictions. For most people, being a conservationist's no more than a matter of exercising consumer choice at the supermarket.'

'But is her position sustainable? If the food runs out, she's going to find she's not perched on the moral high ground, but pasted in a corner.'

'It won't come to that,' Candy said.

High tide had covered the reef crest. On the lee side, Marriot baited a small hook with rice and dropped it into a shoal of fish painted in clown colours. Within seconds, one of them was wriggling on the end of the line.

Boucher looked dubious. 'That won't go far between four people.'

'Sprat to catch a whale,' Marriot said. Taking a much larger treble hook, he impaled the fish on one barb.

'I'm glad Aquila's not watching,' Candy said. Even out here she couldn't shake off her controlling presence.

A tidal surge offered a way through the reef. Here, the

crest was about fifteen yards wide – an exquisite piece of seascape gardening planted with clumps and fronds of yellow, pink and red. On the seaward side the reef shelved steeply past caves and undercuts and polyp masses wrinkled like brains. Fish in extraordinary numbers and variety occupied this zone, radiating streaks and sparks and bubbles of light. One shoal twisted and turned, flashing on and off like a neon sign. Looking past them into the indigo depths, Candy experienced vertigo.

Marriot dropped anchor over a coral outcrop and lifted the fishing pole. He cocked an eyebrow at Boucher. 'Want to give it a go?'

'Okay,' Boucher said, uncertain. Clumsily he dropped the bait where Marriot directed. The fish jerked in wounded circles.

'Jay,' Candy said, 'why do you insist on wearing that silly tie?'

Boucher fingered the greasy strip of silk. 'It's the badge of my calling. I'm still ...'

The line drew taut and water flicked from it. 'I got one,' he yelled. 'I got one. What do I do?'

'Keep the line tight,' Candy shouted, caught up in the thrill. 'Stop it from diving under the boat.'

The pole quivered and bent. Boucher cried out in glee. 'Let them have dominion over the fish of the sea and over every creeping thing.'

The fish swirled red beneath them. With Marriot's help, Boucher brought it thrashing to the surface. Marriot scooped it into the boat and clubbed its head. The fish gave a couple of slow flaps and its eyes filmed and its vibrant colours faded to dross.

'Coral trout. A real beaut. Let's try for another.'

'One's quite enough,' Candy said, not meaning to sound so prim. 'They'll only rot in this heat.'

'We can smoke them.'

'Please, don't push Leo and Aquila too far.'

Marriot's excitement subsided. He shrugged. 'Okay, plenty more where that came from.'

Flushed with triumph, Boucher studied his fish. 'Beautiful,' he said. 'But is it edible?'

'Best eating on the reef,' Marriot said. He grinned: 'Exciting sport, eh?'

'Damn right.'

'If you go fishing on your own, don't eat anything until I've checked it. A lot of the reef fish are poisonous. Pufferfish are the worst. The flesh is okay, but the blood and organs contain a fatal neurotoxin. Handle any fish with care. Some of them have venomous barbs. And never walk on the reef in bare feet. Step on a coneshell or stonefish and even if you don't end up dead, the pain will make you wish you were.'

Boucher winced. 'Isn't anything around here harmless?'

'Play safe; assume it isn't.'

On the way back, Candy let the men row while she trailed her hand in the water. The heat made her languid. Boucher had stripped off his shirt and she couldn't help observing that he was a tauter physical specimen than she'd imagined. Not that she'd given it a moment's thought, she told herself, eyeing the subtle slide of muscles in his arms, the complicated articulations in his torso. Flustered by a sudden flush of warmth, she turned her attention to the underwater landscape sliding past. A splash of green snagged her attention. She jolted upright. 'My rucksack!'

Marriot peered down. 'Shouldn't be difficult.'

'Allow me,' Boucher said. He stripped to his shorts.

Despite herself, Candy sneaked a look.

A splash and he was gone, scissoring down. His hand closed on the sack and he floated up, bubbles like quicksilver trapped in his hair. Grinning, he broke surface and deposited the bag in her hand. She clutched it to her, delighted.

'Jay, you don't know what this means to me.' She pulled out a shirt, 'Look the other way.' She unclasped her bra, stuffed it into the bag, and put on the soaking shirt. 'Okay,' she said. 'Decent at last.'

Boucher slowly faced her and an expression that looked like pain but wasn't crossed his face. 'Decent? Candy, I could see less when you were wearing your bra.'

Blood rushed to Candy's face. Her shirt was as transparent as cellophane and much clingier, revealing her breasts in their entirety, perfectly delineating her nipples. Pulling the material away, she put on the bravest face she could manage. 'After Aquila's exhibition, I'm surprised you even noticed.'

'Ah, but with Aquila, it's all or nothing. With you there's still something to tease the imagination.'

Trying to hide her confusion, she began to sort through the contents of her sack. It was all there – shorts, spare underwear, towel, suncream, medicines, soap, toothbrush – treasures beyond price.

'Women are amazing,' Marriot said. 'They're always prepared for the worst.'

'That's because we're programmed to think long-term,' Candy said. She noticed Boucher's expression had turned wistful. 'You don't have anything, do you?'

He shrugged. 'Come as you are, you said; and lo, I came.'

'I'm sorry, Jay. Look, you're welcome to use whatever you need.'

'Yeah, mate,' Marriot said, 'same goes for me.'

'I'm real obliged to you both,' Boucher said. He looked away, his mood reflective. 'People are basically good, aren't they?'

'As good as they need to be, and as bad as is good for them.' Marriot jerked his chin at Candy. 'Hawk and dove, right?'

She smiled at Boucher's mystification. 'It's a hypothesis in behavioural ecology.'

'Yeah? Explain it.'

Candy gathered her thoughts. 'Suppose you have a population that acts like doves, settling contests over food or mates by ritualized displays instead of fighting.'

Boucher struck a body-builder's pose. 'How's that?'

'I'd have to judge the competition.' Hastily, Candy veered away from this line. 'Right, now imagine that one of the doves begins to act like a hawk. It would always win because the other doves would back down without a fight. The hawk would have its pick of mates, so the gene for hawkishness would spread, and after a few generations every individual would be a hawk. Now, though, there wouldn't be any advantage in being aggressive because you'd have as much chance of losing as winning, and even if you did win, you might be injured. Acting like a dove would be a better strategy.'

'You're forgetting payoff,' Marriot said. 'The bigger the benefits of victory, the more it's worth fighting for them. Take elephant seals competing for a harem. Since the winner gets a huge number of copulations, aggressive fighting is worthwhile even if it carries the certainty of injuries and the risk of death.'

'It's called an evolutionarily stable strategy,' Candy added smartly, trying to blur the image of harems and copulation.

'What's our stable strategy?' Boucher asked. 'Are we hawks or doves?'

'Retaliator's the ideal compromise,' Marriot said. 'When there's conflict, play the dove, but if it escalates into violence, react like a hawk.'

'We're none of those things.' Candy told them. 'We're rational human beings.'

'Except where sex is involved.'

Boucher's eyes explicitly sought hers, and as they met she felt a little collision. For just one moment, but one moment too long, she couldn't break the contact.

'All right, you two,' Marriot said. 'If you can tear yourselves away, I'd like to take a closer look at the mangroves.'

Boucher deflated instantly. Candy didn't relish the prospect of a trip to the inner lagoon either. She opened her mouth to say that Josef needed her, but Boucher beat her to it.

'If it doesn't scare Candy, it doesn't scare me.'

Damn, Candy thought.

Cloying heat embraced them as they rounded the island's southern end. Slowly the water grew cloudier, the bottom siltier and more indistinct, until at last each oar-stroke disturbed clouds of stinking ooze. Shielded from the sea breeze, the atmosphere on this side was suffocating. They rowed to within fifty yards of the swamp. Close up, it was even more forbidding than Candy had imagined – a maze of rank-smelling grey and green, each channel dead-ending in a stew of mud and roots.

Fiddler crabs with one enormously enlarged claw waved at them from their burrows. Bulging-eyed creatures that looked like a cross between a frog and a fish skittered on the tidal flats.

'Mudskippers,' Marriot said. 'Amphibious fish. This is where life began.'

From a dead tree a brown-and-white fish eagle launched off with an eerie cry and flapped heavily up the coast. Swifts scythed across the surface, feeding on the plague of surface skaters. Small but nasty flies burrowed into Candy's hair, her eyes, her nostrils.

Marriot's eyes patrolled the margins.

'What exactly are we looking for?' Boucher asked.

'Croc nests.'

'Is that wise?'

'Not too fond of crocs?'

Boucher shuddered without affectation. 'I think they're loathsome.'

'They're incredible creatures, Jay – one of nature's miracles. People are awed by *Tyrannosaurus Rex*, but salt-water crocs aren't a lot smaller and they're just as ferocious. Plus, they've got something the dinosaurs lacked.'

'Engaging personalities?'

'A winning design. They're as old as anything in Jurassic Park, but whatever killed T-Rex and the rest had no effect on crocs. Some people reckon that's because Jurassic Age species were tiny and only evolved into their final huge form because competitors had been eliminated. But there were small dinosaurs, too, and they didn't make it.'

Candy found herself paying particular attention to half-submerged roots and branches – anything that might conceivably transform itself into a crocodile's snout or orbital ridge. The water was so unfathomable that one of the monsters could have been lurking feet away without advertising its presence.

'How do they hunt?' she asked, her voice pitched higher than she'd intended. 'I mean, how do they locate their prey?'

'Good night vision, highly developed sense of smell, and acute hearing. They're pretty territorial and aggressive during the breeding season. Bulls have been known to attack motor boats. Apparently, the sound of an outboard resembles the bellow of a rival.'

Candy surreptitiously drew in her feet from the slash in the hull and took a firmer grip on the thwart. She was conscious of the craft's flimsiness. 'Maybe we should return before this fish starts to go off.'

But Boucher was transfixed. 'What other monsters live in there that you haven't told me about?'

Marriot sucked air through his teeth. 'Jay, I don't think you want to know.'

'Know what? Come on, give.'

Marriot sighed. 'Okay, watch out for giant carnivorous crabs.'

As Boucher glanced behind him, Marriot winked at Candy. 'There was this old bushman up in Queensland who used to catch giant crabs, bag them up and sell them in Cairns. They make bloody good eating. One day he caught a real beaut, three metres from pincer to pincer, put it in the ute and set off for town. When he didn't show up, they went looking for him. Found him sitting in the driver's seat with his spinal cord severed.' Marriot made a scissoring motion. 'Snip.'

Boucher's jaw had dropped. He shut it. 'Take me back.'

'He's just teasing, Jay. There's no such thing.'

Boucher's eyes switched from one to the other. 'Teasing?' He gave a funny laugh. 'You call that teasing?'

'Sorry, mate.' Marriot fell quiet for a moment. 'Seriously, Jay, we don't know anything about half the animals that live in the rain forest. In museums all round the world, there are cases of specimens no one's even got round to classifying.'

'He's talking about small creatures,' Candy said before Boucher's alarm could escalate. 'Insects and other invertebrates.'

Marriot nodded. 'But the rain forest may still hold a few

surprises. It's less than ten years since they found a new species of deer in Vietnam, and Vietnam's like Earl's Court compared to this patch.'

'How about ape men?' Boucher asked, only half joking.

Marriot grinned. 'Drop Jaeger in there and he'd have taxonomists scratching their heads.'

At that moment, a chorus of monkey shrieks rose from the mangroves, some way south and inland. Candy's gaze traversed the shore. 'Something's given them a bad fright.'

'Probably an eagle grabbed one,' Marriot said. He did another scan, then picked up his oar. 'Jay, you'll be pleased to hear there are no croc nests.'

'Good,' Boucher said, 'Now let's get the hell out of here.'

Candy rowed as hard as the men and didn't feel secure until the water turned blue beneath them.

When they reached camp, she found Nadine being consoled by Dexter. For an awful moment, she thought Fieser's condition must have turned critical or worse, but none of the other castaways seemed upset, and a quick check showed that the pilot was stable.

'Nadine had a fright,' Trigg explained indifferently. 'Says she saw some kind of beast.'

After giving Fieser his medication, Candy went over to Nadine. She was still distraught, her face streaked with tears. Dexter looked up.

'She went off for a walk by herself. Down there,' he said, pointing to the island's southern tip. 'She saw some kind of animal on the other side of the lagoon.'

'What kind of animal?'

'It was in shadow and she couldn't see any detail, but she said it ran fast along the edge of the mangroves, then it dived into a creek and swam inland.'

'Probably an otter.'

Dexter shook his head. 'It was big – longer than a man.'

Candy exchanged a look with Marriot.

'Sounds like she saw what we missed,' he said.

'Crocodiles,' Boucher explained. 'We didn't run into any, thank God.'

'Crocs can be real tricky to spot when they want to be,' Marriot said.

'It wasn't a crocodile,' Nadine blurted. 'I know what a goddam crocodile looks like. This thing was moving too fast and its legs were too long.'

'A crocodile can move faster than a man for short bursts.'

Candy knelt down. 'Nadine, can you remember what time you saw this animal?'

Nadine sniffed and wiped her nose. 'About four-thirty. I'd just checked my watch because I didn't want to get back late.'

'Well,' Boucher said, 'we were right alongside the mangroves at that time, and we didn't see anything bigger than a crab.'

Candy looked round at him. 'It was about then we heard that uproar in the trees.'

'Coming from deep in the mangroves,' Marriot reminded her. 'No, I bet it was a croc.'

'Robert, there are more creatures under heaven than crocodiles.'

He grinned at her. 'Still dreaming of tigers, eh? Well, it's easily checked. There's still enough light left to go and take a look at the tracks. Nadine, can you point out the exact spot?'

Though the day was fading fast, it wasn't the thought of tracking animals in the dusk that put Candy off. In the last three days, she hadn't slept for more than two hours at a time. She was simply dead beat.

'Leave it till tomorrow,' she said.

'By then the tide will have washed away the tracks.'

'Ah hell,' Boucher said, through a yawn, 'I've seen enough wildlife for one day. Whatever Nadine saw isn't going to bother us here. That's a totally different environment on the other side.'

Candy realized that what Nadine needed was reassurance. 'Jay's right,' she told her. 'We're perfectly safe on the island.'

The fishing party, joined by Trigg, made their own fire and cooked and ate separately. The coral trout, wrapped in leaves and broiled over driftwood embers, was delicious – worth putting up with Aquila's black looks.

Before the others had finished eating, Nadine threw down the leaf she'd been using as a plate and stared straight at Jaeger.

'When are we going to send up a flare?'

'How many have we got?' Aquila asked.

'Eight. We'd have to fire two – one to get noticed and another to give whoever sees it a fix.'

'That gives us four chances. I say we wait until we get a clear shot – like if a ship or plane comes close.'

'I agree,' Jaeger said eventually. 'Remember, it's only been two days.'

'But you promised,' Nadine said, gulping back tears. She saw Jaeger glance sideways. 'Stay out of it,' she snapped at Aquila. 'For you this is just a chance to act the earth mother, but me and Dexter have jobs to do, a schedule to fulfil.' She rose, tall in the firelight, and stamped her foot. 'After what I saw today, I want out of here. Now!'

'Nadine, you're going to miss a few engagements. What's that compared to the experience of a lifetime?'

'Dying of heat and bug bites isn't my fucking lifetime ambition.'

'If only you'd try shedding your urban hang-ups, you might start enjoying yourself.'

Nadine's eyes projected venom. 'Remember who's paying. Without Dexter's money, you'd still be selling witch cookies and herbal teas back in Twin Falls.'

'Go easy,' Dexter said, but he too stared at Jaeger without flinching. 'It's been an experience right enough, but Nadine isn't cut out for living rough, and to be truthful, neither am I.'

'Wait one more night.'

'Where are the planes you promised?' Dexter demanded. 'We haven't seen a ship since yesterday morning. I'm telling you, they've called off the search.'

'Don't be crazy,' Jaeger said.

Candy noticed the uncertain set of Boucher's mouth. 'What is it, Jay?'

He smiled guiltily. 'I guess the rigs being so close softens the bad news.' He hesitated a moment. 'Our pilots thought we were about to crash. That was their last radio message. Dexter's right; the search and rescue people have probably written us off.'

Candy joined in the collective sigh.

'Why didn't you tell us before?' Jaeger asked.

'I didn't want to spread unnecessary alarm and ...'

'Unnecessary?' Dexter exploded.

'I'll tell you why he kept it to himself,' Disco said. 'He doesn't want us to get off. You heard him. He's got an interesting story shaping up and he doesn't want to lose it.'

'Damn it,' Boucher yelled, half rising. 'I've had enough of your insinuations. You come out of nowhere, hitching a ride with some bullshit story about being a ...'

'Sit down,' Jaeger ordered.

Slowly, Boucher did as he was told, the object of all

eyes, all hostile. Angry with him herself, sensing resentment crackling like dry tinder, Candy damped it down before a spark could catch. 'Whatever the Indonesians are doing, another night might be one too many for Josef. I'm frightened he'll develop gangrene. He could lose his leg. The sooner he gets to hospital, the better his chances.'

Jaeger's eyes dropped. 'Nine o'clock,' he said. 'Make sure the fire's ready.'

Candy ignored Boucher's covert look of gratitude. Recalling his glib claim about the cruelty of writers, she decided that Disco's accusation might not be so far from the truth. At the same time, she remembered the tender way Boucher had spoken to her and the moment on the lagoon when, looking back into his eyes, she'd found her defences utterly lacking. Contradictory emotions assailed her.

At the appointed hour, she joined the others on the tideline. Behind them the beacon fire had crackled into life. When it was well alight, Jaeger raised the flare gun and fired. High overhead an incandescent medusa formed.

Darkness sifted back and they all watched the horizon. Along the reef something splashed. Candy saw fish moving in the lagoon, their luminous bodies swirling like comets' tails.

'If they'd seen it,' she said eventually, 'they would have sent up an answering flare by now.'

Muted, the castaways returned to the fire. An hour later, with the bonfire dying, Jaeger fired a second flare. There was no answering light and no one expected one. The bonfire collapsed in a rustle of sparks. Nadine stayed alone on the beach. When Candy and Dexter went to fetch her, they found her staring into the dark, her face smudged by soot, her hands held stiff at her sides.

'They can't see us,' she said. 'Nobody can see us.'

Gently Candy took her arm. 'Come away now. Things will look so much brighter in the morning.'

As they approached the fire, she heard Bartok reading from the Book of Genesis.

'The Lord God took the man and put him in the garden of Eden to till it and keep it. And the Lord God commanded the man, "You may freely eat of every tree of the garden; but of the tree of the knowledge of good and evil you shall not eat, for in the day that you eat of it you shall die.'

Blinking with weariness, Candy acknowledged the possibility that their stay might be indefinite.

12

It was the little things that Candy missed – the lack of privacy, washing facilities, proper sanitary arrangements. Apart from these inconveniences and her constant worry about Fieser, the living was surprisingly easy. The beach was mercifully free of mosquitoes; the lagoon offered relief from the enervating heat; and there was always fish to eat. But, despite these blessings, Candy was aware of the fragility of their situation. Only Aquila and Jaeger were still tapping into their eco-psyches. For the rest, the novelty of subsistence living was wearing off fast.

Tensions broke on the fourth day, while Aquila was preparing the midday meal.

'Someone's been at the rice,' she announced.

Everyone got slowly to their feet. 'I'm sure you're mistaken,' Candy said.

'I worked out portions for ten days. We've been here four and there's less than a third left.'

Seeing how little remained, Candy experienced alarm. At this rate they'd run out of their mainstay within a couple of days.

Marriot wandered over. He reached into the bag and let the grains trickle through his fingers. His lips pursed. 'Did you stow the rice back in the locker like I said?'

'Of course I did.'

150

Marriot held out his palm. 'Then what's this?'

Aquila avoided his eye. 'I don't know.'

'Animal droppings, Aquila. Rodents. You must have left the sack out in the open or forgotten to shut the locker.'

'You moron,' Nadine said, her face turning ugly. 'We're gonna starve.'

Aquila rounded on her. 'You've got some nerve. This morning you used half the fresh water to wash your goddam hair. Don't talk to me about waste.'

Dexter Smith joined in. 'Just because we're stuck on a desert island doesn't mean we've got to look like barbarians. Nadine's supposed to be shooting a hairspray commercial next month.'

'I'm sick of hearing about Nadine's schedule and her broken fingernails and her sunburn.'

'Stop it,' Candy cried, 'all of you.' She swallowed, unnerved by the passion in her voice.

At that moment Jaeger appeared, carrying an armful of wood. Even with his impaired vision he recognized calamity. He dropped the load. 'What's going on?'

'We're using up the rice quicker than we calculated,' Candy said, staring hard at Marriot. 'We'll have to tighten our belts a bit.'

Jaeger inspected the remaining stores in grim silence.

'No worries,' Marriot told him. 'The fish will never run out.'

For the first time, Aquila lost her composure. 'How many times do I have to tell you? I'm vegetarian. My body rejects flesh. Even the thought of it makes me feel sick.'

'Then start with grubs,' Marriot snapped. 'Work your way up the phylogenetic scale. Stop where your conscience dictates.'

Breathing harshly, Jaeger clutched a bunch of Marriot's shirt. 'Wise guy,' he snarled.

'I'm trying to introduce some sanity. This island doesn't

cater for special diets. For chrissakes, Leo, half the forest *flowers* are carnivorous!'

'How do we know you didn't take the rice?' Disco said.

Candy turned, flabbergasted. Still in Jaeger's grip, Marriot was speechless.

Disco shrugged. 'Maybe you want to prove a point – force Aquila and the rest to do something against their conscience.'

You shit, Candy thought, recalling how Disco had taunted Boucher, how he had raised tensions over the issue of Marriot's leadership. He was like a sharp goad, jabbing right in the most tender spot.

Marriot found his voice. 'You'd better take that back.'

Disco laughed. 'Hell, I'm not serious. I'm just trying to show that going round blaming people cuts both ways.'

Marriot's eyes narrowed. 'Jay said you had a real knack for making trouble, and I'm beginning to see why.'

'He told you that, huh?' Disco said, and turned with thoughtful deliberation to contemplate Boucher fishing out on the lagoon.

Candy intervened with the briskness of a nanny breaking up a nursery squabble. 'Let's search for some edible plants. We know there must be fruits because each night the bats fly into the forest. Robert, you said we might find figs.'

Still eyeball to eyeball with Jaeger, Marriot nodded. 'Okay, but don't expect miracles.'

Jaeger let go and Marriot stepped back, rubbing his chest. Candy released her breath.

'Split into pairs,' Jaeger ordered. 'That way we'll cover more ground.'

Two by two, they went off until only Candy and Disco were left on the beach. Bartok, who usually teamed up with Disco, was gathering materials for the look-out.

'I guess I'm with you,' Disco said.

Candy shook her head. 'Josef can't be left on his own.'

Disco walked over to Fieser. 'Josef, me and Candy are gonna look for some food. Right now, that's the most important thing.'

'The most important thing is to get him into proper care.'

'Sitting here won't help bring that along. C'mon, Candy, I can't find food on my own. I don't know what to look for.'

Candy glanced at the faraway figure of Boucher and felt exasperation. Since that day on the lagoon, she'd been waiting for him to make the next move so she could tell him that, though she was fond of him – which was more than he deserved, she reminded herself – that was as far as it went. Instead, she found herself in the galling position of having rehearsed a response to a proposal that hadn't been made and, judging by Boucher's coolness, wasn't going to be. Maybe he was paying her back for her own stand-offishness. Maybe, she thought with mounting indignation, he was so confident of his charms that he was waiting for *her* to throw herself into his arms. Well, she vowed, remembering the smug way he'd looked at her that morning when she *had* found herself in his arms, he could wait till hell froze over.

Disco was patiently awaiting her decision.

Sod it, she thought resentfully, making her mind up. 'All right, but I must be back in an hour.' She began walking towards the trees.

'Not that way,' Disco told her. 'That's where Leo and Aquila headed. No point covering the same ground.'

Each time Candy entered the rain forest, she expected it to be familiar, and each time she was disconcerted by how quickly all directions looked the same. But the uniformity was an illusion; nearly every tree was different from its neighbour, dozens of species growing in a single acre. After half an hour, Candy's vision was blurred from trying to pick out fruits against the relentless green camouflage.

It was hopeless, she decided, resilience draining out of her. Everything was hopeless. Josef might die unless rescue came in the next two or three days.

'Let's stop and collect our bearings,' she said, sliding down against a tree.

From the shadows a few feet away, Disco regarded her with sympathy. 'Poor Candy's got the blues.'

She nodded, tightening her mouth. 'By now my family will have given me up for dead.'

Disco laughed loudly. 'Be real funny when you show up again.'

Candy found his laughter inappropriate. 'I expect you're giving somebody sleepless nights, too.'

'Nobody waiting up for me,' Disco said, and grinned. 'No one even knows I was on that airship.'

'Someone must be expecting to hear from you?'

'I got no ties.'

The satisfaction he seemed to derive from his detachment made Candy uncomfortable. 'Pontianaka's not exactly a tourist Mecca. What were you doing there?'

'Jay got you asking me questions now?'

'Oh for heaven's sake, I'm just interested.'

In the shadows, Disco's face was unreadable. 'I arranged to meet a girl.'

That sounded reassuring. 'Oh yes? What's she called?'

'Doesn't matter. She never showed.'

'How annoying.'

Disco laughed and came forward so that Candy could see him properly. 'I'm real glad she didn't, because you're a whole lot prettier.'

Candy's heart sank. Being sweet-talked by Disco was

154

the last thing she wanted. 'We'd better push on,' she said, starting to rise.

Disco offered his hand and she felt obliged to take it. He didn't let go when she'd got to her feet.

She checked her watch and smiled. 'Time's nearly up.'

'Josef will keep,' Disco said. Slowly, he reached out a hand to her breasts, and Candy was so taken aback that she made no attempt to resist.

His fingers stopped an inch short. 'Real perky little critters. You got names for them?'

'Don't be ridiculous.'

'I'll soon find names for them. Lemme see, how about ...?'

Candy's wits caught up at last. 'No, you bloody well don't,' she snapped, slapping his hand away.

'Ah, c'mon, honeybun.'

'I mean it,' Candy said, forcing herself into calm. 'Now just stop it.'

Disco looked crestfallen.

'I really do have to get back,' Candy said, edging around him. 'Jay will be anxious when he finds no one on the beach.'

'Keeping an eye on you, huh?'

'Yes,' Candy said, 'he is.'

Moodily, Disco scuffed the leaf litter. 'You fucking him?'

'What?'

Disco raised his eyes. 'I said, are you fucking him?'

Candy brought all her contempt to bear. 'Mind your own business.'

Disco's attitude didn't alter by so much as a flicker. 'No point pussy-footing. May as well know where I stand.'

Candy pushed him aside. 'In my way. Excuse me.'

'Candy, I'm not gonna hurt a sweet thing like you.'

She laughed and continued walking, with no idea where she was going. The nape of her neck prickled at the sound of vegetation swishing behind her. She was a long way from the beach and a shout wouldn't carry far. She looked for a weapon, a stick – anything.

'Hey, you saw how rancid things turned back there. Harsh words have been spoken and sooner or later they'll be backed up by deeds. Once the food's gone, it'll be everyone for themselves. Stick with me and no one will harm you. I guarantee it.'

She turned then and looked back with real curiosity. In the green gloom, he was just a stroke of shadow. 'Where are you from, Disco?'

'Seattle, Denver, San Francisco. I like to move around.'

'Cities.' Candy indicated the unbroken green circle and laughed.

He shrugged. 'Jungles.' He began to close the distance between them. 'I got all the survival training I need.'

Deciding it was pointless to run, Candy stood her ground. Keep talking, she thought. 'You said you were an actor.'

Disco's face went blank. 'I done some stunt work.'

'That sounds fascinating. Was it for films?'

Disco frowned at a fly that had alighted on his arm. 'Hey, honeybun, you're as bad as Boucher. Always asking questions.' His hand moved in a blur. Fastidiously he wiped his fingers clean. 'And you still haven't answered *mine*.'

Rapidly, Candy ran through her options, trying to plot a path between antagonizing Disco and encouraging him. 'Jay and I are friends. He saved me from drowning.'

'Only life Jay's interested in is his own. All he's after is saving his ass so he can see his name in lights.'

'He's got more important things on his mind.'

'Don't believe it. He's writing about me. He's writing about you. He's writing about everyone.' An expression of cunning came over Disco's face. 'That's why I won't tell him who I am. It really pisses him.'

'He's only doing his job.'

'And if he gets off this island, it'll make him rich.' Disco looked aggrieved. 'I don't think that's right – profiting from other people's suffering.'

'You'd do the same in his position.'

'But I ain't in his position. I asked him to give me some lessons on writing and he looked at me like he just trod in something. You heard the way he laughed at me on the airship.' Disco's hand hovered over another fly. 'He thinks I'm *nothing*!'

Candy cringed. 'Remember what Leo said about respecting each other. If you carry on like this, I'm going to have to speak to him.'

It sounded so feeble, but Disco didn't jeer. Instead he turned and stared entranced into the forest. 'You know, this is how it must have been back in the times before constitutions and individual rights and shit like that. We're a tribe and Leo's our chief and I guess I'm like his warrior. I protect him and in return he grants me anything I ask for. Suppose I ask for you. If he says yes, you'll have to agree, because you're part of the tribe, too, and what the chief says is law.'

'Disco, I don't know what comics you read, but this is the twentieth century and I'm not a piece of disposable property.'

'I'll treat you right, Candy. Anything that belongs to me, I take good care of.'

Candy lost patience – and with it, caution. 'I *don't* belong to you. I *am* involved with Jay. There – satisfied?'

Disco's mouth twisted. 'Looks like that man's got everything he wants.'

'*Now* will you leave me alone?'

Sadly, Disco shook his head. 'Some things a man wants, he has to fight for them.'

Candy drew herself as tall as she could. 'You'd have to fight me, too.'

His face relaxed in a smile. 'You've got a strong will as well as a pretty ass. I like that.'

Something like fur blocked Candy's throat. 'Disco, if you were the last man alive on this island, I'd rather throw myself to the crocodiles.'

With what composure she could muster, she began to walk away.

Disco's voice followed. 'Trust me, Candy, when things go wrong and you need someone to stand by you, that scribbler ain't it.'

Candy was trembling inside when Boucher landed with his catch. Oh, Jay, she rehearsed, I hope you don't mind, but Disco was pestering me, so to get him off my back, I told him we were lovers.

In some irrational way, she actually felt resentful that he hadn't been at hand to protect her. Even if she'd misunderstood his body language, he was her closest friend on the island – and a friend was someone who was there when you needed them. And she did need someone, she knew, thinking over Disco's warning about the group fragmenting. She was no go-it-alone feminist; part of her strength derived from the fact that all her life she had been able to rely on strong, gentle men

When Boucher landed, he was too lit up over an encounter with a shark to sense her fraught state. 'It came right up to the boat,' he told her excitedly. 'Not a huge specimen, but a shark's a shark. I guess tomorrow I'll stay away from the deep water.'

'Very wise,' Candy said, keeping her face lowered.

Boucher looked around. 'Where are the rest of the gang?'

'Searching for food. Vermin's been eating the rice. We're down to a couple of days' rations.'

Boucher sighed heavily and flopped beside her. 'Looks like the fun is over.'

'It was never that, Jay.'

Boucher caught the edge in her voice. 'What happened exactly?'

'Marriot blamed Aquila. He said something provocative and he and Jaeger nearly came to blows.'

'Damn, I wish I'd been here.'

Candy glared at him. 'Disco's right. All you care about is your story.'

One corner of Boucher's mouth lifted. 'He's been working on you, huh? Telling you that I'm the only one who's going to come out of this better off than when I came in.'

'Well, it's true.'

'And he never misses an opportunity to remind everyone.'

'Is that why you dislike him so much?'

Boucher shrugged. 'A dog meets another dog and they both wag their tails. They get along fine. Same dog meets another dog and the hackles rise and the fangs are bared. They don't know anything about each other. They've got no philosophical points of difference. It's just animal behaviour.'

Candy traced a triangle in the sand. 'I was in the forest with him.'

Boucher looked at her sharply. 'He open up about himself?'

'Not really. He told me he'd been a stunt man.'

Boucher laughed.

'He thinks you despise him.'

159

'I think he's a wrongo. Why else would he keep his past a secret?'

'Because it makes him seem more interesting than he really is.'

Boucher rose to fetch some water and Candy found herself evaluating him, measuring him against Disco. Physically, they were a match, and she suspected that Boucher was more rugged mentally than his laid-back manner suggested. 'Are you frightened of him?'

Boucher drank. 'There's no reason why we should go up against each other.'

Candy searched for a way in. 'Suppose we had to compete for resources?'

'If it came to a free-for-all, Disco is a guy I'd take seriously. But it isn't going to happen. We've got food and lodging and ...'

'They're not the only resources in short supply.'

Boucher's eyes narrowed.

'The day we explored the island,' Candy said, 'you told me to watch myself. You meant, watch Disco, didn't you? He must have said something about me.'

Boucher darted a glance at her, then looked away. 'He tried to get it on with you?'

'Does that upset you?'

Boucher's jaw tightened.

'You see,' Candy said quietly, 'there is something deeper between you and Disco.' She hesitated, then took Boucher's hand. 'Between us, too.'

Boucher scratched the side of his head. 'Candy, you work so hard and I guess the last thing on your mind is ... well, I figured the circumstances weren't right.'

'Suppose I said they were?'

He looked hunted. 'Candy ...'

'Disco asked if you were fucking me.'

Boucher blinked. He gave a breathy laugh. 'Well, I guess you put him right.'

Candy made no answer.

Boucher leaned closer in puzzlement. 'Didn't you?'

Candy averted her eyes. 'Disco made me an offer. He promised to keep me from harm provided I let him ... let him ... provided I became his woman.' Candy swallowed. 'I told him I already had that kind of arrangement.'

Boucher processed this. 'You told him I was sleeping with you?'

'It's what you want, isn't it?'

'What did Disco say?'

'When I turned him down?'

'When you told him about me.'

A buzzing began in Candy's head as she realized it was going to go wrong. She looked past Boucher – through him. 'It doesn't matter.'

Boucher took her hand, firmly. 'What did he say?'

Candy struggled to release her hand, then let it go limp. 'He said that if something's worth having, it's worth fighting for.'

Boucher released her hand and smiled tightly at nothing in particular. 'Hawk and dove, huh? No payoff without risk.'

Face stinging, Candy stared blindly out to sea, knowing that the mortification she felt now was as nothing to what would come later. She let go a deep breath. 'I seem to have made a dreadful mistake.'

Boucher turned, his expression agonized. 'Candy, whatever I feel for you, I'm not going to start a relationship on those terms.'

Candy smiled brightly. 'I see.'

'No you don't. Disco's trying to get at me through you. This is all a game to him, and he's got you playing by his rules.'

Abruptly, she stood. 'Get at *you?*' she cried. 'Get at *you?* It's *me* he's after.'

'Tell Leo,' Boucher said, rising. 'Better still, tell Aquila. They'll put a stop to it.'

Candy's humiliation unravelled into fury. 'Disco's right. You're spineless and selfish. You're the most pathetic specimen I've ever met.'

Wordless, without expression, Boucher left. But even as she continued railing at him, Candy knew that most of her anger was directed at herself. She had been a weak little fool, panicked along the path of least resistance. Breathing hard, she glared down the beach. Boucher had disappeared and she was alone. So be it, she vowed. From now on, she would fight her own battles.

13

Next morning the sky closed down and a coppery wind blew offshore, piling surf against the reefs and making fishing impossible.

On the pretext of collecting firewood, Boucher went into the forest. He wanted to be alone; he needed space to examine his behaviour. The proposition before him was simple. Candy had asked for his protection. In return, she had offered herself to him and he had rejected her – an act as ungallant as it was a denial of his feelings.

He wanted her. He didn't know when he'd fallen for her, but fallen he had. He recalled the night she came to his room in Jakarta. He *had* been writing about her – some crap about thorny English roses. He remembered her spilling out into his arms the next morning, asleep on his shoulder after the storm, the moment their eyes met in the lagoon.

Half a dozen times since they'd crashed he'd gone dry-mouthed, preparing to open his heart, but each time he'd remembered why he was here and slammed down the shutters.

Also, if he was truthful, he had feared rebuff. He still smarted from her tart put-downs. She was English and she didn't fit neatly into any familiar cultural templates. She had a way of wrong-footing him.

And yet from those refined lips, that classy mouth, had come the most explicit proposal he was ever likely to receive in his life.

Which brought him right round to his starting point. She had offered herself and he had cravenly passed. He hadn't even given a sufficient reason. He could have reminded her that he had a woman back home. But in his heart he knew that Lydia wasn't the antidote. Right now, Lydia seemed like a being on another planet.

It didn't even have to be sex. Candy needed an ally. That's all.

'Arghhh,' he roared. Shame. He was eaten up with shame.

Also, he was lost. He'd been walking at random and didn't have a clue where he was. Through the treetops the wind surged in a hushed roar, but on the forest floor not a leaf stirred. He thought he could hear a voice, but then a lot of jungle riffs had a spooky human quality. This sounded like an incantation. It drew him on.

The chanting stopped. Parting a tress of lianas he saw Aquila standing in a clearing, her arms uplifted and her face raised in the rapt blankness of one who has been vouchsafed a vision. She was in communion with her spirit of the forest. Boucher looked up, trying to imagine what she saw or heard. To him the jungle was a mystery he had no wish to fathom – a place of rot, perpetual racket and pointless swarming. The pale tree trunks steepled over his head, pinning him down, diminishing him. Every time he left the jungle was like coming up for air.

There was nothing there. Only the wind in the canopy. He left Aquila to it.

On the way back, he tripped over a root and lost his shoe. Stumbling to catch up with himself, he trod on something. It bit him. Excruciating pain pierced his foot.

164

He sank down, clutching his ankle, flashing images of pit vipers and foot-long centipedes.

An object resembling a large, glossy beetle had embedded a horn like a marlin spike in the soft underarch. Wincing, he pulled it out. A single bead of blood welled up. He examined the object. A seed case, he guessed, though for all he knew it was some kind of alien life form. The wound looked innocuous and hurt bad. His mind played a fast rewind of Marriot's warnings about minor abrasions ending in amputations.

Favouring his injured foot, he limped back to camp. Candy was bent over a piece of fabric, sewing. She looked tired and strained and in no mood for baring souls. He squared himself. His throat tightened.

'I trod on this,' he said.

Without a word, Candy took the seed case, examined it briefly, then tossed it away. 'Sit down,' she ordered. Without any change of expression, she knelt and took hold of his foot.

Feeling her grip, seeing the cool nape of her neck, Boucher experienced an erotic charge. It was against reason.

'Where, exactly?' she said.

He pointed to the puncture. 'Doesn't look much, but it went deep and my foot is throbbing like hell.'

'I'll put some antiseptic on.'

While she was looking for it, he made an attempt to lighten the mood. 'I saw Aquila talking to the trees.'

Candy absorbed the news without comment.

It was no good. He couldn't leave the atmosphere festering. 'Look, about yesterday.'

'I owe you an apology,' she said immediately. 'I put you in an impossible position.'

'No, no,' he protested, though impossible was exactly

what it was. 'In any other ... Look, it's just not that simple.'

Her voice was flat. 'It's very simple. You're a journalist and you must keep your distance at all costs.'

It was the argument he'd deployed to himself, but though Candy delivered it without any mocking spin, it came out skewed.

'Look, Disco's not going to try anything.'

'Then why did you warn me he might?'

Boucher scrabbled for an answer.

'Suppose he rapes me?' Candy said, putting the knife in. 'Will you describe it objectively?' She twisted the blade. 'I expect you'll want to interview me? I expect you'll want to interview both of us.'

Boucher pulled his foot away. 'Right, I'm going to have it out with him.'

'No you won't,' Candy cried, loud enough to startle Marriot. 'Yesterday I suffered as many humiliations as I'm prepared to take. I'll deal with Disco in my own way.' She stood up, dismissing him. 'Keep that foot clean.'

Boucher didn't know what to say or what to think. 'Don't I get any antibiotics?'

'For a tiny little prick?'

Boucher flushed. 'Robert says you can't be too careful.'

Candy's smile was sweet with contempt. 'Then you'll be fine, won't you?'

Ignoring Marriot's warning, Boucher went fishing. It was punishment therapy, a reckless displacement activity.

Although the sea had moderated, it was still too high for safety. The inflatable was unwieldy at best, and several times the offshore drift threatened to push it on to the reef before Boucher finally got the anchor to bite. Waves chopped at the hull and the lagoon, usually so clear, was turbid. The sea's mood matched his own.

Fish streamed underneath in an endless silver procession. There was a flash as the shoal shot upwards in one co-ordinated reflex. Half a dozen broke the surface and fell back, wriggling frantically. Boucher knew that only a predator could have induced such panic. He peered long and deep, and though he saw nothing, that was scary too. Every living thing had vanished. It was a long time before he lobbed in the bait.

Thinking about Disco, his stomach churned. It felt like rage and he knew fear was involved. It had been there ever since he'd looked into Disco's eyes after he'd insulted him during the lifeboat game. Now, with the constraints of civilization gone and Candy between them, he knew it was only a matter of time before Disco forced a showdown.

Boucher weighed his chances. Strength and fitness wouldn't be the deciding factor; it was the will and readiness to inflict bodily harm that counted. He'd grown up with kids like Disco and envied the way they didn't let thinking get in the way of action – instant gratification. For Disco, violence was payoff in itself and risk hardly came into it, whereas for himself the equation was reversed. Disco was a hawk and he was a dove. That was the truth of it.

Boucher found himself thinking of some way in which he might appease him.

Fuck that, he decided. Start thinking of yourself as a victim, and that's how you end up – your own victim. He would just have to get in touch with the savage inside him.

He tensed as the line moved, relaxed as it sagged, then sat upright as it began to draw tight again. Following Marriot's advice, he counted to three before striking. He met resistance so solid that at first he thought he'd snagged rock.

Then the pole was almost snatched from his hands. 'Whoa!' Whatever was on the other end was big, much bigger than the coral trout. Enormous. He couldn't stop it. He couldn't deflect it. He leaned back, digging in. It was like trying to put the brakes on a motorized beer keg.

His tackle was rudimentary – just a pole with thirty feet of line whipped to the end. Marriot had guaranteed the line was strong enough to handle just about any fish he might encounter. Boucher threw all his weight behind it. The mass yielded a little and he hoped he hadn't got into a moray eel. Marriot had warned him of the hideous damage their teeth could inflict.

He pulled again and saw a glint of bronze, a deep body, a broad tail. A grouper, and therefore excellent eating, though without any device for reeling it in, God knows how he was going to land it.

Water splashed him. Alarmed, he realized the anchor was dragging and he was dangerously close to the reef. His right arm was aching and his left hand, clamped round the butt, had lost all sensation. Give up, he told himself. Another minute or less and he would be aground, the boat a ruin and him with it. His only chance lay in tying the line to the inflatable and trying to tow the fish into clear water.

First, though, he had to win some slack. Grunting with the strain, he pumped up once, twice – and again. For a moment he saw the fish clearly, goggle-eyed, its bottom lip protruding in what looked like glum resignation.

Stalemate. Movement had ceased. The grouper must have jammed itself into a cave. He let the pole dip, released his right hand, grabbed the loop of slack and took one turn around a rowlock. An instant later the fish made another run and the line scorched into his palm. A second earlier and his hand would have been trapped.

Throwing caution aside, he dropped the pole and took

another couple of bights. Then he grabbed the oars and paddled as hard as he could. The line thrummed. He put fifteen yards between himself and the coral. Kneeling, he braced his hands on the hull and peered down. There it was, changing colour with each shift of the sea. He'd have to hand-line it in.

His palm was bleeding where the line had cut it. He unknotted his tie and wrapped it round his hand. With his bandaged hand he took hold of the line. It was as taut as wire.

Now what?

A grey torpedo rolling into white smashed into the grouper. Boucher recoiled from rows of teeth and eyes like discs of graphite. The shark shook its head violently, worrying off flesh. Flecks of tissue clouded the water. The inflatable dipped sharply and Boucher tipped half overboard. Dimly he heard a sharp *ping*. The inflatable righted itself, throwing him on to his back.

For ages he lay sprawled in the bottom, not moving a muscle. He groped for the line. It was slack. That's how it was done, he realized, thinking of Disco.

Marriot was waiting anxiously on the beach. 'I thought you'd had it. What were you fighting out there?'

Boucher elected for nonchalance. 'I hooked a big grouper. A shark grabbed it. I reckon it was the same one I saw yesterday. It's getting familiar with my timetable.'

'You get a good look at it?'

'Jaws like a shovel. Its eyes turned white as it took the fish.'

'Tiger shark,' Marriot said, and gravely shook his head. 'Don't try that again.' He took Boucher's arm. 'You look like you could use a brew.'

Boucher saw he was holding a diamond-shaped piece of airship fabric and some whippy twigs.

'What are you making?'

'A kite.'

'A signal kite?'

'I'll show you this evening. What happened to your foot?'

'Trod on a seed pod.'

'Candy give you antibiotics?'

'She says it's not necessary.'

'Tell her I say it is.'

'To be honest, Robert, I don't have the nerve.'

'I saw you two having a heart-to-heart. She's punishing you.'

'Candy's not that small-minded.'

'For women, no detail is too small to overlook – not where the heart's concerned.'

'We don't have a relationship. That's the problem.' Boucher felt utterly miserable. 'She's really got to me, Robert, but I'm in no position to do anything about it.'

'What's stopping you?'

'I can't afford emotional entanglements.'

Marriot shook his head in disgust.

14

Day 5

'Ready for the test flight?' Marriot asked.

Groggy with afternoon sleep, sore from his struggle with the fish, Boucher was in no mood for another excursion. His foot hurt worse than ever and the site of the wound felt puffy to the touch. His right hand, burned by the fishing line, was another cause of concern. 'I guess I'll give it a miss.'

'Jay, you'll find it really interesting. Of course, if you want some time alone with Candy, I'll shoot off and leave you to it.'

Everyone else had disappeared on another search for fruit. Imagining the mood that would congeal around him and Candy if they were left together, Boucher decided to fall in with Marriot's plan. They wandered up the beach. The sky had cleared and the wind had fallen to a breeze. This was the best part of the day, the only time when Boucher's body felt in equilibrium with the climate.

'Tell me what you've got in mind.'

'Fishing.'

Boucher stopped and crossed his arms. 'I'm not ready to face the lagoon again.'

'No worries, Jay. This is dry-land fishing Sulawesi style. I promise you won't get your feet wet.'

They walked the length of the island. Around the

northern end, Marriot halted, laid out the kite and began to unwind fishing line.

'I get it,' Boucher said. 'You fly the kite over the lagoon. Neat idea, but will it work?'

'Don't know,' Marriot said. 'This is a prototype.' At half a dozen places on the top third of the line he tied short leaders.

The placement puzzled Boucher. 'What sort of fish are we after?'

'Batfish,' Marriot told him, threading bait on the hooks. When he had finished he began to back away, playing out the line. 'Hold the kite into the wind.'

The first three launches were flops. 'Back to the drawing board,' Boucher said.

'It'll work,' Marriot insisted. 'I used this method for a survey in Arnhem Land.'

'I thought you said ... Hey!'

Balanced against the wind, the kite slid up into the sky.

'Brilliant,' Boucher said. He watched the kite curvetting. 'But unless you aim to catch flying fish, there's a basic ...' He stopped, shot a glance to the north, then swung on Jaeger. 'Oh no. Definitely no. Robert, this is not a neat idea at all. It's a very bad idea. Get that kite down.' He grabbed for the line.

Marriot side-stepped. 'The rations have nearly gone.'

'We agreed to abide by the rules.'

'The rules are incompatible with reality. You nearly got yourself killed on the reef today. Suppose it's still blowing tomorrow?'

'Robert, if Jaeger finds out, he'll beat shit out of you.'

'Save wildlife, kill a biologist.'

'I know it's crazy, but humour them. This is their expedition.'

'The expedition ended the moment we crashed. This is survival, pure and simple.'

'Part of surviving depends on getting along.'

'It hasn't sunk in, has it? In five days, we haven't seen a single ship or aircraft.'

'It's just a matter of time.'

'You said it yourself. They gave us up for dead on day one.'

Marriot's stark analysis hit Boucher like cold water. He walked away, leaned against the bole of a tree and slid down. He eyed the pink sky with morose detachment.

On cue, the dark squall gathered and meandered towards them, following the same path as previous evenings. Boucher heard the high-frequency squeals and the soughing of wings, and then the bats were overhead, a swirling black blizzard so dense he couldn't separate out individuals.

Suddenly the kite stumbled. One of the bats had stalled in the air. The kite zigzagged to earth with its flapping load. It dipped faster as another bat hooked itself. Marriot ran to his prey. By the time Boucher reached him, he had broken their necks. With their furry faces and big ears they looked like diabolical soft toys.

'They've probably got rabies.'

'They taste better than they look.'

Marriot unseamed their bellies and spilled out the entrails. A carnal reek affronted Boucher's nose. Deftly Marriot skinned the bats. Naked, they looked like babies.

'That is so disgusting. Aquila's right. If people saw how their meat was prepared, most of them would never look at a hamburger again.'

'Give her another week and I guarantee she'll be queuing for seconds.'

'Want to bet?'

Darkness covered their return to camp. Boucher was relieved to find the Wildguard executive in good spirits.

'We found a tree loaded with figs,' Aquila declared proudly.

'Terrific,' Boucher said, hiding his nervousness under a mask of *bonhomie*.

'Don't eat too many,' Marriot warned her. 'As far as figs are concerned, you're only a temporary agent of seed dispersal.'

Trigg had lit a fire for the carnivores. Marriot prepared to spit the bats whole.

Boucher sneaked a glance behind him. 'Pete's sake, Robert, cut them up so they don't look so goddam mammalian.'

He breathed easier when they were dismembered and their flesh had begun to char. The memory of those embryos dissolved in the savoury fumes. He was very hungry; he was as hungry as a hunter.

Candy joined them. 'Smells wonderful,' she said, and bent over to savour the aroma. She stiffened, then slowly straightened up.

'You idiots,' she said. 'You absolute idiots.'

'Keep your voice down,' Boucher muttered.

Too late. Someone stirred behind him. His back cringed. He prepared for the worst.

'What the fuck is that?' Disco said, sniffing. 'Hey, Leo, get a load of this.'

Jaeger loomed out of the dark. Without his glasses he had difficulty distinguishing anything. He peered at the meat like some myopic Stone Age professor.

'They're fruit bats,' Marriot told him. 'Flying foxes.'

Boucher squeezed his temple as if he'd been struck by a blinding headache. Disco grinned. Jaeger blinked very slowly.

'How did you catch them?'

Marriot produced the kite. 'Aerial fishing line. Ingenious.'

174

'Yeah,' Jaeger said. He kicked the bats into the sand. He kicked again, spraying embers.

'Hey,' Marriot said, brushing sparks off his clothes.

Jaeger walked away and stopped where the firelight ended. 'Come here, Marriot. You, too, Jay.'

Boucher's heart thumped against his ribs. He had an urge to yawn.

'Jay didn't have anything to do with it. I told him we were going fishing.'

'Like hell,' Disco said happily.

'He was going to eat them, wasn't he?' Aquila added. She appeared distressed. 'Those poor creatures. It's so barbarous.'

'I don't want to fight,' Boucher said.

'I don't want to fight,' Disco repeated in a falsetto. He stuck his face close to Boucher's. 'You dumb jerk. Leo's not sending a party invite.'

'No other way to settle it,' Jaeger said, sounding fair-minded. 'You agreed to the rules. I gave you due warning.'

Marriot threw down his knife and stood up in the same movement. He strode forward. 'Listen ...'

Jaeger punched him – not hard – a short jab in the chest that sent him back-pedalling. Instinctively he put up his fists and began to circle. 'Listen, Leo, we may not be rescued before the rations are used up. We have to exploit every resource available.'

Jaeger stalked him at leisure

Marriot was slightly taller than the Wildguard leader. He was younger, fitter, more athletic and he must have known that Jaeger's punishment wouldn't be a mild chastisement. But Boucher knew he didn't have a prayer. Just as he knew he wouldn't when his turn came.

'Stop this,' Candy pleaded. 'Tell him to stop.'

'Teach him the meaning of pain,' Aquila cried.

Marriot lowered his guard and stood his ground. 'Leo, from now on we have to use whatever food we can get hold of.'

With startling speed for such a bulky man, Jaeger charged. Marriot got in one punch before he was borne over. Jaeger slammed down on top of him. He drew back his fist and drove it into Marriot's face.

Candy ran and grabbed at Jaeger. Still holding Marriot by the throat, he sent her sprawling. Boucher's elbow was grasped and he turned to see Disco grinning at him like a junkyard dog. Fear snapped into rage. He lashed out and caught Disco full on the chin. Surprise as much as anything toppled Disco. He lay back for a moment on both elbows, shook his head, and grinned.

'Looks like I must have stepped on your prick.' Unhurriedly, he got to his feet and Boucher knew that he'd already lost. If he'd followed his own advice he would have gone in with maximum force while he still had the initiative. But he didn't have the killer instinct.

'Candy's got the rice!' Aquila shouted.

Eyes locked on Disco, Boucher heard feet scuffing on the sand and then splashing through water.

'Leo, get off him or I'll throw the rice in the sea.'

'Give that back,' Aquila screamed.

'Leo, if you don't let Robert go, I swear I'll dump the rice. Then you can try eating your precious principles.'

'I'll kill you,' Aquila shrieked.

'You're animals. The lot of you. That's what you are – animals!'

'Do what she says,' Nadine yelled. 'Who cares about a couple of fucking bats?'

Everything went silent at once. For a moment it hung in the balance then, from the corner of his eye, Boucher saw Jaeger heave himself to his feet. Marriot groaned. Disco relaxed his stance.

'I'm glad you did that,' he told Boucher.

Battle fever still beat in Boucher's blood. 'Not as glad as I am. That was for Candy. Touch her and I'll kill you.'

'Deal.'

Trigg helped Marriot back to the fire. His nose was broken, his mouth so bloody it looked like a black hole. He went down on to the sand like a sack. Candy began to clean him up.

Jaeger shambled into the light, his chest heaving. He seemed as distressed as anyone. He gulped for breath. 'Against Aquila's advice, I compromised. Catch fish, I said, but Aquila was right. You couldn't leave it alone.' He gulped air again and turned to Marriot. 'I'm giving you one last chance.'

'I'm finished with Wildguard,' Marriot mumbled.

Slowly, reluctantly, Jaeger's spine straightened. 'Okay, go your own way, but make sure it doesn't cross mine.'

Into Boucher's mind came a verse from last night's Bible reading. 'I shall be a fugitive and a wanderer on the earth, and anyone who meets me may kill me.'

'Leo,' Dexter said, 'this has gone too far. You're over-reacting, man.'

Jaeger ignored him. 'The rest of you make your minds up. Go with Marriot or stay with Wildguard. This is a Wildguard expedition, so the food stays with us, and so do all the medicines and tools.'

'What about Josef?' Candy demanded. 'You're so con-cerned about saving animals, but none of you cares a damn for Josef.'

'Candy, I guess you made it clear where you stand.'

'What about the rest of us?' Trigg cried. 'What happens if we get sick?'

'Sounds like you just put your cross against Marriot's name, too. Anyone else?'

'I'm with you,' Disco said.

'Goes for me,' Bartok added.

A house divided, Boucher thought, with a tingle of apprehension and excitement. Now we get down to it.

'I really don't think this is a good idea,' Dexter said.

'No one's asking your opinion.'

Dexter's eyes sought Nadine's, but Boucher knew their choice was a forgone conclusion. The starry couple were conditioned to put their affairs in others' hands, and Jaeger had demonstrated where the power lay.

'We'll stick with you, Leo, but I don't like what's happening here.'

'That leaves you, Jay.'

Boucher's blood had cooled. 'Dexter's right, Leo. You're making a bad situation worse.'

'In or out, Jay. There's no middle ground any more.'

A dissident voice told Boucher to stay with Wildguard, stick with the main story. 'I'm not joining any side with Disco in it.'

'That's it then,' Jaeger said. 'My people, get your things. We're moving base. We'll set up camp near the flag.'

His followers began to gather their possessions.

'What happens to the boat?'

'It's ours,' Aquila said.

'You're not taking the boat,' Marriot said.

'We'll be back for it tomorrow,' Disco told him.

Marriot climbed to his feet. 'Take the boat and it's war. Without food or the means of getting it, we've got nothing to lose. And if it comes to real fighting ...' he gestured at the forest '... it won't be fists on the beach.'

For a moment Boucher thought Marriot's ultimatum would tip Jaeger into fresh violence. Here they were on the threshold of a new millennium and they were acting like it was a rehearsal for 20,000 BC.

'I'll decide about the boat later.' Jaeger eyed his tribe. 'Everyone ready?' He picked up Marriot's kite and led the exodus into the dark. A minute later his voice floated back. 'Marriot, Boucher, Trigg – come on up here.'

'Fuck that,' Trigg muttered.

'Go on,' Marriot told him. He jerked his chin at Boucher.

They walked up the beach and found Jaeger and his tribe assembled near the women's bathing area. Jaeger held out his hand. 'Nadine, give me some lipstick.'

When she handed it over, he took the kite and scrawled a crude image of a tiger's head. He planted the fetish in the sand.

'Everything beyond this point is Wildguard territory. You don't hunt on it. You don't come on to it without my say-so. Trespassers know what to expect.'

'What's so fucking funny?' Trigg demanded as they headed back.

'The irony. Here we have two tribes: the Ecos and the Preds. The Ecos eat grass and are warlike; the Preds eat meat and are pacifist. Actually, Bartok gave us a biblical precedent last night. It was Cain the tiller of the soil who murdered Abel the shepherd.'

'Well, I'm not laughing. Those back-to-nature crazies started the fighting and they keep all the gadgets.'

'That's divorce for you.'

But Boucher sobered when he reached camp and saw what loss they had suffered. Most of the cooking gear was gone, along with the parang, the torch, the flare gun. The Preds' material culture had been set back about thirty thousand years.

Candy had retreated to Fieser's bedside. Marriot, his nose swathed in lint, sat by the fire whittling a spearpoint. Telling him about the Ecos' territorial claim, Boucher eyed the weapon with unease.

'We going hunting tomorrow?'

179

'Unless we get a delivery of manna.'

'So what's on the menu?'

'Bat garnished with sand.'

'I meant tomorrow.'

'Whatever we can catch. It's open season now.'

Boucher took his place by the fire. 'We've still got a better chance than the Ecos, haven't we? This is the stable strategy.' He hadn't meant to sound so anxious.

'Unless we lose the boat,' Marriot said. He slashed a paring off the spear tip. 'And I won't let that happen.'

Trigg looked north. 'I wonder what they'll do when their food runs out.'

A laugh bubbled in Marriot's nose. 'Dexter and Nadine and Disco will be round here the moment their tummies start rumbling.'

Boucher shook his head. 'Not Leo, though. And certainly not Aquila.'

'You really think she'd starve herself to death?'

'For Aquila, eating animals is cannibalism.'

'It won't be the first time people in our situation have eaten each other. Who knows what we're capable of? Starvation's the strongest imperative of all.'

'I really think Aquila and Leo would go all the way. Cultists have a habit of self-destructing when there's no way out.'

'So long as they don't try taking us with them,' Marriot said, jabbing the spear point into the embers. 'Food's ready.'

'I'll fetch Candy,' Boucher said.

She was trying to get Fieser to accept some water. The pilot looked like a corpse, his eyes blank pools in a face fallen in on its bones.

'Bad?' Boucher said.

'Worse than that. The antibiotics haven't killed the

infection. It's out of control.' Candy's shoulders were slumped, and though her hair-covered her face, Boucher knew she was close to breakdown. He wanted to share the burden. He wanted to take her in his arms.

'Josef said there are more drugs on the airship,' she told him, 'in the flight cabin.'

'We'll do what we can.'

Tiredly, Candy wiped a strand of hair from her face. 'Yes, thank you.'

That weary gesture broke the last line of Boucher's emotional defences. All at once, he knew that what he felt for her was love.

She frowned. 'What is it, Jay?'

Regaining control, he remembered why he was here. 'Food's up.'

'I'm not hungry.' She smiled thinly at his tie. 'I thought you weren't supposed to take sides.'

'I wasn't given a choice,' Boucher said. He hesitated. 'I socked Disco, so that's the end of my neutral status.'

'He's really got it in for you. You'll have to be careful.'

'Too late for that.'

She raised a wan smile. 'How's your foot?'

He looked at it. 'Oh, okay. Fine. False alarm.'

'Good.'

'Yeah.'

There was an excruciating silence. From Candy's expression, it was obvious she thought he was going to say more. When he didn't, she looked away quickly. 'Well then, goodnight, Jay.'

Boucher felt like an emotional clodhopper – like he was seventeen again. 'Yeah, sleep well.'

A few yards away he stopped, his back turned. He opened his mouth, cleared his throat, then shook his head and returned to the fire.

They ate like trolls, gnawing on burnt bat and spitting out bones and grit.

'Funny thing,' Trigg said, 'but I miss Kent's Bible readings.'

Boucher flicked a bone away. 'You're not missing much. We're on to genealogy – Adam's descendants. All that Seth begat Noah begat Ham stuff. I told Kent the Israelites ripped it off from the Sumerians. He said I was blaspheming. He believes every word was engraved on tablets by God.'

Marriot wiped grease off his hands. 'Even if you don't believe in Him, you'd better start praying.'

'If there is a God, he's not on this flyspeck. He's gone where the action is.'

Trigg gazed at the sea. 'I can't believe they've stopped looking for us.'

'The Western delusion. A hundred thousand Chinese die in an earthquake and we don't turn a hair. But when one of us gets into a spot of difficulty, we expect the world to turn upside down to help. Aquila's right: each individual imagines he or she is the high point of evolution, the be-all and end-all.'

'Aquila's no different,' Trigg said.

'Maybe not.'

Marriot stretched his arms and yawned. 'I'm for sleep.' He rose and went off with Trigg.

Boucher composed himself for the night. He could hear the murmur of his companions' voices. After a while they stopped and other sounds took their place, interspersed by strenuous bouts of silence. Boucher was led to the conclusion that the biologist and the cameraman were having sex. What the hell. Sex was about all that was left to them – that and a hollow laugh.

15

Fieser's condition deteriorated further overnight. His blood pressure was down and his pulse was weaker. He was no longer aware of Candy's presence and what few words he uttered were in German. Most worrying of all, he no longer seemed to be in pain.

Down the beach, Marriot was conducting a weapons training session. Candy registered how cranky her companions looked – Marriot's face reduced to two black eyes and a patch of gauze, Boucher shirtless, but still wearing his tie and a jacket with one sleeve half torn off, Trigg skipping about with his camcorder.

'You're in pretty good shape,' she heard Marriot say to Boucher. 'Show us how far you can throw the spear.'

Boucher balanced it in his hand. Before he made his run-up, he glanced in Candy's direction. Men were so pathetic, she thought, with their macho posturing and need for approval. She watched as he sprinted a dozen yards, drew back the spear and, with an explosive grunt, hurled it. Less than thirty yards away it came to earth tail down. Boucher didn't check for Candy's reaction.

'Watch this,' Marriot said, holding the spear in one hand and a length of cord in the other. 'First we take the cord, place the knotted end in the notch, take a turn round the shaft, pull down tight so the free end is in the throwing hand. And then ...' Marriot shuffled a few steps and pulled back his arm.

The spear flew sixty yards.

'Hey, let me try.'

Candy decided to interrupt the exercise. The men fell quiet as she approached. 'Very impressive,' she said, 'but completely impractical for hunting in the forest.'

'Who says it's for animals?'

'Enough of that stupid talk. There's going to be no more fighting.' She waited until their eyes dropped before turning to Boucher. 'Did you tell them about the drugs on the airship?'

Marriot stepped forward. 'It's too risky, Candy. The cabin's crumpled and there are cables all over the place. If one of us got trapped, that would be two dead.'

'Josef isn't dead yet, but he will be if we don't act.'

Marriot stirred one foot in the sand. 'I didn't mean Josef. I was thinking about Sixt – the pilot.'

Candy had wiped her mind clear of the face bobbing beside her in the airship. Chastened, she turned away. 'Obviously, I don't want you to jeopardize lives.'

'I'll take a look at the airship later,' Boucher called after her.

'Jay, you'd better stay and guard the camp,' Marriot told him. 'Don't let the Ecos steal the boat.'

'Not much I can do to stop them.'

'Remind Leo of the consequences. He's not stupid.'

'Yes he is.'

Their voices faded. Candy took her place at Fieser's side, drew up her knees and hugged them tight. Staring out to sea, she saw how false her self-image had been. She had thought herself brave and steadfast, but stripped of the security that had cocooned her, she had proved to be a total wash-out.

Sand crunched underfoot. She knew it was Boucher

and she decided that if he made some smart remark she would hit him.

'Life getting on top.'

'Go away.'

He hesitated. 'Stay with it, Candy. You're a rock.'

She gave a little growl. Americans, with their Christmas-cracker assertions of positive thinking. Go for it! Let's do it! Yeah!

'What'd I say?'

'Take over,' she told him. 'I'm going for a swim.'

On the way to the bathing area, she paused and smiled sourly at Jaeger's boundary marker – a child's caricature of the lord of the jungle. The women's bathing area lay beyond it, but the beach was deserted. Stepping past the warning sign, she continued another fifty yards before going to the forest edge and slipping her clothes off. She wrapped her towel around her, ran down the beach, and threw herself into the lagoon as if she were giving herself to a lover. Paddling on her back, she resolved that if none of the men would dive to the wreck, she would do it herself.

The beach was still empty when she emerged.

After drying off, she let the towel drop and ruefully took stock of her body. Nadine was right. Six days' tropical exposure had taken its toll. Her legs were stippled by fly bites and the insides of her thighs were blotchy with heat rash. Stinging vines had raised ugly weals on her forearms. Her crotch itched. She applied some talcum powder and reached for her clothes.

Her hand stopped short. Some sound had infiltrated her consciousness. Keeping her eyes on the forest, she picked up her towel and covered herself. A bird chimed strenuously in the leafy galleries, but that wasn't the noise she'd heard. Butterflies commuted across the jungle plazas. She listened to the fretful silence, switching from sound to random sound.

'Who's there?' she called softly.

Insects nagged at the beams of light.

She made her voice firmer. 'I know someone's there.'

A bird rattled away through branches.

She took a tighter grip of her towel. 'Is that you, Disco?'

Out of the forest stepped Bartok.

Relief vented itself in anger. 'What the bloody hell do you think you're playing at?'

'Aw,' he said, eyes half-on and half-off her, 'we were just horsing around.'

'Well go and horse around somewhere else.'

'Candy, this is our territory. You're trespassing.'

'You silly man.'

All Bartok's blood seemed to collect in his face. 'No call to speak that way, Candy. You know Wildguard land's off limits.'

'Sure she does,' Disco said behind her, 'and she knows the consequences.'

Candy went cold to the bottom of her feet. 'I'll go where I like,' she said, not turning round.

'You know what, Kent? I reckon she came up here looking for me. You hear the way she called out my name.' His voice climbed an octave. 'Disco, is that you Disco? Feeling herself up, too. You see that?'

On Bartok's face, Candy saw excitement and shame evenly pitted. Trying to keep her hands from shaking, she gathered up her clothes. 'I came for a swim. I swim here every morning.'

'We were planning on skinny-dipping ourselves. Stick around. Don't see why us men should have all the fun.' Candy heard the sound of a zip being loosed. 'Hoo, there you go – naked and unashamed. Like that Adam and Eve.'

Bartok shuffled as if he was on coals. 'Disco, you said we were just going to ... you know, look.'

'And I see what looking does for you and I'm impressed. I bet Candy is, too.'

Still, she didn't face him. 'Kent, I'd never have expected this behaviour from you.'

'He's a man, ain't he? Flesh and blood and sorely tempted. Be fruitful and multiply, like what the good book says.'

Bartok grimaced. 'I don't like to hear that kind of talk, Disco.'

Candy seized on his scruples. 'Kent, I don't expect any better from Disco, but you at least know right from wrong.'

'In olden-day times,' Disco said, 'if a tribe conquered an enemy, they got to keep their women. Even in the Bible they did that. Kent, I reckon Candy's ours by the rules of war.'

Bartok snickered anxiously 'You're funning, aren't you?'

Disco closed his hand on Candy's bare shoulder. 'It's like the chief said: we set the rules on this island. This is our territory and Candy invaded it. She's ours.'

Candy looked sideways at Disco's fingers on her bare skin, then searched out Bartok's eye. 'You're heading for serious trouble. Both of you.'

'Only jungle law out here,' Disco said, 'and from the size of it, I'd say Kent's got jungle fever.'

The first note of panic crept into Candy's voice. 'Kent, soon we'll be back in civilization. If I report you, you're going to end up in an Indonesian jail.'

'Need witnesses,' Disco said. 'No witnesses I can see. We can do *any*thing.'

She swivelled out from his grip, but he grabbed her

towel and Candy couldn't tug free without everything coming undone.

'Now, now,' he said, 'don't go inflaming Kent's passions again.'

She aimed a kick at him. 'You still think this is a bit of fun?' she shouted at Bartok.

Troubled, he took a step towards her. 'Leave her be, Disco. You didn't say anything about this.'

'Skip if you want. Me and Candy have to talk.'

'Stay right there,' Candy begged Bartok.

'You gonna listen to me?' Disco shouted at him. 'Or one of the people who started this trouble?' His voice dropped into a soothing register. 'Now I'm telling you, I need to speak to Candy on my own.'

'I don't know,' Bartok muttered.

'I swear it. I just want a private word with her.'

Bartok wouldn't meet Candy's eye. 'I'll only go a little ways off.'

Very rapidly, Candy considered her courses of action. She'd have to run for it, but without clothes, she wouldn't get far in the forest, and she couldn't outpace Disco in the open.

'You see,' he said, watching Bartok trail off. 'He does what he's told. He respects me.'

Candy made her break, but he got her shoulder again and dug in his fingers, crushing a nerve. She let herself go slack and her voice dropped into sullen resignation. 'Say what you have to say.'

'Not here. In the forest.'

Candy turned and looked him full in the face. 'Is this what you mean by keeping me from harm?'

'I offered you a deal, but you didn't listen.' Disco winced as if stricken by an inner pain. 'That's the trouble with people. They never listen.'

Candy's legs began to flutter. 'I'm listening now.'

'Too late, Candy. You put me down, and like I told Jay, I never forget that.'

'You're mad,' she shouted. 'Mad and wicked.'

Disco's eyes seemed to withdraw into his face and Candy knew she had only a moment in which to act.

She threw her clothes in his face and as his hands came up in reflex, she ran. Halfway down the beach her towel fell off and Disco whooped. She want flat out for the lagoon, fought her way through the shallows and began swimming, heading straight out to the reef. She wasn't a powerful swimmer, but neither was Disco. Her hope was to get far enough out to attract Boucher's attention.

Past the end of the sandspit the vacant sweep of beach came in sight. Her rhythm grew ragged. Cramp threatened her right calf. Over the splashing in her wake she heard Bartok shouting.

'Candy! Disco! Hey, Disco.'

She glanced back. Disco had stopped swimming. Bartok was running back and forth. Her breathing was so laboured she couldn't catch what he was saying.

'... out there.'

Disco sucked in a mouthful of water and squirted it out. 'What's that?'

'Saw something.'

'Saw what?'

'Like a shadow underwater.'

'Like your conscience, man.'

'I'm serious, Disco.'

Candy didn't wait to examine Bartok's claim or motives. She immediately began swimming back, taking the shortest route. Disco blocked the way, treading water. He lunged at her and missed his aim and somehow his fingers were in her mouth and she was biting with all her might. His face contracted in pain and for a moment he went under and she heard him ship water. 'Bitch,' he gasped, and clamped his other hand on her wrist. She gouged at his face and then did what she should have done earlier and screamed.

Her scream seemed to drive Bartok to a pitch of frenzy. 'I swear it, Disco! Swear to God!'

Holding her with one hand, Disco craned up. Candy jerked free and though he lunged at her again, his grab lacked conviction. She floundered shorewards.

Bartok was in the water. 'Disco, you'd better come on back.'

Disco said something unintelligible.

Candy contacted bottom and barged past Bartok. He made no attempt to stop her.

'Get going,' he insisted, but he was staring past her as if he was in dead earnest about there being something in the water. She looked back. Disco was still twenty yards out.

'If a shark gets him, don't ask me for help.' She stumbled up the beach and scooped up her clothes.

Bartok waded in. 'Come on, man.'

Disco grabbed him and they both toppled. They came out on to land as if the water had turned to boiling point around them. Disco staggered and turned, his back heaving. He scoured the lagoon and spat. He gave a breathless laugh. 'There ain't any fucking shark out there.'

'I didn't say it was a shark, but there was something. Real big.'

Disco spat again. 'Just a fish shoal.' He looked at his injured hand and grimaced.

Candy had her shorts on. 'Why don't you go back and find out?'

Disco grinned savagely. 'Fuck you, Candy. That's your last let-off. From now on, Hell's Angels' rules mean women are fair game for any man with balls.'

'Oh yes? Well that shark certainly shrivelled *your* dick.'

190

She made her way back to camp in fits and starts, breaking into little runs and gulps of laughter and tears. Elation at having escaped flipped into rage at having got herself into the situation. Her rage was like a bubble she couldn't burst. Once was bad enough, but twice was bloody well asking for it!

Boucher appeared as if from nowhere. He was hurrying, in a state of alarm. Oh God! He must have seen something. She couldn't tell him. She *mustn't*.

'Candy, it's Josef. I'm no doctor, but ...'

Forgetting everything else, she ran to Fieser's side. He was struggling just below the surface of consciousness, his breaths overlapping and occasionally faltering.

Candy rested the back of her hand on his forehead. 'He's been like this since last night.'

'It's not that,' Boucher said. His face was stricken. He could hardly bring himself to speak. 'Candy, it's the smell.'

She looked at him aghast. In his eyes horror mingled with revulsion. Steeling herself, she lowered her face. She caught a waft of putrefaction – an odour marrying the mangrove stench with the unwholesome perfume of the forest flowers that opened at dusk to attract the night trade.

She tried not to recoil. She took a needle and inserted the tip into Fieser's thigh. He didn't flinch.

She swayed back. 'You're right,' she said dully. 'It's gangrene.'

'Three, four days,' Marriot said. 'Either way the leg's beyond saving. If it was below the knee we could at least consider amputation.'

'But it isn't below the knee!'

'Candy, we're all upset.' Marriot paused. His manner was calm. 'Okay, let's run through our options. We can sit

191

here and wait for rescue. It'll come eventually, but it's a good bet it won't show in time for Josef.'

Candy couldn't contain herself. 'I'm not going to wait, Robert. I'm not!'

'Calm down.'

'We've got to go for help.'

Boucher was doodling with a stick. 'How do we do that?'

'Take the boat and try to reach a fishing village or the oil rig. All of us would have to go – Josef included.'

'The Ecos won't let us take the boat.'

'We wouldn't ask.'

Boucher stopped doodling. 'Candy, the inflatable's a wreck. The nearest rig's probably two days off and if we got caught in a sea like we had yesterday, we'd go down. Five people dead.'

'Jay's right,' Marriot said. 'It's the cyclone season. The weather's too unpredictable.'

'Then we'll go inland. For all we know, there are people within five miles of here.'

Boucher looked up. 'And for all we know, there isn't a soul in a week's trek. It's a hell of a gamble, Candy. Lose your way in the mangroves and no one will even find your bones.'

'It's too dangerous,' Trigg agreed. 'There's no way through. Forget it.'

'What other options are there?' Candy demanded.

'There aren't any. That's it. We wait here and take it a day at a time.'

Candy jumped up in a tantrum of frustration. 'I'll go myself if none of you dares.'

'Sit down,' Marriot told her. He was silent for a while. 'Maybe it *is* time to take a risk. We've still got our strength and health, but sooner or later someone will have an accident or fall ill. Also, the Ecos will be out of food in a day or two. If we aim to get off under our own steam, now's the time.'

Candy felt hope surge. 'You'll go? You'll go through the mangroves?'

Marriot didn't answer for a second. 'It's not something I'd try on my own.'

'I'll come with you.'

'No, it's too tough for a woman. Trigg couldn't hack it either.' Marriot turned to Boucher. 'Feeling brave?'

Boucher squirmed. 'I don't want to leave Candy here. God knows what will ...'

Candy jumped up. 'What Jay's saying is that there are good reasons why I should be the one.'

'I'm not taking you, and that's flat.'

Candy had only one argument left and she delivered it at a shout. 'This morning, Disco tried to rape me. Shut up,' she said, squashing Boucher's outburst. 'I can't stay here. I won't.'

They digested this.

Marriot rose heavily. 'Without equipment, it's a hopeless proposition. I'll have to grovel to Jaeger.'

'And where does that leave me?' Trigg complained. 'We only split up because of you.'

'You'll cope.'

After Marriot left, Boucher went off on his own. He was gone forty minutes and when he came back his face wore a pinched look.

'Oh, don't look so martyred,' Candy told him.

'I know why you didn't tell me. I don't blame you, and I want to say how sorry I am.'

'We agreed I'm not your responsibility.'

Boucher was pale with resolution. 'You are now. Depend on it.'

'Even if I could, it doesn't change my mind.'

'You think I can't handle Disco?'

'I don't think anyone can. He's even got Kent caught up in his fantasies.' Seeing Boucher's wounded look, Candy gave an inward sigh at the thinness of men's skins. 'Nothing happened. I was incredibly stupid. I went on to their land.'

'Did he ... hurt you?'

Candy giggled. '*I* hurt him. I bit his hand.'

'It isn't something you can laugh off. The guy's a bug. He should be put down.' Boucher stopped as if he'd jarred an unexpected nerve. Angry synapses beat under his skin.

'That's why I have to get off. I'm a liability, an incitement.'

'Not to me. You're my most important project now.' Boucher spotted Marriot slouching back and shook his head beseechingly. 'Please, Candy, you're letting your heart get the better of your head.'

'No, *you* are.' Candy put out a consoling hand. 'Jay, with me gone, life will be a lot simpler.'

Marriot slumped between them as if his mission had been wearing and fruitless. 'I tried to persuade Leo to send one of his lot with me.'

'And?'

'He said they needed Bartok to climb for fruits and finish the look-out. Disco gave a flat "no". Said he was damned if he was going to throw away his life for the guy who landed us here in the first place.' Marriot's mood was tetchy. 'Part of me agrees.'

Candy felt as if she'd been relieved of a heavy weight. 'You're stuck with me then.'

Under Marriot's bleak stare, her smile withered. 'Don't have any illusions. The mangrove swamp isn't like you imagine. It's not land and it's not water. It's a sink full of shit.'

'I can face it.'

Marriot seemed to look through her, then his focus

switched back. He produced a compass and a whistle. 'Without these, we'd go round in circles. Leo didn't want to part with them; they're an unsecured loan he doesn't expect to see repaid. He wouldn't give up the parang.'

'What else do we need?'

'Food, plenty of water, salt tablets and all the first aid kit we can spare. Can you make up some leggings and overshoes out of balloon fabric?'

Candy nodded energetically.

'We leave at low tide.' Marriot stood up. 'Feel free to cancel.'

THREE

16

A t low water, Candy could see nothing except the small crimson disc of the sun smouldering in the humid vapours shrouding the tidal forest. In the boat ferrying her across, the atmosphere was equally muted, the silence broken only by the the funereal rhythm of the paddles. Peering through the mist, she saw tree shapes loom up like a projection of her forebodings. On some parts of the Sumatran coast, the saline swamps soaked inland for up to thirty miles. Marriot had told her they would be lucky to make five miles a day. They carried only enough food for three days.

'Go right,' Marriot murmured. 'There's an inlet.'

Paddling into it, Candy had the unnerving sensation that she was entering a hot, wet mouth. She smelt a heavy reptilian reek. The trees wafting past rose dark and slender from stilted roots arched like spiders' legs. Fiddler crabs sidled over the grey flats, waving their claws in menacing salute. On a splintered branch above a fork in the canal, a cormorant held its wings in a tattered black cross.

'Which way?'

'Left.'

One direction was as good as another. The mangrove coast was an archipelago of little islets separated by a million rancid waterways. Already the lagoon was out of sight and Candy's only reference was the sun prismed in the branches.

Around the next corner the boat gently grounded. Marriot probed the bottom. Runnels of sweat streaked his neck. Candy raised her hand to ward off a vicious haze of mosquitoes. The heat was a dead weight and in her makeshift leggings she felt as if she was being cooked.

'Now what?'

'That's it. This is where we get off.'

The prospect silenced them all.

'You can't go in there,' Trigg muttered. 'It's a cemetery.'

Marriot looked at Candy. 'It's your decision.'

Faced by the dreadful sameness on all sides, Candy suffered an overpowering lack of will to move.

'This is the worst part. It'll get easier further inland.'

'How the hell do you know?' Trigg cried. 'It's not worth it – not for a dying man.'

'There's a big difference between dying and being dead. We can make it count.'

'Crap. Girl Guide bullshit.'

'Imagine it was your leg,' Candy told him, and settled the issue by stepping out of the boat on to a root mass. Her footing was precarious and her mouth clenched in unease. Marriot joined her. They did a final check on their equipment – food, water, purifiers, medicines, mosquito nets, compass, whistle.

'Candy.'

Boucher had hardly said a word. Now he got out of the boat and, careless of the lurking bottom life, squelched towards her. Assailed by so many doubts of her own, she assumed he would make a last attempt to change her mind and she wasn't entirely sure she could hold firm.

He stood before her, his face grave, both hands resting

on her shoulders. 'Good luck,' he murmured. Gently he kissed her on the lips. 'You'll be taking a piece of my heart with you.'

She didn't really register it. Perhaps her lurch of emotion was just relief that he hadn't tried to undermine her. She hugged him – a fierce little hug.

'Take good care of yourself and look after Josef.'

'We'll follow the sun,' Marriot told her, watching the compass needle settle. 'No point in being subtle.'

'How will we know what's happening to you?' Trigg demanded.

'You won't until you're rescued.' Marriot hesitated. 'If you haven't heard from us after six days, assume the worst. Keep an eye on the mangroves, but don't come looking for us. Sit tight and you'll be able to hang on indefinitely.'

Marriot's casual acceptance that they might be walking to their deaths chilled Candy. She had forced this on him, and if they should perish, the blame would be on her shoulders.

He smiled at her. 'Ready?'

She felt wobbly. 'Yes.'

'See you in Jakarta,' he told Boucher and Trigg. 'You're buying, Jay.'

Candy picked her way after him, using the root clumps as stepping stones. Between the main supports were lateral cable roots that broke surface at intervals like dinosaur vertebrae. She tried to make progress look easy, but her legs lacked reach and before she had gone ten yards she slipped. Sinking to her crotch in stinking mud, she gasped as much in humiliation as disgust. Sweat-drenched and panting, she lunged for the nearest sapling.

Trigg was filming her botched departure. Beside him Boucher stood dismayed, one hand half-raised. Candy put them out of her mind. Forgetting appearances, she fixed her concentration on the next step, the next foothold, the next support.

When she looked again, they were gone.

Snakes aquatic and terrestrial were the most obvious danger. Once they saw five water-snakes together, clumped head to head in jade-green scum as if engaged in some bizarre ritual. More pernicious, and deadlier in the long run, were the leeches and mosquitoes, the razor-edged shells buried in the mud, the columns of ants flowing over almost every tree.

It was impossible to establish a rhythm. Every step had to be considered separately. Some of the cable roots thrust up small growths as sharp as pencils; other areas were booby-trapped with ankle-wrenching stumps like legs severed at the knee. Without the leggings and clumsy overshoes, Candy's feet would have been cut to ribbons.

Worst of all was the clinging mud and sapping heat. The air was as slick and dense as the sweat that coated her.

Occasionally, they heard troops of monkeys scampering overhead like fleeing rioters. On a quaking island they disturbed a roost of fruit bats that rustled on membranous wings semi-transparent against the wan light. Everything in this nether world seemed ill-omened.

In mid-afternoon Marriot called a halt. They chewed fish that was already slimy. When Candy drank, she found her water bottle half empty. Afterwards, Marriot eyed her in a way that touched a shard of female vanity.

'I must look a complete fright.'

His expression was stony. 'Take your leggings off.'

Knowing what was on his mind, Candy obeyed. Half a dozen leeches clung to her ankles. Marriot pulled them off without ceremony and one of them, glutted on her blood, burst in a bright red spray.

'Yuk,' she said faintly.

He faced her. 'It's still not too late. We can be back by nightfall.'

In Candy's mind the island had been transformed into a paradise of clean airs and pure waters. Even Disco was no more than a minor irritant compared to what she might suffer here – what she was already suffering. But the mangrove's insidious rot reminded her that Disco wasn't the reason she had come.

'It's just as easy to go on as to go back.'

'We'll soon be at the point of no return.'

'Let's give it till evening. If we haven't reached dry land by then, we'll call it quits.'

He nodded curtly and they pushed on.

Soon after resuming their slog, the light turned addled and then drained away. Thunder rumbled and rain crashed on the canopy. Candy raised her face to the cloudburst, letting the deluge sluice away the filth. She filled her bottle with water funneling down the leaves.

All afternoon, fits of rain broke over them. The going got no firmer. In fact, the channels were getting deeper as the tide rose. The heat flayed her. Her mouth hung open and she grew careless about where she placed her feet. Cuts and scratches accumulated. Teetering on a submarine root, she grabbed a sapling too late to see the ants swarming on the bark, and before she could pull her hand away, three of four of them bit her, their jaws lancing like red-hot needles.

She began to lag, and though Marriot didn't complain, she could sense his resentment at the futility of their mission. It was certain they wouldn't reach inhabited parts today, and even if they found a village tomorrow, it might take another two or three days to get to a town and mobilize a rescue. By then, Fieser would be dead. This was just running away; staying with him, watching his life ebb away, would have been the real act of courage.

She almost stumbled into Marriot. Ahead of him lay a large pool. On the other side the forest seemed thicker and taller, the trees festooned with ropes of vine and clotted by soft excrescences.

'Light's going,' he said. 'We'd better find somewhere to sleep.'

She nodded, too wrung out to speak.

'You wait here. You're done in.'

'Shouldn't we stay together? It'll be dark soon.'

'Give me fifteen minutes. If I haven't found somewhere by then, I'll head back.' Marriot put the whistle to his mouth and blew a single note. 'One blast every minute means I'm still going. Two means I've found somewhere and you should come after me. I'll keep blowing every few seconds until you reach me. Three means I've run into trouble.'

She nodded like an automaton. 'One, I stay where I am. Two, I come after you. Three ...' She raised her head. 'What should I do if you blow three times?'

'Up to you. It'll probably mean I've got stuck in the mud.'

Miserably, she watched him wade through the pool. On the other side he turned.

'I'm sorry, Robert. I've completely mucked up.'

'We gave it a go.'

The forest absorbed him.

Candy looked at her watch and marked the position of the second hand. The first whistle was reassuringly loud, the second, though audible, was markedly less piercing, and when the third one sounded fainter still, Candy began to worry that he'd have gone beyond earshot by the time the fifteen minutes expired.

Water fell from the leaves in slow drips. No birds called.

All movement had been reduced to the sweep of the second hand. It passed the mark twice before she heard the next blast. She tried to relax. Robert wouldn't be timing his signals to the second.

He had left her parked in a particularly unwholesome spot. The pool smelt like a fever culture and the growths hanging on the sodden walls made her think of a giant's larder. While she waited, her eyes never stopped moving. She imagined leeches looping towards her, homing in on her body heat.

The next signal was louder, as if Marriot was heading back, but the one after that sounded as if it had come from a different direction. Candy guessed the trees were playing acoustical tricks. She prayed for a double blast.

She lost track of the minutes. It made no difference and every second beyond the deadline only piled on the anxiety. Gloom was massing up from the swamp and she knew that Marriot would be hard-pressed to get back before dark. She considered shouting, but even if he heard her, it would only confuse him, make him assume she'd got herself into difficulty. She had to hold her nerve.

Had that been a whistle or a bird call?

In the rain forest, every creature had evolved a system of communication adapted to the gloomy and choked conditions. That's why the birds were so brightly coloured and why the gibbons had such penetrating cries. It wasn't simply a matter of volume; their alarm calls were pitched at low frequencies that travelled ten times as far as a high-pitched shriek. Robert might be blowing his lungs inside out without the sound reaching her.

Given the difficulty of movement, he probably hadn't gone more than a few hundred yards. She tried to put herself in his place, imagined him struggling around obstacles. He would be aware of her anxiety and would be doing everything he could to bring it to an end.

Why didn't he blow?

Candy stood up, nerves shredded, fighting the compulsion to go in search. Stay put he'd said. If she went looking for him, there was a good chance she'd lose contact, and once lost ... She gritted her teeth, trying to blank out the fact she could no longer distinguish detail on the other side of the pool.

Far away the whistle blew. He was still going away. Resentfully she slid back into a crouch. All the light that was left had collected in the treetops. By now he must know it was hopeless. He should have taken her with him. He had no right to abandon her. He had shown poor judgement.

As her reproaches mounted, she heard another faint *peep*. She stood up. It came again and this time there was no doubt. The signal was a double note repeated almost immediately.

'I'm coming!' she shouted, tension bursting out. She fought her way through the water, knowing that if the light went before she caught up, she might still end up benighted. The whistle blew repeatedly, sometimes fading, sometimes louder, but always a double note from the same direction. It had an urgent, excited tempo, as if the campsite he'd found exceeded his expectations. In her imagination she was already there, cuddled over a fire, joking about the fears that had nearly undone her.

Again the double blast, the summons constant. She was racing against the dark, but she was close now, surely no more than a couple of minutes away. A branch clawed her. She struck back at it. 'I'm coming!' she gasped.

Pandemonium broke out in the canopy. Candy froze, rooted in mud. The furious clamour subsided only to erupt again. Long after the main outburst had died, sporadic alarms flared. At last silence settled and lengthened.

Staring into the core of it, Candy groped for the nearest tree.

The last note she'd heard had been a single blast, but the signal must have been cut off by the uproar. Marriot wouldn't have gone on with night almost here.

Almost? It was too dark to read her watch or see her feet. Only the black tracery above remained visible.

'Robert!' she shouted. 'Robert, I'm over here!'

She held her breath, trying to wring a human sound from the monotonous frog chorus. Only a couple of minutes could have passed since the racket in the trees and she might have missed a signal. She began counting aloud: 'One and two and three ...' Her voice grew slower and slower as she fought back the moment of truth. '... fifty-eight, fifty-nine, sixty, sixty-one, sixty ...'

Candy bit her finger. She waited. She waited and she waited.

'Damn you,' she sobbed.

She splashed forward, tripped and sprawled. She scrambled up and clung to a tree, panting with shock. She mustn't panic. He was close by. He must be. She filled her lungs.

'Roberrrt!'

From somewhere not far away came a faint *splosh*. Candy formed an impression of something heavy and sleek, as much at home in water as on land. Her skin crawled.

'Robert?' she said, very softly. 'Is that you, Robert?'

She waited, flinching at every little sound. An internal voice told her to keep quiet and absolutely still, but somehow the silence was unignorable. If she didn't challenge it, it would engulf her.

'Robert,' she cried sharply, 'where the hell are you?'

The silence pressed in. She whimpered. She no longer

cared about finding proper shelter. All she wanted was to be in a human presence.

'Please whistle,' she whispered. 'Whistle and I'll come to you.' The words kept repeating themselves and finally petered out.

After that she didn't call again.

Something bad had happened to Marriot. Something had got him.

As quietly as she could, she pulled herself up on to the root buttress of the nearest tree and drew up her legs as far as possible. Again and again she replayed the splash she'd heard, aware that if it had been made by a crocodile, she had not the slightest defence to offer. It would know where she was. It might be closing in for the kill at this very moment, drifting imperceptibly nearer, watching her as she sat there oblivious of its presence, until ... The image of its final lunge sent Candy's whole body into spasm.

Terror of what might be stalking subsided into a dull awareness of her present afflictions. Her body throbbed from bites and scratches. There was a flux in her stomach and a crab at the centre of it. Her temples thumped. She sensed fever spores circulating in her system. She took a cocktail of pills and tried to swallow a piece of fish. As she chewed, tears of self-pity welled up her eyes. If only she'd listened to Boucher. If only she hadn't been so blind to her inadequacies. She began to weep openly, her misery almost a comfort, but when she caught the self-conscious note in her sobbing she rubbed her eyes fiercely.

'Pull yourself together.'

Nearly twelve hours of darkness had to be got through, and sleep was out of the question. Tomorrow was already louring over her and she tried to push it away, aware that if she dwelt on it she would squander what fortitude was left to her.

Staring into the dark, she imagined home, riding down from the ridgeway on an autumn evening towards the warm lamplight, the dogs barking, a door opening and light flooding out. She imagined a hot bath, a quiet meal, and then the soft bed.

Boucher's parting words came to her. She didn't take them seriously. Jay didn't really love her and she certainly didn't love him. She wasn't sure what she felt for him, but she suspected that if they ever met again in the everyday world, they would be strangers to each other.

And yet she kept returning to his declaration and the way he had looked when he made it. Somehow it lightened her darkness.

Not that it was pitch black. The ghostly phosphorescence of decay misted every surface, and always a faint animation crowded the air – the mindless scrapings and hisses, clicks and burps of the forest recycling itself. Huddled in the roots, Candy pictured herself as the most ill-adapted of creatures – a soft, blind, irrelevant object in a creation that was none of man's handiwork and perhaps not of God's either.

17

Boucher and Trigg stewed by the edge of the mangroves until well after midday, and then, convinced that Candy and Marriot must have made a breakthrough, they rowed back to the island. The pall had drawn back from the sun and the brazen light forecast rain.

Both men were short-tethered. Trigg was still disgruntled by what he saw as Marriot's desertion. Boucher was desperately worried about Candy, bitterly regretful that he'd let her go. Already the island seemed empty without her, and all enterprise dull. Story or no story, it was time to get out. With the material he already had, he was sure he could work up a parable relevant to the times.

Rounding the southern point, he spotted a shape on the sand that hadn't been there that morning.

'Pull in over there.'

'What is it?'

'Looks like a turtle.'

They followed its laborious furrow up the beach. At their approach, it pulled its head in. Its mottled green carapace was nearly two feet across. Boucher touched it with the point of his toe. He'd seen smaller turtles on his fishing trips; underwater they seemed to fly.

'Is it edible?' Trigg asked.

'Only one way to find out.'

'Kill it?'

With Marriot and Candy gone, the mantle of leadership had fallen on Boucher. It wasn't a garment he felt comfortable wearing.

'Yes.'

'How?'

Good question. The horny shell was impregnable to any tool they had at hand. Guillotining was probably the only quick method of despatch, but Jaeger had the parang.

Cautiously the turtle extended its head and peered about. It looked very old and inconvenienced. When Boucher moved, the head swiftly retracted.

He would have to bludgeon it to death. He looked about, at a loss. There weren't any rocks on the island, and he calculated that the oars were too light to inflict a killing blow. Turtles, he guessed, were extremely tenacious.

'Get the anchor.'

'Ah, leave it, man.'

'We haven't got anything else to eat. Fetch the anchor.'

Trigg's expression turned mulish. 'I don't want to.'

Boucher regarded his companion broodingly. What was it Candy had quoted from Darwin? Something along the lines of any variation profitable to an individual engaged in the struggle for existence would tend to the preservation of such an individual. Quite. Trigg might have mastered the right moves for urban living, but out here street-smartness had precious little survival value.

Deciding not to force the issue this time, Boucher turned on his heel. For better or worse, he was stuck with the man.

By the time he returned, the turtle had lumbered further up the beach.

'Let's go fishing instead.'

'Out of the way.'

Boucher hefted the anchor. Apart from the fish he'd caught in the last few days, he had never killed anything bigger than a fly. The turtle pushed out its snout and fastened its little eyes on him.

With a force that jarred his wrist, he brought the anchor down. He struck again, the effort driving a sob from him. The turtle's head pulled back then flopped, blood spilling obscenely. Its flippers propelled it in a half circle and continued to move even when it lost traction and stalled like a clockwork toy.

'That is fucking gross, man.'

Boucher rose pale and nauseous. 'Eat or die.'

Back at camp, Boucher steeled himself for his next sickening task. In the sluggish air, the foul smell of Fieser's decaying flesh hung heavy. Hand over his nose, breathing through his mouth, Boucher put his head into the pilot's shelter, half-expecting to find him dead.

He was conscious, his purple-ringed eyes latched on to his own.

'Josef? Can you hear me?'

Fieser gave a gargling sigh.

'Candy and Robert have gone for help. It won't be long now.'

Fieser seemed to see something astonishing in front of him. His hands reached up as if to grasp it and Boucher shrank away. Then they fell back.

A lump filled Boucher's throat. He took one of Fieser's hands and watched him sink back under.

'Forgive me, Josef. I'm only human.'

When he rejoined Trigg, the cameraman was watching him steadily. Boucher gave one quick shake of the head but didn't speak. Trigg went back to cleaning his camcorder. Boucher looked on, his mind dulled by horror.

'Is that thing still working?'

'Sure is,' Trigg said, and blew grit from the delicate mechanism.

'What have you got so far?'

'Got you coming ashore after the crash, the women bathing, Kent climbing the tree. All sorts. Take a look.'

Putting his eye to the viewfinder, Boucher watched a playback of Candy and Marriot disappearing into the swamp. The image was steady and professionally framed.

'What d'ya think?' Trigg asked.

'Very saleable.'

'Priceless. I got some great tit and bum shots of Nadine and Aquila.'

Boucher looked at Trigg thoughtfully. It hadn't occurred to him that he had a media competitor.

Trigg jerked his head at the turtle. 'Better do something about that thing before it goes off. Smells bad enough round here as it is.'

Boucher's smile was a tic.

Cleaning out the turtle was a revolting task made all the more gruesome by Boucher's discovery that the creature was a female crammed with eggs – dozens of globes like soft ping-pong balls. It might have swum a thousand miles to reach its breeding ground and he had smashed its head in.

'Hey,' Trigg called, 'we've got visitors.'

Through the puddles of heat, Disco and Jaeger were advancing down the beach. Boucher's skin grabbed. This could be it. Casually he got up.

'Let's take a look at the wreck. See if we can salvage those medicines.'

Trigg glanced at the livid sky. 'It's going to piss down.'

'A few drops of rain won't harm us.'

Trigg shook his head. 'I'm no diver.'

'All I want is for you to hold the boat steady.'

'I'm out of it, man. Got a real splitter.'

Boucher held on to his temper with difficulty. 'Look, I can't do it single-handed.'

Trigg's eyes scavenged around. 'Waste of time. Josef's for the chop anyway.'

Only a massive effort of restraint prevented Boucher from throttling him. 'Not if Robert and Candy get through.'

Trigg's mouth began to work. 'This was a bum move. He had no fucking right to leave us. I stuck my neck out for him. We all did. And for what? One day later he ditches us.'

'I'll take that for a "no".'

Trigg cast a narrow-eyed look at him. 'You're not bothered about the medicine. Listen, man, I don't blame you for wanting to clear off, but Disco isn't my fight. Okay?' He glanced in the direction of the visitors and seemed to come to a decision that relaxed him. 'I'll stick around to see what they want.'

Simmering with anger, Boucher stormed down the beach, pushed the boat out and flung himself in. His anger was all the more intense, all the more impotent, because what Trigg said was true. Hearing Disco shout his name, he snarled wordlessly.

His mood calmed somewhat when he reached the wreck. The lagoon was as flat as a mill-pond, its glassy transparency rather sinister in the metallic light. Since Boucher's last visit, the gondola had rolled even further, exposing the flight cabin's wide-open door. He couldn't see the pilot's body and assumed that by now it would have been stripped to bones. Pushing that image away, he tried to fathom out the best approach.

On the beach, Disco was angrily gesturing. Boucher cocked an eye at the baleful sky. He didn't have much time.

His first attempt failed. Too much energy went into the

dive, leaving him no breath for entry. It wasn't wasted effort, though. He got close enough to get a good look at the cabin lockers. They were secured by simple press catches.

He surfaced into a luminous darkness. The atmosphere was charged and any minute all heaven would break. What he needed was a weight, some ballast to pull him down. A bag of sand would be ideal, but Disco and Jaeger were still occupying the beach.

Boucher pulled himself aboard and gathered in the slack of the anchor rope until he felt resistance. Allowing another few feet, he lashed the rope round one of the rowlocks, then hauled up the weight, laying the rope in coils as he did so. He manoeuvred the inflatable until he was looking straight down at the cabin door, dangled the anchor overboard, seated himself on the side and fitted his feet between the tines. With a wriggle he went over.

His descent couldn't have gone better, the anchor pulling him in free fall plumb to the cabin door. Unhurriedly he grabbed the frame. The nearest locker was within reach. It opened at a touch and immediately he saw the green plastic chest and red cross.

With breath to spare, he decided to make an attempt on the other locker. Fish like gold medallions clustered around him. Leaning down, he opened the door, reached in and felt a clutter in the lowest corner. Groping for a hold, he dislodged a bright metallic object. Recognition struck instantly, but his awkward attempt to scoop it up knocked it behind him, over the pilot's seat. Twisting, he saw it wobble end over end in slowish motion, bounce off the flight panel and settle in a puff of silt right in the furthermost recess of the smashed nose cone. In the shadows he could see it gleaming. He marked its position and pushed out and up.

A subdued hissing filled his ears and he broke through

into deafening confusion. While he'd been under, the rain had arrived with a vengeance, whipping the sea into a froth that made it difficult to catch a breath. Thunder detonated right overhead. The beach was invisible. Boucher slung the chest into the inflatable and buried his face against the side.

Lightning ripped. Rain pellets scourged his shoulders. Only vaguely aware of the elements, Boucher had the pistol centred in his mind's eye.

A pistol!

The rain slackened and then ceased as if a switch had been thrown. Ominous streaks of light swirled and through them the island slowly reformed. The camp was deserted. Looking north, Boucher picked out three profiles making their way back to the Ecos' camp.

'Good riddance.'

But his bravado was empty. All his intentions had been stood on their head. He was supposed to be at the centre of events and now he was completely out of them. Candy had subverted him, and she was gone, too. He was on his own, love lost and the story happening elsewhere. He'd blown it on all fronts.

Tight-jawed, he looked inland, towards the retreating squall. Thunder sounded and behind the clouds lightning flickered like a faulty neon sign. Imagining Candy embedded in those dank depths, Boucher experienced a seismic shudder. He could never have faced it. If she made it, she'd be a hero and the story would be hers. She deserved it.

His mind switched back to the pistol. It couldn't have lodged in a trickier place. To reach it, he would have to negotiate the pilots' seats, work his way down into the footwell and then, avoiding the torn bulkhead, manoeuvre round in the confined space before exiting. He wasn't sure he had sufficient lung capacity.

Out to sea another batch of dirty weather was brewing. Boucher's mangrove vigil and exertions had left him drained. He considered returning for the pistol another day, but by then the Ecos might have repossessed the boat. Now was as good an opportunity as any. He sat consolidating his will.

By the time he dived, he had gone over the moves so many times that he didn't have to think. This time, though, his aim wasn't so sure and he wasted precious oxygen getting through the door. Inside, he folded at the waist and kicked down. It was like performing gymnastics in a small sedan. The light was grey inside, the experience claustrophobic. He was going to make it, though. The gun was in his sights, almost within reach. His right hand strained towards it.

Inches away from making contact, he saw the eel.

A moray eel, lying under the seat, motionless. Only its head was exposed, undershot mouth half agape, revealing rows of back-curved teeth. Boucher was paralyzed, desperate to flee but unable to move. It was a nightmare come alive, a creature from his worst imaginings. Staring at that hooded head, the flat, vicious eyes, he felt he was confronted by the oldest, most evil tyrant in the universe.

His breath was nearly used up, his lungs stretched as tight as a drum. He was too buoyant and it was impossible to remain still without fanning his hand. One way or another he was going to have to move, and he was certain that when he did, the eel would strike. Its eyes were vacant, but he knew they were watching him – knew they would only blink in the ecstasy of seizing prey.

Slowly his fingers closed the gap. At his first touch the pistol slid away. Air vented from his lungs with a soft, percussive thud. The eel lay inert. Watching its dead, all-seeing eyes, Boucher strained again and felt the butt. In an agony of stealth he closed his fingers round it. His chest was at bursting pressure. He snatched up the pistol, turning with the same convulsive moment, and as his head came round he was sure he saw the eel shoot forward. An instant later he felt a violent tug on his left leg. Bubbles exploded from his mouth. He lost it. Eyes bulging, hands milling, he kicked frenziedly for the door.

All he could see of the surface was the patch he was aiming for – like a bright hatch. He burst through and drew agonized gulps of air. He tried to elbow himself aboard and slipped back. He shot a look below and saw blood-clouded water. The spurt of fear fuelled his next attempt to pull himself aboard.

Flopping into the bottom, he saw the pistol clamped in his hand, pointed at his stomach. Still holding it, he sat up and gripped his knee in an impromptu tourniquet. Pain as jagged as the tear in his calf caught up with him. He whimpered through clenched jaws. Moray wounds always festered, Marriot had told him. Their jaws were charnel houses and they also harboured toxins from the poisonous fish they ate.

Let it bleed, he told himself. Let it clean itself out. He sat there with the blood mingling with the water sloshing at his feet. His terror abated. The wound seemed clean and didn't look like it had been inflicted by teeth. At last he decided he must have snagged himself on a piece of torn metal. Relief flooded him like a drug. Immediately afterwards a wave of black nausea struck.

He hunched in a kind of stupor, feeling the sun on his neck and the barely perceptible rocking of the boat. With great weariness he opened his eyes and saw the gun. Lucky he hadn't triggered it and blown a hole in himself. Carefully, trying to calm his shaky hand, he laid it on the seat beside him and turned to the medicine chest. His hands were so unsteady it took several tries to open it. Glinting in the light was a compartment lined with miniature syringes. He held one up. Morphine. He put it back and searched for antiseptic.

After drenching the gash thoroughly, he waited until the bleeding had eased. Then he stuck a dressing on.

His breathing slackened. The gun lay beside him, nickel-plated and larger than expected. His hand stole towards it as if it were a ticking bomb, then stopped. He knew the pistol would change things, altering the odds in his favour, but also – in some way he hadn't worked out – raising the stakes.

For a moment he considered ditching it. He was against guns on principle; he'd never even handled one before. But when he felt its weight and balance, a feeling of tranquillity settled on him. The pistol gave him a sensation of being solidly centred.

The beach was empty now and the island looked uninhabited. He rowed ashore, glancing often at the pistol. On dry land his limbs weighed heavy.

Trigg had left a note on his sleeping pallet.

This was a bum move. We're no good on our own. Leo
says he'll take you back if you swear to stick by the rules.
PS – They want the boat and anything you got from the
wreck.

Boucher gave a harsh laugh and raised the gun, recognizing the feeling it gave him. It was like the opiate calm that came on the very rare occasions when he was dealt a pat poker hand.

He dragged himself over to Fieser's bed. The pilot had gone under again; tiny, random pulses beat under the mask. There were more antibiotics in the chest, but Boucher knew it was too late. He picked up one of the morphine syrettes. At least he could give Josef peace. He took the pilot's wasted arm and searched for a vein. He'd never fired a gun or injected himself or anyone else. He'd been around drugs and guns, but he was too controlled, too self-alert, to mess with either.

Deciding that it didn't matter much if he fucked up, he gathered up what he guessed was a vein, inserted the needle and squeezed. The syrette emptied. After a minute, Fieser's tremors died. Boucher thought about giving him lasting peace. Maybe he would. It might come to that.

Bone-tired and sore, Boucher collected the makings of a fire before turning his attention to the pistol. After a week underwater, it might be seized solid and would certainly need an overhaul. First he checked the safety. It was on. Turning the pistol this way and that, he figured out how to eject the magazine. Sea water had rusted the mechanism and silt had found its way into the internals. He rinsed it with rain water, then cleaned all the accessible parts with a strip of lining torn from his jacket. For good measure he oiled it with some sunblock Candy had left him. He hummed as he worked.

Most of the corrosion was superficial, he decided, squinting up the barrel. Sliding the pistol inside his jacket, he took a few exploratory steps, as if he was testing new shoes for fit. The weight of the gun pulled his jacket down and the whole thing felt conspicuous. He couldn't carry it around with him. Tomorrow he would hide it in the forest, somewhere accessible. Until then, he would keep it close. He wrapped it in a square of airship fabric and stowed it under his sleeping platform.

Minutes later he pulled it out again, removed one bullet, shunted the clip in and hid it away.

Weighing the slug in his palm, Boucher recalled what Marriot had told him about hawks and doves. They weren't the only players in the jungle. There were also cheats – hawks disguised as doves and vice versa. The rain forest and the reef were full of cheats – bluffers and counterfeiters and mimics. The harmless mangrove snake dressed up like the deadly krait. For almost every predatory coral fish, there was an innocuous look-alike. Turning deception into a lifestyle, one bug patterned like a wasp spent its life joined head to head with its partner, so that whichever way a predator approached, it was apparently confronted by a stinging thorax.

Darkness was drawing down. Boucher tucked the bullet in his pocket and faced north, where a little eye of fire had appeared. A dove armed with a gun was a cheat with an unbeatable hand.

18

Day 8

Hunched in the dark, Candy gradually sank into an animal suspension of awareness. Fear remained, stalled at a distance. Her eyes stopped roving for things with teeth approaching through the slimy avenues of night. She endured the mosquitoes' torments and blotted out all thought of the leeches. She ignored the rain that soaked her and the cold that seeped into her bones. She must have dozed because dawn crept up unawares. Haggard and shivering, she looked into strands of mist and felt defeated before the day had begun.

Next thing she knew, the forest was splattered with sunlight. Groaning, she massaged life back into her limbs, then undid her leggings and pulled up her trousers. The sight made her moan. The leeches had been and gone, leaving their stigmata from ankle to thigh. Altogether, she was in a bloody wretched state. Her face was knobbly from mosquito bites and one eye was swollen half-shut. Sickness sat in the pit of her stomach like a protest.

A scarlet bird enraged by her presence flitted on the trunk above her. Watching its antics, seeing all that beady-eyed energy go to waste, Candy dragged her spirits from the mire. She was alive and that's what counted.

Maybe Marriot wasn't dead either. In the swamp, pessimism grew like mould and the worst was easiest to imagine; but there were any number of reasons why they might have lost contact.

Like what?

Well, like Marriot losing his whistle or deciding the place he'd found was no good and going on too far to return in the dark and ... After all, she hadn't heard him blow the danger signal.

She checked the time and the shock of how much she'd let slip drove her to her feet. Marriot might have been calling her; he might have gone back to the pool. She stumbled off in the direction of his last summons. Soon the ground grew springy underfoot and she knew she was on the right track because she found Marriot's cleated footprints. Not a crocodile then, she thought, wondering if that made things better or worse.

Ahead, the leaves brightened from olive to emerald. More stealthy now, she sidled into a wide clearing. When her eyes had adjusted to the harsh light, she saw crudely axed stumps. That's why Marriot had sounded so excited, she realized, her own heart racing.

A suggestion of a trail led through the undergrowth. At the end of it was a shape that didn't fit the haphazard jungle pattern. Approaching with caution, she found the remains of a rattan lean-to.

Puzzlement turned to apprehension. If Marriot had run into forest dwellers, he wouldn't have gone off with them and left her – not willingly. And if they had made him captive, they would have come looking for her, too. Maybe they had. Maybe the soft splashing she'd heard had been man-made.

She rejected the possibility. The shelter was rotting and overgrown. Nobody but Marriot had been here for weeks, probably months. And having found the camp, he wouldn't have left it. Nor would he have stopped whistling. Candy's apprehension deepened.

With a furtive backward glance, she got down on her knees and peered into the remains of the shelter. Among the rank weeds, something shone unnaturally. Wary of snakes, she reached in and pulled out a cheap cassette player in mock aluminium. In astonished reflex, she pressed the eject button and slowly it half-opened. There was still a cassette inside, its label obliterated by mould. A bug ran over her hand and she dropped the machine in fright.

After another edgy look behind her, she probed further and discovered a cooking pan and one rubber sandal. She swallowed, digesting their significance. This camp must have been made by hunters or honey-gatherers – people in marginal contact with civilization. Poor people. People who wouldn't have abandoned such valuable possessions. Either they had fled or been struck down by disease or ...

Whirling, Candy saw Marriot's hat, lying in a place so obvious that for one stopped heartbeat she imagined someone must have lobbed it towards the lean-to while her back was turned. Her gaze travelled along the encircling wall. She couldn't shake off the feeling that she was being spied on. Still watching the trees, she sank to her knees, then slowly lowered her eyes to the ground. Peering at a shallow angle, she made out Marriot's footprint. Close to it there appeared to be another impression that took her palm with space to spare.

She stood up, not moving, conscious of the deep-brewed silence and her thudding heart. A trickle of sweat ran into her eyes but she didn't blink it away. Insect motes danced in a shaft of sunlight. A bird tolled in the distance. The sounds only amplified the stillness. Braced against invisible threat, Candy again surveyed the edges of the clearing. On all sides the trees caged her in.

One step at a time, she began to move, letting instinct guide her. She scanned the ground, alert to anything that might flicker into the corner of her vision. A bird flying overhead made her lunge with fright. She found no footprints, no sign that Marriot had come this way except for a slight disturbance that might have been made by something dragged through the litter.

It led towards a dense screen of ferns and saplings. Candy's blood tingled as she drew close. Ten yards short, she balked, senses straining. All she could hear was the buzzing of flies – a drowsy, sated sound. Dry of mouth, she peered through bars of shade and sunlight.

Tiger.

Its image leapt from the thicket in her mind where it had been crouching ever since she'd arrived on the island. Only a tiger could have killed Marriot and carried him away.

It wouldn't have carried him far. It might be watching her right this moment. She might be staring back into its unblinking eyes.

Candy backed away, keeping her gaze turned towards the thicket even when she could no longer see it. She passed the lean-to and kept going. She was nearly out of the clearing when she remembered the compass.

The compass! Without it she was done for.

What steeled her to go back was the awful knowledge that the tiger would have gorged itself and wouldn't need to hunt again for several days. Provided she didn't blunder into it, it had no reason to attack. She searched all around the shelter and then, mustering every fibre of will, worked towards the thicket. Marriot had carried the compass on a cord around his neck. It would still be with him – with what remained of him.

Inch by inch she edged closer. Again the soothing drone warned of imminent menace. She took another step and the buzzing hardened angrily. Her legs began to quake.

Fear shook her like an ague. She couldn't do it. She couldn't go in there.

Fighting the urge to bolt, she retreated to the lean-to. When her nerves had settled, she faced a simple decision – go on or return. Without the compass, either way was hit or miss. She looked inland. Whoever had made this camp must have come from a village fairly close, possibly within a day's walk. The swamp seemed to end here, and further on she might pick up a trail.

Her eyes fell on the cassette player and again its superficial glitter flashed an alarm. Whoever had owned it would have had relatives, and when he didn't return, they would have searched for him. They were natives of the forest, skilled trackers, and yet they hadn't found the camp.

Going on was out of the question; the mangroves were the only course open to her. Her navigation didn't have to be spot-on. Provided she took even the faintest approximation of the right direction, she should strike the coast within sight of the island

She squinted at the sun. It was almost directly overhead and its path wasn't immediately obvious. She stuck a twig in the earth and waited for its shadow to creep. When she was sure of her orientation, she turned her back on everything else. All she had to do was sight on three trees in a line and keep repeating the process until she struck the coast.

She took a last look around. Years might pass before anyone else came to this spot, and by then the forest would have grown back and obliterated any sign that anyone had been here. Twisting Marriot's hat in her hands, she tried to commit his resting place to lasting memory.

'Goodbye, Robert.'

Within minutes of leaving, Candy's confidence began to waver. One false step, one wrong turn, was all it would take to lose her bearings, and once lost there were no landmarks to put her right. Even in the desert there was a horizon to aim for and a sky to steer by. Down here there were walls for horizons and the light jostled in the canopy without giving away its source.

She kept a look-out for some trace of her passage and from time to time looked back, trying to decode the jungle sounds.

Since childhood, tigers had been her favourite predator. She had seen her first wild one on a forest road in Malaysia, ambling in front of the Land Rover, tail switching contemptuously, shoulders rolling as if on oiled bearings. When the driver blew his horn, it had turned and opened its mouth in a silent snarl. Safe in the vehicle, her thirteen-year-old self had experienced a thrill that was almost sexual.

Mud sucked at her feet and she nearly went over. She was beginning to flag and she pushed tigers into the back of her mind, keeping her concentration for what mattered.

She stuck at it for what seemed like a couple of hours, but when she stopped, she found she'd been going no more than forty minutes. Though her stomach was still in revolt, she forced herself to eat. No sooner had the food settled than cramps doubled her over. A wave of vertigo swamped her. She seized a branch and hung on until the nausea passed. It left her sweating unnaturally and very weak. Minutes later her insides turned to liquid and she hardly had time to squat before it squirted out. Flies convened as if all evolutionary history had primed them for this moment.

Too exhausted to feel revulsion, Candy hauled herself upright and shakily fed pills down her throat. Knowing dehydration was the greatest threat, she drank as much as she felt her stomach would accept. Then she checked to see how much time she'd lost.

None. The hands were frozen. She tried to dismiss the breakdown. Clocktime was meaningless here. Looking up into the splintered light, she guessed she had about two hours of daylight left.

She glanced around to orientate herself and frowned. Strange, she thought, blinking in another direction. Her eyes slid from side to side and her heart began to pound. She whirled and searched wildly behind her. Back and forth she turned in growing stupefaction. She fingered her throat. She hadn't a clue which way she was facing.

'Now your arse is really against the wall.'

Back-tracking didn't help. The swamp had absorbed her steps without trace and she ended up more confused than ever. She leaned her head against a tree and tried to think what to do. Her brain was inert. The trees were still, motionless down to the smallest leaf. Time itself had stopped.

'You can't sit here all day.'

Still she waited, stagnating. Her thoughts began to wander. Hearing a sad cry, she fancied it was part of a memory from the island. It grew clearer and her face tilted up as she recognized the haunting call of the fish eagle that patrolled the inner lagoon. Shaking the dizziness from her head, she tracked its course.

After the bird had faded out, she aligned herself to its flight path, but made no move to follow. The eagle might have been returning inland or it might be a bird of passage. This was her last decision, her last chance, and she was afraid to commit herself.

A sigh escaped her. 'Oh, what does it matter?'

Her legs carried her forward again. Depleted in spirit as well as body, she made poor progress, sometimes covering only a few yards before running out of steam. She had a horror that some malign instinct was drawing her back to the clearing. She fell and didn't care what she was falling into. One of her leggings came undone and she couldn't summon the energy to take it off or lace it up. She fell again, struggled to her feet and stood staring blankly ahead.

'Well, Candy, what are we going to do?'

She swayed, sick and faint, and laughed in astonishment at her weakness.

'Well, Candy,' she heard herself say again, 'what are we going to do?'

Apathy settled on her. She wasn't going to get out. She would flounder in circles until she dropped. None of the other survivors would search for her. Each day she was away would count as a day nearer their own release, until the fifth day and the doubts started. By then she would be dead. Josef, too. And Robert. And the pilot whose name she always had to hunt for. Sixt, that was it. Sixt was his name and he had two girls under ten and a boy aged thirteen. Josef's wife was expecting their first baby at Christmas. If it was a girl they were going to call her Lotte; if it was a boy they hadn't decided between Martin and Klaus. Josef preferred Klaus, but his wife wanted to call him Martin, after her grandfather.

Candy came to her senses with a start. 'Get a grip,' she told herself. 'You're not dead yet.'

Only an hour or so of daylight remained and surely she could keep going that long. Even if she had to spend another night in the swamp, it wouldn't be the end of the world. She drained her bottle. From now on she'd have to rely on purified swamp water.

'Right, Candy. One last push.'

She tried, she really did, but her effort was aimless, her vision so fuzzy that she felt she was treading water in a feverish sea of green. Her face was ablaze and her head felt as if would burst. She had heat-stroke and worse. She had stopped sweating.

There was no shortage of water, all poisonous. At the first puddle, she parted the surface scum, submerged the bottle and dosed the contents with chlorine tabs. Twenty minutes she was supposed to wait, but she didn't have time. The light was running low. She took a sip and immediately spat it out and tried to rub the taste from her mouth. Vile. Not just brackish, but stingingly salty. Undrinkable

Despair engulfed her. It was too late to find another source, and without water she didn't think she would last the night. Her mouth trembled. Utterly beaten down, she began to cry – spasmodic gulps like the hiccups of a fuel-starved engine.

When her crying petered out, fatalism settled on her. 'All right,' she muttered. 'All right.'

She began to pour away the water, then stopped, her brow creasing. She stared at the bottle. Her throat bobbed. She took another taste and this time she didn't spit it out.

Seawater! Water that briny must mean she was very near the lagoon. But which way? She cast around. It seemed to her that the light in one sector was subtly different. She felt her way towards it, hands outstretched as if she was playing blind man's buff. She blinked as a light breeze touched her and in one step she was in a gap, tottering, holding one hand up to fend off the giddy sky. Between the trees stretched a taut line of tropic horizon.

There was no island, but it had to be close, hidden behind the mangroves that reached out on each side. Between them the water grew deeper, sometimes reaching her waist. With the recklessness of desperation she plunged on.

At last she cleared the mangrove headland and saw the island no more than a mile up the coast. How beautiful it looked, how serene and pure, the highest trees illuminated like parasols in the last slant of sun. But more beautiful still was the inflatable glowing like a marigold.

It was about quarter of a mile away, going back. She flailed forward and cried out, but her voice was cracked and hoarse. Frantically, she began to wave. After a minute she saw the rower stop. Hope streaked through her. It was Jay, she was sure of it. A surge of gratitude rose. He had come looking for her. He hadn't forgotten her. She waved again and saw him resume rowing. Yes!

She kept her arm raised and waited for the boat to turn her way. She waited, and slowly her arm began to drop. The boat was going on, straight back to the island. Jay hadn't seen her. Steadily, the boat drew away. In silent anguish, she watched its profile shorten as it rounded the point.

Then it disappeared.

A great lump of disappointment filled her throat. Tears stung her eyes. So close, so heart-breakingly close. If only she hadn't wasted so much time. If only she'd got here ten minutes earlier. If only luck had been with her.

She became conscious of her situation, standing up to her midriff in putrid water, surrounded by tidal flats swarming with tiny lifeforms. The nearest trees were forty yards away and were little more than aquatic shrubs, but she had no choice. Already the light had lifted from the island.

Crushed in mind and body, she began wading for a mangrove islet. By the time she'd found a perch, sea and sky were dissolving in a haze of grey and silver. The breeze fell to nothing and blackness ridged the horizon, then the day died and the island was a clear contour under a starry sky. Candy didn't waste her breath calling. Even by day the survivors rarely visited the inner lagoon, and never by night. If Jay didn't return tomorrow, she would have to swim for it, crocodiles or no crocodiles.

There was no room to sit or even crouch. Slumped upright, she hung on. A half-moon slid clear of the forest horizon and lit up a thousand pairs of crab eyes. Candy could hear their pincers scraping. On the water margin a larger animal screeched and thrashed, its throes continuing for a long time. Candy's skin puckered. Mouth pressed to the crook of her arm, she stared into the cavern of her imagination and saw the tiger, glowing like a hot coal.

19

Solitude weighed heavy on Boucher. Having only himself for company wasn't his style or habit. As he ate, he was aware of how primitive he must look — gripping the half-cooked turtle flesh in both hands, jawbones working savagely, staring ahead like an ape. From time to time he stopped in mid-chew and his eyes were drawn behind him. Moon and stars were out, slicing the forest into sharp-leafed silhouette and wells of shadow. The trees were full of nervous whispers. Occasionally, his hand strayed towards the pistol.

All day he had been jumpy, anticipating a raid by the Ecos. They hadn't come, and he didn't think Jaeger would order a night attack, but Disco, though ... Candy's going changed nothing. It wasn't over between Disco and him. Again, he glanced into the forest, remembering Disco boasting about how he'd crept up on him the night he'd fallen asleep on look-out duty. It had been a warning, a declaration of violent intent that had scared him then and scared him even more now. The man was deranged, capable of anything.

Anything?

Boucher sat still, waiting for the voice of reason to overrule his fears, but it was silent. Reason didn't rule here; the unthinkable was free to express itself. It would be easy to get away with murder on this island. Disco could kill him as he slept, drag his body into the forest, and who could say what might have happened? The others probably wouldn't even find his body.

Hairs prickling, Boucher set down his meal, picked up the pistol and altered his position so he could cover any approach from the forest. He couldn't go on like this, he knew, with only fear to take up the slack. No one to talk to, no light to read or write by. Dead time. With glum longing he looked towards the other end of the island, where tonight the Ecos had built a fire large enough to be ceremonial. They had been working on the look-out and seemed to be celebrating. Shadows fluttered across the flames and a sound that might have been drumming trembled the air.

Bored and restless, Boucher mooched down to the lagoon and studied the faint red flush from the oil flares. Just over the horizon, people were watching television, taking showers, shooting pool. Sighing, Boucher tipped his face to the stars. They crowded so densely that parts of the sky were whited out, yet the closest neighbours were light years apart.

In his mind, Boucher strummed a few blues chords.

Apart from the isolation and the strain of living under threat, he was losing copy. He had written himself out of the script. There was nothing for it but to make his peace with the Ecos. Duty required it, and also common sense. Better to be where he could keep his eye on Disco than live every hour imagining when and where he might strike. Yeah, he'd be safer with the others, but he wasn't going to grovel. Pride demanded that he remain outcast for another night.

Again his attention was caught by some stray jungle cadence. 'Be not afeared,' he told himself, 'the isle is full of weird shit.'

The moon had turned the beach into a silver freeway. In the grip of impulse, Boucher strolled to the southern point. Moonlight lay on the polished water and the fireflies' synchronized light-show was in full swing. Boucher studied the black frieze of the mangrove coast, not imagining for a moment that Marriot and Candy were on it. Twice that day he'd paddled into the inner lagoon, the last time shortly before sunset, leaving only when the water between the trees exhaled a dark breath.

His shout was a token effort, pitched at a volume aimed more at avoiding denting the peace than attracting attention.

Seconds later an echo floated back. Odd, he thought. He would have expected the swamp to soak up sounds like a sponge. He tried again, and again his voice returned, from down the coast. When his next shout faded into nothing, he was relieved. Just to make sure, he called twice more.

Slowly the tension went out of him. Nobody there.

Back at camp, he gave Fieser another shot of morphine and felt angry that he was hanging on when there was nothing left to save.

Afterwards, lying on his bed, he fell into bitter-sweet memories. He'd imagined that as Candy's presence faded, his infatuation would grow tepid, but the memories of her had lodged deep – her vigorous smile, her limber walk. He had her preserved in his memory down to the smallest detail – the curve of her belly, the habit she had when tired of brushing the curls up from the back of her head to expose her neck.

Sleep eluded him. The echo played on his nerves. First there had been one, then there hadn't. Maybe some ape mimic had been mocking him, he thought, turning his head to a gust of laughter floating from the Ecos' camp. He lay back and tried to imagine where Candy might be right now.

Shit!

Boucher flung aside his net before realizing that the only way to put his mind at rest was to row down the coast. He'd never ventured on to the lagoon at night and the idea of being alone out there gave him the willies. It made him think of the Styx, a one-way crossing.

And he was the ferryman who'd landed Candy on the other side.

He got into the boat and pushed off. The water shone like bitumen. Rowing close inshore, he pictured the eel, still unblinking, patient as the grave. In some indefinable way, the moray reminded him of Disco – like Disco was *meant*, had always been there, waiting for their paths to cross.

Boucher's extremities began to tingle, but only because he had cleared the island and floating on the lagoon was like creeping over the skin of an animal. The tide was low and the mudbanks lay frosted by the moon. He gave them a wide berth and paddled as softly as he could.

His nerve ran out when he looked back and saw the island sunk low behind him. Pulling his oars in, he waited for his senses to attune themselves. Small creatures were moving on the flats. He cleared his throat.

'Anyone out there?'

Something went *plop*. His head snapped around and his heart beat double time.

'Hello?'

The tide gurgled in the roots.

'Hi!' he shouted, feeling incredibly foolish.

At an answering cry, he convulsed, nearly knocking an oar overboard. Unmistakably a human voice, further down the coast, too faint to identify. Emotions tumbled over each other – shock, elation, disappointment, relief, dread.

At his next call the response was so feeble he only just

picked it up, and when he called again he was met by silence. Grabbing his oars, he began paddling. Mudbanks closed around him, parted and converged again. His eyes probed the mangrove corridors. It was black as hell in there.

He nosed into mud and had to pole back into deeper water.

'I have to go round,' he called. 'Where are you?'

He caught a whisper that might have come from anywhere. His eyes darted among the leaf-shadows, conjuring up hoary figures.

'You have to tell me where you are.'

Quite distinct, a voice said: 'I'm over here.'

Staring, he made out a face like a paper lantern against the shade of a mangrove brake. His heart turned over.

'Candy? Candy, is that you?'

'Hello, Jay,' she mumbled.

His heart rose up in joy. He uttered a tremulous laugh. 'Christ, Candy, what the hell are you doing here?'

'I'm afraid I'm stuck.'

He dug in the oars and snagged comprehensively.

'Candy, this is as close as I can get. Can you reach me?'

He interpreted her sob as a *no*. She was making another noise that he couldn't identify. It scared him.

'Okay, I'll come to you.'

He threw his legs over and his breath caught in his windpipe as he sank deep in sediment. Holding out his arms for balance, he felt his way over roots and a whole lot of bad shit. Every step released a gust of rotten eggs. His mouth set in a rictus, tensed for the jolt of an electric eel or the barbed lash of a sting ray. He thought of the bacilli entering the fresh wound in his leg.

The noise he could hear was Candy's teeth chattering. She was clinging to a tree like a sailor lashed to the mainmast, and he knew she was in a parlous way. Mud smothered her and at first he thought that accounted for her misshapen appearance, but when he peered close he saw her face was swollen and one eye had disappeared.

'Jesus,' he breathed, 'what the ...?' He broke off and peered beyond her. 'Where's Marriot?'

'Dead,' she whispered.

Numbness encased him. Marriot was the jungle expert. He couldn't be dead.

'But ...'

She gave a croak that translated into a plea for water. Devastated, he realized he hadn't brought any. He reached up his arms. 'It's not far. Can you make it to the boat?'

Unaided, she couldn't get down off the roots. He had to support most of her weight as they floundered back. It occurred to him that the row they were making sounded like an animal in distress, and at the rate they were moving, any crocodile within half a mile could have reached them before they made the boat. He tipped her inboard as if she was a sack and then wrestled the inflatable free. He dived in and began to row with all his might.

Candy tried to speak. Boucher thought he caught Josef's name.

'He's clinging on. I got the medicines from the airship, but it isn't going to make a difference. And Trigg's run out on me. It's just us now.' His voice broke. He was on the verge of tears. 'God, Candy, I'm so glad you're back.'

Her head lolled and he was frightened stiff.

'Don't die on me,' he pleaded.

She looked like she was knocking at death's door. It had to be something critical – snake-bite or forest pestilence. Glancing over his shoulder, he sighted on the island and pulled until his arms burned in their sockets.

He hit the beach and dragged her bodily from the boat.

She tried to walk, her feet slurring on the sand, and when he got her to her sleeping platform, her legs caved. She drew herself into a ball, her body in spasm. Boucher felt her forehead and hissed.

He ran for water, cupped her head in his hands and held the vessel to her mouth. Most of it spilled out, but from the painful working of her throat, he knew some of it was getting down. When she had taken enough she rolled her head.

'Cold,' she said.

The fire was nearly out. Boucher ripped several pages from his notebook, twisted them into brands and blew them into flame. He fed the embers with driftwood, then ripped more pages out, dipped the torch into the fire and raised it to Candy's face.

His lips spread back. Her face was bloated like an over-ripe fruit, one eye a mere slit and the other completely sealed. There were bites everywhere. The torch scorched his fingers. He lit another and moved it down her body. She'd lost one of her leggings. He pulled up the cuff of her pants and his hand went to his mouth. Her leg, all he could see of it and more, seemed to be branded by cigarette burns.

'Oh fuck,' he moaned.

She gave no sign that she'd heard him.

He swallowed. 'Candy, I have to clean you up.'

While the water was heating, he rummaged clumsily through the medicine chest. When he'd assembled every-thing, he reached for her belt buckle. At his touch she moaned and her fingers fluttered at his hand.

'This is no fucking time for modesty.'

He stripped her naked, section by section. First he rinsed her in seawater. When he'd removed as much filth as he could, he washed her with soap and fresh water, paying clinical attention to the intimate areas. After drying her as best he could, he applied antiseptic to every bite and scratch he could find. There were dozens – hundreds. Then he dusted her from head to toe with sulphonamide powder, using almost the whole container. It wasn't enough, he knew. Her sickness was systemic. He forced pharmaceuticals down her throat – antihistamines, penicillin, salt, aspirin.

Then he waited, knuckles in his mouth, not daring to turn his eyes from her in case the next time he looked she was gone. The night drew on. A flight of shooting stars snuffed out.

'Jay?'

He sprang forward, but her eyes were closed. He grabbed for her wrist and his eyes squeezed tight in relief as he found the pulse. It was fast but strong, and her breathing, though rapid, seemed to be steadying. He took her temperature again. Still sky-high. He pressed a damp cloth to her forehead.

For the next two hours, he watched over her, swabbing her brow. It broke his heart to see her like this. He shouldn't have let her go. If he really cherished her, he would have taken care of Disco. Inside him, rage and self-loathing grew like a tumour.

Some time later he became aware that one of Candy's eyes had opened. He bent cautiously.

'Are you awake?'

'Grotty,' she said in a thick voice. 'Thirsty. Feel sick.'

When he brought water, she tried to struggle into a sitting position. He cradled her shoulders. After drinking, she fell back, her face on one side.

'I must look so awful.'

Boucher took heart from this gesture of self-consciousness. 'Are you up to talking?'

She didn't answer for a while. She seemed to have gone under again. Then she sighed. 'Get everyone here.'

Alarm ignited. 'Candy, you're real sick. I'm not going to leave you.'

'If I'm going to die,' she said, 'they'd better know what happened.'

'You're not going to die, dammit. I won't let you.'

She pushed him feebly. 'I know I'm not,' she said, matter-of-fact, 'so get a move on.'

The Ecos were still partying, but if Boucher had been expecting a scene of bacchanalia, he was disappointed. True, Aquila was naked and Jaeger as good as, but their dance was sedate, liturgical, Aquila shimmying in a trance and her consort shuffling like a dancing bear that hasn't mastered the steps. Rhythm was provided by Bartok beating a makeshift drum, and Dexter was chanting. On all of them was the sheen of religious fervour. Nadine remained unmoved, smoking a cigarette, examining a piece of paper as if it were a laundry list. Disco was leaning against a tree, his eyes giving back the firelight.

Master of the dance, Boucher thought.

At his entrance, Aquila drew back and moved closer to Jaeger, who pulled her behind him and seemed to expand to meet the threat.

'It's only Jay,' Dexter said, up on his feet.

Jaeger peered defectively. 'You could get yourself hurt sneaking up like that.'

'Feeling lonesome?' Disco called.

Boucher made it short. 'Candy's back. Marriot didn't make it.'

They looked from one to other. Trigg spoke first, his voice squeaky with disbelief. 'Dead? You're saying he's dead?'

'I don't know how. Candy's in a bad way.'

They moved forward as one, bumping into each other like cattle. Boucher led the way. He could hear them

241

murmuring behind him, nobody saying a word outright. As they passed Fieser's sickbed, everybody made a diversion and Nadine furtively raised her hand to her nose.

Candy had relapsed and seemed confused and frightened by the faces gaping down at her. The Ecos drew intakes of breath and shook their heads pityingly. Disco stood back. Aquila knelt by Candy's side and took her hand.

'Oh you poor thing,' she sobbed. 'Whatever happened to you? Where's Robert?'

Candy spoke between laboured breaths. 'Got dark. Went ahead. Blew twice – tell me he'd found a place. Trying to reach him. Terrible noise. Didn't call again.'

'What kind of terrible noise?' Jaeger asked gently.

'Gibbons, birds. Terrified.'

'What did you do?'

'Too dark. Stayed in the swamp. Found a camp. A shelter. Robert been there.' Candy began to fiddle with her sack. 'Hat.'

Boucher, unsettled by Candy's disjointed utterances, fished out Marriot's bush hat.

Jaeger's brows knitted. 'At a camp, you say?'

'Empty.' Candy gave a bemused laugh. 'Found a cassette player. With a tape. And cooking pot. Flip-flop – not Robert's.'

Unable to follow Candy's thread, Boucher grew increasingly worried.

'A cassette player?' Trigg said, hope springing. 'He must have been picked up by the locals.'

Candy's head rocked from side to side.

Jaeger bent closer. 'Candy, are you saying they killed him?'

'Nobody there. Only us.'

Jaeger swayed back on his heels and looked blankly at his tribe. 'Who lives in that jungle anyway?'

Disco shrugged. 'Maybe head-hunters.'

'Head-hunters?' Nadine yelped. 'In *this* day and age? Head-hunters with cassette players?'

Candy rolled her head in frustration. 'Not people. Camp deserted ages.'

Trigg broke the silence. 'Then what makes you so sure Robert's dead?'

'Animal. Found print. Blurry. Must have been tiger.'

Sensing the dubious glances, Boucher intervened. 'Okay, you can see Candy's not up to being interrogated. Let's leave it for tonight.'

Trigg's manner was brutal. 'If you couldn't identify it, how do you know it was a fucking tiger?'

'In the forest. Carried him away.'

'You found his body?'

'Too scared. Frightened.'

'You didn't see the tiger or the body?'

Candy cringed. 'Flies.'

Jaeger turned and raised an eyebrow. Disco delivered his verdict.

'Without a body, we can't be certain Marriot's dead. He could be lost in the swamp.'

'Wouldn't have thrown his hat away.' Candy's voice was colourless. 'Wouldn't have left me.'

'That's enough,' Boucher said, pushing himself between Candy and the Ecos. 'She can't be expected to remember all the detail. It'll come back.'

Trigg walked away a few steps and faced the forest. 'Robert's still in there,' he said, voice trembling. 'We ought to send a search party. I'll volunteer.'

Boucher's distress vaulted into anger. '*You?* You couldn't even wait half a day before scuttling off. Suppose Robert had been stuck on the other side of the lagoon.

Where were *you?*' Boucher's rage spilt out on all of them. 'Where were *any* of you?'

Trigg shrank back. Only Disco met Boucher's eye.

'I saw this coming,' he said. 'I told Robert not to go.'

'And me,' Jaeger added. 'You all heard me tell him there was no necessity and the risks were too high.' He swivelled, blinking stupidly. 'What's so funny?'

Candy's laughter turned Boucher's blood cold. She stopped laughing, and though everyone stared expectantly, she didn't say anything.

Disco wandered forward. 'If she's right about the village, there's got to be a trail. A way in and a way out.' He put his face close to Candy's. 'You're sure about this village?'

'Camp.'

'Yeah, camp, village. Whatever. Think you could find it again?'

Candy shrank away. 'Not going.'

'Get away from her,' Boucher snapped, pulling Disco back.

Disco brushed his arm away and resumed speaking in a steady voice. 'Because if we could reach it, establish it as a base, we could search systematically. Eventually we'd hit a trail, find a village.'

Candy began to strive on her pallet, the words refusing to come. 'You couldn't ... You have no idea. You couldn't ...' Her voice trailed away.

Everyone seemed to forget her. 'It's not all doom,' Jaeger said. 'Now we know there are people within a few miles. People who carry radio cassettes.'

Candy's little tremor turned their heads. 'All dead,' she mumbled.

'All? Who's dead?'

'Killed Robert. Killed the people in the camp as well.'

20

Day 9

Bathed in amber mist, Candy walked through pale phallic groves that grew out of water. Everything sparkled – the gem-tipped leaves, the filigreed spiders' webs, the flies. She could hear Robert crying out. One of the flies flew towards her. The mote grew larger and she saw it was a tiger, panting – a mangy bald creature with the face of a malevolent child and stiletto teeth.

Horror jerked her to the surface, but consciousness was just an extension of delirium. Smothered in hot filth, she gazed up from the bottom of a well.

'Jay!' she cried. 'Jay!'

A shape superimposed itself on the dark. Hands seized her thrashing arms.

'It's all right, Candy. It's all right. Only a dream, a nasty fever dream.' He held her, making gentling noises.

'I thought you'd gone,' she sobbed.

'Me? Hell, no. I'm right beside you.'

Her wits seemed to be floating around her. She couldn't put one thought in front of another. 'I can't remember anything. How long have I been here?'

'Only a few hours. Rest now. I won't leave you.'

She felt something cool laid on her forehead. 'What's the time?'

Boucher's arm moved. 'Coming up to five. Not long till dawn.'

Outside seemed very black to Candy. There could be anything out there. Even the proximity of Boucher didn't provide sufficient reassurance. 'Can we have a fire?'

'Sure.' There was a pause. 'I'll have to collect some wood. Won't be long.'

'No!' she cried as his hand left her. 'Stay there. Stay where I can feel you.' She gripped his arm in both hands.

He slipped it round her. 'Here I am. Nothing's going to harm you.'

She sank back and clutched her forehead. 'I feel crazed.'

'You're pretty ill. Rest is what you need.'

He fell quiet and the silence grew so that it seemed the more immediate presence.

'Josef, is he ...?'

'No. He's drugged with morphine. I got it from the airship.'

'That was brave.'

'It didn't feel like it at the time.'

'That's twice you've saved me.'

'Ah, hell. Tomorrow you'd have come out of the lagoon like a mermaid.'

'Some mermaid.'

He squeezed her shoulder. 'Just shut up, Candy.'

Later, she sensed he was asleep. She could hear his breathing, but she couldn't be certain it was him. Perhaps in the dark, another presence had stolen up on her.

'Jay?'

He twitched and made a sucking noise. 'Huh?'

'You don't have to sit out there. There's room for both of us.'

'I'm fine.'

'I'm scared.'

He crawled in and fitted himself in awkward congruence. She burrowed close and smelt soap and clean sweat.

'How have you been?' she asked, her voice smothered by his chest.

'Lousy.' He gave a husky laugh. 'I was beginning to talk to myself.'

'I was so scared.' She lay wide-eyed against him. 'So scared.'

Soon after sunrise the fever veils lifted and Candy sank into deep sleep. She woke confused to a sky the colour of violets. When she moved her head, the world spun blue, but she knew the worst had passed.

Watching Boucher as he took her temperature, she saw how drawn he'd become, his eyes polar grey in the tan. He'd ripped off the torn sleeve of his jacket and he was still wearing his silly tie.

'Last night,' Candy said. 'Was I delirious?'

'A bit vocal, yeah. How's memory lane today?'

She tried to think back. 'I can remember you rescuing me, and then ...' She shook her head. 'Nothing until I woke in the dark and ...' Her hand darted to her mouth. 'Oh God, I'm sorry. It must have been a hideously uncomfortable night.'

'Torrid. You were burning up.' He took out the thermometer and squinted at the gauge. He raised an eyebrow. 'Amazing. Only a degree above normal. Guess it takes a lot to kill you.'

'My father says I've got the constitution of a horse.' Candy frowned. 'I don't know why people say that. Most of the horses I've known got sick at the drop of a hat.'

'Can you face eating? I made some turtle soup.'

Queasiness returned, and with it the foetid smell that had invaded her dreams. 'Josef ...' she began.

Boucher shook his head in warning. 'Not long now.'

A great burden of sadness descended on Candy. 'I've let everyone down.'

Fever returned in the evening and she passed another racked few hours. By morning her temperature had sunk again, and in the afternoon she felt well enough to get up and wash. Walking was an activity she had to learn all over again.

Halfway back to the camp, a horrid thought invaded her, fixing her to the spot. Seeing her stranded, Boucher hurried over. He peered closely into her eyes.

'What if I was wrong?' she whispered, staring down the beach. 'What if Robert's not dead?'

Gently, Boucher took her arm. 'Come on.'

Her gaze remained pinned to the southern end of the island. 'Do you mind if we go down there?'

'Disco and Trigg have been round the other side a couple of times. It's been three days, Candy. Robert's not coming back.'

'I want to take a look,' Candy said, her voice small. 'Would you come with me?'

Reluctantly, he nodded.

On the way he asked her to go over her story. As she explained, she discerned doubts from his fractional hesitations and mute nods. Her own belief in what had happened hadn't really weakened, but she needed to see the mangroves for confirmation.

At the sight of them, her voice petered out. Gazing at that endless line of battlements, she was appalled by her temerity in thinking she could ever have found a way through, shocked by the knowledge – the guilt – that she had been the foolhardy one, and Marriot had paid the price.

Her eyes panned along the bays of shadow. Imagining topaz eyes boring out at her, she couldn't control a shiver.

Boucher, standing one pace behind her, like someone lending moral support to a mourner, placed his hands on her shoulders.

'I'm all right,' she told him. 'Just a touch of the heebie-jeebies.'

'I know. Imagination works overtime here.'

She glanced at him and then looked away. 'You don't believe me, do you? None of you do. You think Robert and I got separated and I panicked and invented the tiger as an excuse.'

'Hey,' Boucher said, turning her round. 'One thing I know for sure. You're not the running-away type. If you say there was a tiger, that's good enough for me.'

Candy faced the mangrove barrier again, thinking of the things in the swamp she had seen or half-seen or sensed. 'It was very close to me, Jay. It was watching me.'

'Why didn't it kill you?'

'It wasn't hungry.'

Boucher filled his cheeks and let the breath go slowly. 'Tell me about tigers.'

Candy checked to see if he was trying to humour her. Apparently he wasn't. 'They're the ultimate land predator. Apart from us, of course, and we've reduced their population to less than ten thousand. On Sumatra there are probably fewer than five hundred.'

'Lousy luck for Robert to run into one.'

'Where we were is ideal tiger territory. They have huge ranges.'

'I've only seen one in a zoo. It was the sheer size that impressed me.'

'Up to five hundred pounds and ten feet from nose to tail. The Sumatran race is smaller, but small doesn't mean cuddly. A leopard is only half the size and one of them killed 120 people before it was shot.'

'What makes them turn man-eater?'

'Normally they avoid people, but once they lose their innate fear, no one is safe. Humans are easy meat.'

'Easy meat,' Boucher repeated. He moved his tongue around his cheek and his eyes ranged over the lagoon. 'They can swim, can't they?'

'Yes, but this one won't come through the swamp. There isn't any suitable prey.'

He gave an off-centre smile. 'There is now.'

Fighting clear of this thought, Candy steered her eyes south, trying to locate the spot where Boucher had found her.

'I saw you at sunset, leaving. What made you come back?'

'I guess I must have heard you calling out.'

Puzzled, Candy shook her head. 'I didn't. I couldn't. Not after dark.'

'Then I guess some superior power guided me.'

'I thought you didn't believe in divine intervention.'

'Even if I did, I can't call on it because I haven't taken out a subscription.' He smiled at her. 'In any case, I was thinking of a different power.'

Recognizing what it was from the light of his eyes, she nestled against him. It felt right. 'How can I ever repay you, Jay?'

'Having you back's enough.'

Feeling safe in his arms, Candy was filled by a sense of her own unworthiness. 'I don't deserve it. By rights, it should have been me who was killed.'

'Now, now,' he murmured, stroking the nape of her neck.

They stayed like that, resting against each other, until twilight had begun to settle and the gibbons were staking out their territories. The march of shadows across the water made Candy stir from Boucher's arms. She didn't want to be caught out here by night.

On the way back, she sensed from Boucher's silence that he had something on his mind and it wasn't her. 'Something's bothering you,' she said.

He didn't answer for a moment. 'I've been thinking about our situation – you and me and Josef. I need to catch fish for food, but I don't want to leave you alone, and we can't both be away from camp. We're too exposed. It's up to you, Candy, but I think we have to grit our teeth and join up with the others again.'

He was worried about his story, Candy knew. 'Of course,' she said without hesitation. 'These last few days, looking after two invalids, must have worn you out.'

Boucher stopped and made sure he had her eye. 'You needn't worry about Disco.' His expression was as solemn as an oath. 'Take my word.'

She nodded and was quiet for a while. 'We'll go,' she said at last. 'But not just yet.'

They both knew she meant they would return when Josef died.

Day 11

Three mornings after her rescue, Candy woke ravenous, her temperature normal, her system clear. The day was an uplifting one, clear and less humid than usual. She took a dip in the lagoon, staying in the nursery area close to the shore. Paddling lazily on her back, she looked at Boucher stationed on the beach like a lifeguard, eyes patrolling anxiously.

'Nothing's going to attack me,' she called. 'If you want to keep an eye on me, why don't you come in?'

He peeled off and ran whooping until the water took away his legs and he fell full length. They sported like kids, splashing each other, playing tag. And then they waded further out and explored what Marriot called a 'bommie' – a table-topped coral outcrop where fish fry darted in unison among the undulating fronds.

Boucher pointed at a weed-covered piece of coral rubble. 'See that?'

When Candy reached out, Boucher snatched her hand back. 'No!' he cried. Thoroughly alarmed, he wiped his face with his forearm. 'It's a stonefish. Marriot told me it's the deadliest thing on the reef. One jab from those spines and you'll die insane.'

Candy saw now that the lump was animate – a warty, mottled-brown fish armed with a jagged row of dorsal spines.

She turned away and forgot deadly things, struck dumb by the beauty of the island. From this perspective, all the separate elements could be seen – the bright acrylic bands of blue, the massed greens under blinding white cloud towers.

'It's everyone's dream island.'

'It's ours.'

Turning as he turned, she reached for him as he reached out for her.

They kissed.

Hand in hand they walked back to the camp. The air was perfumed. In her hair, Candy wore an orange flower presented to her by Boucher.

She smiled at her feet. 'This is so slushy.'

He grinned. 'Isn't it great?'

Suddenly Candy was sad, remembering youth, the time of hope, when every chance was a chance to change the world. Only a few years gone, but already irreclaimable. She knew the feeling that had invaded her heart wouldn't last. It couldn't. She couldn't let it. In the real world, she and Jay could never be together, and it was to the real world they would return. Apart from anything else, he had this cellist woman. She wanted him, but she wouldn't give in to short-term desire.

With a lover's alertness to emotional nuance, Boucher sensed something was wrong. He stopped.

She squeezed his hand. 'This is only temporary. I don't want you to ...'

He closed her lips with his. When he drew away, she couldn't remember what it was she had been about to say.

'A temporary situation,' he reminded her.

Candy took his hand and swung it energetically. 'Then we'd better make the most of it.'

Before retiring, Candy dabbed perfume at strategic locations. Boucher had drawn his pallet up next to hers and was already lying on it. In the dark she could sense him watching her. When she lay down, his hand stole out and rested on her elbow. She waited on tenterhooks, worrying about the lack of contraception, but he made no move one way or the other. After a while, concluding that she was going to have to take the initiative, she moved up closer. His arms enfolded her.

'That's more like it.'

Still he took it no further. Her passion was whetted and she wondered what was wrong. Running her fingertips down his belly, she was relieved to encounter proof positive of desire.

'Take no notice,' he murmured.

'It's hard to ignore.'

'I don't want to force things. You're still a convalescent.'

Her lips feathered his ear. 'What are the most compelling biological urges?'

'Watching television, drinking cold beer, driving a sixty-seven Mustang down ...'

She squeezed, hard.

'Ouch,' he cried. 'Sex.'

'No,' she said, 'Food is.' She guided his hand. 'But we've had our supper.'

Several minutes later she gasped and pushed him away. 'Jay,' she said, 'would you mind taking your tie off? It's like being fucked by a waiter.'

'I'm not fucking you. I'm making love.'

'I don't care. It still tickles.'

She didn't come. She rarely did. But she wobbled on the brink and she thought, next time ... Next time seemed a foregone conclusion. She laid her head on his chest. 'I knew we'd end up like this.'

'Then why did you make me suffer so long?'

'A woman's prerogative.'

'Of course. Silly me.'

She kept her eyes open in the dark. 'Thank you, Jay. For everything.'

'My pleasure.'

Still tingling, Candy kissed him. 'Not entirely. Not at all entirely.'

21

'Strangers!' Bartok shouted from his treetop perch.

Boucher shaded his eyes from the sun. 'Ah, chrissakes, Kent, grow up.'

'Leo said to warn him if anyone came near.'

'Do we look like strangers?' Candy called.

'I couldn't think what to call you.'

'How about Candy and Jay?'

'They're constructing a separate reality,' Boucher growled. 'Next, they'll be issuing passwords, badges of rank, the whole arcana.'

Construction work had continued apace. Some kind of hut had been erected and out of it stepped Jaeger and Aquila. He had stripped off the last remnants of civilized dress and was wearing a loin cloth. He looked like a Visigoth with bad sunburn. Beside him, Aquila was similarly undressed; her nakedness was natural, hieratic. She had lost weight and her eyes were large against her pallor.

Disco and the others drifted in from several points and stopped at an invisible line. Candy tightened her grip on Boucher's arm.

'Don't lose your temper.'

'Things have got to be said.'

This morning the Ecos seemed out of sorts, bleary-eyed and pale. Even Disco's poise was ruffled.

'Well, well,' was all he said.

Boucher addressed Jaeger. 'When Josef dies, we want to come back.'

Disco laughed.

Jaeger put his face close to Boucher's, as if he was peering through a tiny aperture. 'Why?'

'We need each other. We're all in the same boat.'

Jaeger drew back with a judicial nod. 'You know the conditions for returning.'

'I've got two of my own,' Boucher told him.

Disco smirked. 'You're in no position.'

Jaeger raised his hand. 'Before we get to that, how about admitting what you pulled out of the airship.'

'Another medicine chest. It's for the community. There's morphine and more antibiotics.'

'Is there any Lomotil or anything?' Nadine quavered. She had hacked her beautiful hair short, and her complexion was blotchy. A sore marred the corner of her mouth and her upper lip was beaded with sweat.

'I'll bring you something,' Candy promised.

'These conditions,' Jaeger said to Boucher.

'First, we go on catching fish.'

'We've found fruits and berries,' Aquila said. 'There's no need to kill fish.'

'Yes there is,' Nadine said. 'Those berries we ate were poisonous. From now on, me and Dexter are going to eat fish, same as Candy.' Nadine pointed, almost in tears. 'Three days ago she was positively dying, and look at her now. She's *glowing*.'

'What's the second thing?' Jaeger asked.

'Disco tried to rape Candy. You're the leader. I want you to make sure he keeps away from her.'

Disco uttered an astonished laugh.

Jaeger rubbed his nose with the back of his hand. 'You want to say something about that, Disco?'

'Sure,' he said, relaxing. 'What this is about, me and Kent were having some innocent fun, nude bathing, and we ran into Candy on our territory. Well, we didn't make a fuss about that. In fact we invited her to join us and she took it wrong.' Disco held up a hand as if admitting guilt. 'Okay, maybe it was too strong for her, but hell, this is Eden, ain't it, and a man can go naked in Eden if he wants.'

'That's crap,' Boucher said. He turned on Bartok. 'You were there. Tell them what happened. Tell the truth.'

Bartok avoided all eyes. 'Like Disco says, we were just fooling about and Candy misunderstood our intentions.'

'Liar,' Candy said.

'Cool it,' Jaeger told her.

'Candy's English,' Disco added with satisfaction. 'I guess she's not used to a show of hot blood.' He appealed to the others. 'If I'd come on to her like she says, do you think they'd be begging us to take them back?' Encouraged by their nods, Disco looked coldly at Boucher. 'I think it's us ought to be worried.'

'How's that?' Jaeger demanded.

'Ask yourselves why he wants to come back. I'll tell you. It's so he can get back to writing about us. He's playing God, putting us down in his judgement book. And I know what his judgement's gonna be. First off, he's gonna slander me as a rapist.' Disco pointed at Bartok. 'Kent, he's gonna accuse you of being a God-fearing hypocrite. Leo and Aquila – he's got you down as a pair of crazies who care more about bats than humans. Trigg, you're condemned as a sodomite and coward. Dexter, he's gonna say your biggest live performance was a real let-down. Nadine ...' Disco left a silence, inviting his audience to catalogue Nadine's deficiencies for themselves. 'Playing God, I'm telling you.'

Boucher was rattled. 'So what does that make you?'

Disco spread his hands. 'I'm the spirit of reason, man.'

Boucher pulled loose from Candy's hold. 'You're a fucking psycho.'

'You hear that?' Disco said with satisfaction. 'You hear that? There ain't one thing Jay won't stoop at, and that's how he's going to deal with all of you.'

'Defame me,' Nadine said, 'and I'll sue the ass off you.'

'It isn't right,' Dexter agreed. 'Some bad things have happened here, and I don't want them getting out.'

'No way of stopping it,' Disco said. 'Jay's got all your reputations on the line.'

From the intensity of their silence, Boucher knew what poisonous seeds Disco had planted in their minds.

Jaeger stuck out his hand. 'Show us what you've written.'

Boucher carried the notebook in his pocket, with the bullet. He handed it over.

Too blind to read it himself, Jaeger passed the book to Aquila, who opened it, shrugged, and handed it on to Disco. He riffled the pages from end to end, then looked up sharply. 'There's nothing here.'

Boucher removed the book from his hand and put it back in his pocket. For a moment Disco looked thwarted, then he grinned and nodded, and tapped his head.

It was an acknowledgement, a challenge. No limit poker. And that's when Boucher knew that only one of them would get off the island. He knew it in the same way Candy had sensed the tiger – an electric charge on his skin that worked into his gut and lodged.

'You can come back,' Jaeger was saying. 'You know the rules. You know what happens to those who break them.'

'We won't give you any trouble,' Boucher said, thinking of the pistol.

On the way back, he didn't speak.

'You're very moody,' Candy said.

Boucher had been listening to a monstrous little voice in his head. Kill him, it said. Kill him before he kills you.

That evening, Candy suggested they play *Desert Island Discs*. She was amazed to discover Boucher had never heard of it.

'You choose ten records,' she explained, 'and between each choice you say something about what it means to you. It's potted biography to music.'

Boucher took to the game enthusiastically. Listening to Candy's life story, he had to acknowledge how different their backgrounds and lifestyles were. That didn't bother him. But Candy's taste in music was a letdown. Really dire.

'Vivaldi's *Four Seasons*,' he protested. 'No, no, you can't. I won't allow it.'

'I like it,' she insisted, her mouth setting in stubborn lines. 'I know it's clichéd, but it evokes the countryside perfectly. *My* countryside. Not Illinois or wherever it is you live.'

'It evokes low-fat spreads and photo-copiers and sanitary products. It's the ultimate all-purpose jingle. Look, even if you do dig it, you mustn't admit it. It's like going on to a foodie show and boasting that your favourite meal is peanut butter and jello sandwiches.'

A hint of steel showed in her eyes. 'If it's true, why not admit it? Anyway,' she said, mounting a counter-attack, 'how do I know *your* selection isn't rubbish? I've never heard of these people. I mean, Billie Cage. Who's he?'

'*She*. She's a jazz-rock guitarist. Highly tuned to the *zeitgeist*.'

'Hum some.'

Boucher had quite a true and melodic voice.

'Huh,' Candy said sulkily. 'Give me Vivaldi any day.' She put her nose in the air. 'The truth is, we haven't got a thing in common.'

'I know,' he said, mock despondent, cupping one breast. 'It's tragic.'

She slapped his hand down. 'We haven't finished. You still haven't decided on your one item of luxury.'

'Anything I want?'

'Provided it's impractical.'

His hand slid to her plush slickness. 'I've already got it,' he said. 'What about you?'

She stifled a moan. 'I can't think.'

Boucher was surprised by her avidity – thrilled but surprised. He had expected she would need a long arousing.

'You see,' he said afterwards, 'two hearts that beat as one.'

She looked at him through half-closed eyes. 'No wonder you're always so pleased with yourself.'

'Decided on that luxury item yet?'

'Not an ironing board.'

But Boucher didn't catch what she said. Some discordant sound had intruded. He raised himself on one elbow. 'I thought I heard something.'

Candy's voice was drowsy. 'I didn't.'

'Sort of like a scraping.'

'Branches rubbing together.'

'No wind.' Boucher waited a moment. 'Must have been Josef.' He began to rise, but Candy pulled him back.

'My turn,' she said through a yawn.

After she'd crawled out, Boucher closed his eyes and gave thanks for all his blessings.

'Jay.'

Something in her voice turned all his thoughts to ice. 'Is he ... dead?'

'Gone.'

In his drawn-out sigh, Boucher heard grief and relief mingle – grief for another life lost, relief that it wasn't only Josef's suffering that was ended. 'I'll give you a hand.'

'I mean he's *gone*!' Candy's face suddenly appeared out of the dark. 'The tiger must have taken him.'

22

They huddled close and spoke in disconnected whispers, breaking off at every external sound.

'We can't cower here all night,' Boucher muttered.

'That's exactly what we have to do. We'll never find his body in the dark, and if we did, we'd find the tiger, too.'

'You're certain that's what got him?'

Candy spoke through her teeth. 'How many times ...?'

'Okay, okay.'

They were taking out their terrors on each other. Only an hour ago, Candy thought, they had been so close, melting into each other, oblivious to the tiger dragging Fieser away. It seemed like a judgement on her lust.

She tried to find something to brace on, but inside her was a morass. Her mind refused to concentrate. 'I don't know what we're going to do. I just don't know.'

'The tiger's going to go on killing — is that it?'

'There's no reason for it to stop.'

Boucher punched the ground. 'This is a nightmare!'

For his sake, Candy tried to damp down her despair. 'Things won't look so hopeless in daylight.'

After a few moments of stillness, he gave a hollow laugh. 'At least you've been proved right.'

Candy had a sensation like starting down in a lift. 'They'll say I brought the tiger. They'll say it's my fault.'

Boucher didn't overrule her. Instead, he gripped her by the arm. 'There's no authority on this island, no cohesion. With the tiger here, I think we'll see some serious personality slippage. From now on, things could degenerate very fast. You and me are going to have to stick together, because there's no one else to trust.' He mantled over her. 'I'll bring us out safe, Candy. Say you trust me.'

She gave his cheek a perfunctory touch. 'I trust you.'

Dawn was a long time coming. Every time Candy began to doze, some movement on Boucher's part would set her off. They were feeding off each other's nerves. By the time the cicadas began their scraping, Candy was frazzled. The sea glimmer paled, its blackness fading into the grey of the sky. And then the ridge of the world turned silver and the sun lifted up, blood-red and huge.

When it was half-clear of the horizon, they emerged, rubbing their arms and grimacing at nothing. It was if they were ashamed to meet each other's eye. Candy inspected Fieser's bed. It offered no clues and the surrounding sand was too fine to hold an impression.

'He couldn't have felt anything,' Boucher said.

Candy began to make her way up the beach. At the treeline she stopped.

'Don't go in there.'

Fleshy leaves nodded in a light breeze. Behind her the waves made a gentle seething. She nodded. 'We'd better warn the others first.'

They kept the width of the beach between themselves and the forest and monitored its border constantly. About halfway to the Ecos' camp, a solitary figure came wavering through the heat haze. From under the brim of her hand, Candy recognized Aquila.

'You tell her. I'll wait here.'

While Boucher broke the news, Candy observed the forest. Everything looked so fresh, so full of new life.

Butterflies flirted in spears of light and a bird sang so carefree that Candy's chest tightened with the onset of tears. So beautiful, so transient.

Aquila came to her. 'Are you sure?'

'I'm sure.'

Aquila raised her head, apparently watching something recede in the distance. 'I'll get the others.'

Minutes later Jaeger emerged, carrying the parang. Disco followed, holding a spear. Nadine and Dexter were last to appear and hung back until everybody else had departed, and then they came hurrying after. Nobody exchanged a word, not even when they were all gathered round Fieser's deathbed. Disco idly kicked it. They faced the forest, frowning as if it had moved closer in the night.

'In there,' Candy said, pointing at an opening.

'Fan out,' Jaeger ordered, 'but keep close.'

It was the smell that led them to the body, behind a clump of palms less than a hundred yards from the camp. Its corrupt state had apparently been too much for the tiger to stomach. Only one arm had been eaten, and not all of that. What remained of Fieser's leg had burst into suppurating matter, not recognizably human remains or anything else.

Hands masked against the stench, Candy crouched down. Bile rose in her throat. Trying to keep from gagging, she turned Fieser's head. On the base of the skull were deep punctures. She assessed their depth and spread. She noted raking claw marks on one shoulder.

'A tiger,' she said, 'without doubt.'

The others stood glassy-eyed, hands pressed to their faces like figures from some medieval tableau.

'In some ways it's a mercy,' Aquila said.

Boucher stumbled aside and was violently sick.

Flies were already busy on the corpse.

'What do we do with it?' Dexter asked through spread fingers.

'Bury him,' Boucher said, wiping his mouth.

'Leave it, man,' Trigg blurted. 'While the tiger's got something to eat, it won't come after the rest of us.'

'That's Josef you're talking about,' Candy told him. 'We'll bury him at sea. It's what he wanted.'

Four of them performed the funeral rites – Candy, Boucher, Jaeger and Bartok. They paddled through the tidal passage and stopped over the drop-off zone, where the sharks cruised. On the beach the watchers were incised on the sand. Forest and sea were clearly demarcated. Low over the waves flew a flock of pelicans, strung out like a line from an undeciphered script.

'"And there shall be no more death,"' Bartok recited as Jaeger and Boucher tipped Fieser's body over, '"neither sorrow, nor crying, neither shall there be any more pain."'

'Amen,' said the others.

Down into the deep the body slipped. Looking straight up, Candy spied through her tears birds of prey like pinholes in the sky. They were probably always there, but she had never looked so high before.

'Are we done here?' Jaeger asked.

'We're done.'

Ranged in a circle, they held council. The mood was fractious, like a dog-fight about to happen, and Candy decided to let the others vent their tempers before speaking.

Disco scratched his head and inspected his fingernails. 'I guess you brought the tiger back with you.'

Candy caught Boucher's eye.

'Maybe it wasn't a tiger,' Nadine suggested, lacing and

unlacing her hands. 'Who knows what lives in the swamp?'

'Tigers have incisors three inches long,' Boucher said to the ground. 'They can leap thirty feet and carry a bullock over an eight-foot stockade.' He raised his eyes. 'We don't need to invent monsters.'

'Someone spell out what this means,' Dexter said.

'It means we're all in mortal danger,' Nadine cried. 'That animal took Josef right from under Jay's and Candy's noses.'

'Tigers kill the weak and defenceless,' Bartok said. 'Nobody could have been weaker than Josef. I mean, it didn't touch Candy or Jay and they were only a few yards away.'

'It took Robert,' Trigg cried. 'And he was no five-stone wimp.'

'Until a couple of hours ago, you swore blind there was no tiger.'

'I changed my mind.'

'We don't know it's the same tiger,' Jaeger said. 'Robert disappeared on the mainland, miles away.'

'Tigers can swim,' Nadine said. 'I've seen it on television.'

Disco shrugged. 'Same animal or different, it's here.'

'Okay,' Jaeger said, 'assume we're sharing our island with a tiger. It's not such a big deal. People have been co-existing with tigers for hundreds of thousands of years.'

'And I bet a lot of them got eaten.'

'You're over-reacting.'

'What!'

'Look, if we'd left some meat out there and the tiger had taken it, we wouldn't be getting so worked up. It's a terrible thing to say, but that's all Josef was. Meat.'

'That *is* a terrible thing to say.'

'It's the truth.'

Boucher addressed Aquila. 'Why so silent?'

She hadn't uttered a word since they'd found Fieser's body. Then, she had been as distraught as anyone. Now, though, her huge onyx eyes were calm, radiant with some significance known only to her.

'There is a tiger on the island, but it wasn't Candy who brought it here. It's our spirit guide. We mustn't interfere with it.'

Even Jaeger was startled.

'That's great,' Nadine sobbed. 'A fucking supernatural tiger.'

'Get real,' Trigg told Aquila.

She passed her hand in front of his face. 'Reality isn't confined to what's in front of your eyes.'

There was a concerted howl of derision.

'Whether you believe me or not, your fear doesn't outweigh the tiger's right to live.'

'Oh, dandy. It's got the right to kill us and we do nothing about it.'

'It won't kill us.'

'Wanna test that?' Nadine shrieked, pointing erratically at the trees. 'Go take a walk.'

'I'm not frightened.'

'Well I am,' Dexter shouted, 'and I won't stop being shit-scared until the tiger's dead.'

'We can't kill it,' Jaeger said. During the exchanges, his eyes had darted about like a fire-fighter looking for sites of conflagration.

'Leo's right,' Bartok said. 'We don't have weapons.'

'I don't mean that,' Jaeger said. He pointed at the flag. 'Look. We're Wildguard. The tiger is our symbol.'

'This is how religions start,' Boucher said. 'Start off saying something's sacred and end up offering sacrifices to it.'

'Imagine what the world would say if we killed a tiger.'

'Who gives a fuck what the world says?' Trigg shouted. 'Three of us are dead. How many more have to die?'

'It won't kill any more,' Aquila said.

'You're an expert, are you?' Nadine shouted.

'Candy is,' Boucher said, 'and you'd better listen to what she has to tell you.'

Trigg slammed his hand down. 'The fucking thing's only here because of her.' His face was congested with hatred. 'She's a jinx.'

'You shut your mouth,' Boucher snarled.

As eyes targeted her, Candy felt the blood leave her face.

'I think it's the same tiger that killed Robert. I suspect it also killed whoever made the camp. That makes it a confirmed man-eater – a creature that knows humans are easy prey. It's four days since it took Robert and it didn't eat much of Josef. It's probably hungry.'

'Kill it. Just fucking kill it.'

'We haven't got the means.' Candy glanced at the spear planted by Disco. 'Get close enough to use that and you're already dead.'

'We could trap it,' Dexter suggested excitedly. 'Make a cage and lure it in.'

'We haven't got a bait.'

Dead ends confronted them. Passions seemed to run into the sand.

'This is turning into a real bad trip,' Dexter said eventually. 'I say we bale out. Pile into the raft and find another island. Or try making it to the rig.'

'Quit now,' Nadine agreed. 'This momento.'

'The tiger won't harm us,' Aquila insisted. 'It's here to protect us.'

'Buy that and you'll buy anything.'

'Please be sensible,' Candy begged. 'This is a natural killer. You saw what it did to Josef. We're all soft targets.'

'I know you're scared,' Aquila said in a kindly voice. 'That's only natural. I was scared too at first.'

Reasoning with her was like struggling through quicksand. Candy appealed to Jaeger. 'It's fight or flight,' she said, 'and since we can't kill it, running away is our only chance.'

Jaeger showed irresolution. Aquila took his hand.

'We're not leaving.'

Jaeger nodded. 'We're not leaving.'

'Do what you like,' Nadine said, rising. 'Dexter, get our things.'

'*No one* leaves,' Jaeger said. 'Candy and Robert tried it and look what happened.'

'This is different. The danger's on our doorstep now. We're not safe in our beds.'

'No one leaves,' Jaeger repeated. 'We're gonna see this through, and you'll be glad you did.'

'You can't stop us going.'

A vein fattened in Jaeger's temple. 'Don't try me.'

There was a slow circling of eyes. Dexter scrambled up. 'Stop us and Wildguard can kiss goodbye to my support.' He whipped his shades off, revealing his eyes for the first time since Candy had known him. They were a commonplace grey. 'Shit! Live or die, my involvement with Wildguard is over. This isn't a conservation group; it's a therapy support programme for two.'

'Close up,' Jaeger said, 'people can be real disappointing.' Parang in hand, he rose. 'Try taking the boat and I'll cut it to ribbons.'

'Leave the boat alone,' Boucher said tiredly. 'It's a nonstarter. Half its buoyancy's gone. It'll hold five maximum, and even then it's a death-trap in anything except a dead calm.'

'Leo,' Candy said sharply, 'you're supposed to be

responsible for our safety. That's why we agreed to you being leader.'

'I'm doing what I know is right.'

'The truth is,' Boucher said, 'reality's overtaken you and you haven't got the courage to face it.'

'Want to test my courage, Jay?'

Nadine beat her fists in a violent tattoo.

Again, passion seemed to burn out.

'It's only a dumb animal,' Bartok said at last. 'We can outsmart it if we put our heads together.'

'Make masks from the airship fabric,' Candy said. 'Wear them on the back of your heads.'

Trigg gave an incredulous laugh. 'And say *boo*? What kind of protection is that?'

'Tigers rarely attack from the front. Even deer and wild pigs have defensive weapons. Nine times out of ten, tigers stalk from behind. It's a proven fact that masks deter them.'

'Is that it?' Trigg demanded. 'Wear a fucking mask and keep our fingers crossed.'

'Stay out of the forest as much as possible. Dawn and dusk are the most dangerous times.' Candy scanned the perimeter. 'We should also put some masks around the camp and keep a fire burning at night. The most important thing is never to do anything alone. I mean anything – washing, going to the lavatory, *anything*. Stay in pairs, preferably more.'

'If we can't go into the forest,' Bartok pointed out, 'we can't collect food or wood.'

'Any chance that the tiger could attack me in the boat?' Boucher asked.

'Not in open water,' Candy said.

'Then you're going to see a lot of fish on the menu.'

'I'm not afraid to go into the forest,' Aquila said.

270

For a moment, Jaeger hesitated – only an instant. 'Nor me.'

Candy gave it one final try. 'No one doubts your commitment, Aquila, but this time you're taking it too far. The tiger will kill you.'

Aquila smiled at her. 'Not if we don't harm it.'

'Live and let live,' Boucher snorted, 'the New Age law of the jungle.'

Aquila regarded him equably. 'You can sneer at my beliefs, Jay, but you won't be able to say I gave up on them.'

Boucher laughed dismally. 'While I'm alive, I'll keep a straight record – obituaries included.'

Once the immediate edge was off their fear, the threat galvanized them and drew them together. That, Candy supposed, was what had helped kick-start civilization, cavemen banding together against the megafauna, until such time as non-human threats had been contained and people began to look for enemies closer to home.

Aquila and Jaeger didn't join in the mask-making, but Candy sensed that Jaeger was severely shaken. As their dream of living in harmony with nature disintegrated, Aquila seemed to retreat further into it, leaving blind Jaeger clinging on to her conviction.

Candy's mask showed a conventional snarling face. Nadine revealed a real talent for caricature, creating in eyeliner and lipstick an instantly recognizable portrait of a supermodel rival famous for her tantrums.

'If you dislike her so much,' Candy asked, 'aren't you inviting trouble?'

'She's such a skinny, poisonous bitch, the tiger will take one look and go elsewhere for a meal.'

Candy eyed Boucher's effort. 'Who's that supposed to be?'

He grinned up. 'Clarence Tusser – an ultra-right-wing congressman who commands a lot of support even among those electors he'd like to see shot, castrated or chemically subdued. I don't know about tigers, but he scares the shit out of *me*.'

Disco held his mask up. He hadn't drawn a face – only an eye.

23

Life went on in a tied-down sort of way. The survivors built a communal hut and retreated into it each evening before the sun was off the forest. Once inside, they barricaded the entrance with thorns and didn't come out again until full light. Prisoners of nature, they couldn't relieve themselves unaccompanied, and because no one dared go more than a few yards, the surroundings became fouled and insanitary.

By day they were stalked by fear; at night it besieged them. Candy and Boucher slept side by side amid the sounds of digestive disorders, grinding teeth and muttering nightmares. Understandably, sexual desire had ceased to be a possibility. Boucher was very withdrawn and Candy put it down to tiredness. He spent most of the day fishing – a necessity with the extra mouths to feed. Some days there was barely enough to go round. All of them had grown thin, but more worrying than the threat of starvation was the general deterioration in health. Even with the medicines Boucher had recovered, they were beginning to get low on drugs. They were running out of other basics, too – matches, water purifiers, soap. Their clothes were rotting and falling apart.

Each day, while Candy mouldered with the others at the camp, Aquila and Jaeger went foraging in the forest.

And every day they returned unharmed with fruits and leaves. Their diet didn't seem to be a healthy one. Aquila had lost weight, but the more she wasted, the larger and more luminous grew her eyes. She seemed to have been elected to some higher state of awareness.

Twice, ships trailed smoke at a huge distance.

One blustery afternoon, Jaeger casually let slip that they'd found a bees' nest.

'Something sweet,' Nadine sighed. 'That's what I crave.' Food fantasies had become a tedious staple of conversation.

'You're not plundering my bees,' Aquila told her.

'Don't you even eat honey?' Candy asked.

'Certainly not.'

In the corner, Trigg began to laugh. It wasn't controlled laughter. 'Robert's dead. The pilots are dead. I'm so scared, I can't even take a leak without pissing down my leg.' He dashed tears from his eyes. 'And you're telling me I can't eat honey.'

Jaeger shook his head. 'You couldn't reach the nest anyway. Even Kent couldn't climb this tree.'

'That's irrelevant,' Aquila said.

A stirring in the corner drew everyone's attention to Disco.

'Sounds like there's not much that isn't forbidden. Leaving's forbidden. Eating meat's forbidden. And now even the bees get better consideration than we do.' Disco looked up from under his long lashes. 'Are you trying to kill us, man? Because I ain't no martyr.'

This was the first time Disco had said anything critical of the Wildguard leadership, and Candy sensed his withdrawal of allegiance was some kind of turning point. In the wake of his complaint, a sullen silence spread.

Jaeger rubbed the bridge of his nose. 'Listen, Disco, we ...'

'No, man, you listen to me. You and Aquila may think this island is heaven on earth, but for the rest of us, it's more like the other place.'

An ugly mutter of assent rose.

Jaeger gave way. 'A man's got a right to eat,' he told Aquila, his voice almost wheedling. 'I say we let them take some honey if they can get to it.'

Seeing the force of feeling marshalled against her, Aquila lifted her head in regal disdain. 'You're not worthy of this island.'

Disco looked about enquiringly. 'Feel like risking it?'

'I dunno,' Dexter said. 'I guess not.'

'It's been three days since Josef was took. I reckon the tiger's gone back to the mainland.'

'That's a very dangerous assumption,' Candy warned.

'Leo and Aquila have been out there every day and it hasn't bothered them. How about it, Kent? An unclimbable tree. How can you refuse the challenge?'

'Where is it?'

'Not far,' Jaeger admitted.

Disco rose. 'Hell, let's take a look. We've got a rope.'

Candy was puzzled. 'I never noticed you being so keen on going into the forest.'

'I'm climbing the walls in here. If our ancestors had acted as chicken as us, we'd still be living in caves. There are nine of us. If we stay together, that tiger's not going to come near.'

'I agree it's all or none,' Candy said.

'Count me out,' Nadine said.

'I'm not feeling too hot,' Trigg said.

'Stay then,' Disco told them, 'and mind you look after each other.'

On reflection, after weighing the security each other represented, Nadine and Trigg decided to go with the majority. Only Boucher, out fishing, was absent.

'Bees sting,' Candy pointed out.

'Kent can make a veil from a mosquito net,' Dexter said, surprising everyone with his practicality. 'We can use a smudge pot to smoke them out.'

'Honey for tea,' Candy said, in a fit of daftness.

A hundred feet overhead, the wind poured through the gaps in the canopy. Down below, the expedition jostled in a tight little pack, everyone trying to avoid being first or last – especially last. Candy found herself reflecting on the geometry of the selfish herd. Superficially, their crowding together looked like mutual defence – all for one and one for all. Looked at another way, though, it was every man for himself, each individual using the others as a shield.

They were all reflexes.

Walking in one direction, apparently facing another, they made a bizarre spectacle. All of them carried spears or, in Dexter's case, a bow. Candy was armed with a spear; it might not have offered much protection, but the feel of it gave her some reassurance. Bartok was carrying the rope looped over his shoulder.

The wind plucking on their nerves had worn their enthusiasm thin by the time Aquila and Jaeger halted, deeper in the forest than Candy had anticipated.

Head thrown back, Jaeger pointed. 'I told you.'

Up and up soared the slim trunk, appearing to dwindle to a point before spreading into the crown. The nest formed a pendulous comb under one of the main branches. Candy stroked the bole. It was as smooth as vinyl.

'What does the human fly say?' Disco asked.

Bartok's nose puckered. 'Leo's right.'

'What about the rope?' Disco said.

Bartok shook his head. 'At least thirty foot short, and

276

there's no way of tying it to the branch unless I'm already up there.'

'Aw, hell,' Disco said. 'We come all this way. Don't go disappointing me.'

Candy glanced at a mesh of vines draped from a nearby tree, then at Dexter's bow. 'We could use creepers to lengthen the rope, then tie some fishing line to one end and shoot it over the branch.'

'Should have thought of that earlier,' Trigg said. 'Anyone feel like going back for the line?'

'I'll go,' Candy said, 'if somone comes with me.'

Everyone else looked away.

'Hell, let's forget it,' Dexter said.

'Wait,' Bartok ordered. He seemed to be performing mental calculations. He ran his hand across the bark, then turned and stared at the vines Candy had pointed out. He walked over and hauled on some of the thinnest creepers, tearing them free.

'Okay,' he said, 'all of you help. I need at least a hundred feet.'

Not sure what he had in mind but glad to be doing something positive, Candy yanked and heaved at the vines until Bartok said they had collected enough. He tied the longest pieces to both ends of the rope until its length was more than trebled, then sat down and began plaiting half a dozen strands into a loop about eighteen inches in diameter.

'What's the idea?' Dexter asked.

'Sling,' Bartok said, and looked up with an angelic smile. 'Don't tell my climbing buddies I used technical aids.'

Slipping the circlet around his ankles, he grasped the tree at shoulder height, spread his legs until the loop was taut, then made a little jump. He stuck, splayed on the trunk like a frog, locked to it by the cutting pressure of the vines. Before committing himself, he made a thorough trial, working round the tree about five feet off the ground. Satisfied that the sling gave him the necessary friction, he jumped down, tied one end of the rope around his waist and began his ascent, moving aloft with a series of squats and push-ups.

Watching him made Candy sick to her stomach. His contact was so tenuous that the slightest slip would have been irrecoverable. Mind over body, she thought, and maybe something more than that, because anyone in their right mind wouldn't have hazarded their life on such a hairline venture.

From time to time she glanced over her shoulder. More than an hour had passed since they'd left camp. The wind in the treetops urged haste.

Once Bartok had passed the halfway point, he moved faster and Candy began to breathe more easily. Gaining the fork leading to the nest, he tied one end of the nylon rope to the branch with a slip knot, leaving the length of creeper hanging down so that he could pull the knot free once he'd regained the ground.

'Why bother with a rope?' Disco shouted up. 'You did fine without it.'

'Coming down isn't the same thing in reverse. Different forces are involved. Besides, it'll save time.'

Veiled in the mosquito net, Bartok sidled towards the comb. Candy thought she could hear angry buzzing.

'Are they stinging?'

'No,' Bartok called, 'but they sure pack a nip.'

Reaching the comb, he leaned over and hacked at it with the parang. Chunks began to rain down – wax and grubs and honey together. The castaways rushed to gather up the booty, almost fighting over it. Candy dipped her finger into a piece and sucked. The honey was dark and tangy, so sweet it burned the palate.

'That's enough,' Aquila cried. 'You've destroyed the nest. Oh, the poor bees!'

'Mmm,' Nadine crooned, syrup plastered round her lips.

Something else came flopping out of the air and Candy instinctively ducked and raised her arm. Across her back fell the rope. She turned and saw Disco, and though she couldn't believe it, her brain instantly made the connection.

'You did that deliberately.'

Disco looked back aghast. 'I didn't touch it. Kent must have tied it wrong.'

'You pulled it loose,' Candy insisted. 'How else could it come free?'

'Are you crazy?' Disco shouted. 'Why would I do a thing like that?' He stared up. 'Hey, Kent, I'm real sorry, man.'

Bartok peered back, his face so small that Candy could only infer his features.

'I left both ends hanging down the same side,' he admitted. 'That was pretty stupid.'

'Is it going to be a problem?' Disco shouted. 'Can you climb down without it?'

'Don't have much choice. Give me a minute to think.' Bartok didn't sound worried.

In the long silence, Candy studied Disco, aware that he knew she was watching him. She hadn't seen him pull the rope down, and there was no reason why he should want to put Bartok in danger. Yet she was convinced he'd done it. He was like an emotionally damaged child who pushes another into a fire, just to see what will happen.

Her companions' minds had concentrated on the tiger. They were bunched up, turning in half-circles to keep all sectors covered.

'Does anyone know Blake's tiger poem?' Trigg asked.

'Some,' Dexter said, and began to recite:

'Tiger Tiger, burning bright,
In the forests of the night;
What immortal hand or eye,
Could frame thy fearful symmetry?'

He shrugged. 'That's as much as I can remember.'
  Aquila took it up.

'In what distant deeps or skies
Burnt the fire of thine eyes?
On what wings dare he aspire?
What the hand, dare seize the fire?

And what shoulder, and what art,
Could twist the sinews of thy heart?
And when thy heart began to beat,
What dread hand? and what dread feet?'

Aquila moved away, addressing the remaining verses to the forest.
  'Stop,' Nadine cried. 'Don't.' She gave a titter. 'It's like you're calling it or something.'
  Aquila turned back, witchy in the olive light.

Tiger! Tiger! burning bright,
In the forests of the night,
What immortal hand or eye,
Dare frame thy awful symmetry?

Branches groaned and palm leaves clattered.
  'You worked through that problem yet?' Disco called to Bartok.
  'Kind of tricky. The tree's swaying a lot. I'm not used to having things move under me. Makes me feel insecure.'
  'Coming down's the easy bit.'
  Bartok laughed. 'Sure, I can be down in about two seconds.' His voice seemed to fade out.
  'What happened to the power of prayer?'

280

Bartok laughed again. 'Not this time, Disco.'

'Well, you're gonna have to make a move, because nobody's coming up after you.'

'Okay,' Bartok said after a minute that seemed like an hour. He spat on his hands and wiped them. 'Here we go.'

Heart in mouth, Candy watched him dangle his legs and feel for purchase. No one spoke. For the moment, fear of the tiger had been pushed into the background. Bartok's movements were slow, geriatric, but they were sure, and they carried him to a level where Candy was sure he had passed the worst. There he stopped, resting, Candy assumed.

One foot extended and felt for a hold. Slowly he transferred his weight to it. It slipped and Candy gasped – a dry sucking sound. Bartok's neck ligaments strained like cables.

'He's gonna fall,' Nadine murmured.

But somehow Bartok clung on, and somehow he found the strength to haul himself back into a more secure stance.

'Whoo,' he said, face pressed to the trunk. 'Nearly lost it that time.'

'You were almost there,' Disco yelled.

'The lower I get, the less grip there is.' Bartok looked down, his face oiled by sweat. 'I'm going to have to go back up.'

The light had turned sallow and the wind had got everyone spooked.

'Getting late,' Disco bawled. 'Tiger's gonna be thinking about supper. You can't come to harm up there, but down here backs are beginning to itch.'

'It's no good. It's gone.'

Candy's eye fell on the bow in Dexter's hand. 'Fetch the fishing line from Jay.'

281

'He's out on the reef. It'll be dusk by the time we get back.'

'Kent may as well stay up there for the night,' Disco told her. 'We'll come back for him in the morning.'

'It was you who got him into this mess,' Candy shouted. 'I thought he was your friend. How can you be so callous?'

'He's in the safest place on the island. It's us who need protection.'

'I'll get the line,' Aquila said.

'I'm going back with you,' Nadine said.

Trigg and Dexter moved to Aquila's side with equal alacrity. Disco joined them.

Candy was beside herself. 'What are you playing at? This expedition was your idea.'

'I'm not playing at anything, honeybun. This is life and death.'

'You can't all leave,' Candy cried, almost stamping her foot.

'You've got Leo,' Trigg pointed out.

'Fat lot of use he is. He can't see.' Candy grabbed Dexter's arm. 'You,' she said. 'It's about time you started pulling your weight.'

'Leave him alone,' Nadine yelled. 'He belongs with me.'

For several seconds the two women wrestled with one of rock's biggest properties.

'Oh, hell,' Dexter said, prizing Nadine's hand loose. 'Candy's right. I ain't contributed much.'

'Let's split,' Disco said. 'We're cutting it fine as it is.'

Still seething, Candy watched them desert.

'Don't mind Nadine,' Dexter told her. 'It isn't easy for her.'

Candy's anger died. 'No,' she agreed. 'Nor for you.' Alone with him, she was tongue-tied. 'I think this is almost the first time I've spoken to you.'

'I don't talk much.'

'I saw one of your concerts once. On television.' Candy paused, seeing an image of thousands of hands out-stretched in ecstatic longing to a tiny spotlit figure. 'It was very impressive.'

'It's only rock 'n' roll.'

Conversation lapsed. Candy registered the slow infill of shadows. She glanced at Jaeger. His eyes were desperately unfocused, incapable of forming a coherent image. She looked at Dexter.

'One blind man is bad enough. You can't possibly see anything from behind those glasses.'

'That's why I'm wearing them.'

Candy plucked them off and saw the real person – scared, like herself. She glanced at her wrist, forgetting she no longer had a watch. Fear wormed deeper.

'What's keeping them?' she muttered.

'Ten minutes to the camp, and another ten to bring Jay in. Half an hour at least.'

Candy gauged the amount of light remaining. It would be touch and go.

'This was a dumb idea,' Dexter muttered.

Candy wasn't sure if he meant the whole enterprise or her insistence on rescuing Bartok.

'Kent, I hope you're keeping a good look-out.'

'I'm all eyes.'

'We're going to tie a line to the rope and shoot it up to you.'

'Got you.'

They had backed against the tree, weapons held ready. Candy was so strung out that when Dexter inadvertently bumped her elbow, she nearly fell over.

'Hey,' Bartok called softly. 'I thought I saw something moving.'

Candy's mouth turned to cotton. 'Where? I can't see where you mean.'

Bartok pointed. 'Heading your way.'

'Holy shit!' Dexter squeaked. 'What do we do?'

'Don't run. Whatever you do, don't run.'

'I can't see,' Jaeger complained.

Every nerve in Candy's body was jumping. She saw the tiger in front of her, rumours of a tiger – shadows.

And then a twig snapped. She stiffened. Leaves slithered and Aquila stood before them – an emanation in the green twilight.

Candy sprang forward. 'Thank goodness! Where are the others?'

'They were scared of being caught by the dark.'

'The bastards,' Candy hissed, 'the bloody bastards.'

Dexter was already busy with the rope and line.

'Keep watching,' Candy called to Bartok.

'Yes, ma'am.'

In a fever of impatience, Candy watched Dexter tie one end of the fishing line to the rope and the other to the butt of the arrow. By the time he was ready, Bartok was just a black blob against the lesser darkness.

Dexter's first shot didn't carry. His second was way off-target and the arrow stuck in a clutter of twigs and had to be teased out. With every mis-aim and recovery, the light was leaking away.

'Leo, Aquila, we're relying on you to watch our backs.'

When Dexter made his third attempt, it was too dark to see where the arrow had gone.

'About fifteen feet out,' Bartok reported, 'over a mess of leaves beneath the branch I'm on. Too far to reach.'

'That's my best shot,' Dexter called. 'I can hardly see to aim.'

'I'll give it a try.'

Bartok hauled himself along the branch. He stopped

284

and leaned down and Candy saw his arm come out and grope full-stretch below.

'Nope.'

'We can't wait any longer.'

'Okay, I've got one last move.'

Candy saw him change position on the branch and then he seemed to fall. As she opened her mouth to scream, he stopped, hanging upside down by his legs. She tried to cram her fist into her mouth.

The silhouette swung up.

'Got it. Someone up there still loves me.'

With cheerful briskness, Bartok hauled up the rope. The rest was a breeze. After making the rope secure, he slid down out of the semi-darkness and let go from a height that would have broken most people's legs. For a moment he remained squatting on the ground, grinning up, brushing bee corpses out of his hair.

'Anxious moments.'

'Don't ever do that again,' Candy said faintly.

'Where did Disco get to?'

'He had better things to do.'

'Well, I'm greatly obliged to you folks. Greatly obliged.'

'Can we go now?' Dexter said politely.

There was barely enough light to see by.

'Stay together,' Candy ordered, leading the way. 'If anyone falls behind, call out.'

Fear drove them faster, turning retreat into rout. Vines lashed out of the dusk. Fronds tore at them. It was like running through a cluttered cave.

'This isn't the way,' Dexter panted.

'It's the quickest way to the beach. The sooner we're out in the open, the safer we'll be.' Candy saw Jaeger blundering alongside, bug-eyed. She threw a hasty look behind. 'Where's Aquila?' She stopped, her heartbeat ragged. 'I told her to stay close.'

'She'll be all right,' Dexter said, so anxious to get out that he was almost running on the spot.

'Oh Christ, why won't she listen?'

Jaeger grimaced. 'You go on. I'll wait for her.'

Dexter was already making off. Candy hesitated only a moment before following. She heard surf. It grew louder and the branches gave way and she staggered onto the beach. Rain spattered her and she held her face up and spread her arms to receive it. Boucher had drawn up the boat ten yards offshore. He leapt out and ran to her. Seeing the relief on his face, she folded over, hands on knees. 'Oh, Jay,' she panted, half laughing, 'look at us.'

Jaeger blundered out and Candy's laughter died in her throat. She took one step towards him.

'Where is she?'

'Close.' He was knuckling his eyes. 'I couldn't see to find her.'

Candy's concern flashed into anger. 'The foolish woman! What's she trying to prove?'

Jaeger looked sickly. 'I'd better go back in there.' He didn't move.

Neither did Candy. There was a limit, and she had reached it.

Jaeger took a breath to settle himself. 'I better go.'

He pushed his way back into the forest. The sound of his clumsy passage faded out, and then Candy heard his voice, calling plaintively through the wind and the sucking of waves.

Bartok was performing a delicate shuffle. 'I got dysentery. It started up the tree.'

'Off you go,' Candy told him, all her attention concentrated on the trees.

Darkness seemed to be sifting down in front of her. The forest had turned solid. Up the beach the others had lit a fire and the wind was tearing rags of flame off it.

'Time we cleared out, too,' Boucher said.

Candy gave her head a fierce little shake. 'We'd better wait for that bloody woman.'

'Any minute, she's going to walk out of there like some Minoan goddess on Prozac. Come on,' Boucher insisted, taking Candy's elbow. 'Nothing's going to happen to her.'

Weakly, Candy let him lead her towards the inflatable.

'In any other age,' she said, 'Aquila would have been a priestess.'

'Or burned as a witch.'

Weariness caught up with Candy. It wasn't just physical tiredness; it was the attrition of living under constant threat. She put her arms round Boucher and leaned on him.

'Jay, take me away. Take me home.'

He stroked her hair. 'I've been thinking about that. Patching the bottom of the boat shouldn't be difficult, and we might be able to restore some flotation. If we could make it ride more ...'

A scream rent the dark. Candy staggered. She heard another noise, muffled and unintelligible, and then Jaeger's terrified voice.

'Aquila! Aquila! Oh, fucking hell, no!'

'The flare gun!' Candy yelled, pushing Boucher and sprinting in the opposite direction. 'The torch! Get everyone else here. Everyone!'

She ran straight at the forest, forcing her way through, following Jaeger's hysterical shouts. He was hacking at a covert, the parang rising and falling in glimmers.

'Leo! Is Aquila in there?'

'I can't get to her!' he screamed.

Risking amputation, Candy grabbed for his arm. It was slippery with blood.

'She's alive,' he said, his voice suddenly compressed. 'I heard her.'

No more than a couple of yards in front of them, the tiger growled – a sound pitched between a purr and a snarl. Candy immediately thought of a cat with a bird. Gooseflesh rose on her arms.

'Make as much noise as possible. Distract it until the others get here.'

Jaeger continued to slash at the thicket. Candy made weird ululations, noises drawn from some primitive vocabulary pre-dating speech. Other sounds approached – war cries and drum beats. They drew nearer. A yellow beam darted among the branches.

'Over here!' Candy cried. 'Bring the torch. Hurry! Hurry!'

She grabbed the light from an anonymous hand and aimed it into the thicket. Its light filtered out into a labyrinth of thorny branches.

A full-throated roar shivered her diaphragm. It was a sound to turn blood to water.

Beside her ear there was a sharp crack and hiss and the forest exploded into blinding photo-negative. Candy shut her eyes. Printed on her retina was the image of the tiger, muzzle rucked back from fangs like tusks, one huge pad pressed down on Aquila's chest.

Around Candy a scuffle had broken out.

'It's gone,' Disco yelled. 'I'm telling you, it's ...'

Another crack and incandescent burst.

'You hit her! You fucking hit Aquila, man!'

Through the hiss and reek of chemical combustion, Candy heard a fatty sizzling and the savoury smell of roasting flesh.

Hands seized her, dragging her back. Blinded, she put up no resistance. Magnesium after-images flared under her eyelids – Aquila's throat torn out, her windpipe laid bare. Rain stung Candy's face but she wasn't aware of it. A terrible noise was coming from her – a deep grunting, '*nghh, nghh,*' like an animal trying to express inexpressible pain.

24

Wind and rain slashed into the forest, tugging the flames this way and that, painting the faces of the survivors and bringing the fright-masks in the trees to life. Branches ground together with a sound that set Boucher's teeth on edge. He took a covert look at his companions. They were sitting head-down, lights out, like survivors of a six-day battle. Candy had her hands splayed over her face, only her eyes showing.

Through the keening of the wind, Boucher heard Jaeger ranting.

Bite the bullet, he told himself, tightening his grip on the pistol. Face the wrath before Jaeger returned. In his crazed state there was no telling what he might do.

'Someone ought to go after him,' Dexter muttered, fidgeting with his feet.

Disco snorted. 'He's way beyond reaching. He'd probably waste you.'

'The tiger could get him.'

'He doesn't give a shit.'

Nadine looked round, her face streaked with dirt and tears. 'He really loved her, didn't he?'

She sounded more frightened than moved. Jaeger's grief scared them all. He hadn't let anyone touch Aquila's body. He had driven them away with curses.

'I never thought it would be her,' Nadine quavered. 'I really believed she was charmed.'

Candy hunched her shoulders. 'The tiger's probably been stalking her for days.'

'That's twice it's killed and not eaten,' Disco said. 'It'll be getting mighty mean.'

'Tigers don't get mean,' Candy answered, from behind her hands.

'Hungry, then. This is one *real* hungry tiger.'

Another gust buffeted the shelter. Sparks flew off the fire in streams.

Nadine snickered. 'I'll huff and I'll puff and I'll blow your house down.'

'Glad someone sees a funny side.'

It turned out Nadine was weeping. 'I was thinking of the tiger taking us one by one and not knowing when it would be my turn.'

Disco's face was featureless in the gloom. 'Who'll be last? I wonder.'

Still Candy didn't look up. 'The way you deserted Kent, I'd say you have a good chance.'

'Go butter your ass. If you'd done like I said and left him in the tree, Aquila would still be alive.'

Lifting the pistol on to his lap, Boucher took loose aim. 'Care to repeat that?'

Disco narrowed his eyes. 'I told Candy to go butter her ass, and seeing as how you and her are such ...' Disco's voice ran out like water going down a plug. Slowly he stiffened. His tongue flickered over his lips. 'Is that what I think it is?'

'It's a pistol. It's pointing at you.'

Disco eased back a little. 'You devious prick.'

Everyone's eyes were raised, Candy's showing above the top of her fingers.

'No need to look at me like that,' Boucher said, his voice

shaking. 'I found it in the wreck and figured there was enough bad feeling floating around without tossing a gun into the equation.'

'You devious prick,' Disco repeated, and laughed in what sounded like admiration.

'But that was nearly a week ago,' Candy said. Her voice rose. 'Day after day we've sat here in fear of our lives, and all the time you had a gun.'

'I was ready to use it.'

'You let us go into the forest,' Candy shouted.

'I didn't know you were going into the forest.'

'And now Aquila's dead,' Disco said. He gave a low whistle. 'Man, Leo's gonna make you pay.'

'The way Candy described it, nothing could have saved Aquila.'

She didn't come to Boucher's defence. 'Trust me, you said. Oh, Jay, is that all you meant by trust?'

Guilt fanned his justification. 'You know what I meant,' he shouted.

'It wasn't Disco who killed Aquila or Josef.'

'I had the pistol right beside me when Josef was taken. What use was it?'

'You didn't even tell *me*!' Candy cried, and turned away in disgust.

The others kept on staring at him, their eyes stone cold, and Boucher knew that without the gun, they would have lynched him.

'You know how to handle that thing?' Disco asked.

'Yes,' Boucher muttered.

'Because guns I'm familiar with.'

'I bet.'

'Let me have a look.'

Boucher brought the pistol up again. 'You stay where you are.'

Disco hoisted his hands. 'Hey, don't be so paranoid.'

'Until we decide what to do, it stays with me.'

Disco subsided. 'You check it works?'

'I fired one round. It works.'

'How many shots?'

'Eight left. It's a 9-millimetre Mauser.'

'Will that stop a tiger?' Dexter asked.

'I'm not sure,' Boucher said. 'I guess ...'

'Depends how close you are,' Disco said decisively. 'Anything further than ten yards and the chances of hitting a vital spot are slim.'

'We're never going to get that close.'

'We could if we had a bait,' Trigg said. 'Maybe we could shoot a monkey.'

'We can't hunt with that thing on the loose,' Disco told him. 'Besides, the only bait it's interested in is us. Sooner or later it's gonna come sniffing round here. If we keep watch and ...'

'Ssh!' Nadine hissed. Her eyes were like bulbs. 'There's something at the door.'

'Speak of the devil,' Disco murmured.

Boucher heard a snuffling.

'Jay, do something!'

Shakily, Boucher raised the pistol. He thought he saw a shadow detach itself from the fire. Thorns scraped. His finger began to close.

'Idiot,' Disco said, rising. 'It's Leo.'

Jaeger staggered in, naked and torn from head to toe. He seemed to fill the shelter. He wasn't the least bit surprised to see a gun pointing at him.

Candy half stood. 'You're covered in blood. Sit down and ...'

'Give me that,' Jaeger said thickly.

Boucher knew the only way he was going to keep hold of the pistol was to shoot him. He had a fraction of a second to make up his mind. Jaeger loomed over him and,

293

confronted by irresistible force, he let go. Immediately, Jaeger returned to the door as if he intended going right back out.

'Jay got it from the wreck and kept it for himself,' Disco said. 'How about that?'

Jaeger looked at the silvery weapon. Then in a movement too fast to see, he was crouching in front of Boucher, grinding the muzzle into his temple. Boucher couldn't speak. He tried, but the words got only halfway up his throat.

'Don't,' Candy cried. 'Jay only kept it because Disco tried to rape me and you did nothing to stop him.'

'Liar,' Disco said.

Jaeger was manic, on a hair-trigger.

Candy jumped up. 'Tell him,' she shouted at Bartok.

Jaeger's mad eyes swung round.

Bartok dropped his head. 'It's true. Disco was going to rape her. I lied.'

Disco's mouth curled. 'You pious little fuck. You would have been right in there after me if she hadn't broken loose.'

The gun was still boring into Boucher's skull, but Jaeger's eyes were on Disco.

'What's the big deal?' Disco said. 'You made the rules. Hell's Angel rules. You saying you never fucked some chick belonging to another biker gang?'

I warned you, said the little voice that had taken up residence in Boucher's head. You should have killed him while you had the chance.

Abruptly, the grinding on his temple was lifted. Jaeger walked to the entrance and peered out. 'What you do to each other doesn't bother me. There's only one thing I'm after.'

Disco nodded. 'We figured the way to do it is wait for

the tiger to show up here. What do you say, Candy? Does that make sense?'

'It won't come into the camp. It doesn't have to. It only has to wait for us to come out.'

'Not if we baited it.'

'We've been through all that,' Dexter said. 'No bait and no way of getting any.'

Disco mused for a few seconds. 'Leo,' he said slowly, 'I'm going to float an idea and I hope you don't take it wrong.'

Jaeger was still manning the entrance as if a tiger attack was imminent. He grunted.

Disco's face was in partial eclipse. 'What,' he enquired, 'have you done with Aquila?'

Nadine pulled at her bottom teeth. 'Oh no, that's foul!'

'She's safe from more harm. I wrapped her and hung her in a tree.'

Boucher dwelt on the image.

'You planning on burying her?' Disco asked.

'I'm gonna give her a Sioux funeral.'

'You want that tiger dead,' Disco said. 'Use Aquila as bait.'

'That's a disgusting suggestion,' Candy blurted.

Disco rounded on her. 'Would it work?' he demanded. He waited for her to answer 'I'm asking, would it work?'

Candy's mouth moved soundlessly for a second. 'It might, but that's not the point.'

'Not the point? I thought the bottom line was killing the tiger before it kills us.' Disco ran his eyes over each person in turn. 'Anyone got a better idea?'

Pair by pair, their eyes dropped.

'So what's your decision, chief?'

Jaeger's eyes were glazed. He nodded.

'So how do we fix it?' Trigg asked.

'Candy?' Boucher said.

She glanced at him and quickly looked away. She was quiet for a few seconds. 'Not here,' she said at last. 'We'll have to place the bait in the forest. Sitting over it in the open would be too dangerous. Whoever volunteers will have to use some kind of cage.'

'A cage is a good idea,' Disco agreed. 'That only leaves who goes inside it.'

'Me,' Jaeger said, still looking into the night.

Disco rubbed his scalp. 'No one's got better reason, but frankly, Leo, you couldn't see an elephant at twenty yards, let alone hit one.'

'I'll be a lot closer than that.'

Disco pulled a face at the other castaways. 'We'll maybe only get one chance.'

'One chance is all I need.'

'At least take someone along as lookout.'

Jaeger didn't answer at first. Finally, he turned and, as Boucher had expected, his gun hand pointed at him. He knew the decision wasn't open to appeal or negotiation. Even Candy made no protest.

'Great reporting opportunity,' Disco told him.

'With you around, a cage is the safest place to be.'

'When will you do it?' Nadine asked in a hushed voice.

Candy answered. 'Tomorrow night. We'll need a day to make a safe hide. Leo and Jay should be inside at least an hour before sunset. If the tiger does come, it probably won't turn up until after dark. The moon's about half-full. You should have enough light.'

'Who's going to protect us while you're gone?' Nadine wanted to know.

Nobody answered.

'Everything's ready,' Candy whispered.

Feeling ill-used and frowzy, Boucher sat up and rubbed his eyes. After yesterday's scudding wind, the day had been one of sweltering heat, the air at saturation point. A thunderstorm had broken the tension around two, spreading violet tracery across clouds the colour of bruised fingernails.

He massaged his cheeks. 'You know why I kept the gun.'

Candy kept her face downcast. 'We've built the cage in a clearing about two hundred yards away. We made it as strong as we could.'

Boucher took her wrist, forcing her to meet his eye. 'Remember what you told me about the principle of natural selection? If an individual possesses some variation useful for survival, it will tend to preserve that individual. That pistol was our profitable variation.'

'A gun isn't a variation of natural selection, and Darwin wasn't talking about humans.'

'Until the tiger came along, it wasn't nature I was worried about.'

Candy sank her teeth into her bottom lip and slowly nodded. 'Leo's waiting.'

The thought of the night to come made Boucher short of breath. 'What have you done with Aquila?'

Candy hesitated. 'She's been prepared.'

'This isn't going to work,' Boucher said, getting to his feet. 'Leo's as blind as a bat. He's just as likely to shoot me as any tiger.'

He went out on to the beach. It was the calm time of day, the sea-mirages gone and the sun declining through pink and lavender strata. A few yards away stood his companions, semi-naked and sombre except for Disco, who greeted him with a slim smile. But it was the sight of Jaeger that arrested him. He'd striped himself with charcoal embers and what remained of Nadine's make-up and he looked as close to a tiger as a man could.

'I'm beginning to find the line between us and what

we're hunting increasingly fuzzy,' Boucher murmured.' He looked down at Candy. 'This is hardly an auspicious moment, but I love you. I thought I'd better let you know while I had a chance.'

Candy straightened his lank tie. 'You'll survive. It's in your nature.' Her kiss grazed his cheek. 'I'll be waiting for you.'

Boucher grinned weakly. 'Feels like I'm going to the office.'

'Let's do it,' Jaeger said.

Stars were out, and in their hoary light Aquila's naked body was visible – a pale smudge about five yards away. Looking past it, Boucher made out waxy highlights on leaves at the edge of the clearing, then beyond that, his gaze ran into the crowded zone of imagination. He eased his legs into a more comfortable position, wincing as nerves stirred back into life. The cage was about four feet square and Jaeger filled most of it.

'I was thinking about the tiger I saw in the zoo,' Boucher murmured, 'pacing back and forth, back and forth. Now look who's behind bars.'

They spoke at random, to keep themselves awake.

'You never understood Aquila, did you?'

'That's a fair conclusion.'

'She knew so much, she was so wise.'

'She was one in a billion, Leo.' Boucher made another survey of the clearing. 'Do you know about her family?'

'Her mother ran off with an actor when she was seven. Her father's had two more wives since then. He's a millionaire – president of a company that makes TV snacks and sauces. Junk food. But himself, he's a real gourmet. Goes bingeing in France. He's joined all these wine societies – Chevalier de this, Chevalier de that. Aquila says he's the grossest human being she ever met.'

'Poor Aquila.'

The night was hot and still, the distant surf whispering like a far-off crowd. Stars jostled in the branches above. Boucher couldn't be sure, but he had a suspicion that small things were stirring around, and even on, Aquila's body. She'd been exposed to the tropical heat for over a day, and the musty fragrance of the jungle and the animally smell of Jaeger was overlain by a more malodorous scent.

Jaeger pressed his face to the slot in the lattice door. 'Come on, you cocksucker.'

Boucher was troubled. 'You know, Leo, I'm sure Aquila wouldn't have taken her death so personal. Revenge on an animal is the last thing she would have wanted.'

'I'm doing it for me.'

'But her life was dedicated to protecting nature. Using her body to bring a tiger close enough to shoot it dead goes against everything she stood for – everything Wildguard stands for.'

Jaeger glared at him. 'He took her away from me.'

'He?' Boucher wasn't sure if he'd missed a link. 'You mean the tiger?'

Jaeger took so long to answer that when he did start speaking again, Boucher thought he must have started down another conversational track.

'We were building a cabin up in the mountains above Goose Creek. Aquila planned for it to be a pagan centre. We were gonna raise a family.'

His revelation raised a sour smile in Boucher. Apparently the world wasn't so crowded that it couldn't accommodate Aquila's children. But of course any child of hers would be an initiate, elect, ecologically sound. Only other people's brats were landfill. Given the fragile state of Jaeger's mind, Boucher expressed no view.

'Kids were important to Aquila. They were gonna be

like a blueprint for the future. Trouble is ...' Jaeger breathed so deep, he expanded to almost fill the cage. 'I ain't told no one else before, but it doesn't matter now.' He gave a bitter laugh. 'My name's Leo. That means lion, right?'

The irony hadn't escaped Boucher. 'Right.'

'Lions can copulate sixty times in a row. You know that?'

'I didn't know that,' Boucher said truthfully, wondering if Jaeger had jumped another track.

'Well, I couldn't manage that,' Jaeger said, 'but I came pretty close.'

'Yeah?'

Jaeger cast a grim look at him. 'Only thing is,' he said, 'I couldn't father kids. I'm infertile. Found out about three months ago.'

Enlightenment dawned. 'You didn't tell Aquila?'

Sadly, Jaeger shook his head. 'I was scared to death of losing her.'

'She'd have found out eventually.'

'I think she knew,' Jaeger said, nodding. He gave Boucher a quick, fierce look. 'Nothing could be hidden from Aquila.'

'I don't see what you being infertile has to do with killing the tiger.'

Jaeger went back to watching the clearing. 'I know you think she was crazy.'

'I think,' Boucher said carefully, 'she functioned in a realm of thought outside my experience.'

From the way Jaeger nodded, he seemed satisfied with this epitaph. 'The first night we were here, she said there was a spirit on the island. Remember? She told me what the spirit was – a male tiger. That was long before the man-eater arrived. She used to go into the forest to be in

300

union with him. That's how she described it to me –
union.'

'You mean, as in sexual union?'

'That's why she let herself be killed. She's gone off with
that tiger. She's a tiger herself now.'

It was the middle of the night and Boucher began to feel
as if his head was floating. 'Leo, if Aquila wants to go off
with a tiger and have cubs, why not call it quits?'

Jaeger looked at him calmly. 'She's mine, Jay. He stole
her and I'm gonna kill him.'

Boucher wished he'd kept his mouth shut. 'Well, if you
want to do that, maybe we ought to keep quiet.'

Tiredness blurred his concentration. In the motionless
air a leaf was spinning on its stalk, and though watching
it made his eyelids heavy, he couldn't keep his eyes off it.
Bit by bit, his head began to nod.

'Something out there,' Jaeger whispered.

Boucher jerked back from the drop with a spastic
shudder. Blinking, he saw that nothing had changed. The
leaf was still spinning. He held his breath. The moon had
ridden into view, its pale radiance fraying through the
green-black leaves, bathing Aquila's body in ghostly
luminescence. She lay staring up and Boucher had the
eerie impression that her body was levitating. His heart
thumped his ribs. A long black shadow was slipping
towards her.

'I see it.'

'Where?'

Glancing, Boucher saw Jaeger's eyes screwed into
points. Irritated as much as scared, he guided Jaeger's gun
hand into approximate aim. 'Creeping up on Aquila.'

'You ready with the light?'

Boucher nodded. He felt a sick excitement.

The shadow glided closer, slinking belly to the ground.
It stopped by the body and raised its head, testing the air,

then hunched over. Boucher heard a faint rending and Aquila's body seemed to jerk. A moment later a soft snarl reverberated down his spine and the shadow reared up with a hiss like escaping steam and looked directly at him, its eyes reflecting gold and green.

Boucher flashed the torch and in the same instant the pistol went off, hideously loud. The shadow pirouetted as if it was disappearing into itself and there was a rapid scuffling on the forest debris.

'Did I get it?' Jaeger shouted, leaping up and almost collapsing the cage around them. 'Did I get it?'

Boucher gasped for breath. 'It wasn't the tiger, Leo. It was a lizard, a big monitor.'

Jaeger fell back. 'But it snarled.'

'I'm telling you, it was a lizard.'

Jaeger was trembling. 'Maybe the tiger will come later.'

The adrenalin in Boucher's blood had turned to acid. 'The tiger's not going to show after that rumpus. And even if it did, you couldn't hit it.'

Muttering to himself, Jaeger settled back into myopic vigilance, squashing Boucher in a corner. It was like being stuck in a cubicle with a mastodon.

Some indeterminate time later a nudge in the ribs brought him instantly alert. Jaeger was blinking like an owl in Aquila's direction. Her body seemed to have changed shape, it was still changing shape, growing smaller before Boucher's eyes, a treacly blackness closing over it. The hair lifted on his scalp.

'What is it?' Jaeger whispered.

'Damned if I know.'

'Shine the light.'

Boucher flashed it and something humped fled with a twitter. He held the beam on the corpse and closed his eyes to the sight.

'You make it out?' Jaeger asked.

'Ants,' Boucher said in a drained voice. 'Millions of them, all over her.'

Jaeger slapped his hand down. 'Turn that thing off.'

'Whether you can see or not, they're still eating her. By morning, she'll be nothing but bones.'

'Shut up.'

'We all want the tiger dead, but not this way. Aquila deserves a decent send-off. You said you were going to give her a Red Indian funeral. At this rate, there'll be nothing left.'

Jaeger's body began to shake and Boucher realized he was weeping. He put his arm around him.

'Oh God, why did she go?'

'Leo, we can leave today, straight after the ceremony. Make our way down the coast in stages.'

Jaeger rubbed his eyes with his fists. 'The ritual takes three days.'

'Three days! Leo, we can't wait that long.'

Mournfully, Jaeger shook his head. 'You go. I'm never gonna leave. All I want is to be where she is.'

Boucher dropped his arm from Jaeger's shoulder. 'Stick around and you'll get there soon enough.

25

Day 19

Next morning, Boucher summoned the castaways to test the liferaft's seaworthiness in preparation for evacuation. Jaeger remained ashore with the pistol, collecting wood for Aquila's funeral pyre. One by one the others climbed in. With four aboard, the boat rode reasonably well; with six, it became unstable. Candy was the last person to board, and when she gingerly lowered her weight, the port side dipped right under. She didn't have the heart to tell Boucher it wasn't going to work. Red-eyed and dishevelled, Boucher shifted them about, trying to bring the craft on an even keel.

'This heap of shit will never reach the rig,' Disco said.

'We'll stick to the coast,' Boucher told him.

'We'll still be on the open sea, and we haven't had clear weather more than two days running.'

Boucher slapped his hand down in frustration. 'We haven't got any alternative. Come on, let's make a trial run.'

Candy looked into the sea glare. The swell was still running high, combers bursting with muffled concussions on the reef, the back-tow sucking through the coral grottoes.

'Jay, there are too many of us. If we go out there we'll capsize.'

Disco broke the impasse by getting out. The rest followed, trooping back to the shelter. Hot and hopeless, Candy remained with Boucher in the sagging liferaft. He looked done in. 'You haven't slept. Get some rest and then we'll repair the boat and try again in a day or two.'

He eyed the group on the beach with hatred. 'They don't deserve saving.'

'You don't mean that,' she said gently, and led him back to the dispirited huddle.

'Back to square one,' Trigg said, 'thanks to Jay.'

'Jay did what any decent person would have done,' Candy told him, without much conviction.

'Decent? What's decent about putting one corpse against the lives of eight people? That tiger had come right up to Aquila. Another few minutes and Leo would have had a clear shot.'

Candy herself had discovered the tiger's pug marks, only yards from the cage. The pistol shots must have scared it off. It would be more wary now.

They sat deadlocked.

'You know something,' Disco said, tapping his teeth. 'Candy's right. There are too many of us.'

Some ambiguity of tone made everyone forget whatever it was they were thinking. A fly had lit on Disco's eyelid. He didn't brush it off.

'Oh yeah?' Nadine snarled. 'Well, we're getting fewer all the time.'

Candy looked at Disco on the bias, as if only by indirect study could she read his mind. 'Are you suggesting some of us stay behind with Leo?'

'Any volunteers?' Disco asked brightly. He waited. 'Didn't think so.' He became aware of the fly and flicked it away. It settled again on his neck. Candy watched it with a kind of fascinated repulsion.

'Then what,' Dexter said slowly, 'have you got in mind?'

'The lifeboat game.'

Candy's mouth slackened, then snapped shut. She stared at Boucher, who seemed as nonplussed as everyone else.

'Only this time, because everyone always has good reasons why it shouldn't be *them*, each of us nominates the person they least want on board. Then the rest of us vote.'

Candy made a sound of revulsion. 'You're sick.'

'Maybe it'll be me that gets left behind. Put it to the test.' Disco swivelled round. 'Hey, Leo, we're playing the lifeboat game. Care to join us?'

Jaeger shambled up and sat himself down like an unruly mutant. Under the hair and greasepaint and charcoal, his scratches were turning septic. He hadn't let Candy treat them.

'Trigg, how about starting us off?'

Trigg sniggered. 'You're not serious.'

'Let's see how it turns out.'

'Stop this,' Candy cried. 'Can't you see what he's doing? He's not playing a game. He's choosing a victim.'

Trigg opened his mouth, shut it.

'Go ahead,' Disco said encouragingly. 'Get all that bad feeling out.'

Trigg began to draw a complicated pattern in the sand. 'Well,' he muttered, 'it was Candy who brought the thing here.'

Boucher lunged and would have had him by the throat if Disco hadn't got between them.

'Easy,' he told Boucher. 'Your turn will come.' He smiled reassurance at Trigg. 'What you're saying is that if anyone should be thrown off, Candy is your choice.'

'All I'm saying ...' Trigg fell silent, his mouth working. 'Yes.'

Candy saw murder in Boucher's eyes. She herself felt cold – cold all over.

'Let's put that to a vote,' Disco said, grinning like a game-show host.

No one except Boucher would meet Candy's eye. Her throat pulsed. She felt her blood quickening. Surely they wouldn't ... surely they hadn't ...

No one put their hands up. Relief coursed through her, and then a surge of repugnance. Looking at her companions, she saw how far into primitive savagery they had fallen – their scrounging eyes, their verminous rags, the miasma of fear that hung over each and every one.

'Who's next?' Disco asked. 'Jay, you look like a man with a grudge.'

'I'll pay it off in my own time.'

Disco's eyes widened in mock concern. 'Hear that, folks? Writer-man's still on the case, and that's a worry, because if he gets off, our reputations will be shit. My vote says there's no place on the lifeboat for Jay. Everyone agree?' Disco looked about. 'Anyone?' He looked pained. 'No?' He sighed. 'A time will come when you'll reconsider that decision.'

He'd mesmerized everyone, Candy realized, had insinuated himself into the dark parts of their souls and brought the unthinkable into the light. It was a kind of seduction, she thought, a delicate arousal of an urge that could only be awakened by a sure and experienced touch. And she herself wasn't immune, she realized, sensing foul thoughts trickling through dark channels. Why should I die? My life's worth more than any of theirs. Why not Disco, why not Trigg, why not ...?

Disco smiled like a cat. 'Nadine, you look like you have something you want to get off your chest.'

Nadine was chewing her nails. She looked a fright – her skin scurfy, her hair lank, her face so emaciated the skull showed beneath the skin.

Her voice was only just audible. 'What if one of us did something that jeopardized all our lives?'

'Like what?' Disco asked gently.

'Like stealing food and things.'

Jaeger blinked, his eyes unequal to the brightness. 'Then that person loses his right to our protection.'

'Uh-huh,' Disco said, and took his bottom lip between finger and thumb. 'Who have you got in mind?'

Nadine bit her nail.

'Don't,' Candy pleaded, half aware of what Disco was contemplating even though she couldn't formulate it.

'The name,' he said.

Nadine shook her head. 'Everyone show what's in their bags.'

Someone sighed in relief.

'I haven't got a bag,' Boucher said, sucked into the charade.

'Empty your pockets then.'

One by one they turned out their possessions.

'Everyone, Candy.'

'I told you. I'm having nothing to do with this ... this ...'

'Then I'll do it for you,' Disco said, scooping up her sack. He tipped out the contents. 'Bet you're relieved.' He eyed everyone's pathetic oddments. 'Nadine, I don't see anything here to condemn a man.'

Nadine took a chunk out of her nail. 'Trigg hasn't emptied his camcorder case.'

His laugh made Candy cringe. 'There's nothing in it except cassettes and batteries.'

'Then you won't object,' Disco said, stretching for it.

Trigg looked about wildly. 'I know what this is about.

Nadine's pissed at me because I got some tape of her nude.'

'Sure,' Disco said soothingly. 'So what's this?'

In his palm lay two of the survival ration biscuits. 'And all the time we thought it was vermin.' Disco reached in again and extracted a handful of pills and a couple of morphine syrettes. 'No wonder you've been looking so mellow.'

Trigg's mouth began to quiver. 'I didn't put them there. Honest. I swear to God.'

'You bastard,' Dexter hissed.

'Now we have to decide whether this is more than just a game,' Disco said in the stunned aftermath.

'I warned you,' Candy cried. 'I told you not to listen to him.'

'Shall we vote?'

'What are we voting on?' Dexter asked, his tone subdued. 'The verdict or the sentence?'

'Both,' Jaeger announced.

Silence drew on.

'So what happens if we find him guilty?'

'He has to stay behind,' Nadine said, 'take his chances with the tiger.'

There was another moment of silence, then Disco raised a hand. 'That still doesn't leave enough room in the raft. I say we find a better use for him.'

The conclusion that Candy had already anticipated worked into everybody's mind. 'You fools,' she hissed.

'Jeez,' Dexter whispered, 'you mean ...'

'Stake him out for the tiger. It gives us another shot at it.'

'You can't do that!' Trigg screamed. 'You can't!'

He clawed upright but didn't run.

'Is that the judgement of you all?' Jaeger said.

No one answered, but Candy saw no mercy in Nadine's

face or in Bartok's. She checked Boucher's reaction and saw his eyes were flat. Oh no, she thought, not you.

'Okay, I'll ask you in turn,' Jaeger said. 'Disco?'

'For.'

'Nadine?'

'If it's him or me, I say yes.'

'Nadine,' Candy pleaded, 'think about what you're saying.'

'She already has,' Jaeger said. 'Dexter?'

Dexter's face was screwed into lines. 'I'm against Nadine on this. One day, we'll have to face our consciences.'

'Conscience is an individual matter. What does yours say, Kent?'

'I abstain.'

'What!' Candy shouted. 'This isn't a high school debate.'

Bartok paled with resolve. 'Nobody can force me to vote.'

'Candy?'

She gave a gusty laugh, then another. 'I can't believe you're doing this.'

'He pointed the finger at you,' Disco reminded her. 'He'd have given the thumbs down if it was you who stood accused.'

'I don't live by his rules.'

'No,' Jaeger said, 'you agreed to abide by mine.'

'Not any more. You're insane.'

'Take his place if you want.'

'No one goes,' Candy said. 'No one.'

Jaeger ignored her. 'Jay, you side with Candy?'

Boucher hesitated and Candy froze inside. Please, she begged him with her eyes.

'If you go ahead,' he said, 'you'll be committing murder.'

'And you're a witness,' Disco pointed out. 'I told you writer-man's a problem.'

Candy saw the vote going against her. 'I've got an alternative,' she said recklessly. 'Me and Jay and Trigg will stay with Leo. The rest of you go in the boat.'

'Anyone want to risk a trip in that sieve?' Disco asked.

'I'm not going in any boat,' Nadine said.

No one else even responded and Disco spread his hands. 'Well, Leo, that leaves you.'

'Guilty.'

'That's an even split,' Candy said. 'Three all.'

'Leo has the casting vote. We all agreed.'

'Do this,' Candy said, 'and you'll be crossing a line you'll never be able to go back across.'

'Four of us have already made a one-way crossing,' Disco told her.

Jaeger raised his hand, demanding quiet, and addressed Trigg. 'I'm gonna give you a choice. Go your own way or serve the sentence. Survive the night and that's the end of it.'

'It's a death sentence whatever he chooses,' Candy cried.

'The sentence stands,' Leo declared.

Candy rose and went to Trigg. He pushed her off and reeled away.

'Maybe we should tie him up,' she heard Nadine say.

'Where's he gonna run?'

'Now we have to decide who mans the stakeout,' Disco said.

Jaeger raised the pistol. 'I'll do it.'

'You can't fucking see,' Boucher shouted. 'If you're going to kill Trigg, at least make it worthwhile for the rest of us.'

'Fair point,' Disco said.

Jaeger blinked ponderously. 'You go then.'

Disco seemed surprised to be singled out. 'Sure. Anyone object?'

'Yes,' Candy said with venom. '*I* do.'

'I can shoot straight, Candy.'

'But will you? Maybe you won't shoot the tiger because you're enjoying your game too much, and tomorrow we'll be sitting here choosing another victim.'

From under his lashes, Disco looked at her in dark surmise. 'Got an alternative?'

'Me.'

Disco laughed at her obvious ploy. 'No, no. Soon as we're out of sight, you'd cut Trigg loose and bring him into the cage.'

'I'll take someone else with me.'

'You can't shoot.'

'I've been shooting since I was fourteen. I bet I'm a better shot than you are.'

Disco raised a brow. 'Leo, you decide.'

Jaeger deliberated. 'Trigg, it's your life. I guess you have a right to choose.'

'I'm not ... I'm not ...'

'Disco or Candy. You've got half an hour to make up your mind.'

Trigg took five minutes. He spent them snivelling in a way that tried even Candy's pity. Finally he wiped his nose and looked at her dull-eyed.

'You.'

'Whoever goes in the cage with her,' Disco said, 'it's got to be someone who voted for the sentence.'

'I'm taking Kent.'

'Kent abstained. He's sweet on you.'

'I'm taking Kent.'

Bartok gave her a cornered look. 'Candy, if it's all the ...'

'Shut up, you miserable little worm.'

312

'Do you want to pray with me?' Bartok inquired.

'No thank you,' Candy said politely. 'But why don't you ask Trigg? I'm sure he'd appreciate your Christian fellowship.'

The scapegoat was tethered by one leg only four yards in front of the cage. He had been so hysterical that Disco had forcibly given him a shot of morphine. He was quiet now but apparently awake, the whites of his eyes showing.

'I guess you're angry with me,' Bartok muttered.

Candy kept her concentration on the moonstruck edge of the clearing. 'Anger doesn't describe how I feel. From you at least, I'd have expected mercy.'

'Men pass judgements. Mercy is for God.'

Candy spared him a contemptuous glance and then went back to investigating a mottling of moonlight and shadow that could conceivably have been a tiger. She decided that her eyes were up to tricks.

'Kent, I've been meaning to ask why someone who lives by the scriptures joined a group of pagan nature-worshippers.'

'Genesis 1.29,' he answered. '"I have given you every plant-yielding seed that is upon the face of all the earth, and every tree with seed in its fruit: you shall have them for food", Bartok's tone was earnest. 'You see, Candy, before the Fall, we didn't eat meat or harm animals. Ours was a gentle dominion.'

'You really believe everything began in the Garden of Eden?'

'Yes I do, and God's covenant says that one day we'll return there.'

'Did you think you'd found Eden here?'

'I ... I believed this was a hallowed place.'

'But no longer. You tasted the forbidden fruit, and now your eyes are opened.'

Bartok squirmed. 'I'm sorry about what happened on the beach. Disco said there was no sin in nakedness, so there was nothing wrong in looking on it.'

'He had more than looking on his mind, Kent, and I think you did, too.'

Bartok didn't answer.

'First it was Jay he singled out,' Candy said. 'Then he tempted you. Now look what he's done. I think you were right. This is Eden, complete with serpent.'

Again, Bartok hunched up uneasily.

Candy yawned. 'Well, never mind that.' She blinked and breathed deep in an attempt to aerate her blood. 'What does your church have to say about evolutionary theory?'

Bartok became animated. 'Evolution's a lie and I can prove it.'

'Not now,' Candy told him. She gave another sluggish yawn and rubbed her eyes. 'If there's no change, no evolution, what will become of us? Where does it all end?'

'In annihilation and redemption.'

'Do you have a date?'

'The calculations are a bit complicated, but in eight years time, on June 24.'

Candy stared. 'Golly, that doesn't give us much time.'

'Enough to prepare.'

Her brow ruffled. 'Kent, isn't there anything between Genesis and Revelations?'

'Sure, there's history.'

A long period of time elapsed. The forest was at a standstill.

'Keep talking,' Candy said. 'I'm drifting off.'

'Are you and Jay ...?'

'Having sex?'

'In love?' Bartok said in a pained voice. 'Do you love each other?'

314

That woke Candy up. 'Goodness, I've only known him a few weeks, and soon – very soon, I hope – we'll be off here and go our separate ways.'

'If I had a girl like you, I wouldn't let her out of my life.'

In the dark he was unfeatured, but Candy knew he would be blushing to his roots. She made a cursory scan of the clearing. 'Don't you have a girlfriend?'

Bartok hesitated. 'Yes, she's a teacher.'

'Have you slept with her?'

'We've taken vows of chastity. It's a rule of our church.'

Candy nodded. 'You told Disco, didn't you?'

Bartok's silence was all the answer she needed.

'He certainly knows how to find people's weak points.' She stretched. 'When you get back, Kent, I suggest you break your vows. I wouldn't be surprised if all this death-defying climbing wasn't a way of sublimating your sex drive.'

'Gee, Candy, climbing's like a religious experience for me. It brings me close to God.'

'You never know. Sex might do the trick, too.'

'You're making fun of me.'

'I'm serious.'

Bartok was quiet a moment. 'Sometimes when I'm climbing, I know He's guiding me, bearing me up. Then there's nothing I can't challenge.'

'What happens on the other days?'

'Oh, I climb all the same, but maybe I think twice about the real extreme routes. God isn't an all-risks insurance policy.'

'Damn,' Candy said. 'Damn and buggeration.'

Religious matters had been shunted aside. Clouds were drawing across the moon. Trigg whimpered invisibly.

Bartok shifted. 'I hate to hear you use that kind of vocabulary, Candy.'

'I can't see a thing,' she told him. She turned in the

dark. 'It's no good. There's nothing to be gained by leaving Trigg stuck in the pitch black.'

'Disco said you'd try something like this. If we take Trigg in, Leo will only send him out again tomorrow night.'

'You're not going to tell them.'

'I'd only get us all into trouble, Candy. I'm no good at lying.'

'Then you'd better start practising for when we're rescued, because Leo's so-called laws aren't recognized in any civilized court. If we sacrifice Trigg, we'll be guilty of murder, and however much we try to hide it, the truth will come out. Do you think you could keep it hidden? Do you think Nadine could stick to a story? And remember Jay. He's got no intention of covering up for anyone.'

'You're right,' Bartok said, chastened. 'I keep forgetting there's another world out there.'

Trigg displayed no gratitude at being brought to safety. The wretch sobbed and cursed until Candy's patience snapped.

'Oh stop gibbering.'

Eventually, he shut up. From Bartok's regular breathing, Candy guessed he'd fallen asleep. She felt cut off, and in her solitude she looked into herself and was disturbed by what she found. She had always taken it for granted that what virtue she possessed was absolute and sustainable, but now she saw how precarious it was, how dependent on benign and stable circumstances. If the clouds hadn't covered the moon, Trigg would still be out there. She had pleaded that he be spared, but when the decision went against her, she had gone along with it. At bottom, she was no different from the others. Disco was a manipulator, but he only teased out what was already there. At bottom there was an evil sediment which, if

Disco ever reached it, would release things as rank and scuttling as anything in the mangrove swamp.

Her shudder brought Bartok awake.

'Bad thoughts,' she murmured. The darkness showed no sign of lifting. 'What a bloody hideous night.'

But even the longest night must end and there came a time when wraiths advanced out of the gloom and solidified into sentinel trees. Tendrils of mist clung to them. In the grey-green infusion they appeared to be spaced out with the regularity of formal arrangement – a deadly-still arboretum draped with mosses and laced with glistening spiders' webs.

'Let's call it a night,' Candy said.

Bartok was uneasy. 'Maybe we should give it a few more minutes. You said dawn's one of the most dangerous times.'

'I don't want the others turning up and finding Trigg in the cage.' Candy addressed him as if he was senile. 'We're going to tell them you were out all night. Get it wrong and they'll peg you out again.'

He didn't answer. His expression was not like any she had seen on a human.

'Oh, come on,' she snapped, unlatching the entrance.

Outside, she stretched, straightening out her cramps. Trigg stumbled away. Around them the forest was waking up. A troupe of parrots flared through the canopy and a hornbill performed its flamboyant routine. A monkey chattered near by. The first spindles of sunlight fell through the clearing.

Leaves shook overhead. Startled, Candy looked up and then smiled. A leaf-eating monkey was scolding them from the end of a branch. It sprang to another perch, leaning out and chattering fiercely, teeth bared.

Suddenly, her smile went out. She looked in the

direction that was provoking so much agitation and her heart began to gallop.

'Wait,' she murmured, laying a hand on Bartok's arm.

At the edge of the clearing, Trigg had slumped on to a fallen tree.

'It's only a monkey,' Bartok whispered.

'It's not us that's scared it.'

Candy's nostrils dilated. Her eyes began to patrol. The pattern of branches and sunlight was maddeningly cryptic, and several times her heart skipped as she constructed a striped flank from random arrangements of vegetation. Her gaze tracked across a picket of saplings, moved on, came back and stopped.

Then she saw it.

It was so diabolically camouflaged that she had been looking at it for several seconds before she registered its presence. If it hadn't flicked its ear, she might have missed it.

It was no more than fifteen yards away, crouched to spring, its eyes burning into Trigg, who was unconscious of anything amiss. Candy clasped the pistol in both hands and slowly brought it up.

'See it?' she whispered.

'Yes,' Bartok breathed. 'Lord have mercy.'

From the corner of her eye, Candy saw that Trigg still had his head in his hands. She considered the risk to herself if she called out.

'Trigg,' she said in an unconcerned tone. 'Come here, will you?'

Trigg's sozzled eyes settled on the gun. 'What for?'

'Don't argue. Just walk over here as slowly as possible.'

The tiger turned its magisterial gaze on her for a moment, then resumed its watch on Trigg.

'Fuck off.'

'The gun's pointing at the tiger.'

318

Trigg rose unsteadily, groping for balance.

'One step at a time. Slowly now.'

But Trigg was riveted.

Candy's mouth was bone dry. The tip of the tiger's tail had begun to switch rhythmically, hypnotically. A ripple crossed its shoulder. Its ears flattened back on its skull and its pupils narrowed to strokes. In a moment it would charge.

'Shoot it,' Trigg said, his voice a subdued shriek. 'What are you fucking waiting for?'

But the range was too great – a wounding shot at best. Trigg's teeth began to chatter. His eyes bolted sideways, looking for an avenue of escape. Realizing that his nerve wouldn't hold, Candy consolidated her aim. Her breathing shortened.

'No!' she screamed.

At the same instant Trigg broke, the tiger exploded forward, a golden strobe, moving so fast that Candy's snap shot came nowhere close. The tiger had about twenty-five yards to cover, and it closed the distance in four or five bounds, launching itself at Trigg before he'd gone twenty feet. It took him full in the back and Candy heard him gasp under the impact. The tiger bunched up over him and there was a muted crack.

Candy was running, shouting, trying to divert its attention. It picked Trigg up by one shoulder and bounded off as if completely unencumbered. Candy whipped up the pistol, knowing it would be her only chance. The tiger launched into a thicket and the puppet in its jaws caught in a fork. Whirling, it saw Candy and crouched low, tail lashing, generating a sound that stopped her dead. It dropped Trigg and menaced her with spread jaws. Rooted in her tracks, Candy stared into its plush red mouth.

'Shoot!' Bartok yelled, his cry cut off by the tiger's cough.

She fired, fired again as it sprang, and once more as it hurtled into her, sending her sprawling. As she fell, the gun discharged by accident. She went face down and tried to cover her neck in a pathetic gesture of defence. She squirmed right way up, waving the pistol.

There was nothing there – only Bartok, running towards her. Her head was ringing. Dirt and leaves filled her mouth. She spat them out and sat up in a daze.

'Are you hurt?'

'I don't know,' she said, her voice startling her. 'I don't think so.'

Hauling herself round, she saw Trigg lying on his back, eyes fixed in a frozen upward stare. Bartok went to him and looked down, then came back. White with shock, he dropped beside her as if his legs had been severed at the knees.

'It broke his neck.'

They sat, leaning against each other, unable to speak. Candy heard Boucher call her name, and then other cries. It was Bartok who acknowledged them. When the other survivors appeared, they drifted into the clearing, peering around like rag-tag marauders in hostile territory. Boucher ran to her and held her. She couldn't speak.

Disco inspected Trigg briefly, then glared around the empty clearing. 'Shit,' he said.

'She hit it,' Bartok told him. 'More than once, I reckon.'

Disco held out his hand. 'Let's see how many are left in the clip.'

Instinctively, Candy tightened her grip.

'Wounded, it could be even more dangerous,' Disco told her. 'Someone's going to have to go after it and you're too beat up.'

She raised her hand to Boucher and he pulled her upright. She felt wobbly and sick and altogether peculiar. 'I shot it,' she said, finding her voice. 'I'll go after it.'

'There's blood here,' Dexter said, squatting.

Casting about, they found a trail. Bunched together, they followed. At one point the tiger had lain down and in the scrape it had made was a froth of pinkish blood.

'Lung shot,' Disco said.

It didn't take them long to catch up. The tiger had gone to cover in a close-set clump of rattan. They could hear it – a broken, liquid snoring, like a drunk sleeping off a binge.

'Drowning in its blood,' Disco said.

'Maybe we could burn it out.'

'Let's wait. Keep back.'

After half an hour the sounds ceased. Eyes turned on Candy. She ignored them. After another few minutes had gone by without any sound from the thicket, she knew there was only one way to find out.

'The rest of you stay back.'

Sweat greased her palms. Nerves jangling, she advanced, parting the branches one by one and pausing between each move. She saw gold and black and brought the gun up. The barrel wavered then fell away.

'It's dead,' she said.

The others crowded in and stared. She'd hit it three times – in the leg, in the shoulder and in the chest. It was a creature in its prime, well-fed, flawless; bullet wounds like obscene flowers bloomed on its skin.

'It's beautiful,' Boucher murmured.

'Smaller than I expected,' Disco said.

A pulse crossing its flank threw them into a frightened knot.

'It's still alive!'

Another little spasm rippled its fur. Then another. Candy leaned to touch its belly and dropped to her knees.

'It's a tigress. A heavily pregnant tigress. Those are her cubs moving.'

A look of childish panic swept Jaeger's face. His mouth quivered. His eyes watered. He uttered an incoherent sob and began to back away, bulldozing through the undergrowth. Turning, he covered his eyes with his hands and barged off.

'No pleasing some folk,' Disco said.

Boucher let a sigh go. 'He thinks you've shot Aquila.'

Disco was regarding Candy with frank admiration. 'I'd better watch my step, you being so handy with weapons.'

Shoving the pistol into Boucher's hand, she walked away.

FOUR

26

Because none of the castaways wanted to be around Jaeger and the remains of Aquila and the tigress, they moved camp, throwing up a haphazard bivouac further down the beach. After that flurry of activity, they occupied the hours one by one, performing only tasks immediate to their survival. Jaeger laboured from dawn to twilight, fuelling the fire that would convey Aquila and the tiger to their next lives. For reasons none dared enquire, he had cut off the tiger's head and impaled it on a tall pole next to the pyre, under the look-out tree. Bartok, who spent much of each day in scriptural study atop his tree eyrie, was the sole witness of his erratic comings and goings and outlandish oratory.

Boucher alone acted beyond immediate necessity, working long hours on the liferaft to render it fit for ocean travel. After two days he declared it more or less sound and invited Candy to accompany him on a shakedown cruise to the reef. Wordlessly she accepted and sat mute in the stern while he rowed.

'Three weeks,' he said. 'That's how long we've been here.'

She merely nodded. A force field seemed to have sprung up around her. Inside it, Boucher sensed a great anger. Whenever he woke at night, she was always lying clenched and wide-eyed. He didn't dare touch her, feeling that if his rough hand made contact she would explode.

But then, as if she'd divined his concern, she said: 'I'm sorry, I haven't been very welcoming lately.'

'I understand.'

'Part of me feels dead.'

Boucher stopped rowing. Water nuzzled at the hull. 'Everything heals.'

'At bottom, we're just animals, but I never realized how close to the bottom we were.' Listlessly she looked away. 'Three weeks.'

'Candy, it's time we got out of here.'

She turned then and tried to raise a smile. 'You've done wonders with the boat, but it won't take us all.'

'I'm talking about you and me, Candy. No one else.'

'We can't abandon the others.'

'We won't be abandoning them. We'll be going for help.'

'Let's discuss it tonight. If they say yes, I'll come.'

'They won't agree. They can't. Disco's got them too scared of what I'll reveal about the things that happened here. And the longer we stay, the more he'll play on their fears. He's out to harm me, Candy. You, too.'

In the look-out tree, Bartok gave a wave. Eyes on Candy, Boucher made a distracted response. 'We'll do it tomorrow. We'll make out we're going fishing.'

She leaned forward. 'Jay,' she said quietly, 'Jay.'

He waited, but she didn't continue and it became apparent that her attention had been captured by something behind him. He swivelled on his seat and his jaw dropped. A schooner with sails furled was motoring from south to north no more than a couple of miles offshore.

'A ship,' he murmured, hardly able to trust his eyes. He opened his mouth in a glorious shout and began to row for land. 'A ship!'

The others came racing out, ran into a wall of their own disbelief, then leapt deliriously. In mid-cavort, Dexter suddenly seized up.

'Leo! He's got the flare gun!'

'I'll go,' Boucher said, already running. 'The rest of you, get the fire lit.'

'Oh quick,' Nadine wailed.

By the time Boucher reached the north tip, his heart was bursting. Bartok was still up the tree, waving the tiger flag.

'Where's Leo?'

'Don't know. In the forest.'

Boucher whirled. 'Leo, a ship! We're rescued! Do you hear me? A ship.' His exertions had brought constellations to his eyes. He folded over until his vision cleared. He straightened, searching the treeline. 'Leo, where are you? We need the flare gun. I know you can hear me, Leo. Even if you don't want to leave, think of the rest of us. Nadine and Candy and Dexter don't deserve to die because of what happened to Aquila.' He waited, conscious that each second the ship was sailing by. As he backed on to the beach, tears of frustration mounted. 'Fuck you. Stay here and die, you crazy bastard.'

He stumbled back, nursing a stitch. Anger and despair raged in him. Their first real chance, and that maniac had blown it.

His companions' jubilation had congealed into a desperate anguish.

'He's hiding,' Boucher panted. 'He heard me, all right. He must have seen the ship. He doesn't want us to get off.'

Nadine whimpered. Smoke had begun to rise from the smudge fire. Only a trickle, not enough to attract attention unless the crew were searching for it. Even then, it didn't look like a distress signal. Bartok was still frenziedly flag-waving.

'Everyone shout,' Nadine said. 'Everybody wave.'

They began to whoop and holler and leap like savages. They danced and yelled until at last they had no breath left and they stood mute, knuckles clenched in their teeth, watching the boat come level and then draw past. Candy pulled the gun from her waist and pointed it at the sky.

'Relax,' Disco said. He had Trigg's camcorder trained on the schooner. 'They've seen us.'

Nadine began to bawl, but no one else uttered a sound. They had endured beyond certainty of release and now even hope was no longer their entitlement. Boucher felt Candy's arms link around his waist and he pressed her head to his shoulder.

Slowly the schooner came round until its prow aimed straight at them. In the acute light, Boucher could distinguish the bottle-green colour of its patched sails, hear the beat of its engine, make out figures on deck. It anchored half a mile outside the reef, and as its motor died and the air went still, salvation could no longer be doubted and everyone went mad. Dexter Smith and Nadine rolled on the sand. Bartok, down from his look-out and racing to join them, performed a double handspring. Boucher nearly found himself slapping Disco on the back. Candy's eyes glistened; her teeth were sunk in her bottom lip. Emotion welled up in Boucher, too. 'We made it,' he said softly. 'We fucking made it.'

'About ten of them,' Disco said. He must have had the camcorder on maximum zoom. 'Fishermen, I guess.'

In the heat, the schooner's masts seemed to warp and the hull to shimmer and melt into the sea. Boucher shielded his eyes.

'They're lowering an inflatable.'

The craft fired up and accelerated, foam combing up from its bows. It smacked across the waves, the hard, flat engine note bouncing back from the forest. Bartok cheered.

'That's a fucking powerful launch for a fishing boat,' Disco said.

Dexter punched the air. 'The faster we're out of here, the happier I am.'

Disco kept his eyes to the viewfinder. 'Yeah?' he said. 'Well, I'm not happy.'

Boucher's eyes snapped round. 'What are you trying to pull now?'

'Ask yourself why they need a boat that powerful.'

'Any number of reasons.'

'Yeah, and I can think of a few.'

'Hell, maybe they do some smuggling on the side. So what?'

'And maybe piracy, too. There are pirates on this coast.' Disco glanced round. 'You know that?'

'Around China, the Philippines. Not here.'

'Where the fuck do you think we are – Nova Scotia? I'm telling you, there are pirates in these seas, and I'm not talking about punks rolling rafts full of boatladies. These guys are major league. They hijack cargo boats; they board yachts and throw the crews to the sharks. They're called bogeys.'

'Bugis,' Candy said.

'Bugimen, bogeymen. Pirates.'

Nadine exploded. 'After what's happened here, after what we did ... Just because we can't trust each other ... I don't know how you dare ...'

Disco made no response. His speculations had poisoned the mood and there was a thick silence as the boat reached the first reef and slowed, going from flat out to a crawl almost in its own length. Its crew were looking for the way through. Boucher could make out five men, dressed in a variety of jazzy casuals.

'I'm telling you, that's an assault boat,' Disco said. 'That's a craft for hit-and-run.'

Some of his misgivings had rubbed off on Boucher. 'Can you see if they're armed?'

'They're not gonna hit the beach waving weapons.'

A sailor in a red shirt stood at the bow, acting as leadsman. They were through the first reef, speeding up towards the second barrier.

'We can't stand here dithering,' Candy said.

Disco lowered the camcorder. 'I propose we get off the beach until we see what kind of guys they are.'

'This is madness,' Nadine protested.

Boucher caught Candy's eye and saw his own uncertainty written there. Disco began to move away and Boucher and Candy tagged after, followed reluctantly by the others, Nadine included. The man in the red shirt hailed them.

'They must think we're crazy,' Dexter said, looking back over his shoulder.

The castaways put more than a hundred yards between themselves and the camp before they halted. The boat nosed into the lagoon and cruised to shore. It beached in front of the camp and four of the crew jumped out. One of them wore what looked like a turban and did, in fact, give a buccaneering impression. The fifth remained at the helm and backed out at least twenty yards. The landing party took a few cautious steps up the beach and halted.

'See the way they're fanned out,' Disco said, 'like they're expecting trouble.'

'No shit?' Nadine snapped. 'A bunch of castaways signal for help, then when it comes, they fuck off into the jungle. Those fishermen must be wondering what we're trying to pull. I wouldn't blame them if they climbed back in and just sailed away.'

The man in the red shirt turned to the helmsman, gesturing incomprehension.

'Nadine's right,' Dexter said. 'For all they know, *we're* the ones trying to spring an ambush.'

Two of the men made their way to the camp and inspected it. Another checked the liferaft. There was a shouted interchange with Redshirt in a language nobody recognized. Redshirt, who was obviously the leader, summoned his men back. He shouted again and cupped his hand to his ear. Even from this distance Boucher could infer his shrug.

'They must have heard about the crash,' he said. 'If they're fishermen, they'll report us.'

Dexter rounded on him. 'If they're simple sons of the sea, why would they bother? I tell you, we'll feel fucking sick when they pull out.'

Candy stood decisively. 'I'm going to ask one of them to come over.'

'What they tell us doesn't impress me,' Disco said. 'We won't know if they've got bad intentions until we're on their boat, and then there's squat all we can do about it.'

'Hello,' Candy shouted in her clear English voice. '*Selamat.*'

'Hey,' Redshirt yelled.

'Who are you?' Candy shouted. '*Anda tinggal dimana?*' Boucher caught the word *ikan.*

'They say they're fishermen from a place called Bangka.'

'They're not going to own up to being slavers and dealers in body parts.'

'Ask him to step over here,' Boucher said. 'No one else.'

'Come,' Candy shouted, beckoning with her hands. '*Tidak,*' she ordered, when all four men began to move. She held up one finger. 'One.'

Redshirt seemed to understand. He waved his companions back and they dropped on their haunches while he trudged forward.

'Better hide that pistol,' Boucher told Candy. 'Give it to me.' He stowed it inside his jacket as Redshirt approached.

None of them could recognize his provenance beyond the fact that his home belonged somewhere in the vast Indonesian archipelago. He was a tallish man of middle age, his hollow face seamed from exposure to sun and seaspray. His shirt was woven from coarse cotton, his pants baggy and cut off above bare ankles. He spread his hands to show they were empty and grinned warily. No wonder, Boucher thought, remembering what they looked like – half-naked and harrowed, dressed in jungle fronds and mildewed remnants of airship fabric.

Redshirt pointed at Nadine. 'American?'

'Yes we are,' she declared. 'We crashed here. We crashed in a ...' Her hands attempted to describe an airship. Her voice broke. 'We've been here for weeks. It's been terrible, just terrible.'

Redshirt nodded, his eyes roaming as if he was trying to reconstruct what had happened on the island.

'He looks like an ordinary working stiff,' Dexter said.

'You see that necklace he's wearing? Gold.'

'It's probably his entire personal wealth,' Candy said.

Disco pushed to the front. 'Hey, buddy, has your boat got a radio?'

Redshirt frowned. '*Raddio?*' He waggled a finger. '*Tidak raddio.*'

'No radio.'

'Bullshit,' Disco said. 'There are at least ten men on that schooner and wherever they come from, they had to cross a lot of water to get here. You think they'd equip themselves with a fifteen-thousand-dollar inflatable and forget about a goddam radio?'

'*Tidak raddio,*' Redshirt said sternly. He pointed to the schooner, then made a gathering motion to indicate they should come with him.

'Ask him how far it is to the nearest town,' Boucher said. 'Tell him we want him to contact the police or army. Tell him we'll reward him.'

There followed five minutes of cross-purposes and linguistic cock-ups.

'He doesn't understand,' Candy said at last. 'All I can get out of him is that he must land his fish tonight. There is no radio where he lives.'

'You believe him?'

'There's no reason not to.'

'That fucking does it,' Dexter said. 'I'm gone.'

'Me too,' Nadine said. 'Goodbye, hell.'

'I mean what's the worst they can do?' Bartok said. 'Steal our clothes?'

Disco shook his head. 'My gut says this guy's a badass.' He aimed the camcorder at Redshirt's impassive gaze. 'Yeah, I've got your number, pal.'

Boucher looked longingly at the schooner. Disco's suspicions were contagious but almost certainly baseless, and perhaps contrived for some other purpose.

'Let's shift it,' he told her.

But at that moment Redshirt seemed to lose patience. He took hold of Candy's wrist and tugged her forward. In simple reflex, Boucher reached out and checked him. Redshirt's deep-set eyes turned on him and for a moment, just a moment, Boucher thought he detected a spark of malice.

'No offence, skip, but before we commit ourselves, we'd like to know what's in your boat.'

'Yeah, check it out,' Disco told Dexter.

Redshirt's bemusement gave way to irritation when it became clear that only a trio of castaways intended to accompany him. He began to harangue the fainthearts. At last he gave up and left, looking back every few yards, sharply gesturing for the others to follow. Boucher was ashamed of his misgivings. 'Nadine's right. This place has driven us crazy.'

'Someone else should have gone instead of her,' Candy said.

As the three castaways reached them, the sailors rose from the sand. They closed up and Boucher could see them patting arms and shaking hands. Nadine stood a head taller than any of them except Redshirt. Dexter looked back, grinning.

'When he starts signing autographs,' Boucher said, 'it's time to go.'

Dexter made a trumpet with his hands. 'They say come now or stay here.'

A lurking worry pushed to the forefront of Boucher's mind. If he stayed behind, Dexter and Nadine would be back in the world days before he reached civilization. By then their story – *his* story – might already be beaming around the globe.

'Last chance,' Dexter warned them. 'They mean it.'

Boucher hardened his resolve. 'Candy, we're evacuating.' After a moment's hesitation, he turned to Disco, who was still filming. 'You coming?'

'Not until I'm sure.'

Nothing would suit Boucher better than to leave Disco marooned. Hand in hand with Candy, he walked down the beach. One of the men held Dexter's elbow and was obligingly guiding him into the water. Another man assisted Nadine. Boucher came to a halt as Bartok suddenly left the group and began jogging up to the camp, followed by the third man. Redshirt watched him go.

'It's okay,' Boucher said. 'Kent's forgotten his Bible.'

Dexter was nearly at the boat, Nadine a few yards

behind, almost waist-deep. Bartok was rooting through his possessions. The helmsman had come to the bow to offer Dexter a hand up. He saw Boucher and Candy, snatched his hand away and pointed at the latecomers as if he was upset. Redshirt snapped an order. Ignoring Dexter's upstretched hand, the helmsman reached instead into the boat.

'Something's ...' Candy said, and stood stock-still.

Redshirt began to walk towards them, grinning. The men with Dexter and Nadine seemed to be holding them close. Dexter appeared confused. The helmsman crouched down and again offered his hand. Dexter took it. It was the helmsman's left hand. Before, he had used his right, which remained hidden.

'Dexter,' Boucher called, pitching his voice in neutral, 'the guy in the boat has a gun in his other hand.'

Nobody stirred for a moment, then everything became hyper-animated at once. Dexter – all credit to him – wrenched down, toppling the helmsman into the water. Nadine tried to break loose and failed. On the beach, Bartok threw his escort aside and began running towards the melée in the shallows. Redshirt was running back, too, screeching like a carrion bird. Somehow Dexter had managed to break free and was floundering to shore, pursued by the helmsman who had the gun held above his head.

Immobilized by shock, Boucher saw Dexter trip, pick himself up and stumble on to the beach. Making no attempt to go after him, Redshirt splashed into the sea, screaming abuse at the helmsman. Dexter turned, looking for pursuit. Boucher could hear his sobbing breath.

Candy shoved Boucher. 'Get back,' she shouted for Bartok's benefit. 'Run for it!'

At the edge of vision, Boucher saw Redshirt snatch the gun from the helmsman. Bartok had reversed direction and was sprinting for the trees. Redshirt pivoted, the gun coming up to his shoulder. Forty yards from him, Dexter jinked. He was still twenty yards short of cover when the gun made a quick tapping and he pitched on to the sand. He struggled to rise and his arms collapsed under him. Boucher reached the trees and dived flat, Candy alongside. Breath sawing, he bellied round. Dexter's face was turned in his direction, and even from eighty yards Boucher could see it distorted by shock and pain. Bartok and Disco had disappeared. Redshirt was walking up to Dexter.

Boucher blundered to his feet, clawing the pistol from his jacket. Candy dragged him back and shook her head. Redshirt stopped by Dexter, looked up the beach, produced a parang, pulled Dexter up by the hair and, with three strokes, hacked off his head. His body straightened out and seemed to relax. Redshirt waved Dexter's head, bent over the corpse and stripped off the Rolex. From the boat came Nadine's muffled screams.

'Oh no,' Candy said in a small voice. 'Oh no. Oh no.'

'The bastards,' Boucher said. 'The fucking murdering bastards.'

'I fucking told you,' Disco shouted.

Redshirt twirled his gun so the barrel pointed up. Two of his men had climbed into the boat with Nadine and they, too, were armed. Boucher pushed Candy flat beside him. Bullets rattled through the trees. When the shooting stopped, Redshirt walked away, looking back over his shoulder, mocking them in sing-song. His pirate band laughed. More weapons were distributed.

Candy grabbed Boucher's arm. Crouched and weaving, they retreated up the beach and flung themselves down beside Disco.

'Did they get Kent?'

'Dunno,' Disco said. 'He moved pretty fast.'

'We'd better do the same.'

'They're returning to the boat.'

'Sons of bitches ain't going anywhere. They're gonna question Nadine – find out how many of us there are, what sort of stuff we've got.'

'What do you think they'll do to her?'

'Ain't too difficult to work out. Can't say I know what they'll do after that.'

Candy sat up, distraught. 'We've got to try and rescue her.'

'No chance. The bogeys will be coming after us any minute.'

Candy rounded on Boucher. 'Jay, we've got to get her back.'

Boucher's thoughts were in tumult. 'We have to save ourselves before we can do anything for Nadine.'

Candy pounded the ground. Boucher shook her shoulder. 'We have to hide. If they don't find us by nightfall, they might give up.'

'Not these guys,' Disco said. 'They'll hunt us down one by one for as long as it takes.'

'The mainland,' Candy said. 'Hide in the mangroves until they've gone.'

'All they have to do is anchor round the nearest headland and come back tomorrow, or the next day, any fucking time they choose.'

Candy jumped up. 'They won't risk the reefs at night, and they can't get into the lagoon by daylight without us seeing them.'

'They've got our food and gear,' Disco pointed out. 'They'll starve us out.'

'Three of them are staying in the boat,' Boucher said.

'Going round to cut us off.'

Out of the greenery crashed Bartok, stunned and tearful. 'You see what they did to Dexter?'

Disco patted the camcorder. 'See it? Man, I got the whole scene on camera. The whole fucking thing.'

Redshirt and the other remaining pirate seemed in no hurry to come after them.

'We don't have to make it easy for them,' Boucher said. We know the island. They don't. And we've still got the pistol.'

Disco spat. 'One handgun against five AK-47s. They'll be shitting themselves.'

'Not all of them have rifles,' Candy said. 'The man with Kent had a shotgun.'

'You sure?'

'I know what a shotgun looks like.'

Disco's eyes narrowed. 'How many slugs you got left?'

'Two.'

'Two?' Disco laughed and rolled his eyes.

Boucher remembered he'd left his jacket with the other bullet in the camp. He aimed the Mauser in the general direction of the pirates. Disco knocked it down.

'What the fuck you doing?'

'Advertising budget. Make those bastards a little less enthusiastic about creeping around in here.'

'Start shooting now and they'll hunt in a pack. So long as they don't know we've got a gun, they're gonna think we're easy prey and maybe spread out. That gives us a chance of jumping one and grabbing his weapon.'

'I can't see any other way,' Candy said.

Redshirt still hadn't moved. His partner, dressed in a yellow sweatshirt and green baseball cap, was hunkered down, smoking a cigarette.

Disco's eyes switched to the pistol, became calculating. 'Okay, give it to me.'

Boucher took a quick back-step. 'Candy keeps it. She killed the tiger.'

'Killing animals isn't the same as killing a man.'

'How the fuck would you know?'

'Work it out.'

'Where's Leo?' Candy demanded. 'He must have heard the shooting.'

'On his own,' Disco said. 'Same as us.' He extended his hand. 'Now gimme the gun.' He advanced slowly. 'Candy's got more balls than any chick I know, but this is man's work.'

Boucher kept his eyes on Disco. 'Candy, tell him you won't hesitate to shoot.'

'If my life's threatened.'

'If? They cut Dexter's head off and she's talking "if". What you gonna do, Candy – give 'em a jury trial?'

Disco lunged for the pistol and Boucher only just jerked it away. He levelled it without thought of consequences.

'Back off, Disco. I risked my life to get this thing. Candy risked hers to save all our asses. The gun stays with us – not just for now, but for all time.'

Two shots cracked the air on the other side of the island. Disco turned to face the sound.

'Ain't much of that left. They've got us squeezed.'

The pirate in the baseball cap flicked his cigarette away, stood up and took a comfortable grip on his gun.

Bartok shifted in apprehension. 'What's the plan? Do we stay together?'

'Split up into pairs,' Candy said.

Disco took a last look at the pistol. 'Anyone still alive by nightfall, try and make it to the look-out tree.' He bestowed a crimped smile on the Bible clutched in Bartok's hand. 'That thing any good against bogeymen?'

27

Ducking through the forest, Boucher found himself thinking of hide-and-seek when, faced with a hundred choices, you end up with none. You choose a place, but as the seconds tick by, doubts form. If it seemed so secure to you, it'll be the first place your pursuer will look. You abandon it and search for another. Time's beginning to run short. You dive into another hideyhole, only this time something about it isn't quite right, and you dash away again, your time nearly up.

Already Boucher had lost his bearings. A minute earlier they had passed a tree hung with one of the fright masks. As he ran, he wondered what the bogeymen would make of the masks and Aquila's funeral pyre and all the other pagan totems. But any superstitious hackles they might raise would be more than cancelled out by the bogeys' arsenal. Still running, he pushed the pistol at Candy.

She came to a stop, her breast heaving.

'Take it, Candy. I never fired one before.'

She looked at the pistol. 'Perhaps we should have let Disco have it.'

Anger spurted. 'Candy, think of Dexter, think of Nadine. Think of yourself.' He forced the gun into her hand. 'Please. We're depending on you.'

'I'll do my best.' Her eyes ranged about.

340

'Got anywhere in mind?'

'There's a dense patch near where I saw the clouded leopard's tracks. It's about five minutes. We mustn't leave a trail. Watch where you put your feet. Don't break or bend anything. I'll go first. Watch behind you.'

She led and he followed. Now that his adrenalin surge was spent, he felt surprisingly calm. Though they were near the south tip, their precise location was a mystery even to him, and that gave him some reassurance. The bogeys would never be able to scour the entire island in the few hours of daylight remaining.

'Here,' Candy said.

Storms had gashed open this part of the forest, triggering an explosion of new growth. Saplings thrust up through sprays and tangles of ferns and epiphytes. Splotches of sunlight and wells of shadow baffled Boucher's eyes.

'You sure? It looks no different from a dozen other places we passed.'

'Close your eyes and count to twenty.'

'What?'

'Count to twenty and then come looking for me. Remember, try not to disturb anything.'

When he opened his eyes he was alone, but he had heard Candy move away behind him. Carefully he began to search in that direction. She couldn't have gone more than a few yards. After a minute he decided she must have bluffed him and circled round. He returned to where she had left him and started again. Every spot his eye fell on could have harboured a person. A rotted tree trunk leaned through the understorey, its belly hung with a curtain of creepers. That had to be it, he decided.

'Bang,' Candy said behind him, 'you're dead.'

'Whew. We might pull it off yet.'

But after the game was over and the waiting began,

optimism ebbed. Survival today would only be a postpone-
ment of the inevitable. There was no way off the island
and they had no access to food or water. Already he was
dehydrated. Killing the bogeys was their only means of
deliverance, and that would be impossible.

Some trick of sunlight and shadow created a tunnel
effect ahead of their hiding place. Staring down it,
Boucher convinced himself that it would be along there
that the bogeys would appear.

'What happens if there's more than one of them?' he
whispered.

'Stay tight, and if any of them comes close, avoid
looking directly at him.'

'Pretend he isn't there?'

'You know when you get the feeling someone's staring
at you and you look round and see that your instinct's
right?'

'Candy, I lived all my life in cities. If I worried about
people staring at me, I'd be in an asylum.'

'Cities blunt the senses. Take my word, if one of them
gets close, you'll know it.'

Half an hour had passed since they'd fled the beach. By
now the bogeys would be well into their search. Boucher
relived the murder of Dexter Smith and helpless rage
flooded him.

'How could anyone do a thing like that?'

'I know,' Candy said. She was quiet for a while. 'It's
Nadine I'm thinking about.'

Facets of sunshine danced in the canopy. Boucher
looked at Candy's profile and realized with gut-wrenching
certainty that the woman he loved, the woman he loved
without qualification, would soon be dead. He studied the
fragile dome of her temple and thought of the two bullets
in the pistol. His jaw clamped. Better that than let her fall
into the bogeys' hands. It wasn't a proposition he dared to

make, and he knew it wasn't one that Candy would accept. Not yet.

Waiting – even waiting to be killed – became tedious. His mind grew impatient, almost willing the bogeys to appear.

'Candy, if they don't find us today, we have to decide on a strategy.'

'Join up with the others.'

'Then what?'

'Swim to the mainland.'

Candy's account of her ordeal in the mangroves had invested them with a quality almost as nightmarish as their present situation. 'Stuck between a rock and a hard place.'

Candy tensed. He frowned in enquiry, his heart palpitating. She cocked her chin, indicating a point ahead of them and some way over their heads. She didn't look scared. After a minute, he located a lime green snake drooped round a bough. His pulse rate dropped.

Minutes tolled by. The snake had vanished. Something stung him on the thigh. When he reached to scratch, Candy pushed his arm down.

Her mouth was parted, her gaze riveted. His heart began to thump, but no sight nor sound nor sense of anyone reached him, and after a while he rested his head on his forearm to relieve the ache in his neck.

Suppose they evaded the pirates. Suppose they swam to the mainland. Suppose they got through the mangroves. Suppose ...

Some minor but significant shift in Candy's attitude swept his speculations aside. He followed the direction of her stare and saw only a web of green. Scale and distance were impossible to gauge. It was like one of those visual puzzles where you can only decipher the hidden object by letting it surprise your eyes.

His stomach cramped.

One of the bogeys was standing at the far end of the tunnel, only his upper half visible, and not all of that. In the underwater light it was impossible to identify him. For a good half minute, he remained motionless then, with a faint *swish*, he parted the undergrowth and stepped into a shaft of light. It was the pirate in the baseball cap. His yellow shirt had a cobra's head on it and the shadow cast by his headgear made him faceless. He held his AK-47 at the ready, a parang stuck in his belt. No one else appeared behind him and he gave the impression of a man relying on his own initiative. He stopped again, only his eyes moving, rotating in their sockets, examining every stem and leaf. For a moment that seemed eternal, his roving gaze rested on their hiding place. A bird called raucously in the upper storey and the bogey raised his head. Boucher exhaled slowly.

Lifting his feet as if he were stepping over mines, the bogey advanced another few feet. Every step led him straight towards their hiding place. It was as if he was being guided by antennae tuned to their fear. Boucher remembered what Candy had said about avoiding looking directly, but it was impossible to shift his gaze. Like a rabbit entranced by a stoat, he watched the bogey come closer. Now he could make out the man's features – thin jaw with wispy beard, thick lips, yellowish eyes that were blank only because they were utterly receptive. Insects clouded around his head and from time to time he abstractedly took one hand off his Kalashnikov to disperse them. Only the insect whine marred the silence. The bogey didn't make a sound. With each step, Boucher's courage drained away.

Fighting the instinct to flee, he clutched fistfuls of leaf litter. It was a test of will not just within himself, but between him and the bogey. The bogey knew they were there and was telepathically urging him to break and run. Boucher tried to reverse the advantage by imagining the bogey as nothing more than a target. He pictured the muzzle of Candy's pistol pointed at the cobra's head.

Very slowly the bogey got down on one knee and inspected the ground. His hand made a slow pass over the litter as if he could divine evidence of their presence from the air itself. Delicately he touched a leaf. Just as slowly he looked up and stared straight at them. Boucher's endocrine system flooded.

In one smooth movement the bogey rose. Boucher discerned a change in the man's expression. He took one more step in their direction, then half faced the way he had come and put his hand to his ear as if filtering out sounds. He couldn't be more than forty feet away, Boucher reckoned, but Candy held her fire. She wanted to be certain. God, he thought, she was cool. His own quaking nerves would have triggered the pistol long before now.

The bogey went back – only a couple of steps, but Boucher had the impression that he had picked up signals from elsewhere. Anxiety overlapped relief. They had to kill him, and his slight withdrawal had made him a difficult target. Another move like that and it would be hit or miss.

With the bogey's attention still elsewhere, Boucher risked a glance at Candy. She was sighting along the pistol, her left eye screwed shut.

The bogey had turned completely away, his back square on. There wouldn't be a better chance. Boucher braced himself for the shot. His nerves screamed for it.

'Now,' he breathed.

Candy's profile was contorted in concentration.

'Do it.'

Boucher saw to his horror that every part of her was

paralyzed except for her gun hand. Perspiration drenched her face. He snapped a glance at the bogey.

'Give me the gun.'

Candy didn't stir. The tip of the gun shook.

Boucher put his mouth to her ear. 'Give ... me ... the ... gun.'

Her knuckles were white and he feared the pistol would detonate spontaneously. A turquoise and gold butterfly had settled on her arm, its wings opening and shutting in drunken ecstasy. Boucher reached out as though he intended to swat it. As his arm extended, the pirate glanced to one side – a devastatingly alert move. Boucher froze off-balance, aware that any unconsidered motion on his part would be picked up in the man's peripheral vision.

By infinitely small degrees, never taking his eye off the bogey, he groped towards the gun. His hand touched Candy's wrist and eased down. Her fingers were locked on, incapable of relinquishing their grip. He willed her to look at him and at last she met his grimace with an expression of anguished apology. He smiled – not much of a smile. All of a sudden the pistol went loose.

And in the same moment, Candy sobbed – the tiniest little expulsion of breath. But the pirate heard it. His head jerked and his gun came up in a blur and Boucher didn't have time to aim.

Even as he fired he knew he'd missed, and before the second concussion jerked his wrist a storm erupted over him. The functioning part of his brain told him that the bogey had aimed blind and a couple of yards to his right. Boucher rolled and squirmed to his left in a desperate bid to cover enough ground for Candy to get away.

He heard the bogey's quick steps and a scream that meant *Stop!* in any language. Rolling, he saw the bogey's legs, straddled for balance.

'Drop the pistol,' Candy shouted.

Boucher threw it away and fell on his back.

The bogey jabbed the rifle into his chest, then immediately swung it at Candy, who was crouched ten feet away, her hands in the air. He screamed again and Candy scurried forward. The bogey scooped up the pistol, stuck it in his waistband, then backed off to bring them both within a short arc of fire. With one gesture he made Boucher get up. With another he commanded him to come forward. The third gesture was a brisk downward motion.

'He's telling you to kneel,' Candy said.

'Fuck him.'

'Do it.'

Boucher dropped, his mind dulling.

'Money,' Candy said. 'Dollars.'

Boucher looked into the bore of the bogey's gun, and then beyond it, to the bogey's vacant face. He closed his eyes.

A violent commotion accompanied the shot and Boucher collapsed and was knocked sideways, borne down by the bogey's weight. He glimpsed the tiger, orange pelted and striped, a blade that chopped down into the back of the bogey's head with a splintering of bone. Jaeger reared up, the blade bloody, and struck again.

Boucher's legs were trapped under both men. As he tried to wriggle free, he saw the gun. A foot from it the bogey's fingers clutched and unclutched, trying to get purchase even after death. With all his might Boucher pulled loose, but it was Candy, quick as a rat, who scrabbled the weapon up. He staggered and turned. Jaeger's lips rolled away from his teeth, and as he smashed down he arched and his neck writhed and he roared. Boucher backed away, his own mouth a terrified version of Jaeger's. The bogey's head was no longer recognizable.

Jaeger lifted his head and roared again. Blood and bone and brain matted his chest.

Boucher stumbled into Candy. Her hand dragged him. They ran without thought, the jungle reeling past like a green kaleidoscope. They burst into a clearing. Boucher pulled right, but Candy yanked him left.

'This way.'

28

Horror and jubilation warred in Boucher. Violent obscenities spilled out. Kill the fuckers. Blow them away. Bloody images burst like starshells – the red gape of Jaeger's mouth, the pirate's bolting eyeball, his twitching hand.

Candy tripped and fell, grunting as she struck the ground. A thorn had slashed her ear, but when Boucher reached out, she fended him off.

'Did you hear it?'

All Boucher could hear was his blood pounding.

'Someone screaming.' She looked towards the inner lagoon. 'That's where Nadine is.'

Moving more cautiously but still too fast for safety, they headed for the landward shore. Boucher glimpsed water. He crept forward and held up his hand against the dazzle.

'There's nobody there.'

The inflatable was floating on the lagoon, apparently empty. The surface of the lagoon was mirror flat. A plastic drum floated about thirty yards from the boat. Something about the arrangement chilled Boucher.

Candy's voice was hushed. 'Maybe they're lying in the boat.'

'No, it's empty.'

'It must have drifted away from the shore.'

349

'Nobody could be that careless. Besides, they wouldn't have left it. And why would they bring Nadine ashore?'

'I don't know. To use her as a hostage. It must have been her I heard screaming.'

Out of Boucher's perplexity rose a single fact. 'Candy, that boat's our deliverance.'

'They might have left it to lure us out.'

'They don't need that kind of contrivance.'

'Well, something isn't right.'

'I know, but if we can get the boat, no one can touch us.'

'We'd have to swim. We'll be sitting ducks.'

'They'll have heard the shooting and gone to investigate.'

'They may come back.'

'So we'd better make our minds up quick.' The boat was so tantalizingly close. 'We've got to risk it.'

'We can't both go. You take the gun and keep watch.'

'No, I can swim better than you.' Boucher handed her the weapon. 'This time, no debates. Just do it.'

Candy cast her eyes down. 'I don't know what happened. My eyes blurred, it was the ...'

'Waiting. I know. Which is what we're wasting time doing now.' He kissed her cheek. 'I love you.'

Trying to balance the need for speed against the risk of alerting the bogeys, he waded in. He was hideously exposed, and knowing it would only take a minute to reach the boat didn't help. Fate might have allotted him the wrong minute. Mud clutched round his feet and he prepared to swim.

'Jay,' Candy murmured.

The softness of her tone suggested she was about to reciprocate his parting declaration, but she wasn't looking at him. She was staring out over the tannin waters.

Impatience shook him. 'Candy, they could show any second.'

'I think a crocodile got them. Remember what Robert said about crocodiles attacking boats?'

Boucher's groin contracted. 'God, you certainly choose your moments.'

The inflatable looked much further away now, and with every passing second, the more it seem to drift.

'Shit,' Boucher said, and cast off, using breast-stroke for least disturbance and maximum field of view. Recalling what Marriot had told him about crocodiles, he felt boneless, all shrinking flesh. He wasn't sure whether they attacked stealthily, underwater, or came surging along the surface. He reached the midway point and forged on, the boat beginning to grow large in his sights. The closer he came, the harder it was to maintain an even stroke. Only fifteen yards short, he checked the shore.

Candy was flapping her hands and capering like a creature possessed. Terrified, he reared in the water and searched around, not knowing what she'd seen or whether she was urging him to hurry up or get back. Her arm made a desperate sweeping gesture. Back! Now! He filled his lungs, lowered his head and ploughed for shore, not looking up until every scrap of breath was gone. Candy was still throwing a fit, the bank still miles away. When he next filled his lungs she was gone.

He thrashed into the shallows and hurled himself on to land. Picking himself up, he saw Candy crouched behind a tree, waving a hand for silence. He collapsed beside her, gulping air in great whoops.

'Keep it down,' she hissed. 'I heard voices.'

They waited, held on each other's gaze, Candy's finger pressed against her lips and her expression agonized by his spastic wheezing. A fluting whistle made him choke back a gasp. It was repeated several times and followed by a rustle of vegetation, the sound coming from the near distance. Boucher's breathing returned to some sort of order. He glanced at the lagoon and winced. Mud stained the surface and ripples spread far from shore – perfect semi-circles with him and Candy located at the centre. He took the gun from her.

Down the waterline the bogeys had gone quiet. The ripples died, but that didn't mean they hadn't been noticed. Boucher checked the weapon.

'How do you switch it to auto?'

'It's done.'

Boucher heard a subdued splash. Seconds later a scrap of red appeared amidst the greenery. Boucher shifted to get a better vantage. Redshirt was standing in the lagoon, searching along the edge. Boucher sighted on him. Not a clear shot.

Another bogey, the man in the turban, came into fragmentary view. That left one more. Boucher knew he would have to shoot all three. He had no qualms. He jabbed a finger towards the forest and then raised two more to indicate they had three bogeys to deal with. Candy nodded.

Redshirt and Turban had begun to argue. The boat had drifted in the imperceptible current.

'They know what happened,' Candy whispered. 'They're not too keen on going out there.'

Eventually, Turban took the plunge, his actions dainty, his gun traversing for as long as he could hold it level. He extended it over his head and swam in a clumsy sidestroke, the gun raised clear. Redshirt had followed him until he stood thigh-deep, gun at the ready. He paid no heed to anything behind him, confirming Boucher's suspicion that number three was still on shore, covering their backs.

He tapped Candy's shoulder. 'They're going to bring the

boat in. I'm going to have to get closer. I'll wait until all three are on board.'

'I'm coming with you.'

They sidled through the forest. At one point Boucher lost sight of the lagoon. When it came in sight again, Turban was elbowing himself aboard the inflatable. He seemed jittery and made a thorough inspection of his surroundings before starting the engine. Before returning to Redshirt, he salvaged the drum of gas, rolling it over the side with effort. Watching all ways, he motored to shore.

Under cover of the rasping engine, Boucher and Candy gained another ten yards. Any closer and they risked running into number three. Boucher saw Redshirt stepping into the boat. Turban was out of sight in the stern, hidden by foliage. Boucher realized that even this close, he would have to move very fast to get them all. The moment number three got in, he decided, he would dash for a better firing position.

Redshirt was standing up, holding on to a branch to stop the inflatable drifting. Boucher smelt cigarette smoke through the exhaust fumes.

'Come on,' he prayed.

Redshirt began to move backwards. The inflatable was leaving. Boucher couldn't even swear that number three wasn't in it. Cursing, he fought his way towards the water's edge.

No more than thirty yards away the inflatable glided into plain sight. Only two bogeys were in it. Boucher raised the gun and held Redshirt squarely in his aim and knew he couldn't miss.

'Not yet,' Candy whispered. 'They'll probably wait offshore for the other one.'

'What if he doesn't show?'

'Use your judgement.'

'Damn,' Boucher said. He kept the gun steady as Redshirt began to diminish in his sights. He drew a mental line across the lagoon. If they crossed it, he would fire.

Close to the spot where he'd retrieved the boat, Turban switched off the motor. The lagoon settled back into stagnation. The bogeys were waiting for number three.

Boucher's arms began to ache from holding the gun. A matrix of sunlight danced on the waters and the bogeys had slumped into jigging silhouettes. He blinked sweat out of his eyes. At this rate he would freeze up like Candy. He lowered the gun, let his breath go, then jerked round.

'You nearly got yourself shot,' he hissed. 'How did you find us?'

Disco dropped his hands. 'You came storming by ten feet from where me and Kent were holed up. We heard shooting – *pop-pop*, then a burst of semi-auto and another shot and weird howling. We figured you were dead.' His eyes illuminated at sight of the gun. 'Christ, man, I underestimated you.'

'It was Leo. He jumped one of them and pulped his brains. That was him you heard raving.'

Disco whistled in awe. 'You don't want to piss old Leo off.' He shaded his eyes to view the lagoon. 'What the fuck are they doing? Where's Nadine?'

'We think she and the bogey holding her were attacked by crocodiles.'

Disco's mouth made an O. He looked from Boucher to the boat in short takes. 'You're shitting me.'

'When we got here, the boat was floating empty fifty yards out. Those two came back and they freaked.'

'A crocodile,' Disco said, and uttered a short laugh. 'Wow, that couldn't have been much fun for Nadine.'

Redshirt began to shout.

'They can't wait to skedaddle,' Boucher said, 'but one of them's still on the island.'

Disco peered at the boat. 'Yeah, doesn't appear like they're in the mood anymore.' He punched Boucher's arm. 'We did it, man. We did it.' He eyed the AK-47 with reverence. 'That thing loaded?'

'It certainly is.'

'You're holding fire until number three shows up, right?'

'We've got to get them all.'

From the forest came a faraway cry. Redshirt called back.

Boucher adjusted his grip. 'Any minute now.'

The inflatable began to make way. Candy's eyes flicked towards Boucher. 'They must be going to pick him up on the other side. We'll never get across in time.'

'Take them,' Disco ordered.

As Boucher assumed a fresh firing stance, a string of thought unreeled very quickly. He wanted to kill the pirates, but if no one returned to the schooner, the remaining crew would send out a search party – not immediately, perhaps, but sooner or later. The survivors would never be able to sleep without the dread of seeing another party of armed men coming out of the sea. But they wouldn't return if they knew what had happened on these few acres – or rather, if they left with only the darkest intuition of what had killed two of their number. A tiger, a sea monster – inexplicable terrors that would grow more dreadful with each telling.

'What are you fucking waiting for?'

'We should let them go. When they describe what they found on this island, no one will ever – *ever* – dare set foot on it again.'

Rage strangled Disco's voice. 'The man who butchered Dexter is getting away and you're talking diplomacy. And something else, you moron. We need that inflatable.'

Already the boat had cruised past their position.

355

'Give it to him, Jay.'

Disco snatched the gun, at the same time pushing the camcorder into Boucher's hand. 'Crank up the zoom. I wanna see the look on those bogeys' faces.' Deftly he flicked the setting to single shot and settled into his aim. 'Oh, man,' he said, and squeezed off two shots.

Through the viewfinder, Boucher saw Redshirt dive flat. 'Missed,' Candy said.

Return fire came from the boat, which suddenly dug in its stern and accelerated. Disco loosed a fusillade.

'If they make it, Boucher, I swear I'll ...'

His threat was drowned by a soft *whoomph* as the inflatable ignited in a ball of orange flame that rolled aloft on a column of black smoke. Bits of fabric and other debris pattered sizzling on to the water. From the mangroves came a chorus of squawks and screeches.

'What'd I do?' Disco said.

'You hit the gas tank.'

Disco let out a whoop that abruptly tailed off. His face set into petulance. 'Fuck, that was our transport.'

Flames still burned in a circle where the inflatable had been. Smoke hung in the air.

'One of them's swimming.'

Boucher couldn't have said who it was. The man in the water was charred black and virtually incapacitated. Disco fired and water spouted feet away from the target.

'I could have taken them clean if you hadn't crapped out.'

'He won't survive,' Boucher said.

Disco sighted again, then relaxed. 'Yeah, save the ammo. Let the crocs finish it.' He cradled the gun as if it were a baby. 'Don't ask for it back.'

They fell quiet, watching the man in the water, all sharing the same expectation – an oily swirl, a scaly tail, a saurian head. But no crocodile appeared. The pirate's movements got weaker and more spasmodic. His arm came up like a broken marionette and flopped. He floated for a few seconds, then disappeared.

'You get that on film? Lemme look.' Disco glued his eye to the viewfinder. 'Aw,' he said, 'the battery's dead. I was looking forward to the replay. Hey, you sure you got me blowing the boat up?'

'Who cares? One of them's still on the island.'

Disco patted the gun and grinned. 'This evens things up.'

The smoke from the explosion had dispersed into a dirty fog. The air stank of burnt gas and plastic and things that could only be inferred.

'We'd better find Kent,' Candy said. Her ear had bled profusely, was still oozing, and threads of blood had dried on her cheek.

They began to make their way back, Disco jaunty and alert, drawing beads on imaginary targets, Boucher and Candy trailing behind like his prisoners. Another tortured howl rose up out of the forest.

Disco smiled, at peace. 'Sounds like Leo just snuffed number five. Man, ain't he a piece of work?'

29

Day 21

By the time they reached the seaward side, the schooner had hauled anchor and moved further out to sea, beyond range of Disco, who ran along the beach brandishing his gun and screaming challenges to combat. Dexter's body lay where it had fallen and a vulture, the first Candy had seen on the ground, stood on it. She shooed it away but it flew only as far as the nearest treetop, alighting on a twig that gave under its weight and made it dip and bow like a genuflecting priest.

Hurrying to the camp, Candy found it hadn't been touched. There had been nothing to steal. The liferaft was still in one piece, too. Candy found a container of water and drank greedily, the liquid dribbling pink from her chin. Boucher moped by the waterline, back hunched against the carnage.

Disco returned, swagger gone and a new authority in his voice. 'Call Kent,' he ordered.

After about ten minutes' shouting, Bartok emerged from the trees, cautious and round-eyed. Disco looked up from cleaning the gun.

'While you were keeping your curly head down, me and Leo were cleaning up.' He stuck four fingers in the air. 'Leo took out number one with his bare hands. Number two got eaten by a crocodile – yeah, a croc. And I sent three and four to kingdom come. We heard Leo hollering again, so maybe he got the other one.'

Candy noted how Disco ignored the part she and Boucher had played in the battle. 'Nadine's dead, too.'

'Yeah,' Disco said, banging home the magazine. 'Fucking rough.'

Anger scoured Candy. 'Is that all you have to say?'

'No,' Disco said, cold-eyed. 'If Boucher had shown more guts, we'd be halfway to Jakarta by now. He had a chance to grab the inflatable and he chickened out.'

Bartok's eyes darted in the hostile cross-currents. He turned towards the schooner. 'Do you think they'll hit us again?'

Disco snorted. 'Would *you*?' He gave Candy a flat stare. 'Would *you*?'

She shook her head.

'Those bogeys are never coming back. When they crawl in to whatever hole they call home, we're gonna be a legend of the south seas.' Disco's eyes shone. 'Christ, I'd have given something to see that croc. Man, it must have been huge.'

Boucher wandered up like an old man and stood behind him. 'You'd better ask Jaeger about the missing pirate.'

'You do it,' Disco said, without turning.

'I'm not armed.'

'What happened to the pistol?'

'I dropped it.'

Disco stood up. 'Come here.'

'I haven't got it. It's empty.'

'Come here.'

Expressionless, Boucher stood while Disco frisked him. His eyes turned to Candy. 'Now you.'

She submitted to his search. From the corner of her eye she could see the tension in Boucher. Disco's hand lingered on her breast.

'Where did you drop it?'

'Get your hands off her.'

Disco cupped his hand tighter.

'It could be anywhere,' Boucher said. 'I threw it away after I grabbed the Kalashnikov.'

Still holding Candy, Disco elevated the gun. 'Liar.'

'The pirate took it,' Candy admitted. 'Probably Leo has it now.'

Disco rolled his tongue around his cheek, then loosed his hold. 'Okay, but from now on, you all do what I tell you. *When* I tell you. That's been the problem all along. No leadership.' He eyed Dexter's body with distaste. 'Clean this place up,' he told Boucher. 'Kent, you come with me.'

'We've got no protection,' Boucher told him.

'Now you know how it feels,' Disco said, turning on his heel.

Candy forced herself to her feet and stood looking at Dexter's body.

'What shall we do with him?' Boucher asked.

She nearly suggested they drag the corpse into the forest and leave it for the scavengers. The proprieties of civilization no longer seemed important. She was running on empty.

'Bury him off the reef.'

While they were sheeting him up in what was left of the balloon fabric, the schooner raised sail and got underway. Down the beach, Disco shook his gun, his shadow stretched long on the sand.

'He should have signed up with them,' Boucher said.

Candy watched the schooner set course, and as its hull grew shorter, an abyss of despair opened before her.

They waited until the vessel was out of sight before rowing to the reef. The funeral rites were brief and no tears were shed, though both of them had nothing against Dexter.

'The world will mourn for him,' Boucher said.

After regaining the lagoon, they shelved oars and contemplated the island, knowing the worst was still to come. Finally, Boucher voiced the thought uppermost in Candy's mind.

'There's no stopping Disco now. We've got the boat. We don't have to go back.'

'Kent's still there. We haven't made preparations. We need more water, and we have to get the flare gun off Leo. Tomorrow evening is the earliest we can go.'

'Disco's in party mood. You know what he's got in mind for you.'

'Tonight I'll sleep in the forest.'

'There could be an armed pirate in there.'

'I'll slip off as soon as it gets dark. Nobody will be able to find me.'

'I'll come with you.'

'Stay. Don't give Disco any excuses to hurt you.'

'You can't keep out of his way for ever.'

'One night is all I need.'

'Candy, he's going to rape you.'

She smiled tiredly. 'Worse things have happened.'

'Christ, Candy, doesn't it bother you?'

'Being fucked by Disco? I'll tell you what bothers me. Dexter and Nadine and Trigg and Robert and Josef and Aquila and – have I left anyone out? Oh yes, the pilot whose name I can't remember. That's what bothers me. Being screwed by Disco seems almost normal.'

Boucher turned his head as if he'd heard a voice from another quarter. He remained looking in that direction. 'I'm going to have to kill him.'

Candy felt no shock. 'How?'

Boucher fingered his jacket and marked the angle of the sun. 'If the pistol's still with the pirate, can you get it for me?'

'It's empty.'

'No, there's one bullet left.'

'Are you sure?'

'Positive.'

When Kent and Disco returned, just before sundown, Candy was composed. She had secreted water and food by a tree fifty yards from the camp.

Disco flopped on the sand and closed his eyes, the gun across his chest. 'Better stay out of Leo's way. He's in a delicate frame of mind.'

'Did he kill the other pirate?'

'He's not making a lot of sense, but I guess not.'

'Terrific,' Boucher said. 'How does my idea of letting them get away look now?'

Disco opened his eyes a fraction. 'Hey, Kent, you got a good look at the bogeys. Who are we looking for?'

For the first time since Candy had known him, Bartok was surly. 'How should I know?'

'Process of elimination. The boatman's dead, and so's the fucker in the red shirt and the mother in the head-dress. Jay, which bogey did this gun come off?'

'The one with the head man – the guy in the baseball hat and yellow sweat shirt.'

'That make things easier, Kent? Come on, shape up.'

'It must be the one who was with me. He wore blue jeans. He was just a kid. Spoke a bit of English – you know, "Hello, America, America good". He didn't look tough.'

Disco pulled himself into a sitting position. 'Candy, didn't you say he was the one with a shotgun?'

'Yes.'

'Well, if he didn't seem tough when he was part of an army, he'll be a whole lot tenderer now. Wouldn't surprise me if he's already checked his options and decided to swim to Singapore.'

Boucher let sand pour from his palm. 'And it wouldn't surprise me if he was watching us right now, waiting for dark so he can come out and slit our throats.'

'We'll post a watch, and tomorrow we'll have ourselves a man-hunt.'

'You hunt him,' Boucher said. He looked done in, his eyes no brighter than an ape's.

Disco seemed to be in top spirits. 'You know, Jay, the more time I spend with you, the more I see what's gone wrong with America.'

Boucher began to laugh without restraint.

Disco uncoiled from the sand. 'You think it's funny, fucker? Candy here, she went off to look for help and shot the tiger. Kent risks his neck every time he climbs. Leo kills a man with his bare hands. But you, you get a chance to hijack the inflatable and that fucking marsh-mallow conscience fucks it up.' He leaned on one elbow, the gun propped against his thighs. 'One way or another, we're gonna flush out that bogey and Jay, you're walking point.'

'Inside the forest he's got all the advantage,' Candy said. 'I don't think he'll attack us if we leave him alone. He's shocked and frightened, and he knows he can't escape.'

'Desperate, too,' Disco said. 'And we know what desperation does to a man. Hey, where d'ya think you're going?'

'To call him.'

'Get back here.'

'He knows this coast. He'll know where the nearest town is. He can help us.'

Disco thought about it. 'Bring him in then, but whatever he says, his life is forfeit.'

Night had imposed its curfew, stark and still. Candy passed beyond the forest wall.

'Hello!' she shouted. 'Come out. We won't hurt you. We need your help.'

Disco laughed delightedly.

Candy walked deeper into the forest until everything before her eyes was a mystery. Looking back, she could just make out the trio on the sand. Disco was holding something up.

'Jay, how much would people pay for a video of Dexter having his head cut off?'

Boucher was just a glitter of eyes. 'I don't know.'

'How much are they paying you for the Dexter Smith story?'

'Eight thousand dollars.'

'That all? Hell, if one picture's worth a thousand words, then what I've got on here must be worth a million.'

'It's not yours to sell. It's Trigg's camera and videotape. He shot most of the film. Copyright law's very complex, Disco. I'd say the film belongs to Trigg's heirs or the Wildguard foundation.'

Disco rose and for a moment Candy thought he'd been provoked into violence. He disappeared into the dark and she heard a faint splash. A few seconds later he strolled back.

'Who says I shot it on Trigg's machine? Who says this is his film?'

That was when Candy knew that Disco wasn't going to stop at rape. That's when it sank in that he intended to be the only one off the island.

'Time's up,' he called. 'Come on out now. It's not safe in there.'

Hands outheld, she felt her way deeper into the dark.

'I said get your ass back here. What do you think you're playing at? You can't hide from me.'

30

Day 22

Steamy heat filled the forest once the sun had climbed out of the dawn mists. Thinking of the pirate still at large, Candy moved haltingly, starting at every bird cry and leaf fall.

And she could be going out on a limb for nothing. Before her tiger vigil, she'd counted the bullets left in the pistol. Seven. She was almost certain that she'd fired five, and Jay had discharged the remaining two.

But he'd sounded so certain. Positive, he'd said. Memory was such an unreliable witness; the question was, whose was at fault?

A contented sawing – zzz-zzz – advertised the resting place of the dead pirate. His head was an iridescent green casque, and as she approached, flies lifted off in ones and twos and buzzed drunkenly towards her. Edging closer, she saw ants marching and counter-marching up the corpse, their columns winding into the undergrowth for as far as she could see. Stifling her revulsion, she levered the body on to its side. The flies rose from the oozing head in a black torment. Candy glimpsed the silver automatic, plucked it out and ran, swatting at the flies that swarmed after her.

Away from that abominable place, she slid out the

magazine and checked it. Bright hope dulled, and for a moment her mind was as vacant as the clip.

Then despair rushed in. 'Oh, Jay,' she groaned. 'You fool.'

Now what could they do? Boucher had described the pistol as the variation that would guarantee their preservation. Without it they had no weapons offensive or defensive, no survival mechanisms except their brains.

She looked up, frowning. Wait a minute. Brains weren't to be sneezed at. Humans had triumphed by brain power – the adaptive intelligence that permits infinite variations in behaviour. Flexible behaviour was the key to survival. A tiger always behaved as a tiger, a mouse was always a mouse, but there was no natural law that said Candy always had to behave like Candy.

Behind her a twig snapped and the muscles bunched in the small of her back. For several seconds she remained braced for a blast of shotgun pellets. When it didn't come, she slowly raised both hands in surrender and turned.

Looking for a face in that green amphitheatre was like searching for a flaw on an endless circle of hectic wallpaper.

'*Selamat*,' she called. 'Hello.'

Birds twittered.

'You must be hungry and thirsty,' she said. 'Do you want some water?' She laid down her flask. 'Here, take it.' She waited. 'Look,' she said, 'we won't hurt you. Stay out of our way and we'll stay out of yours. Deal?'

Still the forest didn't answer.

'I'm going now,' she said, sliding the pistol into her waistband. 'If you shoot me, my friends will come after you.'

She gave it another few seconds.

'I'm leaving now. Goodbye. *Selamat tinggal*.'

Feeling about ten feet wide and made of glass, she

began shuffling away. Ten yards she covered, twenty, and still no shot. Risking a look behind, she saw only the usual botanical confusion. Spinning on her heel, she fled and didn't stop until she was back at the forest edge.

There, anger at Boucher's miscalculation caught up. Looking at the pistol, she had half a mind to junk it. Instead, she buried it in a clump of ferns and then stood, in a funk at the prospect of returning into Disco's hands. A snake, that's what he was, a venomous snake.

Of their own accord, her eyes shifted to the lagoon. A pulse beat in her brain. Every poison had its antidote, every creature had a fatal weakness – even a snake. And she'd find it. With a last look at the lagoon, she went to face the music.

From a long way off she saw Disco rise, his outline pulsating in the heat shimmers – squat one moment, then grotesquely elongated. When she was close enough to see him properly, she halted. His face was expressionless, his gun aimed at her stomach. Boucher and Disco remained sitting. Boucher had a weeping bruise on one cheekbone and his eyes made her think of an animal in a cage.

She met Disco's stare head on. 'Would you mind pointing that thing somewhere else?'

'Where's the pistol at?'

'You mean the automatic?' She hadn't meant to sound quite that stupid, but Disco's pre-emptive thrust threw her into a panic.

Quick as a lizard, he grabbed her, swung her around, locked one arm round her neck, and roughly patted her all over.

'Where d'you hide it?'

'I haven't hidden it anywhere. Either Leo's got it or it's still with the pirate.'

'Leo ain't got it. That much I did establish.'

'Then it's with the pirate.'

'That's what worries me.'

'Go and get it then. Why stand here talking about it?'

He slapped her and she didn't see the blow coming. Shock stung as much as the pain. Nobody had ever struck her before. Not one person.

Disco's eyes narrowed to slits. He aimed the gun at Boucher. 'Show me where that pistol is, or I'll shoot Jay where he sits.'

She almost told him to go ahead. The fool had almost got her killed twice over for a useless lump of metal.

'You're welcome to have it,' she said. 'The bloody thing's empty.'

'It can't be,' Boucher said, rising stupidly from the sand.

'You can't even count.'

Disco grinned at Boucher's discomfiture. 'Show me, honeybun.'

Wordlessly, Candy turned and marched back to where she'd cached the automatic.

'There,' she said, pointing. She crossed her arms and stared daggers at Boucher.

Disco picked up the pistol and pointed it at her head. 'Empty, you said.'

'Go ahead.'

'Don't!' Boucher cried.

Disco pulled the trigger.

'Good as your word,' he said, 'unlike writer-man.' He looked at Boucher with an expression twisted between condescension and disgust. 'Remind me never to rely on you.' He shook his head. 'But empty or not, it doesn't change the facts. You were planning to do me harm.' He blew out his cheeks. 'What's a man to do?'

Candy said the first thing that came into her head.

'I met the pirate in the forest.'

'Met him? Hell, you make it sound like you shook hands.'

'He had me at his mercy. He could have shot me.'

'Why didn't he?'

'He knows that would have been a declaration of war.'

Disco nodded. 'And he's only got a shotgun.'

'Leo only had a parang,' Boucher reminded him.

'Let's get off here,' Bartok pleaded.

'Feel the same way?' Disco asked Boucher.

'If I were you, I'd quit while I'm ahead.'

Disco weighed up the arguments. 'It's gonna be wearing on the nerves having that bogey around day and night.' He inclined his face to the sky while he pondered. 'Okay,' he said at last, 'we pull out tonight.'

'We haven't got any food for the journey,' Candy pointed out. 'Someone will have to catch some fish.'

Disco looked put out. 'Problem is, now we're all back together, I'm reluctant to see us break up. I can't help feeling that if Jay goes out in the boat, the last I'd see is him heading for the horizon.'

'I'll catch something,' Candy said, forestalling Boucher's interruption and giving him as hard a look as she dared. 'You know I wouldn't desert Jay.'

'There's a first time for everything,' Disco said, giving her a thoughtful look. He relaxed. 'But I guess this isn't it.'

Out on the lagoon the sun struck with full force. Candy rowed almost as far as the reef before turning and following it down to one of the coral nurseries.

Fish the size and colours of postage stamps issued by emergent republics sported among the stems. Fish in op-art patterns flaunted themselves. Clown fish peeped from anemones with the engaging smiles and infantile eyes of friendly aliens. A reef shark about two feet long coasted by and all the little gems vanished in a twinkling. None of these wonders fully engaged Candy's attention. She was trying to find a visual match for the decaying mineral image she carried in her head.

'Where are you hiding?'

On the point of trying another outcrop, she spotted her quarry – a stonefish, a visual misshape so at variance with conventional fishy anatomy that at first she couldn't make out head nor tail. Then it came into focus – the head like a scowling gargoyle, the warty body guarded by a palisade of spines.

'Now how am I going to get you out?'

Reassuring herself that the heat haze hid her activities from any shore-bound onlooker, she wrapped a piece of airship fabric around her palm and carefully submerged her hand. The water was so translucent that she'd underestimated the distance to the stonefish and had to reach deep. It didn't budge. Mobility wasn't its mode of defence. Ever so slowly she moved her hand closer. Apart from the fluttering of its gill feathers, it gave no sign of life. Her hand stopped right behind it.

Salt sweat stung her eyes, but she was in no position to wipe them. Marriot's warning made her bare her teeth. *Even if the poison doesn't kill you, the pain will make you wish you were dead.* Grab it by the tail, she thought, but then realized that if it struggled, she might easily be punctured. All or nothing, she thought, praying that the fabric was thick enough to protect her.

There!

The stumpy little body was in her grip. In almost the same movement she pulled it out and threw it into the furthest corner of the boat. It flapped and jumped and she drew up her feet on the seat as if she was trapped naked in an empty bathtub with a burning tarantula.

Gradually its struggles weakened. It gasped pathetically for a while, then suffocated. Not knowing if its poison died with it, Candy immediately pulled out the syringe she'd taken from the first aid box. Wrapping her hand again, she picked up the stonefish and examined its thirteen spines. There were grooves on each side of the barbs and she deduced that the venom must be channelled up them under pressure from basal poison sacs. When she'd worked out the delivery system, she laid the fish down on the seat. Still holding it, she took a short length of wood and pressed down on the tip of the most forward spine, gently increasing pressure until a thread of fluid appeared in the channels. Tongue held between her teeth, she inserted the needle and drew up the plunger.

Next to nothing, but further pressure didn't yield any more. One by one she milked the spines, and when she'd finished, the syrette was less than one-eighth full.

The pain will drive you mad.

Exhausted, she rested before pulling for shore. The atmosphere was like a sauna. She felt sick and headachy and guessed another bout of fever was on its way.

In the sultry air, the camp seemed to be at siesta. But when Candy reached it, only Disco was lounging. Boucher and Bartok were slumped like captives whose master hadn't decided their fate.

'What you catch?' Disco asked.

Candy shook her head. 'The fish aren't biting. It must be the weather.'

'You were in the wrong place,' Boucher muttered.

Candy assumed a petulant tone. 'You try and do better.' She jerked her head in the direction of the reef.

'Storm's going to break soon,' Bartok said. 'Maybe we should postpone.'

'Wait until tomorrow and there'll be another reason to stay. This island breeds a jail mentality.'

'We need good visibility if we're to reach the rig,'

Boucher said. He spoke to Disco but his eyes were signalling to Candy.

'Storm may clear the air,' Disco said. He brooded for a moment, then jerked his chin at Boucher. 'Go catch fish. You keep Candy in mind, now.'

With a bemused glance at her, Boucher made his way to the boat. Watching him leave, she wondered if he'd interpreted her gesture as an instruction to sail off into the blue.

Disco waited until he was just a tremble in the heat.

'Looks like this is our last day together,' he said. 'On this island.' His eyes trawled around as if cataloguing the scenery for his holiday album. 'I'm gonna miss it. Miss this heat that warms a man up without any exertion on his part.' His cheeks bunched in an explicit smile aimed at Candy. 'Together again at last.'

Knowing what was coming, her interior drew tight. 'Disco, please.'

'Take your clothes off, honeybun.'

'You must know you won't get away with it.'

'Disco,' Bartok said, making to rise.

The casual sweep of Disco's gun dumped him back. 'Stick around, Kent.' He clicked his fingers at Candy.

'Why?' she pleaded. 'Why like this?'

'Time's running short and I made a promise.'

Slowly Candy stripped. 'I'm surprised you didn't make Jay stay.'

'I want to concentrate on what I'm doing.'

When Candy was naked, Disco stood. 'Come here.'

Like a slave doing a tyrant's bidding, she obeyed. He ran his hand over her from neck to navel and she tried not to flinch. Gently he laid his free hand around her neck and forced her to her knees. As she looked up, she remembered the pirate who had made Boucher grovel before execution.

372

'Don't do this,' Bartok begged. 'It's a terrible sin.'

'If it is, it's one you're gonna be committing right after I'm through.'

'Never. For pity's sake, have some respect. What harm did Candy ever do you? She saved our lives.'

'I do respect her,' Disco said, unzipping his pants. His gun jerked up. 'Kent, I told you to stay put.' Rifle still trained on Bartok, he smiled down at Candy. 'Go on.'

Detached, that's what Candy felt. Mercilessly detached. The thing in her mouth, the creature joined to it meant nothing. She thought of the stonefish poison working up the spines.

'I'm warning you,' Bartok said behind her. 'Leave her alone.'

'You hear Candy complaining? Truth is, she's got a taste for it. Kent, you're in for a treat.'

'Stop it.'

'What's your problem?'

'It isn't right. It's evil.'

'In every person's life, there comes a time when they do the exact opposite of what they know to be right. It's a very liberating moment. Some people like it so much they keep on going.'

'You won't tempt me again, Disco.'

Disco cocked the rifle. 'I'm counting on this to do the job first time, temptation thereafter. Because once a man falls, he stays fallen. As I am, Kent, so you will be.'

Behind her, Candy heard the shuffle of sand.

'You're right on the line,' Disco warned. 'Cross it and I'll shoot.'

'Damn you to hell.'

Candy never heard Bartok's last fatal move. All she heard was a single shot, and when she turned, he was already falling, collapsing as if his bones had turned to liquid. He hit the ground and she expected to see him bounce back with his tumbler's elastic grace. But he didn't. Bartok, who could climb a sheer precipice on a fingernail and a prayer, was dead before he hit the ground.

Disco yanked her head back. 'I didn't tell you to stop. Go on. Go on. Yeah, like that.'

Under his ferocious urgings, Candy responded with vigour. Glancing up, she saw his eyes closed, his jaw clenched. Feeling behind her, she picked up the syringe from her discarded shirt. Holding it, she grasped his thigh.

'Good,' he said.

Moments later he gave an involuntary moan and she sensed the tide beginning deep within him. In her hand she aligned the syringe and grasped tighter. His cramped breathing signalled the end. At the climactic instant, she pulled back.

'Bitch,' he said, yanking her head.

'I'm sorry, I got scared. I didn't mean ...'

'Bitch,' he said again. But he was helpless, reduced to brute unconscious function, and as his convulsions began, she slid the needle under his skin and squeezed the plunger.

'Aah!' he said, rhythmically spurting.

And then the pain hit. Still gripping her, he straightened up as if he'd been shot.

Then violently doubled over.

'What the fuck d'ya do?'

She gawped in frightened incomprehension. 'Do? Did I hurt you?'

'You stuck me with something, you bitch. Oh ... Oh ... Jesus.'

She shook her head idiotically. 'I don't ... What's wrong?'

The poison invaded his central nervous system and he shuddered in what seemed like orgasmic aftershock. His

374

eyes stuck wide open and then squeezed shut. 'Oh,' he said, 'oh, oh, oh,' – his cries fading like a reprise of his climax. 'Oh, Christ!'

'What is it?' Candy cried. 'Tell me.'

'Oh, Jesus, man. Ahhhh. Something ... oh ... It's killing me.'

'Where? Show me where.'

He sagged to the sand, still holding the rifle, taking Candy with him.

'Oh Jesus,' he moaned. 'Oh fucking hell.'

'You've been bitten by something,' she shouted. 'Don't move. I'll get some painkillers.'

Tearing loose, she ran towards the first-aid box, spilt the contents out and grabbed the first item that came to hand. The forest was ten yards away and Disco still had the gun aimed at her.

He struggled up on to one elbow. 'Get back here,' he said through clenched teeth.

'I only want to help,' she cried, hurrying towards him.

His eyes closed, but as she reached him, they flicked open and she saw glowing coals through the glaze of pain.

'You fucking poisoned me,' he screamed, bringing the gun up.

Evading his clawing grasp, she vaulted clear and dived naked for the trees.

'Murdering bitch!'

Bullets whipped past her ears. Throwing herself full length, she crawled and scrabbled like a wounded invertebrate. The shooting stopped and she scrambled up and darted behind the nearest tree. She listened for pursuit. Instead there came a muted whimper, the sound of Disco swallowing pain until he could swallow no more and it burst forth in a bellow. For minute after minute, he raved.

Silence fell. Candy didn't move a muscle.

His voice when it came was dulled. 'What have you done? I can't feel my leg.'

'I injected you with the poison from a stonefish.'

He began to pant, completely at the mercy of pain, then he stopped and again spoke with resignation. 'Am I going to die?'

She spat and wiped her mouth and spat again. 'I hope so.'

There came a hideous keening and she put her hands over her ears. Disco couldn't be faking, but while one breath remained in his body, it took every bit of will to force herself closer. He was contracted into a ball and moaning. And then he stretched and arched as if high voltage had been passed through him, and lay still. His gun, no longer in his hand, lay within arm's reach. Through the trees Candy glimpsed a tatter of yellow. Boucher was returning.

'Jay,' she shouted, 'keep away. Don't go near him.'

The inflatable passed out of view. Disco lay completely still. Candy considered making a rush for the gun and rejected the idea. Quietly she moved away.

The inflatable had been beached. Boucher was nowhere to be seen.

'I'm over here,' she called.

She realized she was still naked and tore off a handful of leaves and scrubbed at herself. She was still scrubbing when Boucher appeared and looked at her in a way that made her burst out crying.

'He shot Kent. Just shot him. Kent didn't do anything. He's never even slept with a girl.'

'Okay, okay,' Boucher said, tentatively holding her. 'What did you do to Disco?'

His accusatory tone made Candy cry even harder. 'I poisoned him with stonefish venom.'

'Is he dead?'

She stopped crying. 'I don't know.'

'He looks dead.'

'I'm scared he's bluffing.'

Boucher took off his jacket and draped it over her shoulders. Hefting the anchor like a club, he stalked forward.

'Be careful.'

Boucher closed up on Disco as cautiously as Candy had approached the wounded tiger. Holding the anchor in readiness, he kicked the assault rifle aside, scooped it up, and took aim at Disco's head.

'I think you've killed him. His eyes are open, but he doesn't seem to be breathing.' Bending, Boucher pulled the pistol from Disco's waist and shoved it into his jacket pocket. He dropped on one knee and felt Disco's wrist. 'Still a pulse – just.' He looked up.

Hands to her mouth, Candy came to see for herself. The sight of Disco's face made her shy away. His jaws were set in a snarl and his pupils were fully dilated and stared blackly into her.

'Finish it,' she said, and turned her head.

Eyes averted, she tensed for the shot. The moment stretched into seconds.

'Please,' she said.

'I can't. Not like this.'

Candy whirled in a rage. 'You know what he did to me. What he did to Kent. Don't you realize what he was going to do to all of us? As soon as he got hold of that cassette, he was going to be the only survivor.'

'He made the decision before then,' Boucher said.

'Then get it over with.'

'We're not like him.'

'That's what he counts on,' Candy cried, hitting Boucher. 'He's the hawk among doves. He'll always win because he always strikes first and strikes to kill. This is our only chance.'

Boucher weathered her buffeting. 'Not in cold blood, Candy.'

Her hands dropped. 'Then give *me* the gun.'

Backing away from her, Boucher fumbled the magazine out, ejected the clip and scattered the bullets into the forest. Holding the weapon by the barrel, he pounded it to scrap against a tree.

Candy gave an astonished laugh. 'I know what this is all about. You want Disco dead as much as I do, but you're disqualified from writing the story if you kill off one of the characters. So much for your fucking conscience.'

'I'm thinking about *your* conscience. Do you want to live your life with a murder on it?'

'I *am* a murderer,' she shouted. 'I planned it in cold blood. I performed like a slut so I could get the opportunity to kill him.'

Briefly, Boucher shut his eyes. 'Wait to see if he dies.'

'And pretend it was natural causes?'

'Only you and I need know the truth.'

'And if he doesn't die?'

The question hung in the air.

Candy wilted. 'You said you had to kill him. *You* said that, and because I believed you, I went into the forest for an empty gun. The pirate could have shot me. Disco nearly did. If you didn't mean it, why did you risk my life?'

'I meant it,' Boucher said wearily, rolling a bullet between finger and thumb.

31

$\mathbf{A}$ll afternoon the approaching storm stoked up on energy, but by nightfall the catalyst needed to trigger it was still missing. Disco lay in suspended animation, bound hand and foot. Boucher took the cassettes off him and searched his pockets. They were empty. He returned to Candy. She was very pale, ghost-like, her feelings more veiled than he'd ever known.

'He's not carrying any identity,' he told her. 'So far as the world is concerned, he doesn't exist. That's where his power comes from. He can be anyone he wants to be.' Boucher misinterpreted Candy's shiver. 'He can't hurt us now.'

'It's not that. I'm running a fever.' She gave an on-off smile. 'Not very good timing.'

Boucher felt her forehead and was alarmed. He glanced towards the glow from the rig reflected on the overcast. Without Candy's active help, he doubted if they would reach it in one night, but he was primed for departure and the idea of backtracking was hard to bear.

'We'll call it off until you're feeling better.'

'I think it's malaria. Tomorrow you might be stuck with an invalid. It's now or never.'

Looking into her febrile eyes, Boucher recognized the responsibility resting on him. The thought of Candy sinking ever deeper into illness decided him. 'If the sky's clear by midnight, we'll take our chances.'

Over the horizon, lightning rippled and thunder growled. Disco smacked his lips. Boucher stared hard at him. A steady tapping in the forest drew his gaze further, past the body of Bartok, into the moist darkness that he knew would always be with him.

'We'll never be able to put this behind us.'

'My father's seen some dreadful things, but he never talks about them. Forgetting is an art soldiers have to cultivate.'

'I'm no soldier and I don't see this sitting lightly on the memory.'

Candy focused on him properly. 'You still intend to write about it.'

'We can't pretend it didn't happen. Dexter Smith and Nadine Wells were murdered. The world has to know how and why. It's my duty.'

'Your duty?' Candy jumped up and pointed at Disco. 'Is it your duty to tell the world what he did to me? What I've done to him?'

'I'll find a way to keep you out of it.'

'Lie, you mean. What else will you draw a veil over? The fact that we stood by while Trigg was tied up for the tiger?'

Boucher found no ready answer.

'You see, you'll never be able to tell the truth, so why bother? Forget it.'

'Am I supposed to forget you, too?'

The unhealthy light in Candy's eyes went out. She sat down in front of Boucher and took his hand. She ran a finger over his palm, as if tracing his lifeline. Out to sea the barrage was drawing nearer, finding its range.

'I like you, Jay. I do. But you can't be part of my future.'

For the first time, Boucher realized what a complex

place the future might be. 'If I dumped the project, would it make a difference?'

As Candy's lips parted in reply, a crackling made them draw apart. An orange orb had appeared to the north.

'Leo's lit the fire,' Candy said. 'You'd better tell him to get ready.'

'He's not going to come with us.'

'He's got the flare gun.'

'I know. I've been wondering how to get it off him.'

'Wait until he's finished. He'll be calmer then.'

Lightning stabbed and thunder crashed. A rush of wind blew Aquila's pyre into boisterous life. Another spasm of shivering shook Candy.

'We haven't settled the main issue,' she said, and looked with bleak loathing at Disco. 'We can't leave him like that, and we're not taking him with us.'

Boucher had been wrestling with the dilemma for hours. 'If we leave him, we have to leave him dead. Because if we don't and he survives ...' His voice trailed the awful possibilities.

Hope and fear trembled on Candy's face. 'Does that mean you've decided to ...'

'No,' Boucher said, cutting in quickly. 'We have to take him with us.' Exploiting Candy's dumbstruck silence, he hurried on. 'A dozen people have died here, and that's going to take a lot of explaining. The Indonesian police aren't the most sympathetic listeners. They'll be swarming all over this place. They're going to find some incriminating stuff, and we can't lay it all on the pirates. Disco murdered Kent, and he has to pay for that.'

'He killed him because Kent tried to stop him from raping me. I'm not going to relive that in court.' Candy jumped up and stood over Disco's prone form. 'If it's justice you want, here it is for the taking. Disco's right. On this place *we* make the laws.'

Boucher held out his hand as if warding off a bright light. 'Candy.'

Deadly calm, she faced him. 'Him or me. That's flat. You'd better make your mind up.'

The storm had crossed the horizon. Forks of lightning stood in jagged articulations. Boucher's chest felt spongy. 'Okay,' he said, reaching for the pistol, 'but I don't want you around. Check the drinking water.'

She backed off slowly, caught in freeze-frame by the intermittent flashes, then turned and hurried away. Boucher went to Disco and stood over him, looking at the filmed eyes. Amidst the tumult of the approaching storm, he wondered if murder was the tie, the erotic blood knot, that would bind him and Candy together. He lifted the pistol, dropped to his haunches and placed the muzzle to Disco's temple.

A crack directly overhead jerked his eyes up. A ball of white fire lit the beach, and in the bloom of its opening he swung round and saw his disbelief reflected on Candy's bleached face.

'The fucking flare gun!' he shouted, shoving the pistol away. 'Come on!'

Another burst of phosphorus threw his running shadow down the sand. He shouted, his shouting drowned by the peals of thunder and the incendiary roar of the funeral pyre. He hadn't realized what a massive send-off Jaeger had staged. Great tongues of flame curled up from the pile, licking towards the flapping canopy. Smaller fires had jumped to the look-out tree and were scampering up the woven vines. Tiger-striped in the tigerish light, Jaeger stared enraptured at the Wildguard flag tugging in the updraught.

'Leave it to me,' Candy cried, pushing Boucher back. 'Leo!'

Slewing round, Jaeger peered through his perpetual

shroud of fog, brandishing the flare gun as if an invisible army had him at bay.

'It's me,' Candy cried. 'We're leaving. We've come to fetch you.'

'Stay away. No one's gonna take me from her.'

'Aquila's gone now. She's at peace.'

'She left me. I've got to find her.'

'You're ill. If you stay, you could die. There's still an armed pirate on the island.'

The look-out tree was well ablaze – a flaming candle a hundred feet high. Gases trapped in the trunk escaped with a demonic screech. Air rushing into the vacuum whirled burning debris over the forest. The canopy ignited with a *whoosh*.

'You crazy bastard,' Boucher shouted. 'You'll torch the whole island.'

Candy retreated from the singeing draught. Jaeger held up his arms.

'Tiger, Tiger, burning bright ...'

'Come away,' Candy called. 'You're not well. You need help.'

Jaeger turned, backlit by the blaze. Behind him, ribbons of fire fell hissing to the ground. Thunder rolled in stereophonic waves.

'You thought Aquila was crazy, but her prophecies came true. Man will kill himself. The world will end in fire.'

'Get away from him,' Boucher yelled. 'He's out of his mind.'

Jaeger scooped a handful of sand and threw it in his direction. 'Mock on, Jay, mock on. You throw the sand against the wind, and the wind blows it back again.'

'Stay then,' Boucher yelled. 'Just give us the fucking flare gun.'

'Shut up,' Candy ordered, moving closer to Jaeger. She

held out her hand. 'You don't need it now, but we do. I don't want to die on this island.'

Behind her, Boucher drew a bead, though he guessed that stopping Jaeger in his present frame of mind would require a calibre of weapon much greater than he possessed.

Jaeger approached dangerously close to Candy.

'Don't hurt her,' Boucher yelled. 'I'm warning you.'

Jaeger smiled sadly. 'Aquila liked you, Candy. That's why she signed you up, though you ate flesh and hunted animals. She believed that given a chance, you'd come to see things through her eyes.'

'I do, Leo. Aquila's changed the way I see everything.'

The Wildguard flag combusted and burned to tarry tatters in a matter of seconds.

Gently, Jaeger placed the gun in Candy's hands. 'Go then. Share her vision with the world.'

As they staggered back, the heavens ripped apart, falling in curtains of rain that boiled on the inferno. Boucher and Candy sheltered from the watery bombardment until, as suddenly as it had struck, it swept past, dragging an onshore wind in its train. Stars appeared and the light from the rig came back on. Along the reef, the sea was showing its teeth.

'It's going to be helluva tricky navigating through there,' Boucher said.

Candy couldn't stop her teeth from chattering. 'We can do it.'

'How many flares do we have left?'

'One.'

'Oh boy.'

Boucher tried to reckon up the odds, but there were too many variables. The only constant was Candy's deteriorating condition. Another day and she might be in no state to travel at all. The possibility of her dying left him no choice.

'Leave the preparations to me.'

They didn't take long. Two hours before midnight, the inflatable was as ready as it would ever be. Only one thing remained to be settled. Candy sat forlorn, some distance from Disco, and Boucher decided he would not trouble her again with his scruples. Get it over with.

Pistol in pocket, he went up to Disco. His eyes were shut now, and that made it mercifully simpler. The phrase "putting a dog to sleep" entered Boucher's mind. His face set. He began to reach inside his jacket.

'Hey, Jay, you're not planning on dumping me.'

Boucher jumped as if a snake had leapt out of a sack. Disco's eyes were pain-drugged slivers. He said something else in a hoarse whisper. Boucher caught the words "sweet" and "poison". Flattened by despair, Boucher backed away and sought murderous counsel with Candy.

He crouched down, blocking out the sight of Disco. 'He's regained consciousness. Whatever you decide, I'll do.'

She crossed her arms tightly over her chest and looked away. 'Kill him.'

Boucher went on looking at her, but didn't speak.

'When I was about eleven,' she said, 'I saw a fox hanging about the henhouse. My father would have shot it, but I thought it was beautiful, and I begged and cried and promised to make sure the house was shut every day before sunset. For two weeks I kept it up, but one afternoon I had to visit a friend, and when I came back the fox had got into the coop and killed five chickens. For some reason, it didn't get the sixth one, but I was so upset I forgot about the door, and the next night the fox came back and killed that one, too.'

'Tied up, Disco can't do anything.'

'I've got a rotten fever and you can't keep your eyes on him all the time. What happens when we sleep?'

'He needs us more than we need him.'

'Once rescue is in sight, he'll get rid of us.'

Boucher touched the pistol under his jacket. 'That's what this is for. He doesn't know I've got it.'

'Pray he doesn't find out.'

'We've got some morphine left. The moment we get in sight of the rig, we can sedate him.'

Turmoil showed on Candy's face. 'You're making me walk a tightrope.'

'It's still your decision.'

She passed her hand across her eyes. 'I'm too sick to think, Jay. Do whatever's right.'

Boucher stood and looked down on her for several seconds. 'Okay.'

He left Candy and went back to Disco, who regarded him with the fearful but quizzical expression of a man who knows his fate has been decided.

'What's the verdict, Jay?'

'I'm taking you back to civilization. I want to see you back in the cage. Get in the boat.'

Disco held up his hands. 'I can't move like this. My legs are gone.'

'Then crawl.'

Boucher relented only to the extent that he tipped Disco into the stern once everything else had been stowed. He cast off, aiming for the white tooth marking the tidal surge. Though stars showed, it was darker than he'd anticipated. Disco was little more than a slouched shadow at the other end of the boat.

'One wrong move, piss me off in any shape or form and you're shark fodder.'

The deluge had doused the blaze, but embers were still smouldering where Jaeger had conducted Aquila's last earthly rites. Disco watched them. 'Last person off, turn out the lights.'

Boucher reserved his concentration for the passage through the reef. The first gap was easily threaded. The second was rougher, the swell hitting obliquely and stirring up cross-eddies and general confusion. Candy roused herself and took an oar. The inflatable bucked in the broken water.

'You'd manage easier with another hand,' Disco said.

'Candy, keep an eye out for rocks on your side.'

Undertow threatened to suck them on to the coral.

'Get aft,' Boucher called. 'Push us off.'

With Boucher rowing and Candy poling from the stern, they fought their way clear. They were through, bouncing on the choppy swell of the open sea. Boucher laughed triumphantly. 'Why didn't we do this before? The door's been open all along.'

At that moment, a breaker hit, swamping the boat and nearly throwing them back on to the reef.

'Quick,' he called. 'Get back here. Get rowing.'

Candy half stood and Boucher saw her outlined against the sky, shifting to maintain balance, almost dropping her oar.

'Here,' Boucher cried, leaning forward. 'Take my hand.'

Candy reached out, still off-balance, but couldn't make contact. As Boucher pulled his oar in to free both hands, another wave staggered the boat. One moment she was leaning towards him, the next she was teetering back, one hand milling. He lunged for her and managed to seize her oar. For a moment he took her full weight and thought he had her, but suddenly the oar came away in his hand and Candy was poised at an irrecoverable angle – poised then falling, toppling overboard with the inexorability of nightmare.

He sprang to the stern. 'Candy!'

'It wasn't me,' Disco cried. 'Honest to God.'

'Candy, grab the oar.'

But the current was sweeping her back on to the reef. She seemed powerless against it.

'Candy!' Boucher shouted, sculling desperately. 'Candy!'

She was nearly gone from sight. He tore off his jacket and jumped. When he came up, he couldn't see her. All was foam and blackness.

'Get back,' Disco shouted. 'If this thing hits, I'm done for.'

Boucher could just make out the boat. He splashed towards it and dragged himself up. Grabbing the oars, he rowed like a madman towards the reef.

'You'll kill us,' Disco pleaded. 'There's nothing you can do. She's gone, man. You'll get us both drowned.'

'I don't care. I'm not leaving until I've found her.'

For half an hour, Boucher rowed back and forth along the coral wall, shouting out Candy's name. Several times he thought he heard her answer, but it was only a cruel siren cry. With the last of his strength, he rowed clear of the rough water, then sank over his oar.

'We'll stand off here and go back in at first light.'

'She never made it. This is shark zone, and it's feeding time.'

'We're going back,' Boucher shouted.

'She's dead.'

Then it hit. Boucher stared at the broken line of surf. 'What have I done? Oh God, what have I done?'

'The best you could, man.'

'I've lost her.' Boucher looked up into the heavens. 'I've lost Candy. I've lost the only thing that matters.'

'No you haven't,' Disco said. He struggled into a more upright position and jerked his chin at the horizon. 'Look, man, there's the light from the rig. We can reach it by dawn and they can send a helicopter. If Candy's still alive, they'll pick her up.'

Boucher stared at him and began to quake. He and Candy had survived brute nature and man's savagery, and now she was dead and he was left adrift with the chief cause of his fear and pain – this germ, this fucking irrelevance.

The boat was pitching, jigging on the waves.

'Cut me loose man. You can't get clear on your own.'

'A paralyzed psychopath offers his help.'

Disco thumped his thigh with his fists. 'Only this leg. I can still use my arms.'

It was meant to be, Boucher realized. Him and Disco alone on the vast deep. He leaned forward and untied the wrists. They were face to face.

'Thanks, man.'

In silence they pulled clear of the reef. When the island was barely distinguishable from the mangrove coast, Boucher rested on his oars. The sea breeze chilled his sweat and he put on his jacket. He patted the pocket and then studied Disco with almost scientific objectivity. An odd feeling akin to pity rose in him. Disco was the greedy monkey which, having thrust its paw into the bottle for the candy, didn't have the wit to unclench its fist so that it could withdraw its prize. Really, he was a simple soul, all appetite and primary urges. No higher thought was allowed to overrule them. That's what made him so terrifying.

'Why you looking at me like that?'

'Give them back, Disco.'

'Give what back?'

'The cassettes.'

'I haven't got any fucking cassette. How could I?'

'I'm not interested in the how,' Boucher said. Casually, he reached inside one of the lockers.

When he turned, the bore of the flare gun was trained on his chest. Disco stuck out his legs.

'Cut 'em loose.'

'You'll kill me anyway.'

'I'll kill you if you don't.'

Boucher obeyed and then resumed his place.

Holding his aim with one hand, Disco rubbed his ankles and flexed his legs. He groaned luxuriously.

'There's nothing wrong with them,' Boucher said.

Disco's eyes glinted. 'Oh, they hurt, Jay. They hurt like hell. I could end up like Josef.' He settled himself. 'Just you and me now, playing the lifeboat game for real.'

'Winner takes all.'

Disco held up a cassette and laughed. 'Yeah. Every last damn thing.' He began to tuck the cassette away.

'Disco, before you scoop in the winnings, I have to declare my hand.'

Disco leaned forward, frowning slightly. 'Show me.'

Boucher revealed the pistol. 'Straight flush.'

'Ah, not that old thing. Why didn't you keep the Kalashnikov, hold on to real privilege?'

'Disco, how many slugs does this automatic hold?'

Disco shrugged. 'None.'

'How many originally?'

'Nine.'

'And how many were in it the night I first showed it to you.'

'Eight. You fired one to see if it was working.'

'I did say that, didn't I?'

A faint caution disturbed Disco's nonchalance.

'I took it out, Disco, the day I found it, after your first attack on Candy. It was my talisman – my ace in the hole. Now it's aimed at your heart.'

'Bluff.'

'Call me.'

Disco elevated the flare gun fractionally. 'I am calling.'

'You're holding a dead man's hand.'

Disco's laugh betrayed unease. 'Suppose that thing does have something up the spout. You'd better be a surefire shot, because wherever this flare hits, it'll burn to your backbone.'

'Show time.'

'I pass.'

'On the count of three,' Boucher said. 'One ... two ...'

The click of the flare-gun's trigger stamped itself on Boucher's consciousness like a full stop. He picked up the flare cartridge from under his seat and balanced it in his palm.

'What terrifies me, Disco, is your dime-store mentality and basic stupidity. If they measured your IQ, it wouldn't break the speed limit.'

'You certainly won that one,' Disco agreed, handing over the gun.

Boucher placed it behind him. 'Now the cassettes.'

Smiling tightly, Disco did as he'd been told. 'Are we done now?'

'We're only just starting.'

'Hell, you've got what you asked for. Candy tried to kill me, and you're not much better disposed. You can't blame a man for getting himself some protection.'

'Candy didn't fall. You pushed her.'

Disco mimicked bound hands. 'You're fabricating evidence. You had me trussed up like a chicken.'

Boucher could barely restrain his trigger finger. 'That's why she was swimming away from the boat.'

Disco licked his lips and began to speak rapidly. 'Killing me won't bring her back. I know how gone on her you were, but hear me out a minute.'

'I can spare a minute.'

'Maybe it's for the best. No, listen – like, you're a writer, right, and you've got a story to tell. Because of Dexter, it's gonna be mega, right?'

'Carry on.'

'But with Candy alive, you'd be squeezed out. She'd have ripped you off, man. Who gives a shit about a sharp sentence when you can have Candy instead? Okay, so you know how to string words together. Who doesn't? But Candy, she's the hero and she's classy and cute. Whose face do you think the publisher will want staring out from the stand? Tell me whose ass the talk-show host will want on his screen.'

'I see. You were acting in my interests.'

'Don't get me wrong. I didn't push her. I'm saying that Candy dead makes you better off – financially speaking. I mean, that's why you're here, isn't it?'

Boucher fingered his ragged tie.

'But to cash in, you need to get to the rig, and you won't make it single-handed. You'll go round in circles.'

'You may be right.'

'No doubts of it. You need me.'

A blood-red mist fell across Boucher's vision. 'So you want to play another hand.'

Disco's eyes flicked right and left. He spread his hands. 'I guess this is the only game in town.'

'What are you going to play with?'

'You lost me, man.'

'It's a zero sum game and you've got nothing left in the kitty.'

Disco pondered. 'What about my hundred dollars? Remember, I bet you'd never find out who I was.'

'I didn't accept the bet, Disco. I told you I wasn't interested in you.'

'You're interested now.'

'Whatever you tell me, I won't believe it.'

Disco considered this, then reached behind and felt in

his waistband. When he brought his hand round again, it held a passport.

'Proof,' he said.

Boucher stared at it. 'Where did that come from?'

'Never mind, Jay. Here it is. Here *I* am. Put the two together.'

Boucher looked from the passport to the face and felt very weary. 'It doesn't matter any more. To me you're Disco – nothing else. It's easier to kill a man who doesn't have a proper name, a history – any connection to the human race. You came into my life anonymous, and that's how you're going to go out. Like I said on the airship, you're nothing.'

'Wait! I can give you a marker – something you really need.'

Boucher's trigger finger was at squeeze point.

'Supporting evidence, Jay. You tell people what happened back there, they might not believe you. Hell, they might think you offed some of those characters yourself.'

Disco sat expectantly, hopefully.

Suddenly, Boucher could hardly see for rage. 'No,' he said, 'that's it for you.'

The impact of the shot seemed to somersault Disco over the stern. Boucher threw himself forward, but he was already gone. He hurled the pistol and howled as if Disco had somehow got away. But it was only frustration that he couldn't inflict more pain, extract a harsher vengeance. He stared at the black water, imagining Disco's body slowly falling into the depths, and when it was beyond the reach even of imagination, he continued staring into the abyss.

Much later, he turned lifeless eyes towards the false red dawn. A zero sum game indeed. He'd staked Candy in a game where only his life was for the winning. That, he thought, lifting the oars, was an unbearable prize.

32

Dawn found Boucher becalmed no more than three miles offshore, the island still in sight, a thin column of smoke from Jaeger's blaze leaning against the sky. Boucher never even considered returning; with Candy dead, the emptiness ahead was preferable to the vacuum behind.

He rowed in snatches. The sea was like a hard blue wall, and he thought that if only he could get to the top of it, he would see the oil platform on the other side. Imperceptibly the coast sank into a tremulous line that rose up again at midday and floated upside down on the burning sky. Heat flooded in from all directions. Cowled under a section of fabric, Boucher rested until the light had calmed. His hands were raw and he had difficulty straightening them out. He wrapped them in fabric and waited for the beacon to show him the way through the dark. When it appeared, he rowed on.

In spite of losing Candy, he wanted to live. Survival for its own sake was the strongest imperative. Like the meanest blob of protoplasm, he toiled towards the light.

He wondered where they had gone wrong. Perhaps if they'd crashed with nothing, the peril of their situation would have concentrated their minds and enforced co-operation, but the supplies on the raft, coupled with their own sense of importance had made them complacent. They had looked on the island as a playground, a gentle diversion from the harsh reality of the world they knew, the world to which they would return once the novelty wore off. How could he have known on that first day that, less than one month later, everyone but himself would be dead.

He spread out and rolled his eyes up to the stars. Candy's accusatory eyes looked down on him. If he survived, he realized, he would have to come to a new accommodation with himself.

Day 24

Fixed in its orbit by gravity, the world turned in its cycle while Boucher slept and woke and slept again. At dawn he was too feeble and dispirited to move. The beating sun eventually forced him out of the doldrums. Through swollen eyes he saw that all quarters were empty. The world had flattened into two dimensions, a boundless mirror with him pinned at the centre.

Aimless, he made no attempt to row. His only hope was that he might drift into a shipping lane. He kept watch and twice saw trails of smoke rising from below the earth's curve. Behind him, clouds bubbled up along the invisible coast, never lifting clear of the horizon.

In the cruel heat of the vertical sun, he curled up and let his mind play over memories. He heard voices, Candy's among them – acerbic, gentle, blaming. Her voice became so insistent that he sat up and called her name. For a long time he looked for her in the refractions, lips moving soundlessly. Then, like an old man, he lay down.

At evening he turned his blistered face to a glorious vision, the sun pouring like smelted gold into bands of rosy clouds. A fly marred the radiance, sliding across his vision and disappearing into the sun. His sluggish brain caught up and told him it was an aircraft. The chopping sound of its engine reached him.

A helicopter.

It emerged from the sun's core, flying low on a course that was taking it further away each second. Boucher hesitated, aware that he'd already left it too late. In an agony of indecision he raised the flare gun. Tomorrow there might be a better chance, but by dawn he might be dead in the water.

The flare popped in the sky and hung there. The helicopter held its course. Boucher held his breath.

Through the throbbing of his blood he heard the engine change note. He picked up the atom and saw that it had deviated from its line. It grew bigger and the stropping of rotors got louder. It was coming straight at him, the flat rays of the sun reddening its underside and illuminating the pilots. He spread his arms in welcome. The helicopter grew huge, filling his vision as it roared past in a deafening burst of dirty thunder. Swinging round, he saw it make a flashy turn and sidle back to hover directly overhead.

The gale from its rotors flayed his face. A crewman in helmet and visor stood braced in the door. Boucher raised a hand and the man cocked his thumb, then pointed at himself and made a jabbing downwards gesture. Turning his back, he jumped out and descended like a god, landing inch-perfect in the centre of the inflatable. He unbuckled his harness. From what little Boucher could see of his face, he appeared to be Asiatic. Whatever he said was lost in the churning of machinery, but Boucher nodded anyway. Signalling the 'copter to hold position, the winch-man strapped Boucher into the harness, rotated his hands and stood clear as he was borne aloft.

Hands reached for him. They belonged to an Asian in aircrew gear. Behind him was a burly white civilian who helped pull him in and lay him out on a seat. The winch-man swung back inboard, took off his helmet and flashed his teeth in a grin. Weakly, Boucher shook his hand. The chomping blades grew muffled as the door slid shut.

'Your lucky day,' the burly man said in an antipodean twang. 'Let's take a look at the damage.' He checked Boucher's vital signs, pulled his eyelids up and examined his pupils. Boucher stared back in a nervous stupor. The Australian produced a liquid-filled plastic bag with tube attached. 'Try getting some of this down you.'

The cocktail tasted like warm, sweet seawater.

'Can you speak?'

Boucher's throat was as rough as hemp and his tongue felt like a piece of overcooked liver. But the main impediment to speech was the knowledge that from now on, whatever he said, he would have to stick to. He got the easy bit out of the way.

'Jay Boucher,' he croaked. 'American.'

'Pete Cullen,' the Australian said. 'What's the story, Jay? Your boat go down?'

Whole sentences were beyond Boucher. 'Crashed,' he said. 'Wildguard.'

'What's that, mate? Did you say Wildguard?'

'Yes.'

Amazement dawned on his rescuers' faces. 'The airship? You were on that airship?'

Boucher nodded. It felt strange to be the cause of so much astonishment. He supposed it was something he'd have to get used to.

Cullen wiped his brow. 'Christ alive, that was weeks ago. You're all supposed to be dead. You haven't been floating since then.'

'Landed on island. Still someone there. Got to go back.'

'Not possible. We're at the limit of our range. We pushed our luck stopping for you. Give me the position of this island and we'll rustle up some assistance.'

'Close to coast. I don't know exactly. Can't be far.'

'How about some visual reference? What are we looking for?'

Boucher's system was coming back on line. 'Shaped like a tear-drop, about a mile long, fire scar on north end.'

'How long were you in the raft?'

Boucher had to think hard. 'Two days and nights.'

'Within a hundred kilometres then. How many left behind?'

'One, possibly two.'

'And the rest?'

'Dead.'

Cullen glanced at the crewman. 'What about the pop star you had on board?'

'Dead.'

'Christ. How?'

Boucher shook his head.

'All right,' Cullen said, and turned to the crewman. 'Got that? You'd better call Palembang and tell them to send a search and rescue team.'

Boucher was left alone with him. 'I haven't thanked you. I don't even know who you are.'

'I'm a petroleum engineer working on a survey. Fortunately, this bird is equipped for rescue, otherwise you'd still be floating.'

'Where are you headed?'

'Singapore.'

That was a vast step-up on Jakarta or any other Indonesian enclave.

'You look pretty used up, Jay. How long were you on the island?'

'Nearly four weeks.'

Cullen whistled softly. 'What the hell happened?'

Again, Boucher shook his head.

'Okay, Jay. You get your head down.' Cullen began to rise. 'Is there anyone you want me to contact – wife, family, girlfriend?'

Boucher gave him Lydia's name, then had an afterthought. 'There's also a woman in Los Angeles. Delta Glenn. I don't have her number, but she isn't hard to track down.'

'A girl in every city, eh? Okay, I'll give it a go.'

Darkness had gathered at the windows. This was the only opportunity Boucher would have to do something about the cassettes. He fumbled for them.

'There's something else. These cassettes. It's important Delta Glenn gets them.'

Cullen glanced at the cabin door and sat down again. 'What's this about, Jay?'

'They're video tapes. I'm a journalist. They're a record of the Wildguard expedition.'

Cullen shook his head. 'I don't know. There's bound to be a crash investigation and God knows what else. You were big news. Those tapes could be evidence.'

'Big news,' Boucher repeated. 'Yes, they are. They're worth a lot of money. If you get them to Delta Glenn, I promise you'll be well rewarded.'

Cullen turned them over in his hand. 'Are they suitable for home viewing?'

'They contain some explicit material.'

'Tell you what. I'll look at them myself and then decide what to do.'

Boucher was in no position to bargain. Cullen continued staring at him as if he was an object of fascination. Boucher found it unsettling.

'Anything interesting happen while I was away?'

Cullen shook his head. 'Been pretty quiet, mate. Everyone's waiting for the end of the world.'

Boucher woke up in hospital. His hands were bandaged. That was the first thing he noticed. The second was the uniformed police officer at the door. As soon as the policeman saw the patient was conscious, he disappeared, returning a few minutes later with a dapper man in a suit. The shrewd cast of the man's face announced his business before he introduced himself.

'Good evening, Mr Boucher. I am Chief Inspector Lee of the Singapore police. How are you today?'

'Did they find Candy?'

'Mr Boucher, I'm sorry. This afternoon, we received a report from the Indonesian rescue team that searched the island. They are sure that no one is left alive.'

Boucher faced the wall and clenched his fists. 'Did they recover her body?'

'I do not think so.'

Boucher's head rolled back. 'What do you mean – think?'

Inspector Lee regarded him with gravity. 'The team found certain items on the island.' His eyebrows shuffled as if he expected Boucher to supply an inventory. Receiving no help, he itemized the objects himself. 'A semi-automatic rifle – badly damaged. Unfired cartridges believed to be from that rifle, plus cartridge cases from another gun. Wreckage from an inflatable boat.' He let silence hang. 'And human remains, Mr Boucher.'

Boucher nodded, skimming over the account he'd plotted in his waking moments.

Lee consulted a fax. 'Two bodies, both male. In the beach area was the body of a young, fair-haired man. First indications are that he was killed by a single bullet wound. The second body was discovered in the forest and was too decomposed for cause of death to be established on the spot. But the head appears to have been mutilated by a heavy blade.' Lee placed the fax on his knee. 'You are not surprised.'

Boucher had already decided that he couldn't say Disco had shot Bartok because he had tried to stop him raping Candy. That would establish a motive for revenge. He had to keep Candy out of it. Nor was it safe to claim that Disco had murdered Bartok for some other reason. If he did, Lee would wonder why he had left on the boat with him. Candy had been right. Whole swathes of truth would have to be sacrificed.

'Kent Bartok is the young man on the beach. He was shot by a pirate – Indonesian, I guess. The dead guy in the forest is one of them. Leo Jaeger killed him in self-defence. Jaeger was still on the island when I left. He's sick – ill in the head.'

Lee consulted another sheet. 'He is not there now.' He frowned. 'The rescue party found the burnt head of a tiger on a post. Please, can you explain this strange thing for me? I require a full statement.'

'Inspector, it's going to take a long time and I'm not up to it right now.'

Lee observed him with a brooding expression, then tapped his papers into alignment. 'I will return tomorrow morning. In view of what you have already told me, a lawyer will be present.'

'Fine, but I want to see someone from my embassy.'

'The American embassy knows you are here and is being kept informed.'

'Are you holding me incommunicado?'

'You may see relatives. No one else.'

'Are there journalists waiting to speak to me?'

'Interviews with the Press are not permitted.'

'The pirate killed by Jaeger was one of a gang who

murdered Dexter Smith by decapitation. You do know who Dexter Smith is? Was.'

Lee's eyes narrowed. 'Decapitated?'

'Head cut off.'

Lee gave himself a little shake. 'There is certainly a clamour for information, Mr Boucher. But until we have established the facts, you are not allowed visitors.'

'You want the facts,' Boucher said, 'get a friendly face here.'

Next morning, Inspector Lee returned with the aforementioned lawyer, an American attaché and several police underlings. The lawyer had a flat, passive face that suggested he took a broad view of human nature. The embassy official was a sporty-looking fellow called Arnold, who greeted Boucher with wary friendliness. The lawyer warned Boucher that, though no charges were being considered, anything he said might be used in future proceedings.

When the police minions had wired him for sound, Boucher began his account. He had worked it all out and thought the structure was watertight. No conscious thought intervened as he described the terrible disintegration of the Wildguard expedition. Nobody interrupted. He spoke until his voice was husky.

After he had finished, Lee picked at his cuff. 'The man who left the island with you and the girl – Disco. You say you do not know his full name.'

'He wouldn't give it. Nobody knew who he was. The Wildguard people met him for the first time the night before we left Pontianaka.'

Lee nodded vaguely. 'Kent Bartok was a friend of yours.'

'Yes. Not a close friend, though. He and Disco hung out together.'

'Your other friends – Dexter Smith, Ronnie Trigg. You buried their bodies at sea with proper ceremony.'

'Yes.'

'Mr Bartok was a man of strong religious beliefs. It seems very strange to me, Mr Boucher, that you left his body on the beach. Why did you not show him the respect you gave to the others?'

'There was no time. We were frightened the pirates would come back.'

'But the pirates murdered Mr Bartok the day before you left the island. You had plenty of time. You had more than twenty-four hours. At the very least, you could have buried him in the sand and marked his grave.'

'I know it seems callous, but we were in shock. We'd just seen three of our friends brutally killed.'

'Not so shocked that you couldn't find time to bury Dexter Smith at sea. He was killed on the same day as Mr Bartok. You say that the man called Disco was a friend of Mr Bartok's, yet he left his body lying on the sand.'

Seeing water seeping through the seams, Boucher began baling with the only tool he could come up with. 'We weren't behaving rationally.'

'Was Disco a friend, Mr Boucher?'

Some lies were impossible to stomach. 'No.'

'Was he a friend of Candy's?'

'No.'

'Why not?'

'I didn't trust him. He was a fly-by-night.' Lee didn't understand the expression. 'A creep,' Boucher explained. 'Maybe a criminal.'

'That's why you destroyed the gun he used to shoot the pirates. You believed you were in danger from him.'

Boucher saw the crack beginning to open. 'I didn't like the idea of him having a weapon.'

'So you took the rifle off him. How did you do that?'

403

'We got it when he was asleep.'

'You and the English girl stole a gun off a man you feared, then you left the island with him.'

'We couldn't just leave him there.'

'You left Leo Jaeger.'

'Leo chose to stay. I told you, he'd cracked up. Nothing could have forced him off.'

'Perhaps you forced Disco to come with you, or perhaps it was the other way round.'

'All three of us just wanted to get the hell off that place.'

'But tragically, your ... the English woman who was your friend, and the man who wasn't ... died in the accident on the reef.'

'I tried to save Candy.'

Inspector Lee looked at, or maybe through, the window. 'What happened to the pistol you took from the airship?'

'It was empty. I threw it away.'

'Where?'

'In the sea,' Boucher said, and saw his mistake. 'In the lagoon.'

'When?'

'After ... after the pirates left.'

'After you destroyed the rifle?'

'I'm not sure. Yes.'

'Mr Boucher, four of your companions were killed by a tiger. You said that you were frightened that the pirates might return. But despite these dangers, despite the fact that you feared Disco was a criminal, you destroyed the rifle and threw away the pistol.'

'I've told you. The pistol was empty.'

'Lies are what you have told me. I think you knew the pirates would not come back. I think you were more fearful of Disco. We have found the rifle, but not the pistol. I think you took it with you on the boat and then ...' Lee left an all-too-scrutable silence.

Leaky as his story was, Boucher knew it wouldn't sink unless he holed it himself. 'That's not what happened.'

Lee held him under pensive scrutiny.

'When can I go?'

'By your own admission, serious crimes have been committed.'

'Not by me.'

'These crimes were committed on Indonesian territory. Naturally, the authorities in Sumatra have a particular interest in the case.'

Arnold stirred. 'They want to talk to you, Jay.'

'Can they force me?'

'There are channels they can go through.'

'Extradition, you mean?'

'Depends if they can hang something on you.'

'If they're so concerned about what's happening in their backyard, they should try looking over it once in a while. Three weeks we were stuck on that island, and the only Indonesians who showed up came to kill us.'

Lee was lost in reverie. He looked up. 'Did you kill the man called Disco?'

'No.'

Lee smiled thinly and left.

Next time Arnold pitched up, he looked harassed. 'There's a woman demanding to see you. She claims you asked her to visit. She's been here two days and is a thorough pain in the ass.'

Lydia, Boucher thought, the yawning sensation in his chest reminding him of the gulf that had opened between them. Try as he might, he couldn't think of a way to bridge it.

Then he remembered that the only visitor he'd requested was Delta Glenn. Cullen must have done his stuff.

'Let her in.'

In his mind he'd constructed a portrait of a collagen blonde dynamo in the intermediate thirties. Delta, it turned out, was a middle-aged redhead who looked like a power-dressed housewife with poor colour vision. That was the first impression. The second, based on speed of entrance, directness of approach and all-round energy coefficient, was that she did indeed run on high-octane fuel.

'I got them,' she said, sitting down after the rapid introductions and stock health enquiries. 'They're in a secure place.' Spotting a bowl of fruit, she helped herself to a banana. She breathed out as if it had burned her tongue. 'Whoo! Splatterfest. Poor Dexter. What's the old world coming to?'

'They won't let me find out. They're still talking about shipping me off to the Indonesians.'

'We're taking care of that. Forget about it. Let's talk work. You're already headlining. Run the story past me.'

After hearing Boucher's account, she had only one comment.

'Why you? How was it you were the one who survived?'

The question caused acute pain. 'I don't know. I'd say luck, except that luck isn't what it feels like.'

'I ask because it's a question you're going to get sick of hearing. Try and come up with a more positive response.' Delta frowned. 'Are you religious?'

'No.'

'Never mind.'

From Delta's expression, Boucher deduced there was more coming.

'What makes the situation really sensitive is Dexter. A sizeable chunk of the youth population is in mourning. If there's anything that might rise up to haunt you, tell me now.'

Boucher shook his head. He was beginning to see what he'd let himself in for.

Delta's mouth compressed in a bud. 'Good,' she said at last, then stood. 'Time I was going.'

'Where?'

'Shopping. Then I'm flying home to prepare the market.' She winked. 'Lots to do.'

Inspector Lee and his team returned twice more. Each interrogation ended with questions about Disco. What had his behaviour been like after he shot the pirates? How, exactly, had he fallen from the boat? Lee knew foul play when he smelt it, and though there was damn all he could do about it, it was a sore he couldn't stop scratching.

During one session, he dismissed his junior officers. When the door closed, he put his notebook away. 'You can tell me now, Mr Boucher. There are no witnesses, nobody. You are the only survivor and you cannot testify against yourself.'

'Everything that happened is in my statement.'

On the fourth day of Boucher's confinement, the door swung open and Congressman Clarence Tusser, whose image Boucher had selected as a surefire defence against tiger attack, swept in as if borne on a strong wind. Silver quiff agleam, prognathous jaw sunk in his chest, he advanced on Boucher with right hand stuck straight out.

A flashgun ignited. Boucher felt his hand pumped

'Hi, Jay. Surprised?'

'On reflection, no.'

'I was out here on a mission, finding out how these Asiatics are sneaking jobs from our boys. Your face came up on television, and I thought: hell, I know *him*. He's the guy who tried to make an idiot of me.'

'Come to take your revenge?'

Tusser spun towards an aide, index finger stuck out like a comedian responsible for a scintillating piece of repartee. Turning, his eyes gentled. An expression appropriate on a man contemplating a war-wounded baby settled over his face.

'Come to take you home, Jay.'

33

Day 22

Struggling for balance, Candy had heard Boucher's frenzied cry and then her legs had been swept from under her. Falling, unable to save herself, without even the time to call out, she had glimpsed Disco's face sinewy with effort and malice. In that instant she knew he'd won, knew that even if she managed to get back into the boat, she and Boucher were doomed.

Ignoring Jay's desperate shouts, she swam straight for the reef. The tide sucked her through the gap like a cork. In the calmer water she could no longer hear Boucher's voice. She struck out for the next line of reef and found the way through, but a wave lifted her and threw her against coral. Ignoring the pain, she swam doggedly for shore.

Her strength gave out as she reached it. She crawled halfway up the beach and collapsed, retching. Wiping the acrid taste from her mouth, she pulled herself round to examine the tear in her leg.

She forced herself up and hobbled to the abandoned camp. Cold and sick, she lay down, and then the full extent of her plight hit home. She had no medicines, no food nor means of obtaining any, no water, fire-lighting equipment – nothing. From high hopes she had gone

slithering down the snake to square one and beyond –
stuck in limbo with a madman and a pirate.

Trying to string some strategy together, she realized
that if Disco made a safe passage, he might try to keep the
island secret. He could get away with it, too. There was
nothing to link him with the Wildguard expedition, and
by now memories of the crash would be fading, the
passengers presumed dead weeks ago. Disco could pass
himself off as the sole survivor of a yachting disaster.

Then Candy remembered the videotapes. To sell them,
Disco would have to reveal his involvement in the
tragedy. His ego would demand it. There would be little
risk to him. As far as he was concerned, she was dead,
and even if Jaeger was rescued, he was ignorant of Disco's
last crimes and too unhinged to give any credible
evidence. No, Candy decided, there would be a search and
she would be found. All she had to do was hang on for
another few days. Deranged though he was, Jaeger
wouldn't harm her. As for the pirate, she would just have
to stay out his way.

Hanging on to these slim hopes, she drew herself into a
ball and tried to find rest. She couldn't. She was too poorly
and wet and cold. A fire, she thought. She needed fire.
Jaeger's blaze would still have sparks left in it. By morning
they might be dead; she would have to steal some now.
Groaning with effort, she began to rise.

She froze, still on hands and knees.

Planted in front of her was a pair of bare feet. Hardly
able to raise her face above ground level, she stretched her
neck back and peered up at a figure whose head seemed to
be set in the stars.

'You.'

The pirate dropped into a squat and lifted her head so
she was looking into his eyes. She couldn't read his
intentions. He raised something to her mouth and she

410

found herself slurping from her own water bottle. When she'd drunk, she flopped back, but the pirate shook her roughly, making a sibilant warning sound. He pointed up the beach, then indicated that he wanted her to accompany him into the forest.

'I can't,' she groaned. 'Can't you see?'

With a disapproving click, he put both hands under her arms and locked them round her chest, cruelly abrading her nipples.

'Get off,' she moaned.

She felt herself hoisted and found herself swaying on her feet. Her head reeled. The pirate cupped her chin in one hand and made it known that staying on the beach was dangerous. She let him lug her away, into the forest, guiding her useless legs over obstacles.

Deep in the trees, he stopped and lowered her to the ground. The darkness was total and he was completely invisible. She heard a brisk rubbing and smelt smoke. A tiny spot of red appeared, glowing hotter as the pirate blew on it. A thread of flame appeared. The pirate fed it, and when the fire had taken hold, he made a sound of satisfaction and placed a package on the flame.

In the firelight, she could make out the coppery curves of his face. He looked very young. He took the package off the fire, juggled it to show it was hot, unwrapped it and presented it to her with odd formality. It was a leaf with a few morsels on it. He insisted she eat – wouldn't take no for an answer. She picked up one of the titbits, placed it in her mouth and brought her teeth together. It popped, flooding her mouth with oily liquor. She thought it might have been a grub. The pirate watched her.

'Bad shits,' he said.

'Bad shits,' she agreed, and crashed into oblivion.

Half asleep, she studied her abductor as the watery light

began to strengthen. He *was* young, probably no older than sixteen, with the fine oval face of a Javanese princeling, a soft adolescent down on his lip. She touched his knee and he jumped, flustered. She smiled at him and he smiled uncertainly back.

'Candy,' she said, pointing at herself.

'Kemal,' he responded. He touched her forehead. 'Good?'

'Better.'

She did feel better – about sixty per cent normal, a significant improvement. She spotted Kemal's shotgun – a sorry piece of ordnance spliced with wire and tape, its scarred stock ornately carved. He indicated that it was defence against Jaeger.

'Bad mans,' he said.

'Sad man.'

'Bad crazy mans,' Kemal elaborated, and made a gesture apparently designed to ward off the Evil Eye.

Candy saw something else beside the gun – a blue nylon sports bag. For a moment, it was the incongruity of the object that struck her, then, with a lurch, she remembered that she'd seen the bag before, at Pontianaka airport, in Disco's hand. Shakily, she pointed at it.

Kemal laughed sheepishly.

'Where did you find it?'

Once he understood the question, he gestured vaguely in the direction of the lagoon.

'Can I look at it?'

'Yours?'

She shook her head and slowly reached for it. Reluctantly, he passed it over. She stroked the slippery material and examined it for labels. There were none. She could feel soft luggage inside. She felt sick and Kemal saw her anxiety and frowned. She took a breath and unzipped the bag. There were clothes inside, still wet from their long immersion. One by one, Candy pulled them out, searching each pocket, peering at each collar for a name.

Every item was unmarked. The pockets were empty. She looked at Kemal.

'Did you take anything from the bag?'

With vehement gestures, he told her he was innocent.

She knew he was lying, could see it in his eyes and over-emphatic sign language.

'Give it to me,' she screamed. 'Whatever you've taken, give it to me.'

Like a chastened dog, he turned his head and felt inside his pocket. He brought out a notecase.

Candy took it from him and opened it. A sodden wad of Indonesian rupiah and American dollars filled one side. In the other was a batch of credit cards. Like a gambler picking up a deal that might fill a winning hand, Candy took one out.

The name on it was Norman Richard Cass. All the other cards were in the same name.

Candy sat staring at them, unable to take it in. She knew who Disco was; she'd stolen his power. She looked up at Kemal's sullen face and smiled. 'Here,' she said, handing him back the wallet without the cards, 'I've got what I need.'

Once Kemal understood that he could keep the cash, he became communicative. Sticking to sign language, he sketched the gravity of their situation, rubbing his stomach ruefully, then gazing round and spreading his arms to convey emptiness and futility.

Candy nodded and pointed up. Her hand made a feathering motion to indicate that salvation would come from the sky. Cottoning on, Kemal stuck his bottom lip out and shook his head with slow emphasis. He sprayed the forest with imaginary machine-gun fire and prodded himself in the chest to indicate who would be on the receiving end.

'Where are you from?'

He became evasive. From a long way across the sea.

'How will you get back?'

His hand undulated in imitation of a boat. Smiling at Candy's puzzlement, he beckoned her to follow him. He trod with assurance, never putting a foot wrong, moving so fast that Candy could hardly keep up. The path he took was dim and strange, but eventually she discovered they were heading for the inner lagoon. Not far from the shore, he made her take cover while he scouted ahead. He whistled to sound the all-clear. She caught up with him contemplating three saplings felled with his parang.

Candy surveyed the makings of his raft and her heart foundered. The timbers were about six inches in diameter, cut from a balsa-like tree. Seeing her despondent expression, Kemal tried to encourage her. He hadn't finished; more logs would be required.

'You're going to sail home on a *raft?*'

The notion tickled him. He pointed down the lagoon.

'No,' Candy said, the memory of the mangroves flooding up. 'Absolutely not.'

He indicated that their escape would take them south along the coast until they reached a river. They would ascend the river and in due course arrive at a city.

'A city?'

Kemal's teeth flashed. 'Sure, big city. Dancing. Beer.'

'How far? How many days?'

Dubiously, Kemal examined his fingers. With patent lack of conviction, he extended three.

'At least five, I bet.'

He was keen to get to work. What he wanted Candy to do was keep watch for Jaeger while he felled the remaining trees. He stationed her about fifty yards from

414

the site. As she waited, she listened out for the sound of an aeroplane engine, wondering what Kemal would do if rescue arrived.

Once, Jaeger appeared. Candy warned Kemal just in time and they hid like children, watching Jaeger turning in the jungle.

'I know you're there.'

That night, Candy woke to find Kemal petting her and moving against her suggestively. She pushed him away and he made a plaintive sound, hardly distinguishable from the cry of an infant. A little later, his hands stole around her again but kept away from any contentious zones.

'I don't mind a cuddle,' Candy told him, 'but that's your lot.'

Next morning, her fever had risen and it was all she could do to drag herself up. Giving in would be fatal, she told herself, forcing herself to find a level where she could brace on her sickness.

Again, Kemal made her keep watch while he went to work. Dizziness washed over her. Shrunk down at the base of a tree, she passed into a conscious black-out from which Kemal roused her without ceremony, tugging her up as if angered by her dereliction of duty.

'I'm sick, okay?'

But something else had alarmed him. He led her past the raft and Candy saw it was taking shape – a platform about twelve feet long and four wide, lashed together with rattans. At the water's edge he stopped. Kites and vultures were thermalling in numbers larger than Candy had ever seen. The charred smell of burnt vegetation caught in her nostrils. What a mess they had made of the island. What a vile mess.

Kemal hadn't spoken. His attention seemed to be fixed on a semi-sunken log.

'Oh, my God,' she said, stepping back.

The crocodile was floating tail heavy about twenty yards offshore. Only its nostrils and orbital ridges protruded above the surface.

Kemal lobbed a branch into the water. The instant it hit, the crocodile came alive, gliding noiselessly forward with one invisible sweep of its tail. A ripple spread back from its snout and died as it lost way and hung in the water again, no more than fifteen feet from shore. Through the pea-green water, Candy could see its beautiful mottling and the armoured crests running down its back. Though the end of the tail was lost in the broth, she estimated its length at about fifteen feet. A membrane slid across its brassy eyes and then slid back.

Hingeing her hands at the wrists, she mimicked jaws snapping shut. Then she opened her palms in a gesture of defeat.

Kemal shook his head and patted his gun, but he didn't look a picture of confidence.

By mid-morning the next day, he had put the finishing touches to the raft. Straightening from his labours, he gave Candy the small but decisive nod she had been dreading.

'I'm not up to it,' she stammered. 'Don't be cross. You go.'

Tut-tutting at her faint-heartedness, he took hold of her arm. She dug in her heels, but her resolve was insecure. Three days had passed since Disco's escape and there had been no sign of a search. Maybe he'd decided to play safe and wait until he was back in the United States before selling the cassettes. He was more than capable of putting together some non-incriminating explanation of how they'd come into his hands.

Mouth set, Candy looked into the forest, aware that there was no fallback position. This morning her fever was in remission, but she wasn't cured. If rescue didn't come soon, she would die in a lonely huddle.

Kemal was waiting patiently. For all his youth, he was a real child of the wilderness, deft of hand and cunning in jungle lore and the ways of the sea. He wouldn't hazard a coastal passage unless he was confident of the outcome.

'Oh, bloody hell,' she said, 'what does it matter?'

She helped drag the raft to the bank and slide it in. Kemal stepped on and offered her his hand. Before accepting it, Candy reconnoitred the lagoon. It was another broiling day, the water smooth as silk, but at places and intervals too random to predict, fish rising to insects nudged the surface into rings. Candy's eyes darted from one potential danger spot to another. Kemal shrugged. The crocodile could be anywhere, and where there was one, there would be others.

'Lap of the gods,' Candy said, taking his hand.

Delicately, he pushed off with the reverse end of his makeshift oar. Standing up, Candy felt as precariously poised as a camel in a hammock. She crouched, grasping the rattan ties, her gaze working back and forth. Kemal's eyes were equally busy, scanning the waters between each stroke. The *plop* of a fish jumping made them both jump in turn. They exchanged sickish smiles. Kemal passed her the parang.

Before yesterday, Candy had only seen crocodiles on television. She remembered one documentary sequence – a wildebeest manacled round the head by a crocodile that had propelled itself vertically out of the water to a height not much less than half its length. Her feet shifted. Don't think about it, she told herself, unable to do anything else.

Stroke by stroke, they punted on. A pair of gaudy butterflies waltzed beside them. The surface was a burning mirror of the sun. Candy pushed back her damp and clinging hair and looked back to check how far they'd come.

Oh, shit,' she said.

Jaeger was standing on the shore.

Kemal stopped poling and unslung his gun.

'Don't,' Candy cried, half rising, teetering in the line of fire.

'Candy, is that you?'

She was tempted not to answer. In the weighty silence she could hear the ebb and flow of her breath.

'What do you want, Leo?'

'Take me with you,' he said, his tone bereft.

Candy turned to see Kemal's face contorted in a snarl. She pointed at Jaeger, then at the raft. Kemal shook his hand angrily and resumed poling.

'We have to take him,' Candy cried.

Kemal began to jabber, slapping the raft and miming the consequences if Jaeger boarded it. He was right, Candy saw. The craft wouldn't support Jaeger's weight.

There he stood, slump-shouldered and naked, peering out like a savage on the brink of a future that holds no place for him. She couldn't leave him like that.

'Take me back.'

Holding the shotgun in one hand, Kemal continued poling with the other.

'I said, take me back.'

Kemal ignored her. Candy estimated the distance to shore at about sixty yards. She trembled with indecision and fear, and fear deterred all else.

'Leo, there isn't room. The raft's not big enough. Help's on the way. Hang on.'

With a mighty splash, he waded into the water.

'For God's sake, go back! There are crocodiles!'

Jaeger couldn't have heard her, and even if he had, she doubted if he would have paid heed. Throwing himself forward, he began to swim, using a clumsy, straight-armed action that beat the water to foam. Kemal had put his gun away and reversed his oar and was paddling for all his worth.

Despite Jaeger's lack of technique, it soon became clear that he was outpacing them. At the rate he was closing, he would catch them in the middle of the lagoon. Candy imagined the turmoil when he did, saw them all pitched overboard and a flotilla of crocodiles homing in from all directions.

Dropping to her knees, she began paddling with her hands.

For every three yards they made, Jaeger gained one. Candy cast a glance over her shoulders and gave a throaty moan. He was less than thirty yards astern, thrashing on with relentless strength.

'Damn you,' she gasped, and redoubled her efforts.

Kemal shouted, drawing her attention to the parang. Taking one hand off the oar, he made a slashing motion.

Jaeger had narrowed the gap to a point where Candy could hear his spluttering breath.

'Keep away,' she shouted.

He kept coming.

She grabbed the parang and dashed the sweat from her eyes. 'I'm warning you, Leo.'

He was oblivious to everything except the raft.

Her voice rose in panic. 'Leo, I mean it. You're not ...'

Her final warning was swallowed in a gulp. Her eyes stuck wide. She gulped again before she could speak.

'Kemal.'

He didn't hear her the first time.

'Kemal, there's a crocodile.'

He saw it and stopped paddling. He unslung his gun. The crocodile was coming up behind Jaeger and he hadn't seen it. There was no chance of him making the raft before it caught him.

Candy swung on Kemal. 'Do something!'

Unmoved, he gave a dismissive sweep of his hand.

She cupped her hands to her mouth. 'Leo,' she called, 'Leo, there's a crocodile behind you. A crocodile!'

His pace didn't slacken.

There was nothing they could do. In helpless terror, she watched the point of the V close on him.

In the final yards, the crocodile seemed to gather itself and catapult forward. The jaws hinged open and smacked shut on Jaeger's thigh, the momentum behind them shunting him through the water as if he were a bathtime toy. He cartwheeled bodily as the crocodile spun on its axis, dragging him under. A moment later he shot up, pushed high out of the water, and hung shrieking, arms beating at the crocodile's head, before he was pulled down like a duckling grabbed by a pike. Somehow he managed to break loose and flailed a few feet before it grabbed him again. A blood-tinged spout erupted. The crocodile's tail lashed and a rainbow formed in the spray. The creature spun again and Jaeger disappeared under the roiling water.

Twice more he burst through the surface, and when he went under for the fourth time, Candy couldn't believe that he wouldn't reappear. But the waves slopping against the raft settled into soft weals, and from the cloud of mud where Jaeger had gone, bubbles broke winking in a chain that headed back to shore. The lagoon had been stunned into silence.

'Tsk,' Kemal said.

Senses overpowered by what she had witnessed, Candy looked at him unseeingly.

'Tsssk!'

Kemal's eyes were fixed wide, but they weren't aimed in the direction Candy expected. Following his gaze, she saw three more crocodiles vectoring towards them. In shocked reflex, she clutched the parang.

One of the crocodiles was well ahead of the others, its thrusting tail driving it like a torpedo. Water gurgled in its wake and slid with a silky rustle down its flanks. Frozen, motionless, Candy counted down. Twenty yards, fifteen, twelve.

Ten yards from the raft, it switched off power and coasted, its momentum carrying it to within five feet. Its jaws were fixed in a crooked grin and a few bubbles escaped from them. It was watching her, the irises stopped down to vertical slits against the harsh sunlight.

It drifted closer, almost nudging the raft. Kemal said something, repeated it louder and, as if on command, the crocodile opened its gape. As Candy reared back, Kemal fired both barrels down its throat.

The raft tipped, flipping Candy into the water. She surfaced into a maelstrom, saw the raft and grabbed it. Kemal had managed to hang on by throwing himself flat and grasping both sides while still holding on to the gun and the oar. He bellied forward and hauled her up by one wrist. Fifteen feet away the crocodile plunged and corkscrewed as if it had been plugged into 40,000 volts. The other crocodiles were nearly on it, converging with grunts.

Kemal was already paddling away when the first of them hit the animal he'd shot. A second later the other crocodile struck. A titanic tug of war broke out, the convulsions so frenzied that Candy couldn't distinguish one beast from the other. She closed her eyes and kept them closed until the turmoil had faded. When she looked again, the crocodiles were telescoped by distance, still working out their violent ends, locked in a struggle for which they seemed predestined from before the dawn of man.

She glanced at Kemal, but he paid no attention. She kept glancing at him, afraid to break the silence, knowing words were inadequate even if they had been spoken in a common tongue.

FIVE

34

Day 25

Slowly the island merged back into the coastline until by noon Candy could no longer distinguish it from the mangroves. Soon afterwards, Kemal landed to search for food and water, leaving Candy by the raft. The unseen sun was too high in the sky to afford shade, and under its narcotic effect, her mind gradually lapsed into the same slack rhythm as the waves.

Birds exploded in alarm as Kemal fired his shotgun somewhere deep in the swamp. When the commotion had died down, Candy thought she heard another sound – a mechanical jarring harsher than the counterpoint of insects. Squinting south, she pinpointed a helicopter, miles away, flying up the coast. She knew it was heading for the island, and she knew she had enough time to attract its attention. All she had to do was scull out fifty yards and wave.

She faced the mangroves and held her breath, trying to filter out some signal of Kemal's presence. Deciding he wasn't close, she jumped up and began pulling at the raft, each tug moving it no more than a few inches. She had got its front edge into the water when the consequences of rescue hit her. For her, the helicopter promised deliverance, but for Kemal it guaranteed imprisonment at best, and more likely a sentence of death. They had made an undeclared pact, and for better or worse she couldn't break it.

Close to fainting from her exertions, Candy watched the helicopter approach. As it clattered past, she raised a hand in melancholy salute, then slowly lowered herself on to the raft and remained staring into the blank white heat until Kemal came panting out of the swamp. He stopped dead, eyes darting first to Candy then to the raft, measuring how close she'd come to ditching him. Abruptly, his manner changed to unconcern and he flourished the monkey he'd shot as if it were a soft toy he'd won at a fairground shooting booth. Wondering whether he'd have stood by her if their positions had been reversed, Candy stretched her mouth in an admiring smile.

By unspoken consent, they stayed closeted behind the mangroves for the rest of the day. Another helicopter showed up, and out to sea a warship appeared, confirming that this was no casual exercise. Disco had reached a haven. The possibility that it was Boucher who had raised the alert never seriously entered her mind.

She took out the credit cards and looked again at the name on them. As the only survivor, Disco or Cass or whatever he called himself would be the chronicler of everything that had happened. The thought of him twisting events to his own advantage filled Candy with a visceral hatred that whittled all her reasons for living down to one. *Revenge!* Just the sound of it quickened her blood.

She needed every scrap of resolution next day. Dawn broke slowly, the sun emerging from sea mists in a black corona. When it was only halfway up the sky, scudding clouds overwhelmed it and the sea turned choppy, forcing the voyagers to beach on a mud bank littered with the skeletons of toppled trees. Kemal sank into an animal insensibility, but Candy was acutely conscious of time ticking away, painfully aware that the coral wound in her leg had become infected beyond the stage where it would heal by itself. They had lost half a day already, and today's inertia meant the estimated five-day journey had stretched to seven. She coughed – a wet rattle that startled her and made Kemal open his eyes in concern. She laid her cheek on her hands and closed her eyes. He thought she was miming sleep until he shook her and she pretended not to wake up.

In late afternoon the wind dropped, a window of light opened, and they resumed their journey down the long and empty coast, Kemal rowing on long after the sea had turned opaque and Candy couldn't separate sky from land.

Next morning the sun was back to full strength. For Candy, running a fever and with no overhead protection, the day's voyaging was purgatory. But it was their last on the sea. That afternoon the mangrove barrier parted around a broad olive channel, flat and glossy like the stretched skin of a snake. Candy thought it was a passage between islets until Kemal announced they had entered the promised river. It wasn't the main artery, but a sluggish vein in a huge delta system – a doodle of meanders and oxbows so convoluted that the sun was constantly changing places, one minute dazzling Candy's eyes, the next roasting her neck.

There was no current to speak of and channels beckoned on all sides, but though Kemal could never have travelled this waterway before, he navigated as surely as an otter. Gradually the trees grew taller and more various, some boasting colourful blossoms and leaves the size of tabloid pages. Plying through a green bloom of algae, Kemal scooped a handful of water to his mouth, indicating that they had left the saline zone behind.

After the stupefying emptiness of the coast, the river was teeming with life. River dolphins sported around the raft. Orchids festooned the overhanging branches that offered brief respite from the sun. Kingfishers darted in azure flashes. On a mud bank, a carpet of butterflies flicked their wings as if they were practising synchronized callisthenics. Several times, the travellers disturbed crocodiles basking in the shallows or slithering from flats. One individual entered the river like an elderly matron taking the waters at a spa, while in a tree above it a monkey sat scratching its head in puzzlement.

Kemal greeted the creatures as if they were neighbourhood acquaintances, calling out to them in their own languages and telling Candy their life-stories, both slapstick and tragic. He had a hunter's eye, often pointing out animals she would have missed. One morning he directed her attention to a python lying curled between the buttresses of a waterside tree. At their approach, it began to uncoil, easing out length after length until ten feet of its front end was probing through the water, while the rest of it still lay in folds, like a casually stacked fire hose.

Another time he gesticulated at the bank, and when Candy looked, she saw a tiger crouched to drink, looking back at her with a stare that seemed to probe her soul.

Kemal asked who had shot the tiger on the island, but as she opened her mouth to tell him, she realized that in this relationship, he was the hunter. Leo, she said, the man who was killed by the crocodile, and from the way he nodded, she knew she'd given the right answer.

She was a helpless passenger. All she did was sit back while Kemal paddled on, and on, and on. For long periods she simply watched him, registering the play of reflected light on his skin. Then she would turn and gaze at the perpetual forest and feel like the last woman in the world. In a strange way she was content. The few square feet of wood under her had become home. At night they slept on it. Creatures hitched rides on it – insects and frogs and once, a snake that Kemal killed and cooked.

Their staple food was fish that Kemal speared in the shallows. Unlike the firm-fleshed coral species, most of these river fish had the texture of cotton wool crammed with needles. Their diet was supplemented by fruits and roots gathered on excursions into the forests. These trips were brief and undertaken with caution. Apart from tigers, Kemal told her, there were men-monsters that would tear his entrails out and copulate with her.

Once he shot a duck out of a flock that came hurtling downstream with a pinging of wings that made Candy think of colder skies.

The three-day odyssey had stretched to six before the river broadened and acquired a current. Kemal spotted something that excited him so much he nearly lost his balance. Expecting to see a particularly exotic animal, Candy finally made out a hut on stilts in the encroaching forest.

'How far to the city?' she asked.

Kemal showed two fingers.

The current developed muscle, and it took all his efforts to make any headway. Candy's fever had worsened and her mind began to slip away. She no longer had the sense that she was moving; instead, she was fixed on an axis while a dream slowly spooled around her, the wild green walls slipping back, the trees turning to watch as they passed downriver. Moments of lucidity were seamlessly incorporated into hallucinations. She saw a motor boat with three men in it, one garlanded with birds, another holding a dead turtle.

Later, she woke to the thump of an engine and the reek of exhaust gases. She drifted back under to the sound of waves slapping in the riverside roots. Next time she regained consciousness, it was dusk and her senses had achieved a preternatural clarity, absorbing everything – the lightning that flickered like distant arc-welding on the pewter sky; the fishy odour of the boat and the sharp tang of dung and woodsmoke; the yipping of dogs and the special frog chant that heralded rain. Above her, Kemal's face was suspended like a planet, and ranged behind him in a fish-eye effect, a host of other faces craned down with unrestrained curiosity.

She gave a liquid cough and tried to smile. 'Big city.'

Kemal didn't answer for a moment. Solemnly, he pointed upriver, then addressed her in a formal tone she hadn't heard him use before. She was dimly aware he was saying farewell. Her own lips moved, but the sound she made got lost in her throat. Kemal placed a hand on hers, then withdrew, his eyes still fixed on her as he stepped back through the throng.

That was the last time she saw him.

She was aware of being lifted out of the boat and carried up a log ladder into a room lit only by splinters of light. Around her gathered a sombre crush of people – women with pendulous breasts and pot-bellied kids peeping from behind their mothers' knees.

Things became very hazy after that. She registered bitter concoctions being forced into her mouth and something being applied to her injured leg. For some reason, this triggered an image of maggots. There was no connection between her thoughts. Each one had an arbitrary existence, unconnected to the image that came before and the one that followed.

A pig squealing. A man with a gun leering down at her. The women of the village standing in a line. A high-pitched lamentation. A boat. A ship with black sails.

35

Chicago was grey and cold, clamped in freezing fog. When Boucher entered his apartment, he found it empty, Lydia's suitcase in the hall. He had phoned her from Singapore after tracking her orchestra to Philadelphia. Starting today, she had two days' compassionate leave, but her tour didn't close until the weekend before Christmas – a warped trick of scheduling that meant she would be returning home after him. It was hard to believe that he'd been away less than five weeks.

Walking softly, like a trespasser, he went into the lounge. On the table, next to fresh flowers, squatted the typewriter gifted to him by Tom Brack. Seeing it gave him a queer haunted feeling. Then he remembered it was part of the luggage he'd left at the hotel in Pontianaka – dead man's effects.

A sheet of paper lolled in the rollers. 'Welcome home, darling Jay!'

The feminine exclamation touched a soft place in his heart and he turned, smiling round at the unfamiliar familiarity. Home, he thought, a lump filling his throat. Life starts here again, he told himself. Candy was dead, and though he wouldn't forget her, he would preserve her memory in a place open to no one else.

His face ambushed him in a mirror.

'So how are we?' he asked it.

Pretty good on the surface. He was excited – an edgy

euphoria that made it difficult to stay still. Only when he looked into his eyes did he sense the black hinterland.

Work was the cure, he decided. First a vacation with Lydia – Paris or Rome or Prague, somewhere civilized and temperate. But once old masonry and grand music and midnight cafés had exorcised the jungle voodoo, he would shut the door on the world until he'd written the whole thing out of his system.

As he paced and changed seats and picked up letters and put them down unopened, his eyes kept gravitating to the blank television screen.

In a trade-off for his release, he'd agreed to appear shoulder to shoulder with Clarence Tusser at a Kennedy Airport press conference. Checking the time, he saw that the early evening news had just started.

Unable to resist, he switched on and immediately backed away from his own presence. There he was – top item, front page, block capitals – running the gauntlet of microphone booms and cameras. He winced at his appearance. It wasn't the skinniness and over-bright eyes that bothered him. He looked furtive. He looked like he had something to hide.

Through spread fingers he watched Tusser, huckster's eyes ablaze, extolling Boucher's courage, durability and steadfast refusal to give up in the face of oriental wiliness. Sweat popped on Boucher's brow. He seemed to be agreeing with the lunatic.

A tough trade-off, but no tougher than the ordeal by media that followed. Delta Glenn, dressed in eye-smarting orange, tried to keep the pack to heel, telling it that Boucher had been sent to Borneo on a magazine assignment and would honour that commitment. Subsequently, he would write the full account of the Wildguard expedition in book form.

But the moment she'd finished, everybody started

baying at him, addressing him not as a colleague, but as raw material. Most of the questions were about Dexter and Nadine, and he'd stuck to a diplomatic line, stressing their solidarity as a couple, Dexter's uncomplaining nature and all-round niceness. He sounded sincere.

'Can you talk us through Dexter's murder?' a female reporter asked, jostling to the front.

Delta intervened smartly. 'Like I told you, Jay will give the full facts in his own way, in his own time.'

'How did you manage to get out, and no one else?'

'Luck. Luck of the draw.' As Boucher said this, memory flashed an image of the king of hearts that had given him the winning hand against Henry Ritter. Well, he'd won that one, too, and lost his best friend.

The next question came out of left field, leaving Boucher's wits spreadeagled.

'You've talked about the part played by the English woman – her courage and so on. Did you have a personal relationship?'

'What other kinds are there?'

'Did you have a sexual relationship?'

Before Boucher could find out how he'd parried that one, the elevator bell pinged and he lunged for the remote control as if he'd been caught one-handed watching hard-core porn. He stood, wiped his palms on his hands, took two breaths, then two more. Different expressions jock-eyed on his face.

Lydia came in, saw him, and carefully dropped the shopping she was carrying. Ritter's jibe about Boucher being better off with a saluki wasn't as grotesque as it sounded. With her long, nervously elegant face and silver-blonde hair, Lydia did bring to mind some rare and highly-strung pedigree breed. Her mouth broke into a tremulous smile.

'It *is* you.'

'It is,' he agreed, 'though there's not so much of me as there was.'

As if they both saw the gap that needed to be closed, they moved together, hiding their faces behind each other's shoulders. Holding Lydia, Boucher felt her hot tears on his cheek, the delicate scalloping of her bones. He was back where he belonged and, believing things were going to be all right, he blessed the fickle ways of the heart.

Breaking from the embrace, Lydia sat on a couch, while Boucher took a seat opposite, on the other side of the room.

'It's hard to take in,' Lydia said through a sniff. 'All those weeks I thought you were dead. And now you're here. It's kind of eerie.'

It kind of was – like being a ghost. 'You were probably getting used to not having me around. I'm sorry to put you through two traumas.'

Lydia made a helpless little gesture. 'You're all over the newspapers. You're famous. This isn't much of a home-coming. I feel I should have arranged something special, but you said that ...'

'Hey, this is exactly what I want – just you and me.'

Over supper, which Boucher cooked himself, Lydia picked around the edges of his island experiences. What did they eat? How did they keep clean? The gory details were never enquired into, and Boucher was glad that Lydia lived in a realm where pain was a fluffed note or a reproachful glance from the conductor. Actually, they talked mostly about her – her performances, the petty antagonisms of orchestral life, her run-in with the conductor over his interpretation of her part in Tchaikovsky's *Variations on a Rococo Theme*.

It soothed the way to bed where, by tacit understanding, nothing was expected or demanded of him. Honestly weary, he fell asleep almost as soon as the lights were out.

In the depth of night, a galvanizing shock threw him up in a fit of shuddering. The dream had died with sleep, and all that was left was a pervasive submarine light and sour fragrance.

'Jay, you're boiling. You were calling out. You sounded frightened.'

'I'm fine.'

He leant and kissed her and eased back, leaving a tiny but critical gap between their bodies. His skin seemed to have taken on the texture of suede. Gradually, the formless terror that had jerked him from sleep faded away. Breathing Lydia's perfume, he found himself recalling the scent that had spilled out from certain trees at dusk, the quavering of insects, the nightjars that skimmed like spirits through the forest shadows. Turning over the memories, he was surprised how many good ones there were, and for a moment he was solaced. Then a wave of remorse struck.

'Jay?'

'Hm?'

'It was Candy's name you were calling.'

On the second night of their reunion, Boucher initiated sex and carried it to a conclusion. Sleep didn't come so easily. The room seemed airless, suffocating. He tossed and turned until four, then got up and sat by the window until dawn. Later that morning, he and Lydia went their separate ways – she to rejoin her orchestra in St Louis, he to rendezvous with Delta Glenn at Time Warner's headquarters on New York's Sixth Avenue.

The metropolis was gridlocked for the last Christmas of the millennium – the last Christmas, some predicted, of all time. But if Armageddon was coming, the crowds of shoppers seemed to be treating it as nothing more than an excuse for a retail orgy.

Delta was waiting for him in the lobby, suited in a magenta outfit that seemed to have been spun from strontium or some other exotic metal. She eyed him with concern.

'You look exhausted.'

'Four walls and a roof take a bit of getting used to.'

She continued her appraisal, then she patted the bag containing the two video cassettes.

'There's some nasty stuff on these. I'm not sure you should relive it.'

'I promise I won't throw up.'

She nodded. 'I've told them to go easy on the questions at this stage.'

An editor and two assistants escorted them to a small film theatre, where another six or seven people were waiting. Most of the men and women wore suits and had a legal mien; the senior editorial presence was a large, loose-limbed man called Pulman. Beverages were offered and declined.

'Are we ready to roll?' Delta asked, after the exchange of introductions and pleasantries.

'Any time.'

'Let me remind you,' Delta told them, 'this isn't a show and tell. The purpose of the film is to provide corroboration of Jay's story.'

As the lights dimmed, Boucher's heart pumped harder. Delta gave his hand a reassuring squeeze.

Cassette one opened with a confused drama – the camera tracking from the sunken airship to the beached survivors. There was Jaeger wandering through the background, plaintively demanding to know where his glasses were. Out of view, Fieser was moaning and Nadine sobbing on a single, nerve-scratching note. The camera stopped briefly on himself, looking more shocked than he remembered feeling at the time. Then it panned to Candy and Aquila, semi-nude, hugging each other.

Scene two was background stuff. Picture and sound quality were excellent, and for a moment, seeing the succulence of the vegetation, hearing the murmur of distant surf, Boucher was beguiled by the beauty of the place.

The tranquillity of the scene put the audience at their ease.

'Great beach.'

'Who's the cutie in the bra?'

Next, the audience were treated to Kent Bartok's virtuoso climb to raise the Wildguard flag. Trigg had been good, Boucher realized, combining technical flair with a *paparazzo*'s guile. Somehow he'd managed to capture Nadine and Dexter naked, sporting in the shallows. He'd sneaked a sequence of Aquila, also naked, performing some private liturgy in the rain forest. Seeing himself again, returning triumphant from a fishing expedition, Boucher felt an odd little pang of nostalgia.

The screen turned a murky green. They were in the mangroves and Boucher felt with perfect recall the stupefying heat and sense of threat.

'What's happening here?'

'Candy and Marriot are leaving to search for a settlement inland.'

'Why did you send the girl?' someone asked.

'No questions,' Delta said.

As if caught in a dream, Boucher watched himself saying goodbye to Candy. He swallowed as she gave him the quick little hug that was one of her trademarks. Suddenly he felt his heart was breaking in pieces.

Thunder rolled and he saw himself outlined on the

lagoon against an apocalyptic sky. That was the afternoon he'd retrieved the gun.

The next few scenes were strange to him, having been taken after Trigg had decamped back to the Ecos. There was a clip of Jaeger and Aquila performing a ritual dance around a fire. Disco was in the background, and when he noticed the camera, he thrust his face right up to the lens in a distorted mock snarl. Boucher's own lips curled.

Suddenly the screen blacked out. Loud and terrible cries rang out. The screen exploded into burning white and shadows loomed across it. There was a roar and the scene tilted.

'What's going on here?'

'That's the tiger with Aquila.'

'Can we run it again? I can't make it out.'

Frame by frame, the projectionist reversed.

'Back a bit, a bit more. There.'

'Still don't see it.'

'Left of centre. Jesus! It's ripped her throat out.'

The audience watched in silence as Dexter was killed, shifted uneasily as Disco blew up the pirates to the accompaniment of his threats against Boucher.

There was a collective expulsion of breath as the lights came back on. The audience blinked and shook their heads.

'Wow,' Pulman said.

'There are potential copyright problems,' Delta warned. 'The material was shot by three people on equipment owned by Ronnie Trigg, who was the Wildguard expedition's cameraman. Jay lays no claim to the video. His personal wish is that any profits be shared among the families of the deceased.'

One of the lawyers scratched his ear. 'Could be tricky.'

'That problem aside, I would like a decision on our proposal.'

438

'Why don't we give you lunch?' Pulman suggested.

'Let's skip the foreplay,' Delta told him. 'I need a decision now. I have to be back in Los Angeles this evening.'

Pulman smiled. 'I'm sorry, we don't move that fast.'

'Well,' Delta said, 'that's a shame.' She began to get up.

Pulman's smile went out and he looked anxiously at his colleagues. 'Give us half an hour to talk it over.'

'Sure,' Delta said. 'Can I have a peppermint tea?'

Over her *tisane*, she took the opportunity to conduct two other strands of business.

'It's not the script I'm worried about,' she told an actor. 'It's the director. The guy's flyblown.'

She called one of her associates. 'A million and a half? You got a fix on that? Well, don't take his word, and if you can't screw him down, tell him to take a hike. But nicely.'

She packed her phone away as one of the executives came out and beckoned her forward. Understanding that he was being sidelined, Boucher asked for some coffee while he waited. Worry assailed him. His lie about Disco's death distorted the entire story.

Twenty minutes later, Delta reappeared, took his elbow without pausing and steered him doorwards as if she'd just pulled off a scam and wanted to exit before the mark discovered the Swiss chronograph they'd just bought had been knocked out in a Kowloon lock-up. In the elevator, she leaned her head back on the padded wall, closed her eyes and gave what looked like an orgiastic shudder.

'We have to talk some more, but we've got a deal roughed out – book, film, serialization rights.'

Boucher wasn't surprised. Like most writers, he'd leapt ahead of his end-product to the contract, the critical notices, the royalty cheques.

'You're supposed to ask how much.'

Boucher glanced at the elevator's other occupants, who were pretending not to listen.

'How much?'

'Four million. I said we'd get back to them tomorrow.'

It made no impact.

The doors opened and they spilled out, Boucher increasing his pace to keep up with Delta. She stopped, fast-idling. 'You hungry?'

Boucher felt a bit sick, but he could hardly turn down an invitation from the woman who'd made him a millionaire.

She took him to a private dining club and displayed a healthy appetite.

'I could have got more elsewhere, but they're straight players, and keeping all the balls in one place means we retain some sort of control. Oh, by the way, they want you to go to LA to talk to some studio people.' Delta smiled girlishly. 'Got any preference for who plays you?'

At that moment, Boucher couldn't have cared less.

Delta must have detected misgivings. 'I hope you're not having second thoughts.'

Back in Chicago, Boucher sat beside the telephone, a bottle of whiskey to hand. Delta had strongly advised him against calling any of the castaways' relatives. He'd be treading an emotional minefield. Leave it to the lawyers.

Darkness drew down outside, and when Boucher could no longer see anything but shades of black, he reached for the phone.

'My name's Jay Boucher. I was on the Wildguard expedition with your daughter.'

Candy's father was brusque. 'I know who you are. I've read about you in the papers.'

'I got to know her well. We were friends. She meant a lot to me. A great deal.'

'I understand you were with her when she died.'

'We were trying to row to an oil rig. There were three of us – Candy, me and a man called Disco. The sea was pretty high and it was dark. We caught a wave and Candy and the other man went over. I dived in, but she was already gone. We were right on the reef.'

'Did you see her drown?'

Boucher hesitated. Put a line under it he thought, for both your sakes.

'Yes.'

'I'm grateful to you for telling me. It couldn't have been easy.'

'No, it isn't. Look, there are some other things I want to talk about, but the phone isn't the right place. Could I come and see you some time?'

There was a silence.

'I understand that you're writing a book.'

'This hasn't got anything to do with that. It's personal.'

'I'm not sure how you can separate the two. In the circumstances, I think it's better if we don't meet. I'm sure you understand. If you'd care to write, that's another matter.'

'I'll do that.'

'Goodbye, Mr Boucher.'

'Goodbye.'

At that point, Boucher poured his first drink. Several hours later, he woke in the dark and wished he was dead.

36

Day 42

Candy floated to the surface of consciousness and drifted there. Eventually, she decided that the faint tricklings and hummings she could hear weren't coming from inside her head, which meant she must be in some kind of room. On an experimental basis, she opened her eyes and blinked in the lights shining from oblong lamps set in the ceiling. Moving her head even slightly required prodigious effort. Walls slid into view – glass at the front, gull-white at the sides, hung with restful paintings. Screwing her neck round further, she saw screens and hoses and wires.

A hospital.

Trying to work out how she'd got here, she ran into a blind alley and for a moment felt the scrambled panic of amnesia. Then some of her neural pathways cleared. Kemal, the river, faces peering out of a stormy evening sky. That was as far as memory took her.

A drip tube had been connected to her left arm. With her right hand, she felt under the sheets. She was dressed in a cotton shift and her right leg had a dressing on it. Unable to reach further, she wiggled her toes. Unless she was suffering from phantom-limb syndrome, she seemed to be in one functioning piece.

More or less. With the return of consciousness, she

became aware of the poison still in her system. Her mouth tasted foul, her joints ached cruelly, and the backs of her eyes felt as if they had been worked over with small rubber mallets. All in all, she felt like a bio-engineering prototype cobbled together by scientists with inadequate funds and no scruples.

The door gulped with a pneumatic sigh. A starchy rustle moved towards her.

'Candy?' a soft voice said. 'Candy, are you there?'

Opening her eyes, Candy smiled back at a lady who reminded her of a favourite Scots aunt.

'Are you awake, or are you dreaming with your eyes open?'

'Awake, I think.'

'Delighted to have you back with us. You're in a ship's hospital – a very superior ship's hospital. I'm Dr Laing – Penny. You've been with us since yesterday, since we took you off the schooner.' Dr Laing paused. 'I don't suppose you remember.'

Candy shook her head.

Dr Laing checked the readouts on the monitors. 'How do you feel?'

'Ghastly. Like I'm filled with sludge.'

'You've been in the wars, but you're quite safe now. Safe and a lot sounder than you were. Don't worry about all this plumbing; we're giving you a wee spring clean.'

'How long did you say I've been here?'

'Since yesterday evening. You're the talk of the ship. Everyone wants to know who you are, but we've decided to keep you to ourselves for the moment.'

'Have you told my family?'

'Captain Ainsley spoke to your father in person. He's flying to Singapore at this very moment. You'll see him tomorrow.'

'When can I go home?'

'For Christmas, perhaps. It will be a week or so before you're up and about.' Dr Laing produced an ophthalmoscope and smiled. 'Let's see if all the parts of your brain have woken up.'

When she'd finished her tests, Dr Laing expressed satisfaction. 'Of course we don't know exactly what unpleasantnesses you've been exposed to.' She paused. 'Is there anything you want to tell me?'

Candy didn't understand the question.

Dr Laing's tone was light. 'You were taken off a boat with a male crew.'

Candy caught on. 'I don't remember that bit.'

Smiling, Dr Laing put away her instruments. 'In that case, there's nothing *to* remember. I just wanted to confirm the results of my own examination.'

'Kemal,' Candy said, suddenly realizing who had arranged the black-sailed ship. 'He's going home, too.'

Dr Laing straightened her bedclothes. 'Good. Rest now.'

Candy's relationship with reality was flirtatious; now she saw it, now she didn't. The captain came to visit her, and for a moment she thought he was her father. Next time she woke, she must have been staring into space for several seconds before she became aware that it was occupied by another visitor – a portly, rumpled-looking man with pouchy eyes.

'Hello,' she said drowsily. 'You a doctor?'

His hands implored her not to make any physical effort. He looked at the door before parking himself at her bedside. 'Barry Pitman,' he whispered. He pulled his chair as close as it would go. 'Candida?' he said hoarsely. 'Candida Woodville?'

'Candy.'

'Thank you, Lord,' Pitman breathed, closing his eyes in

gratitude. He produced a notebook and wet his lips. 'Candy, I'd like to ask you some questions.'

'Already told the doctor.'

'About your terrible ordeal.'

'Not now. Not important.'

'Not important? Candy, you are the biggest story in the world. You're a marvel, a miracle, an inspiration.'

'Feel like shit, to tell the truth.'

Pitman made another check on the door. 'The truth. Right. That's what we want.'

His eyes made Candy think of soft-boiled eggs. He pulled himself even closer, close enough for her to smell his boozy breath.

'Have they told you about the other survivor?'

'Disco?'

Pitman frowned.

'Cass,' Candy said. 'His passport said Cass, but Jay didn't believe him.'

Pitman scratched his forehead with a ball-point. 'It's Jay I'm talking about, the writer, the one they pulled off the boat.'

What he was saying finally penetrated the fever mists. 'You mean Jay's alive?' Candy fought to sit up. 'Jay's alive?'

'Ssh!' Pitman pleaded. 'Ssh! Yes, Jay's alive. He's front page. Until tomorrow.'

Candy fell back under a wave of giddiness. 'Where's Disco?'

Pitman consulted his notebook. 'Dead. He went overboard with you and drowned. Don't you remember?'

'Didn't.'

'Didn't what? Didn't fall overboard or didn't drown?'

Candy smiled. 'Jay killed him.'

Pitman laughed and glanced nervously at the door. 'I think you're still delirious.'

'Had to kill him,' Candy said dreamily. 'Was a murderer. Shot poor Kent. Tried to murder me. Pushed me out of the boat.'

'Pushed you? Why did he do that?'

'Hated me.'

'And because of what he did to you, Jay killed him.'

'Had to. Would have killed him.'

Pitman licked his lips. 'That's a very serious allegation, Candy.'

Dimly, she was aware that she was getting into murky water. 'Are you a policeman?'

'I'm a journalist.'

'Oh.'

'Why didn't Jay come back and look for you?'

'Don't know. Can't ... Don't want to talk any more.'

'Are you saying he abandoned you?'

Candy began to strive on the pillow. 'Where's Doctor ... Penny?'

'Okay, okay. Forget Jay and Disco. You were pushed out of the boat and then somehow you got back to the island. Then what? Did the ship pick you up?'

'Rowed down the coast on a raft.'

'On a raft? Oh this is good, Candy. This is great. How many days were you on the raft?'

'Six, seven. Not sure.'

'And that's when you met the ship.'

'Went up a river. To a village.'

'Better and better. Bloody brilliant. Right, you rowed up a river until you reached a village.'

'Kemal rowed.'

'Who's Kemal?'

'Pirate. Sort of apprentice pirate.'

'One of the pirates who killed Dexter?'

'Nice boy. Friend.'

'A friend? Fucking hell! You made friends with a pirate?'

446

'Tired.'

'Tell me more about this friendly pirate.'

'No more.'

'Please, Candy, this is a great story. The world has a right to know.'

Pitman's face had shrunk to the red orifice that was his mouth. Candy rolled her head. 'Go away.'

'One last question.' Pitman's expression grew especially earnest. 'Tell me, did you ever give up hope?'

'Yes.'

Pitman chuckled richly and stood up. Candy thought he'd gone, but then she heard her name called once more. Light flashed in her eyes, flashed again.

'Candy, you have made me rich and restored me to my tribe. And in return, I shall make you a star.'

'Don't want to be a star.'

The door sucked shut. Not a nice man, Candy thought. Thoroughly cheesy. But Jay was alive. How about that?

Fifteen hours later, Candy was stretchered off the *Gloriana* and united with her father. The meeting was virtually wordless. Just a lot of tears and smiles and hugs. As the family escorted her towards the waiting ambulance, a knot of men broke towards them.

'Candy! Hey, Candy!'

Flashguns sputtered.

'How the hell did they get here?'

'Candy, is it true that Jay Boucher killed one of the airship passengers?'

'Don't answer, Candy.'

'Why did he leave you?'

'Get out of the way, damn you.'

'Candy, love, give us a smile.'

'Bugger off, will you?'

'Sir, how does it feel to have your daughter back?'

37

Letters began to arrive for Boucher. Some of them were from well-wishers, admirers even, including one from a woman who wanted to go off with him to a desert island and bear his children. A lot more were in childish script demanding to know why he hadn't done more to protect Dexter. There were two death threats among them. Boucher began to feel in jeopardy.

Three days after the publishing deal had been roughed out, Lydia's tour ended and she came home. She seemed reserved, tense, and Boucher put it down to his own peculiar state of mind. He slept very little, woke in thrashing night-sweats and couldn't concentrate on simple tasks. Since his second night home, he and Lydia hadn't made love, but she didn't seem to resent his impotence.

Plans for their vacation went ahead. They had decided on Prague and were studying travel brochures one evening when the phone rang. Still undecided about choice of hotel, Boucher distractedly cradled the receiver under his chin.

'How does it feel now?' a muffled voice said.

'Who is that?'

'Your conscience.'

'Get lost.'

'Conscience never quits. See you around, Jay.'

Eyes frozen on a photo in the brochure, Boucher laid the phone down. He saw Lydia looking on with anxiety and forced his features into a smile.

'Wrong number.'

He got two hours' sleep that night, then flew to Hollywood to discuss the Wildguard film project with three script-developers – Brad, Ethan and Jerry. Brad wore clerkish specs, looked about seventeen and, from his starchy pallor, seemed to have spent his entire life in a cinema. Jerry was fat and bearded and intense. Ethan wore horn rims and a tweed jacket that gave him the appearance of an East Coast academic.

'This is going to be a great book,' he said, patting Boucher's outline, 'but great books often make lousy films.'

'Lousy film-makers make lousy films.'

The trio laughed at this sally. 'You know what I mean,' Ethan said. 'What works in print doesn't always translate to screen. We've come up with a couple of areas where we think a few tweaks and fixes are called for.'

'Such as?'

Ethan ran his pen down a lengthy list, frowning as if he faced a difficult menu choice. 'Okay,' he said, 'let's start with the tiger.'

'What's wrong with the tiger?'

'Tigers are endangered, protected. In the public perception, they're cuddly, and in the cinema, perception is all.'

'You want to get rid of the tiger?'

'Modify it,' Jerry said. 'Make it a specimen that's been grossly disfigured in a forest fire started by poachers. That way we make it scary while retaining audience sympathy.'

Boucher saw everything slipping out of his control. 'The real thing's pretty terrifying. It killed four of us.'

'Great,' Ethan said, as if that was one problem wrapped up. 'Let's move to the main issue.' He steepled his fingers and looked over them. 'Dexter and Nadine. We have to focus on them, but according to your treatment, they played minor roles.'

'I guess we protected them a bit. Nadine found the island ...'

449

Brad cut in. 'Understood, Jay, but for the film we have to build up their status. Get them into the action.'

'How?'

'You say Dexter was shot and cut down by the pirates without much of a struggle.'

'He didn't have a chance to defend himself.'

'Let me bounce this one off you. Dexter Smith kills two of the pirates trying to protect Nadine. Then, when he's murdered, Nadine, preferring death to sexual slavery, throws herself into the crocodile-infested waters.' Brad opened his palms to show how simple it was once you'd grasped the basics. 'In a way they're together again. United in death.'

'I like it,' Jerry said, staring pointedly at Boucher.

Boucher gave a winded laugh. 'But it's pure fantasy.'

Ethan steered his ballpoint around his notepad. 'That's what we deal in, Jay. Even in life, Dexter Smith was a legend and in cinema legend to fantasy is a short jump. It's Dexter and Nadine who are going to sell this film. The audience has to identify with them and they can't do that if all they see is Dexter mooning under the palm trees while Nadine polishes her nails.'

'What I write will contradict what you screen.'

'Don't worry about that. Film and books are separate worlds. There's not a lot of cross-over.' Ethan moved on briskly. 'Good. Hey, we're getting there. Now, Dexter's music will be a major attraction. We'll use the *Dirty Old Man* album as soundtrack. Dexter's also got some un-released material. We thought we could work it in as songs he came up with on the island.'

Boucher had to pinch himself. 'You're planning to turn it into a fucking *musical?*'

They looked uneasy, then Brad had an inspiration. 'A requiem,' he said. 'A requiem, Jay.'

'How do you plan to deal with me?'

Ethan was pleased to show they had covered all angles. 'Okay,' he said, making a frame with his hands, 'we see you in the dark, just a shadow in the boat, looking back at the island. Big swell of music – Dexter's – orchestrated for strings. It's uplifting, it's optimistic. It says that though Dexter Smith is dead, his dreams of a cleaner planet live on.'

'What about Candy?'

Ethan looked sombre. 'Got to scale her down, Jay.'

'Scale her down,' Boucher repeated.

'We've got to target the market, Jay.'

Boucher rose like a ghost and walked to the door.

'Jay, we're not through.'

'I am.'

'You're contracted,' Ethan reminded him. 'You're on the payroll.'

Flying home that evening, Boucher wondered if there was still a way out. He hadn't signed the contract yet and there must be plenty of film companies that wouldn't mangle the truth.

But watching the wintry plains slipping past below, he knew it was only the in-flight whiskey talking. By summoning Delta Glenn, he had uncorked a genie he could never get back into the bottle. Besides, what right did he have to criticize the script team? Like them, he was planning to cut, splice, water down and generally adulterate.

Oppressed by doubts, he took a cab home. He was keying entry to his block when a figure stepped out of the shadows.

'Are you Jay Boucher?'

Startled, hand on heart, Boucher found himself confronted by five or six youngsters, none older than twenty, most of them girls, all wearing mournful expressions.

'Yes,' he admitted,

'Why did you let Dexter Smith die?'

Boucher wondered if it had been one of these kids who'd menaced him on the phone. He made his tone reasonable.

'Dexter Smith was killed by pirates. Nobody had a chance to save him.'

'He was killed while you filmed him. That's such a terrible thing.' 'The guy who filmed him was called Disco, and he's dead too. Now excuse me.'

'It was you sold the film.'

Fatigue nailed Boucher to the spot. 'Look, I kept that film as a record of what happened. I won't make a cent out of it.'

'You cut a five-million dollar deal. It's in the papers.'

'Four million. I'm truly sorry about Dexter, but it's cold and I have to go in.'

'We want you to stop this book.'

Something snapped. 'I can't stop. I won't stop. It's what I *do*.'

They shrank back, then the girl who had spoken took a step towards him. Almost timidly, she said: 'Why can't it be you who died?'

When he reached his apartment, the phone was ringing inside. As he opened the door, it stopped. Lydia was waiting, holding it out to him. 'Some man.'

Boucher took it warily.

'I told you, Jay. And it'll get worse. A lot worse.'

Smashing down the phone, Boucher crossed to the window. Dexter's fans were still holding vigil. Turning, he was dismayed by the fright on Lydia's face.

'Some nut. Some fucker.' He couldn't contain the tension any longer. 'Christ, people are treating me as if I'd stolen something.' He made a sweeping gesture and headed for the drinks cabinet. 'Ah, forget it. Let's think about Christmas in Prague.'

He had filled his glass and his lips were poised to sip before Lydia's silence got through to him.

'What's wrong?' he asked, lowering his glass.

'I'm not coming to Prague.'

'Not coming?'

She sat down, composed, hands in lap. 'You had an affair with Candy.'

Boucher gave a good-natured laugh. 'An affair? On that godforsaken place? You make it sound like we were enjoying candlelit dinners and afternoon romps.'

'Did you fuck her then?'

The humour fled Boucher's face. Shaking with anger, he turned his back. 'This is absurd.'

Lydia jumped up. 'Did you fuck her?'

Boucher stared out of the window. 'She's dead, Lydia.'

'Not in your memory she's not. All those hours when you lie awake, it's her you're thinking about.'

Suddenly, Boucher's grief crystallized and shattered. 'Yes,' he shouted, 'I loved her.'

Lydia sprawled back on the couch and threw up her arms – a gesture that Boucher thought at first was hopeless despair, but then realized was relief. He peered at her askance. 'My God, this isn't about Candy at all.'

Lydia took her time answering. 'Six months ago I met someone else – another musician, Diethe. I wasn't unfaithful, Jay, I promise, but after I was told you were dead, Diethe and I ... Diethe helped comfort me.'

Boucher felt nothing. 'How nice,' he said stonily. 'How very nice to have a man on hand to help you through your recent bereavement.'

'Please, Jay, it's not as if you were innocent.'

'My source of comfort is dead, Lydia.'

Lydia looked down. 'I'm truly sorry, Jay.'

Boucher had an urge to trash the apartment. Instead, he stalked to the phone and dialled Henry Ritter.

'Henry, I know I'm not your favourite person, but right now you're the only person I can turn to. Lydia and I have split. Can I stay over for tonight? I'll fix proper accommodation first thing.'

'Hey, stay as long as you like. Stay for Christmas. I'll get a new deck of cards in.'

'Now's your chance, Henry. The play's running against me.'

Ritter still lived in the rough old neighbourhood where they'd both grown up. When he opened the door, a buxom and bonny young woman Boucher hadn't seen before stood behind him, grinning for all she was worth.

'Ah, hell, Henry, you should have said. I'll check into an hotel. No trouble.'

'You stay. Nancy's dying to meet you. She can't believe you're as bad as I've painted you.'

Nancy was a poet, a published poet, and she seemed to have wrought a remarkable transformation in Ritter's outlook.

'You never stop smiling,' Boucher told him. 'You must be on a winning streak.'

'Lost another hundred last week. I'm beginning to think I should take up another game.'

'Henry's had a novel accepted,' Nancy announced.

Silently, Boucher went and embraced his old friend, his old sparring partner. 'You bastard, you brilliant bastard.' Ridiculously, he couldn't suppress a twinge of envy.

'It'll sell a thousand copies, tops.'

'But a novel. Out of your own head. Come on, this calls for celebration.'

'What about Lydia?'

'Two calls for celebration.'

He sent out for a bottle of fifteen-year-old malt. Around midnight, when the whiskey had been reduced to half its original volume, Nancy left them to it. By this stage Boucher had grown contentious.

'Why can't I write my fucking story?'

'Because you're too close to it.'

'Are you saying people can't do a job of reportage out of their own experience? That it's got to be certified and processed by a third party?'

'Writers skirt round the margins of things. They don't tackle events head on. They hit their targets at a tangent, a glancing blow here, a feature illuminated there.' Ritter stifled a hiccup. 'But never the whole ...' his arm windmilled '... fucking thing. Take war. War is big, the biggest, and a lot of writers have seen war, but how many ever write about it? Fucking few. Some subjects are *too* big.'

Boucher's alcohol-fuelled high deserted him, leaving him stranded on some arid plateau.

'Even *you* think I should walk away from it.'

'It'll take you over. It's not just the writing. There's all the collateral shit. I read that Wildguard's contesting copyright. Nadine's family is threatening an injunction. It'll eat you up. You'll never be able to go back to doing what you're so good at.'

'Wonderful. Hello, smart-ass magazine articles; goodbye, four million dollars.'

'You came back, Jay. The only one. There's your reward.'

'My life's worth shit,' Boucher said, suddenly sober, and stared for a long time into the dregs of his whiskey. 'The story's the only way of making sense of things. If I have to take it to the grave, it'll drive me there.'

'Maybe you should try therapy, get it out that way.'

'See a shrink? *Pay* for the privilege?'

Laughs were hard to come by, but Boucher laughed at that.

At some godawful hour of the night, Ritter shook him out of a stupor.

'It's that agent. She sounds ballistic.'

Too drunk to engage his brain, Boucher worked out by trial and error which end of the phone to put to his ear.

'Where have you been? I've been trying to reach you for the last three hours.'

'Personal crisis.'

'Your day's going to get worse. You're booked on the 06.20 flight to New York. A car will meet you. Got that?'

'What's up?'

'What isn't? Be there.'

Ritter looked on in concern as Boucher fumbled, groped and finally crash-landed the phone to its rest.

'Trouble?'

'Got to be.'

Hungover and apprehensive, Boucher jetted to New York, turning over various scenarios that might conceivably have led to his undoing. His best bet was that Disco's body had been found. The guy was like a virus he couldn't get rid of.

This time, there was no honour guard to meet him. An editorial junior escorted him upstairs. Another office, same people, expressions running the gamut from embarrassed to grim. Among the grimmest on show was Delta's.

Boucher's smile came out as an incriminating leer. 'Nice to see you, too.'

'Sit down, Jay,' Pulman ordered. He was holding several sheets of paper. 'Today's copy of the London *Daily Express.* We received it just before midnight, too late to make the morning editions.' He handed it over. 'By this afternoon it'll be splashed across the nation.'

ALIVE! said the banner head – a cliché fleshed out with a grainy blow-up of Candy semi-comatose in a hospital bed.

Boucher glanced up in incomprehension. He stared again at the picture. Still it wouldn't click.

Pulman cleared his throat. 'Candy was picked up off a fishing boat on the fourteenth. Her ship docked in Singapore yesterday. Some shipboard hack managed to inveigle his way into her room and interview her.'

Quite unable to help himself, Boucher began to cry. He fought for air and tried to apologize for this unseemly display, but every time he opened his mouth, he broke down again. Someone passed a tissue and he laughed through his tears. 'Why the doomy faces? Candy's alive!'

'Read it,' Pulman told him.

Abandoned by her friends, Candy Woodville survived a terrifying raft voyage with one of the pirates who brutally murdered rock icon Dexter Smith. For seven days, racked by fever, she and the killer she told me became a friend ...

Unable to take it in, Boucher looked up.

'You told us you saw her drown,' one of the lawyers said.

'I was wrong. And I'm rejoicing.'

'There's more,' Pulman warned him. 'There's worse.'

Pages four and five were splattered with photographs. Most were of Candy, but it was his own image, looking haggard and untrustworthy at Kennedy, that leapt out at him. 'Did this man kill a comrade?'

With chill fascination, Boucher read on.

Still bearing the ravages of her nightmare journey, Candy told me that Jay Boucher, the American journalist believed until today to be the sole survivor of the Wildguard disaster, killed Disco in a feud ...

A fist closed around Boucher's heart as he realized what Candy had done. Very quickly he began mounting a salvage operation. 'This flake is making it up,' he sneered, flicking the sheet. 'Look at the state of Candy. She's drugged, unconscious. Besides, she couldn't know what happened to Disco because he'd already ...'

'Pushed her off?'

Seeing the faces ranged against him, Boucher knew he was sunk.

'Don't look so cornered, Jay. If this Disco character murdered Kent Bartok as Candy alleges, why are you protecting him?'

The horrible irony hit like a fist. He had done his best to shield Candy and had only succeeded in absolving Disco. For a moment the truth was on his lips.

'I'm not saying another word until I've spoken to Candy.'

Pulman sighed. The senior legal figure stepped forward. 'Jay, this is a can of worms. We'll want to review our agreement in the light of more solid information.'

Boucher rose. All the way to the door, he could feel their eyes following him. Delta joined him outside and they were halfway to the ground floor before he broke the silence.

'That's it, then.'

Delta shrugged as if she didn't much care. 'Maybe there's something we can salvage.'

'One garbled accusation and they pull the plug.'

'Jay, it's not just the allegations that are worrying them. Not unless they're substantiated.' Delta left a hook in the air that Boucher ignored. 'What's pissing them off is the fact they thought they were getting an exclusive, and it isn't that any more. The media is flocking down on Candy from every corner of the globe. Do you realize her market value? A young and good-looking woman given up for dead by her own friends floats down the coast and sails up a river with one of the pirates who killed Dexter Smith.'

'I told you she was remarkable.'

'She's a star, and you ... Well, Jay, you were second last off, and that's like winning an Olympic silver. Who cares?

Who can remember your name?' Delta stepped back in alarm. 'Why are you smiling like that?'

'Disco warned me that Candy would be the darling of the media if she made it.'

The elevator doors opened. 'Okay, Jay, we'll put it on hold until we clarify Candy's story. Hey, where are you going?'

'Where do you think?'

38

Weak and wasted, weighing twenty pounds less than when she'd left for Borneo, Candy lay in a Singapore hospital oblivious to the media hysteria whipped up by news of her rescue. Each time she raised the subject of her island ordeal, her father headed her off, saying that the emotional wounds were still too raw to touch. On the third day, she insisted that he listen.

'You'd better read this first,' her father said, handing her a newspaper cutting. 'It's the fullest account by Boucher we've been able to get hold of.'

He went and stood at the window, hands in pockets, and from his reluctance to face her, Candy was convinced that Boucher must have given the whole story. She began to read, at first with dread and then with mounting astonishment. Hardly a mention of Disco. Not a single reference to his crimes.

'This is ...' she began, and then saw the strain on her father's face and realized why Jay had edited Disco out. She tried to smile. 'Journalists don't half go over the top.'

Her father nodded and gestured into the grounds. 'They've got us under siege. There must be half a dozen television crews out there and at least a hundred journalists. One of them nearly got in here yesterday.'

'Is that why there's a policeman at the door?'

It was some time before he spoke, and then it was on

another subject. 'If I'd known what sort of people you'd got mixed up with, I wouldn't have let you go.'

Candy smiled weakly. 'If *I'd* known, I might not have been so keen either.'

'Jumping into something with your eyes closed? That's so unlike you. Was it some kind of rebellious gesture?'

'Nothing so dramatic,' Candy said, wondering if there *had* been an element of wilfulness in her decision. 'Borneo was simply too good an opportunity to miss.'

Her father shook his head in incomprehension. 'All the terrible things that happened. I don't understand why you couldn't have co-operated.'

'At first, being on the island seemed like an adventure, and then,' Candy choked back a sob, 'things broke down.'

Her father examined his feet.

Candy collected herself. 'Daddy, when can we go home?'

He extended one hand, then let it drop. 'I'm afraid it isn't for me to say.'

Slowly, Candy sat up. 'What's wrong?'

Her father made an awkward shrug. 'It's this Boucher fellow.'

'Jay? Have you spoken to him?'

Something in the hospital grounds seemed to have claimed her father's attention. 'I spoke to him briefly on the phone soon after he returned to America. He asked if he could come over to see me. I didn't think a meeting would be appropriate.'

'You thought I was dead,' Candy said, her voice rising in astonishment, 'and you refused to meet the person who was closest to me.'

Her father flinched. 'I assumed it was for his book. What was I supposed to make of him? Three or four days after getting back, he was signing a book contract. The man's a bloodsucker.'

'He was my *friend*.'

Her father went still. 'Close friends?'

'You mean, did I sleep with him? God! Yes, if you *must* know.'

Her father closed his eyes briefly. 'With your consent?'

'With pleasure, actually. What's that got to do with anything?'

'Are you in love with him?'

Candy turned away and studied the antiseptic décor. 'It isn't some mad passionate thing.'

'You're a grown woman. Who you choose to ... Well, that's your affair. But this man's an exploiter. He's merchandising suffering.'

Anger streaked through Candy. 'Jay saved me from drowning. When I was lost in the mangroves, it was him who came looking for me. He nursed me when I was ill. If it hadn't been for him, I'd be dead.'

Her father went to the door, checking that the policeman was still there. When he turned, his manner was urgent. 'You told that reporter on the ship he may have murdered the other chap – the one you said pushed you overboard.'

Shock blanked Candy's mind. 'I don't remember that. I can't remember anything I might ...'

Her father sat beside her and seized her hand. 'Is it true? Answer me, Candy. Why did Disco want you dead? What in God's name really happened on that place?'

Looking into her father's face, seeing the desperate concern in his eyes, Candy was suddenly sick of this deception. She felt her face grow ugly. 'Disco tried to rape me. He murdered Kent because he wouldn't join in.' She met her father's appalled gaze. 'He didn't get very far, I'm glad to say.'

Her father grew old before her eyes. With an effort, he found his feet. 'This mustn't get out.'

'Worried what they'll say at the Cavalry Club?'

'Damn that,' he said, and began to pace. 'Candy, when Boucher heard you'd been picked up, the fool flew to Singapore. He was arrested at the airport and remanded in prison. The official line is that he smuggled out some videotapes crucial to the investigation, but the real reason is that the police believe Kent Bartok and Disco were murdered. They suspected it from the beginning, then you went and blurted it out to that journalist.'

Candy's hand went to her mouth. 'Oh, Jay,' she whispered.

Her father took her hand. 'Now look, I've spoken to a good lawyer. If Boucher keeps his nerve, the police can't make a serious case against him. Without Disco's body, it doesn't really matter what they think. The important thing is that you confirm Boucher's story. I've tried to visit him, but the police won't let anyone near him until they hear your account.'

At the thought of facing police interrogation, Candy quailed. 'Do I have to?'

'You have no idea what efforts have been made to spare you this. The ambassador himself has intervened, asking for your immediate repatriation. But the Singapore government is coming under a lot of diplomatic pressure from Jakarta. The Indonesians have lost face over their failure to find the Wildguard survivors. They're attracting terrible publicity over those pirates. If they can prove that you or Boucher or the others committed crimes on their territory, it'll take some of the sting out of the attacks.'

'What will happen if I tell the truth?'

'Almost certainly, you and Boucher will be sent back to Indonesia.'

Candy thought of what that would mean and braced herself. 'When do the police want to see me?'

'Tomorrow morning. Plenty of time to learn your lines.'

'My lines,' Candy said in a toneless voice, thinking of Kent Bartok.

Her father reached out and patted her shoulder. 'We're all terribly proud of you,' he said, not quite meeting her eye.

After he'd gone, Candy's mouth curved down, stayed down-curved and began to tremble. Tears squeezed out. Try as she might, she couldn't stop the floodgates from opening. She cried and cried. Each time she thought she'd wrung the last tears out, her heart would fill afresh and she'd start again. That's for Kent, she thought. That's for Nadine. She had tears for all of them. Only for Disco was her heart cold.

Inspector Lee heard Candy's sanitized version of events with polite anger. When she had finished, he fiddled with a gold cigarette lighter for a minute. Smoking was virtually a political offence in Singapore, Candy knew. Lee must be a terribly frustrated man.

'Let us go back to Disco,' he said inevitably.

'I think his real name is Cass. Norman Richard Cass.'

Lee stopped fiddling. 'Boucher told me no one knew his identity.'

'I only found out after I'd swum back to the island. Disco lost his luggage in the crash. I remember him telling Jay to look out for it. Kemal found it and kept the wallet. Inside were credit cards in the name of Cass.'

'Passport?'

'No, just money and cards – a lot of money.'

Lee took a notebook from one of his officers. 'Please, write this name down for me.'

Candy did so. Lee studied it, then handed it back to the officer with a command in Chinese. Lee watched him leave before returning to the central issue.

'Boucher admits he was afraid of Disco. Why?'

'I can't speak for Jay. That's something you'll have to ask him yourself.'

Lee's eyes narrowed. 'Were *you* afraid of him?'

'I didn't like him. His manner was ... unpleasant.'

'Did he molest you in any way?'

Candy gritted her nerve. 'Not physically.'

Lee agitated his lighter and Candy noticed the nicotine stains on his fingers. 'The night after the pirates attacked, where did you sleep?'

That was the night she'd taken refuge in the forest. She wondered if this was a trick question. 'At the camp, with Jay, Disco and ... that's all.'

'This was the same camp you left from the following night – after the storm, around midnight.'

Aware of the pitfall in her path, Candy had no way of avoiding it. 'Yes.'

Lee compared her statement with another sheet of paper. 'Both you and Boucher say that Kent Bartok was killed by the pirates at this camp. The Indonesian police have forensic evidence to support your statements.'

Finding herself in a hole, Candy could only continue digging. 'Then we all agree.'

'Confirm something else. The night after the pirates left, and all next day, you stayed in a camp less than ten metres from Kent Bartok's body. During this time, you made no attempt to bury him, or even move him.' Lee left a provocative silence. 'Miss Woodville, you know how quickly a body rots in the tropics.'

Candy retreated to her fall-back position. 'I had a fever. The last thirty-six hours on the island are just a blur. My memory simply can't be trusted.'

'The rifle used to shoot Mr Bartok was recovered twenty metres from his body. Unfired cartridges from it were found scattered nearby. Bullets fired from the same weapon were recovered from trees in the immediate vicinity. This was the rifle you say Jaeger took from the pirate who threatened you and Boucher – *after* the pirate had shot Bartok.'

Candy's lawyer gave her a minuscule warning signal. 'I'm not sure what you're getting at, Inspector.'

Wearily, Lee stood. 'The pirates did not shoot Mr Bartok. They had already left. Nor did Jaeger. He was not at your camp. The only people with Mr Bartok at the time he was murdered were you, Boucher and Disco.' Lee wasn't a tall man, but he suddenly seemed to grow two inches. 'Miss Woodville, did you kill Kent Bartok?'

'No.'

'Did Boucher?'

'No.'

'Then it must have been Disco, as you told the journalist.'

Candy forced herself to look Lee in the face. 'Inspector, Dr Laing will confirm that I was delirious when that journalist forced his way into my room. You can't take anything I might have told him seriously.'

'You are right,' Lee said at last. 'I cannot take your statement seriously.' He put his notebook away.

'Have you finished with me?'

Lee looked down on her, his expression a distillate of contempt. 'You are fortunate that your family has influential connections, Miss Woodville. If it was my decision, I would not let you go. I do not like you giving the true tale to some unimportant journalist, and lying to me.' Lee shrugged. 'I have no further interest in you.'

Candy squared her shoulders. 'I'm free to go home?'

'The sooner you leave Singapore, the better.'

'And Jay?'

'Mr Boucher does not have influential friends.'

'You can't keep him in prison out of spite.'

'You call the search for truth an act of spite?' Lee

paused at the door. 'Miss Woodville, if you want to help your friend, I suggest you tell me a story I can believe.'

Wavering, Candy caught the stern warning on her lawyer's face. 'I've said everything I intend to say.'

When Candy was alone, she threw herself on the bed in a rage and pummelled her pillow. She was still distraught when her father came in. She rolled over and stared at the ceiling.

'He doesn't believe me.'

'It doesn't matter. He can't force the issue. We've fed the media with the story that you're being interrogated in hospital, and they're outraged. The jackals have their uses after all.'

'Then tell them to get Jay out of prison.'

'The fool shouldn't have come here. There was no need.'

'No, there wasn't,' Candy shouted. 'And there was no need for him to cover up Disco's attempted rape. He only did it to protect me. And you!' Suddenly, Candy saw that Disco had won. Jay was in prison and Disco's crimes would never come to light. They would fester inside her all her life. She sat up.

'Daddy, are those journalists still out there?'

'They'll get bored in time and find someone else to pester.'

'I want to speak to them.'

Her father recoiled. 'I thought we'd agreed that ...'

'You said they'd helped us. I think they deserve something in return.'

'No, Candy.'

'I'm not asking your permission. If you won't arrange it, *I* will.'

'Inspector Lee is not going to like this one bit.'

'If I'm free to go where I want, I can talk to whoever I like.'

The news conference was scheduled for eleven next morning, in one of the hospital lecture theatres. Candy stood in the corridor, listening to the hubbub within, only half hearing her father's attempts to talk her out of going through with this circus. 'I know what I'm doing,' she insisted, her palms damp with apprehension.

'Ready?' someone said.

The door swung open and she advanced into a burst of lights and applause. When her vision cleared, she saw that the hall was packed – every tier occupied and every aisle crammed. The crowd pressed forward like a single organism. A line of policemen moved to contain the crush. Candy spotted Inspector Lee at one side of the stage.

Flanked by her father and lawyer, she sat down at a table in the centre of the stage. Directly in front of her, a photographer swung a punch at a rival who was trying to steal his line of sight. Out of the ravenous babel, she singled out an English voice.

'Tell us how you are, Candy.'

'Glad to be alive. My only regret is that Jay Boucher isn't here.'

The clamour subsided slightly. Inspector Lee was staring straight ahead. Candy tried to put him from her mind.

'How do you feel about Jay Boucher being in prison?'

'Shocked. Devastated. Heart-broken. Jay's done nothing wrong. He saved my life.'

'You told the *Gloriana*'s press officer that he killed Disco and left you for dead.'

'Rubbish. Jay would never abandon me.'

'What about Disco?'

Candy's voice dried. 'I ... I ...'

'Inspector,' a voice called, 'has Candy confirmed Boucher's version of events?'

Lee took a step forward, but Candy beat him to it. 'Jay Boucher lied,' she cried. 'He lied to save my family from embarrassment.' Candy paused in the momentary hush. 'I also lied.'

'To Barry Pitman?'

'No,' Candy said, and gripped the edge of the table. 'To Inspector Lee.'

'For God's sake!' her father hissed.

One of the policemen took a step towards her, but Lee waved him back. Candy looked into the crowd without focusing on it. 'I told Mr Pitman that Disco killed Kent Bartok. It's true. He shot him and then attempted to rape me.'

'Please, Candy,' her father implored her through the outcry. 'Stop!' He rose. 'Gentlemen, ladies, my daughter is ill. She's been in ...'

'I poisoned Disco,' Candy shouted. 'He deserved to die. He was a monster.'

'Oh boy,' some scribbler said happily.

'*Did* you kill him?'

Candy's head drooped. 'No, Jay insisted we take him with us.'

'Did he go overboard with you?'

'No.'

'Then it's possible Jay did murder him.'

'I have no idea. I wasn't on the boat.'

'I was!' a voice cried.

It was drowned by another. 'Boucher knew that whoever saved himself stood to gain millions. That's a mighty powerful reason to push a man overboard.'

'That's the truth,' cried the voice Candy had heard seconds earlier. '*That* is the truth.'

She peered into the sea of faces, the uproar in her ears fading to a hum. 'I'm sorry,' she said in automatic response to another question bellowed from only a few feet away. 'Could you repeat that?'

'He used the gun you gave him,' the voice cried. 'He kept one bullet back for me.'

As Candy staggered back, her father leapt up. 'What is it?'

'It's him,' she whispered. 'It's him.'

'Who?' her father demanded, whirling round.

'Disco. He's here.'

Her father furiously beckoned to one of the hospital staff. 'My daughter's ill. Get her out of here.'

'You can't hide from me,' the voice cried.

Candy held out her arms towards Lee. 'Inspector, it's Disco. He's alive.'

'My God,' her father groaned, 'what a bloody shambles.'

Candy beat at his hand. 'No one else knows about the pistol,' she screamed. 'I'm telling you – it's *him*!'

Lee scanned the heaving multitude. 'Where?' he demanded.

'I'm not trying to hide,' the voice cried. 'I'm right here.'

Sensing drama, the crowd had fallen quiet. Lee went to the front of the stage and peered towards the back of the hall. 'The man who spoke. Identify yourself.'.

'David Stilcho,' the voice said.

'Come here, Mr Stilcho.'

Candy bit her knuckles. Around the voice, the mass reluctantly began to give way, move apart. She saw a dark-haired young man fighting his way forward. She pressed closer to her father as the man came closer. He was limping badly, using a walking stick, his pale face down-turned. The crowd stood in murmuring mystification.

Near the centre of the hall the man stopped.

Lee pointed at him. 'Is that the man you call Disco?'

Candy still couldn't see his face. 'Look at me,' she said in a trembling voice.

Slowly the man looked up from under long lashes and she saw his eyes – such unusual eyes. Candy's legs turned to water and the faces around Disco reeled. Her father caught her as she began to fall.

As if in a distant dream, she heard Disco's voice. 'My name is David Stilcho,' it said. 'I'm the other man on the island, the one who didn't make the newspapers or TV bulletins. I'm the man you've just heard accused of terrible deeds. I'm standing up here to tell you what ...'

'Come here, please,' Lee shouted over the hubbub. 'Now!' Angrily, he gestured at his officers and they began to struggle towards the figure.

'I didn't rape Candy and I didn't kill my friend Kent Bartok. That's a lie she and Boucher concocted to hide their own crimes. It was them who murdered Kent. That's why Candy poisoned me. Why do you think she's changing her story now? It's because the police have found the flaws in ...'

'The press conference is over,' Lee shouted. 'Everybody, please leave the hall.'

Dimly, Candy was aware of screaming and jostling and things breaking. When her eyes came back into focus, she saw the last of the mob swirling through the door under the raised batons of Lee's men.

And then they were gone, leaving the hall dominated by a lone figure resting on a stick halfway up the central aisle, guarded by a policeman who had his hand on his holster. Along the front of the stage, Lee was walking back and forth. He fumbled for his cigarettes, lit up, and resumed striding, smoking furiously. He took one step towards Candy, glared at her, then turned and stabbed his hand at the man in the centre of the hall.

'Is this the man you call Disco?'

471

She stared at the sick and frail-looking figure and turned away, feeling sick. 'Yes.'

Lee marched off-stage and planted himself before Disco. 'You confirm that is your name?'

'It's what my friends call me. My full name is David Stilcho.'

'Identification, please.'

Out from his pocket, Disco drew a passport. Lee snatched it, walked away a little and opened it – began to flick through it. He summoned one of his officers and thrust it at him. The man left.

'How did you get to Singapore?' Lee demanded.

In a daze Candy listened as Disco explained how he had swum ashore after Boucher's attempt to shoot him. He described how he had reached the coast and struggled through the mangroves until he stumbled on a village whose inhabitants had nursed him and taken him to a road where he managed to get a lift to Palembang. From there he had flown to Singapore.

His speech was more articulate and better-educated than Candy remembered.

'How were you able to enter Singapore?' Lee demanded.

'I have a valid visa.'

Lee was striding about the lecture theatre as if his anger could only be kept in check by perpetual movement. 'Where else have you been on your travels?'

'Thailand, Java, Bali. I went to Komodo to see the dragons. Then I flew to Kalimantan and met the Wild-guard expedition. The trouble with Boucher started on the airship after the storm and we were sinking. He suggested that I should be thrown off to save weight.'

Lee frowned in bewilderment at Candy.

'It was a game,' she said, her voice colourless. 'A stupid game.'

'Even then,' Disco said, 'he was boasting about how he

472

'No, definitely not.'

'Norman Cass and Ann-Marie Becker made this voyage.'

Annoyance sharpened Disco's voice. 'A journey I never took with two mid-westerners I never heard of. Can't we get back to the important thing?'

Lee held him under lengthy regard. 'Yes,' he said at last, stepping back up on to the stage. 'You will accompany me to police headquarters.' He gripped Candy's elbow.

'What about her?'

Without answering, Lee led Candy off the stage and into the corridor.

'Are you arresting me?'

'You have admitted poisoning Disco.'

Candy dug her heels in. 'Those people – Cass and the girl. What happened to them?'

'That is no concern of yours.'

'They're dead, aren't they? Disco killed them.'

Lee bent his face to the window in the door. 'Look at him,' he ordered. 'Is that the face of a murderer?'

Candy peered through the window and saw Disco sitting in the empty lecture room, gazing alertly around. His face turned to the door and for a horrid moment she imagined he could see her. Into her mind came lines from Blake's tiger poem:

> Did he smile his work to see?
> Did he who made the Lamb make thee?

She straightened up. 'Yes,' she said.

39

Boucher had flown to Singapore with only one thought in his mind: to see Candy. After that, he told himself, he didn't care what happened to him.

In fact, he didn't even clear immigration. The official checked his passport, stared hard at his face, then made an invisible signal that summoned two police officers who escorted him to a detention room. He was kept there on his own for three hours before being led out and driven to police headquarters.

Lee was waiting for him. It was the middle of the night and he looked tired and vindictive.

'Mr Boucher, you are under arrest.'

'On what charge?'

'Hampering my enquiries into the murder of Kent Bartok.'

Boucher had hardly slept for two nights and he was as short-tempered as Lee. 'That's not a crime committed under Singapore's jurisdiction.'

'A warrant for your extradition is being prepared by the Sumatran authorities.'

'What about Candy? How is she? Can I speak to her?'

Lee stood dismissively. 'Due to the serious nature of the crime, you will be remanded in custody.'

Boucher was handcuffed and placed in a van. Dawn was beginning to streak the skyline as he arrived at Queenstown Road Prison on the north-east edge of the city. Stepping from the van, he saw high grey walls bristling with barbed wire and machine-gun towers manned by Gurkhas.

He was hustled inside, strip-searched and deprived of his valuables. Then a jailer escorted him to his cell. Inside were four other remand prisoners – an Australian called Keith, a Dutchman by the name of Jan, and two Malaysians.

'What they got you for?' Keith asked.

Boucher was almost out on his feet and couldn't face laborious explanations. 'Fraud.'

'How much?'

'Four million.'

Keith whistled. Out of politeness, Boucher felt obliged to ask him the nature of his own crime. It turned out he'd been arrested for urinating in a public place while drunk, and was looking at a sentence of between three and six months' imprisonment. Jan had been caught at the airport in possession of seventy grams of marijuana, and both the Malaysians were charged with murdering a compatriot – all crimes that carried the maximum penalty of death.

Boucher knew that if he was sent back to Indonesia, he might face the same fate, but he couldn't mount any defence without speaking to Candy first. His greatest fear was that she, too, had been arrested, and it wasn't until Arnold from the embassy turned up that he learned Candy was being allowed to fly home. Arnold, while sympathetic to Boucher's plight, explained that the US government would not be pressing hard to block his extradition. This time, there would be no Clarence Tusser coming through the door at the end of a handshake.

No more visitors came to see him. Boucher tried not to fall into despair, tried to take each hour and day as they came. His cell-mates were already resigned to guilty verdicts and, certain that he would go down too, tried to cheer him up by telling him how comfortable Changi jail was compared to the remand prison.

On the fourth day of his incarceration, a guard summoned him and marched him in silence through barred gates, down grim stairways and along dingy corridors. At the end of a passage, he swung open a door and waved Boucher through. Inside, seated at a table on the other side of a glass screen, was Candy. She rose and smiled and Boucher thought how stunning she looked. Only when he got close did he see how gaunt her face was, how strained the expression in her eyes.

Her voice was hushed. 'I'm so sorry, Jay. I've really landed you in it.'

'I got here all on my own.'

They fell silent, each witnessing their own experiences etched on the other's face, then Candy briskly wiped her eyes. 'I'm afraid we've only got half an hour, and there's so much to tell you. Are they treating you well? You're awfully thin.'

'I can't complain. It's like old times. I'm sharing a cell with two murderers and a dopehead. Sometimes when the door opens, I half expect Disco to walk in.'

'He's alive, Jay.'

'I always knew he couldn't be killed. I should have made sure the slug I kept back was solid silver.'

'I mean it. He's here in Singapore. Two days ago, he walked into my press conference.'

At first, Boucher could only frame the picture of Candy facing the media. He glanced at the guard and dropped his voice. 'I shot him, Candy. You were right, I should have done it when you said. What you told the journalist, it's ...'

'You're a rotten shot, Jay. You missed him completely.

He swam ashore and somehow managed to get through the mangroves.'

Boucher wondered if Candy's ordeal had unhinged her. 'That's not possible. You know it isn't.'

'Jay, I saw him with my own eyes.'

Boucher began to wonder if it was he who was deranged. 'The hand groping up from the swamp,' he said. 'I've been suffering from that syndrome, too. Someone kept calling me in Chicago. I had a nightmare that it ...' He broke off, transfixed by the look on Candy's face. 'Sweet Jesus, you're serious!'

'I fainted, Jay. I passed out.'

'But why would he show up again after what he did?'

'Our stories were in every newspaper in the world. Imagine what that must have been like for Disco – reading how you'd signed a multi-million contract, seeing me hailed as some kind of heroine. In any case, he had nothing to fear. As far as Lee was concerned, he'd done nothing wrong.'

The ghastly truth hit Boucher. 'Christ, I let him off.'

'So did I at first. Then I thought of Kent dead and you in prison and I felt so *angry*. I didn't care if they put me in jail, too, so long as the world knew what Disco had done. That's why I called the press conference. I was explaining exactly what did happen when he stood up.'

Boucher swallowed. 'What did he say?'

'He turned everything on its head. He said we murdered Kent and tried to kill him. He said you were after his cassettes.'

Boucher's mind had stalled. 'But no one's going to believe him. We can verify each other's stories.'

'Jay, the only story we agreed on was a pack of lies.'

'Yes, but ...'

'You weren't there when he killed Bartok and tried to rape me. It's his word against mine, and you know how much the police think ours is worth. He sounded very plausible, Jay, full of hurt and indignation. He sounded like a different person. Remember how you scoffed when he told you he was an actor? Well, it's true. And this was his big moment, his starring role.'

As it sank in, Boucher uttered a laugh of despair. 'If they believe him, I'm going to have to find some absorbing craft hobby to keep me occupied for the next twenty years.'

'It isn't the end, Jay.'

Boucher looked at her.

'After I got back to the the island, I found Disco's bag and credit cards in the name of Cass. No, that isn't an alias; his real name is David Stilcho. Cass was a librarian from Kansas who went to Kalimantan with a girl called Ann-Marie. She used to write or call home every week, but in October the letters stopped.'

Boucher was trying to wrench his mind on to the new track.

'After a few weeks had passed without any word, Ann-Marie's family contacted the police in Borneo and discovered that she and Cass had returned from a river trip near Samarinda on the twentieth of October. They hadn't gone back to their hotel. That was the last anyone saw of them.'

Boucher considered the date. 'That's only a few days before we arrived in Pontianaka.'

'Three weeks later, the police found a body in a monsoon drain. It was Cass's. He'd been dismembered.'

Boucher's skin began to crawl. 'What about the girl?'

'They haven't found her.'

'Christ!' Boucher breathed. 'And Cass's credit cards were in Disco's bag.'

Candy bit her lip. 'I lost them, Jay.'

Boucher was bewildered. 'Then where's the evidence connecting Disco to Cass?'

'One of the the river boat crew remembers seeing Cass and his girlfriend in the company of a young American. Lee sent Disco's photograph to Samarinda. The crewman swears it's the same man.'

Boucher didn't dare hope. 'Is that enough?'

'Disco denies he was anywhere near the place, and the police haven't been able to prove otherwise.'

From hope, Boucher shot into despair. He punched the glass. 'Jesus, he's going to walk away from it. He's going to walk free, while I rot in prison.'

'In Ann-Marie's last letter, she told her parents she'd met another traveller – an American.' Candy's voice began to tremble. 'She gave his name – Disco.'

Boucher sagged back. 'A name and a photograph to match it,' he murmured. 'They've got to take that seriously.'

Candy nodded. 'Disco can't account for his movements around the time Cass and his girlfriend disappeared. There are four days missing in his life. Also, Disco says he left his personal effects in a private house in Pontianaka, but claims he's forgotten the address. The police are searching for it. When they find it, Lee thinks that they'll come up with more evidence.'

Boucher punched the palm of his hand.

'The Indonesians have demanded his extradition. If he's found guilty, he could face the death penalty.'

Boucher recalled the crawling unease Disco had stirred at their first meeting. 'How many others do you think he ...?'

'Don't,' Candy said quickly. 'I can't bear to think about it.'

Boucher's excitement subsided. 'Where does that leave us?'

'This afternoon, I'm going to give an interview for Indonesian television. It was their ambassador's idea. He suggested I make a grovelling speech thanking the Indonesians for their attempts to find us. He wants me to stress that there's no proof the pirates were Bugis. He's hinted that, in return, Jakarta will consider dropping extradition proceedings.'

It would have to suffice, Boucher decided. Candy's half-hour was nearly up and there were more important things to discuss.

'How's it been, since you got back?'

'I get quite weepy at times,' Candy admitted. She gave herself a little shake. 'God knows why. It's so much worse for you. Has Lydia been to see you?'

'That's over. Nothing to do with you.'

'I'm very sorry,' Candy said, her eyes slipping from his. 'How do you pass the time?'

'I play cards. I debate global affairs with my fellow prisoners. But mostly I find myself thinking about the island. In some ways, I miss it. I suppose that being so close to death makes everything more intense.'

'Well, you can write your story now – the unexpurgated version. There's nothing stopping you. I've already spilled the beans.'

Boucher shook his head.

'But you have to live up to your name,' Candy said. She laughed at his puzzlement. 'The scientific name for jays,' she explained, 'is *Garrulus*.'

Boucher considered the possibility and felt a twinge of regret. 'No, Candy. I'd rather let it go. Too many ghosts.'

'Poor Jay, you've lost everything.'

'Have I?'

Candy dropped her eyes. 'I do love you. I suppose. In a way. But ...'

'Stop there,' Boucher said, reaching out, 'before you talk yourself out of it.'

'But we're not suited,' Candy continued. Her voice had an edge, as if she'd been going over this proposition in her mind and was annoyed because she couldn't entirely refute it.

'You said that once before, and look what happened.'

Candy blushed ever so slightly. 'Things were very different then. All we had was each other.'

'It was enough for me.'

'For me, too,' she said, and met his eyes full on. 'I'm glad our paths crossed, Jay, but we both know that they lead in different directions.'

Boucher nodded and was silent for a while. 'Well,' he said, 'yours will take you anywhere you like now. You've got the world at your feet.'

Candy laughed. 'Nothing has changed. I've still got to find a job. I'm flying home in a few days. Once I'm properly fit, I'll move to London.'

Boucher tried to imagine Candy in the big city. 'It's been a long time since I visited London. When they let me out of here, maybe I could fly home the long way and stop off for a few days.'

'Oh yes,' Candy said, 'you must.'

An awkwardness descended on both of them, and before Boucher could find words to end it, the warder indicated it was time to go.

Candy's hands came to meet his against the screen. 'I'll be back tomorrow,' she said, standing up. 'Oh, I brought you a present. I'm not allowed to give it to you personally.' She backed away, a sad, yearning expression on her face. 'Goodbye then, Jay. I'll be thinking of you.'

At the door she stopped, face downcast as if she was about to deliver some crushing last word.

'A goose-down pillow.'

'A what?'

'My luxury item. Remember? That's what I want on my desert island.'

Boucher laughed. 'You shall have it.'

She looked up with a grin. 'Since you're coming to stay, you'd better make that two.'

After she'd gone, Boucher continued staring into space. In his heart, he knew he wouldn't be able to keep her, but his heart also told him that whatever measure of herself she allowed him would enrich his life for ever.

On the walk back, the warder showed him Candy's beautifully wrapped gift package. Inside was a silk tie in a design loud enough to stop traffic. The warder wouldn't let him take it in case he used it for a suicide attempt.

Boucher's cellmates were aghast when he told them what Candy had given him.

'Your girl showed up and all she brought you was a lousy tie. Christ, Jay, she's trying to tell you something.'

'It's a private joke,' he said, and went to stand at the window. Staring at a little patch of tree and sky above the barbed wire, he found himself turning over memories.

'You want to play cards?'

'Sure,' Boucher said. He saw an island shaped like a teardrop, surrounded by six gorgeous shades of blue and green, and in the water, fish shoaling brighter than any painter's palette. He saw Candy on the beach, shielding her eyes from the sea dazzle, waiting for him to return with his catch. 'Why not?'

'Five card draw,' Keith said, 'jacks to open.'

Boucher saw other figures ranged on the sand – Bartok and his luminous smile, Aquila expatiating on man's inhumanity to beasts, Leo nodding in myopic agreement, Nadine and Dexter and Marriot and ... Boucher's throat tightened.

'Hey Jay, are you in or out?'

The vision misted over. Smiling crookedly, Boucher turned, sat down, drew a deep breath and patted his knees.

'Deal them.'

All Orion/Phoenix titles are available at your local bookshop or from the following address:

Littlehampton Book Services
Cash Sales Department L
14 Eldon Way, Lineside Industrial Estate
Littlehampton
West Sussex BN17 7HE

telephone 01903 721596, *facsimile* 01903 730914

Payment can either be made by credit card (Visa and Mastercard accepted) or by sending a cheque or postal order made payable to *Littlehampton Book Services*.
DO NOT SEND CASH OR CURRENCY.

Please add the following to cover postage and packing

UK and BFPO:
£1.50 for the first book, and 50P for each additional book to a maximum of £3.50

Overseas and Eire:
£2.50 for the first book plus £1.00 for the second book and 50p for each additional book ordered

- -

BLOCK CAPITALS PLEASE

name of cardholder ....

address of cardholder ....

....

....

....

postcode ....

delivery address
(if different from cardholder)

....

....

....

postcode ....

☐ I enclose my remittance for £.............................

☐ please debit my Mastercard/Visa (delete as appropriate)

card number ☐☐☐☐☐☐☐☐☐☐☐☐☐☐☐☐☐☐

expiry date ☐☐☐☐

signature ....

prices and availability are subject to change without notice